ZEE EDGELL was born in Belize City in 1940 and grew up in
Belize. One of her first jobs was as a reporter on the *Daily
Gleaner* in Kingston, Jamaica. From 1966-8 she taught at St
Catherine Academy in Belize, during which period she was also
editor of a small newspaper in Belize City. After travelling
widely – apart from Jamaica, she has lived in Britain,
Afghanistan, Nigeria, Bangladesh and the USA – she returned
to Belize to teach, and in 1981–2 was appointed Director of the
Women's Bureau in the government there. From 1986–7, Edgell
was Director of the Department of Women's Affairs, and she
lectured at the University College of Belize from 1988–9. She
now lives with her family in Belize.

Beka Lamb, Edgell's first novel, won the 1982 Fawcett Society
Book Prize, and was the first novel by a Belizean to reach an
international audience. It is available in the Heinemann
Caribbean Writers Series.

ZEE EDGELL

IN
TIMES
LIKE
THESE

HEINEMANN

Heinemann International Literature and Textbooks
a division of Heinemann Educational Books Ltd
Halley Court, Jordan Hill, Oxford OX2 8EJ

Heinemann Educational Books Inc
361 Hanover Street, Portsmouth, New Hampshire, 03801, USA

Heinemann Educational Books (Nigeria) Ltd
PMB 5205, Ibadan
Heinemann Kenya Ltd
Kijabe Street, PO Box 45314, Nairobi
Heinemann Educational Boleswa
PO Box 10103, Village Post Office, Gaborone, Botswana

LONDON   EDINBURGH   MADRID
PARIS   ATHENS   BOLOGNA   MELBOURNE
SYDNEY   AUCKLAND   SINGAPORE
TOKYO   HARARE

© Zee Edgell 1991
First published by Heinemann International Literature and Textbooks
in the Caribbean Writers Series 1991

Series Editor: Adewale Maja-Pearce

British Library Cataloguing in Publication Data
Edgell, Zee
In times like these.—(Caribbean writers series)
I. Title   II. Series
813. [F]

ISBN 0–435–98927–8

Phototypeset by Wilmaset, Birkenhead, Wirral
Printed in Great Britain by
Cox & Wyman Ltd, Reading, Berkshire

92 93 94 95   10 9 8 7 6 5 4 3 2

Chapter 1

Pavana Leslie stretched cramped legs full-length on the narrow operating table in the basement of a private London clinic. She smiled ruefully, remembering with discomfort her twenty-first birthday celebration which had taken place only a few weeks before this cheerless December day in 1968.

The nurse and her assistant moved around the table in the unhurried, familiar pattern of their daily routine. There were no windows in the room, no paintings on the pale yellow walls. The atmosphere was sterile, like the instruments laid out in a gleaming tray on a trolley beside the table.

Pavana stared at them uneasily, speculating on the precise purpose for each one, reflecting on the appalling ease with which it is sometimes possible to depart from one's values.

'Nurse,' she said apologetically, 'I've changed my mind.'

'Changed your mind? A big girl like you afraid of a little operation like this? You won't feel a thing and you'll be right as rain in no time.'

'Do you suppose I might . . .'

'I wouldn't if I were you, lovey – *suppose* I mean, much the best course I've found. Doctor will be along in a minute. Now be a good girl and stretch those legs out as far as they will go.'

Pavana thought back to yesterday afternoon, when she had sat to the rear of a red double-decker bus moving slowly along the streets of London's West End. Festive crowds thronged the sidewalks outside shops and stores lit by a million lights. Shoppers gravitated to window displays glittering in an extravagance of tinsel. In her leather handbag, the drawstrings intertwining her gloved fingers, she had well over a hundred pounds to be spent this year on a purpose contrary to the spirit of Christmas.

The bus idled for a minute near the entrance to a large department store displaying in its windows a representation of the stable at

Bethlehem, with life-size figures of the infant Jesus surrounded by Mary, Joseph, the cattle, shepherds and Magi. The perfect family, their example sculpted, painted or written about for nearly 2,000 years.

'Lucky Mary, and *so* intelligent,' Pavana had muttered to herself.

She envied Mary who, on finding herself pregnant, was able to call on the assistance of the Angel Gabriel and the Holy Spirit to help persuade Joseph that marrying her, and caring for the baby, would be the right thing to do. But those, Pavana consoled herself, must in many ways have been simpler times indeed. In this more permissive and complicated era, she had only her own judgement on which to rely.

Tears blurred her eyes so that the lights illuminating the *crèche* shimmered for an instant like a million shiny soap bubbles. On the alert, lest her hard-earned resolution should lose its sharp, cool edge of reason, Pavana shifted her attention to windows on the opposite side of the street. There, silver-coloured balls engulfed an artificial evergreen tree, its branches bearing boxes in a variety of sizes. Each box was alluringly wrapped in satin-like paper of red or gold or green and tied with wide, shiny ribbons in contrasting hues.

Pavana examined the wet tips of her boots, in which her stockinged feet felt like blocks of ice. Her fingertips ached. Removing the glove from her left hand, she examined her fingernails, bitten to the flesh the evening before in her flat, a short walk from Primrose Hill near the zoo-end of Regent's Park. To the rear of the refrigerator, almost empty since Gail's departure for America, she had found a bottle of champagne brought home from her birthday celebration, and had drunk some of that while neatly packing her overnight bag.

'I can't go home to Belize either, Pavana,' Gail had said, 'That lot has everything to return for. It's easy for them.'

More than one hour later, Pavana emerged from a second bus into one of the meaner, uglier streets of London, a long way from the glittering façade and glamour of the West End. In some confusion, she walked first one way and then another, before at last locating the busy grocery store to the rear of which, she had been told, was the reception area for the clinic. As she approached the counter, the proprietor, a tall man with an apron wrapped twice around his slender waist, glanced at her overnight bag and said, 'Straight through the doorway to your right, miss.' Returning to his customer, he asked, 'Was it Cheddar you were wanting then, Mrs Simpson?' On his transistor radio, concealed among tins of cocoa and bags of coffee, the recorded voices of a boys' choir sang softly and sweetly that 'Christ was born on Christmas Day'.

'Thank you,' Pavana said.

Christmas Eve was still two weeks away. Then, among the people she knew, there would be an excess of merrymaking, of parties and of gift-giving. And when the church bells pealed for midnight mass, some of them would troop exhausted and bleary-eyed into the nearest church to continue celebrating the birthday of the Baby Jesus. The group was not particularly religious, but they did enjoy attending parties together. Within reasonable limits, it seemed anybody's birthday could provide them with a legitimate cause for celebration.

In the new year, Alex, Helga and, later, Moria would be returning to Belize, with Stoner following not long behind. They were all impatient to begin their careers, which, as most of their friends agreed over countless dinners, in a variety of pubs and at innumerable all-night parties, were bound to be brilliant. 'Absolutely, bloody brilliant,' had been Julian's comment last summer, at a dinner party held in his flat. In a few months he too would be leaving London, to take up a position in East Africa.

The hands of the electric clock on the wall opposite the operating table moved with a jerk to seven. Feeling unaccountably cold and shivery in the heated basement, Pavana was reminded of the debilitating bouts of malaria she had suffered periodically as a girl in her homeland, Belize. The cold, clammy feeling pervading her body had little to do, however, with the temperature in the room or with the memory of ancient malarial symptoms. It emanated rather from a disease of the spirit, with seemingly inoperable roots of anger, rejection and isolation.

In a fever of anxiety she sat upright, swinging her legs over the edge of the table, but the floor dropped suddenly away. The nurse pushed her gently down against cold sheets, wet with perspiration, while the other spread-eagled her legs before hoisting them into stirrups which descended from the ceiling to dangle before Pavana's terrified gaze. The doctor picked out a needle from the tray and lifted Pavana'a arm. Unable to stifle her feelings of doubt, of rage and of terror, she sank her teeth into his wrist, retching with revulsion as hair passed through the spaces between her teeth and as she tasted the saltiness of his flesh. A nurse replaced the needle spinning across the floor, and as the doctor

3

pushed firmly against her chest Pavana shouted, 'I'm not sure any more. Please, I'm not sure.'

'Easy there now, easy,' the doctor replied. 'Of course you're sure." There was no hint of annoyance or impatience in his voice. 'Understandably apprehensive, perhaps,' he said soothingly, 'but sure. Relax now, accept your decision.'

'And the consequences?' Her large brown eyes looked with remorse at the teeth marks on the arm expertly guiding the needle beneath the flesh of her own. The doctor examined the thin face almost obscured by an abundance of tightly curling black hair. He noted the ashy tint to her dark skin, the jerking of the lips attempting a smile of apology. Observing the swell of her breasts heaving beneath the white hospital-like shift and the slim, shapely legs extended towards the ceiling, he said, 'Those, too, of course. Don't we all?' He chuckled softly, closing one eye in a heavy-lidded wink.

'A bit late now for regrets, though, isn't it? You should really have thought of all that before, shouldn't you?'

Pavana heard the doctor's mild voice as though he bellowed in her ear through a microphone. The words echoed and re-echoed around the room: 'Too late, isn't it? A bit too late.'

Through the haze before unconsciousness, she screamed again knowing full well that the power of her voice echoed so loudly only within the hemispheres of her brain.

'It can't be too late. I've changed my mind, tell him, nurse, I've changed my mind.'

Chapter 2

Pavana sat up with a start, her muscles taut. Then she leaned back, sighing out loud with relief that twelve years ago it had not been too late to change her mind. In the aeroplane the twins, Eric and Lisa, were sleeping soundly on the seats beside her. The dream, one that frequently recurred, had as usual left her shaken. She would be glad to get home to

Belize City, to the apartment in which they had now lived for several months ever since their return the year before from East Africa.

Through the windows of the plane she could see, far below, the sparkling waves of the Caribbean Sea, foaming across the barrier reef before rolling towards the coral cayes scattered up and down the coast.

A week earlier, they had travelled from Belize City to visit Gail and her husband Robert Figueroa, a Belizean she had met at the University of Wisconsin. Delightful though it had been, the brief holiday had not dispelled, as Pavana had hoped, her grave misgivings about her decision to accept a position with the Ministry of Community Development in the government of Belize. The furore which her appointment had generated among certain cabinet members had been disquieting, serving only to refuel her worst suspicions. But Gail had been quite firm.

'What did you just say?' she'd asked, dumping large boxes of disposable diapers into the cumbersome metal cart, its wheels squeaking as Gail rolled it up and down the bewildering quantity of aisles in the supermarket of a shopping plaza in White Rapids, a small mid-western town a few miles north of Green Bay.

Gail strode along wearing a flaring black cape over a paint-spattered maternity dress, and fashionably high leather boots. Her red woollen beret was pulled low over her right eyebrow, which was pencilled into a dramatic arc. The honey-coloured amber beads Pavana had sent to her from East Africa looked completely at ease among the variety of gilt chains draped around the neck of her black sweater.

She glanced sharply over her shoulder at Pavana, whose voice had risen with agitation. Without waiting for a reply, Gail said, 'Don't even think about letting Mrs Elrington down at this stage of the game. The cabinet is her worry after all. It's obvious, from what you say, that she has faith in your ability to do the job. In any case, it seems a bit late now for all this shilly-shallying. I suggest you go in there and do your best, win, lose or draw.'

Which was all very well, Pavana reflected. But Gail was not the one who would be swimming at unknown depths surrounded by seasoned sharks. Impatiently she reached overhead, switching off the cold air pouring steadily into her face.

'Ah, that's better,' said the short, thick-set gentleman sitting in the seat on the aisle. He pointed to his nose as he picked up her heavy grey overcoat which had fallen to the floor.

'So sorry, Mr Grant,' Pavana said. 'I didn't realize the cold air was bothering you.'

'Oh, don't worry,' Mr Grant replied, stifling a sneeze. He spoke again, but so softly that Pavana was obliged to lean closer to hear his words above the rustling of packages and the clicking of seatbelts.

'A few government ministers are on board, I believe. A delegation returning from a conference in London, so I was told, a break-through in the Anglo-Guatemalan dispute!' He sucked in his breath as he struggled to keep his face neutral, but disbelief showed in his eyes bulging behind thick-lensed glasses.

Interrupting Pavana's exclamations of excited interest, he added with emphasis, 'Apparently.'

'But how wonderful, if it is true,' Pavana said. 'I had no idea talks were being held in London, did you?'

'A surprise to the entire country, I believe.' Mr Grant blew his nose loudly. 'Of course,' he said, examining the damp handkerchief before refolding it carefully and sliding it into a side pocket of his trousers, 'it's hardly the kind of thing that would have been broadcast too widely beforehand. I did gather something was afoot before I left on medical leave.'

'In your position you would, of course,' Pavana said.

'Even so, in my position it doesn't do, you understand, to be overly curious. Not these days anyway, as I've already explained. Sent you to sleep, didn't I?'

'I wasn't really asleep,' Pavana said. 'I feel very concerned and I do understand how disappointed you must be. Still, you never know, perhaps things will improve, eh?'

Mr Grant poked out his bottom lip and said, 'Perhaps.'

Pavana studied his face thoughtfully. She wondered how much, if anything, Mr Grant knew about her own situation.

An assistant secretary in the Ministry of Works, Mr Grant feared that he was in danger of not attaining the rank of permanent secretary, the top public service job and a position to which he had aspired all his working life. The draft constitution, Mr Grant had explained, said so in no uncertain terms. As soon as Independence Day had come and gone – as soon as the last British bagpipe had wailed its farewell dirge on the governor's seafront lawn, as soon as the last cocktail had been drunk by

6

foreign dignitaries – in this very year, 1981, all senior appointments such as his own in the Belize public service would be decided upon not only by merit but also for political expedience.

Mr Grant sat hunched over his packages, looking thoroughly depressed at the prospects he saw before him.

'No,' he was saying, 'it doesn't pay these days to be over conscientious or too public-spirited.'

'Doesn't it?' Pavana asked.

'It doesn't,' Mr Grant said, removing his glasses to dab at his streaming eyes. 'It might be misunderstood – excuse me.' He sneezed again. 'Misinterpreted,' he said, encouraged by Pavana's solicitous and enquiring expression. 'There can be unfortunate repercussions, apparently, for such as myself, draped as I am in all the wrong colours of the political linen.' He looked expectantly at Pavana, then sighed when she asked, 'And how long have you been in your acting position, Mr Grant?' Her eyes watered in sympathy with his obviously miserable situation.

'Not as long as some I could name, but it's a year exactly today, an anniversary . . . so to speak.' He glanced sideways at Pavana, wondering why she had not as yet mentioned her difficulties with the cabinet; after all, the cabinet's displeasure over her appointment was fairly common knowledge within certain ministries.

He decided to raise the subject, but cautiously. He didn't want to alarm her unduly, and he approved of her discretion. After all, one never knew, these days, who was really who.

'As I understand it, you may be joining us shortly – after a fashion, anyway.'

'Oh yes, I will, Mr Grant,' Pavana said, surprised to find that her voice sounded confident, even optimistic. 'I expect to start within the next few days. But how did you know?'

Mr Grant blew his nose loudly, shaking his head from side to side before giving her his gloomiest smile, his eyes mournful, as once more he refolded his wet handkerchief.

'These things drift like air along the corridors of the ministries, Pavana. There are few secrets in Belmopan, as I think you will find.'

Pavana gripped the armrests as the plane hit another air pocket.

'Really?' she asked, smiling.

'Really,' Mr Grant agreed.

Pavana gazed at him attentively. With one hand she fiddled with the

7

thick plait hanging over one shoulder. With the other she clutched the overcoat against her body.

He uncapped his inhaler and sniffed at it meditatively before he said, 'An unfortunate time to be entering the public service, I'm afraid, and age too, if you'll forgive me.' He cleared his throat. 'A bit over thirty now, if I remember correctly?'

Pavana nodded. 'Thirty-four next birthday.'

'Yes, well. You'll have to proceed with caution, you know. No racketing about like you did as a young girl. Erline and I, we remember the job you had getting down from that golden plum tree in the corner of the yard. Climbed on to the kitchen roof as I recall to get the plums from the higher branches. Of course, that tree went in the hurricane of '61, like so many trees and homes in the neighbourhood.' He leaned back in his seat and observed Pavana's face, but she only laughed and said, 'What a thing to remember, Mr Grant!'

Erline and Hubert Grant had no children of their own. Their home and garden on Kiskadee Avenue had, since the earliest days of their marriage, been like an oasis to a number of neighbourhood children fleeing the humidity and tensions of their own homes, the consequences of misdemeanours, or unpleasant household chores. Some dropped by for a drink of iced water, others sat at the kitchen door giving Miss Erline blow-by-blow accounts of street fights, or of brutal beatings in their homes with broom handles or sash cords, soaked overnight in water.

There were a special few who on Saturday afternoons helped Mr Grant, an amateur carpenter, to make tables and chairs for sale on a profit-sharing basis. The back porch where this activity took place was shaded by several coconut trees; and the pungent scent of varnish, mingling with the smell of wood shavings and turpentine, hung permanently in the air of the four-room house.

Sunday mornings had always been the best time for Pavana to visit the Grant's garden, simply for the pleasure of being there. She would read for hours in their Mexican hammock tied between two of the several thick posts which supported the house. Miss Erline started her cooking early and the aroma of chicken, stewing in onions and garlic, wafted towards Pavana's nostrils with every stray breeze that blew. The hammock ropes creaked loudly whenever she pushed her foot against the ground; seashells tinkled in the cool sand, a most comforting sound and a link to holidays spent on the islands offshore, far away from Kiskadee Avenue – a treeless, narrow, noisy street in the centre of the city.

About mid-morning, when Miss Erline returned to the garden, Pavana helped her to wind string around fragrant bouquets of sweet peas, stephanotis and roses, kept fresh in buckets of water. Together they positioned the delicate maidenhair ferns in thick circular wreaths or tied them layer upon layer on crosses made of wire. As they worked, customers came and went through the gate to the street. After lunch, Pavana tied bows of mauve or purple crepe paper on to the wreaths until the bells of the Anglican cathedral on Albert Street, a five-minute walk from Kiskadee Avenue, began pealing for that afternoon's funeral.

'It was such a beautiful garden, Mr Grant,' Pavana said, remembering the ease and dignity with which Miss Erline had conducted her small business, making it seem entirely an absorbing hobby rather than the necessary second income it must have been. She had never seen Miss Erline lugging buckets of water from the public faucets as other women in the neighbourhood had to do, but she always had a full vat of rainwater for household use and for sharing with her neighbours, and rows of galvanized drums filled with river water for her garden. That possibly had been Mr Grant's contribution. Pavana looked at him now with renewed interest.

'Indeed it was,' Mr Grant said. 'And profitable too. We rebuilt our house and had a number of little vacations abroad. Once we even toured Guatemala, a country blessed with great beauty, I must say.' Here he looked apologetically at Pavana. 'Not that we approve of too much consorting, under the unfortunate circumstances, if you understand me. Of course, now the arthritis has gotten to us both, but we still do what we can. You should visit us one day soon.'

'Oh, but I will, Mr Grant, I certainly will. Please give my best regards to Miss Erline.'

'She'll be delighted to see you and the children. So many of our young friends have gone abroad – not that I can blame them. Not many return to stay. There's nothing Erline loves more than talking about the old days. We were so sorry when your parents moved up north – Corozal, wasn't it? Would you believe, Pavana, Erline still talks of how you cried as if your heart would break the day Edward Kelly and Sylvia Johnson got married? Of course, it was a sad day for all of us.'

9

A note of wistfulness crept into his voice. 'Odd to think,' he said, 'that Mr Edward Kelly is permanent secretary in your ministry-to-be, isn't it? He and I, well, we entered the service at about the same time.' Mr Grant examined his fingernails, perfectly clean, neatly pared, as if he expected to find something wrong with them.

'Isn't it, Mr Grant?' Pavana said, her voice echoing the wistfulness in his. She was amazed to find that she had succeeded in forgetting that Saturday afternoon in June, nearly twenty years before, shortly before the rainy season set in.

Chapter 3

It was to have been such a grand wedding. Pavana had accompanied Miss Erline to stand, with other uninvited but interested persons, at the arched entrance to the Anglican cathedral, opposite the green, tree-fringed lawns of Government House and the unkempt Yarborough Cemetery with its crumbling nineteenth-century gravestones.

From where she stood that day – an undersized thirteen-year-old, her hair freshly washed and plaited, in her best print dress and whitened tennis shoes – the inside of the small brick cathedral resembled the receiving hall of a storybook great house.

Miss Erline bent her head and whispered, 'There's space just inside the door, Pavana. Move forward. We'll stand there.'

In the afternoon sunshine the mahogany pews glowed, and the open windows framed the flaming blossoms of several poinciana trees planted in the grounds of the cathedral. Miss Erline's flowers, which Pavana had helped to twist into a heart-shaped bouquet for the bride and six posies for the attendants, looked as fresh as when they were picked by Miss Erline early that morning. A stem of maidenhair fern, nearly a yard long, cascaded down the front of the bride's gown of ivory satin embroidered with beads. She felt extremely pleased when Miss Erline, her plump face alight with pride, said, 'Your fern does look pretty, Pavana. We'll use that idea again.'

Miss Erline straightened her straw hat to the correct angle on her head. She pulled a handkerchief from her bag, polished her glasses and glanced around the church to see if anyone was admiring her handiwork. The triumphant booming of the organ subsided as the bride reached the altar. The officiating minister, an angular Englishman with half-glasses on his nose and multiple folds in his cheeks, stood ready.

Turning her attention to the groom, Pavana was again struck by his height and broad shoulders. She had seen him on the streets any number of times, at the head of scouting parades, his chin up, his shoulders straight, his chest forward, looking very military and very correct. Mr Edward Kelly was known for the care he always took with his appearance; but he had outdone himself that day. His hair, parted in the middle, had been neatly cut, brilliantined and brushed so that the tight waves rippled and gleamed. In the lapel of his dark blue jacket he had placed a red rosebud from Miss Erline's garden.

Just as the ceremony began, the bell in the church tower began the most mournful tolling: dirgelike notes, clang, clang, clang, clang, the sorrowful signal given for a burial service. Startled, members of the congregation turned their heads towards the rear of the cathedral where, to Pavana's astonishment and distress, a slender young woman, not more than twenty years old was standing. She was holding aloft an infant who was howling piteously, its mouth wide open, its tiny fists beating the air.

The woman, wearing a crumpled black dress reaching almost to her ankles, advanced further into the church so that she could look down the aisle at the couple standing in splendour before the altar. The broken zipper at the back of her dress left her skin exposed, and the greenish plastic slippers on her feet were caked with mud.

'It's Junie Silver,' Miss Erline whispered, 'She's taking her revenge. Just look how she has come down . . .'

The woman's face was twisted in rage, defiance and fright as she shouted above the tolling bells, 'Here is your baby, Edward Kelly. God will never give you another!'

Two boys, about Pavana's age, their clothing dishevelled and torn, came rushing out of the entrance to the bell tower, screaming obscenities at the church attendants who were desperately trying to catch hold of them. Separating, the boys fled through the side doors of the church. Several members of the congregation surrounded Miss Junie Silver, who

11

left the cathedral quietly with them, clutching the crying baby tightly against her chest.

After a while, the wedding ceremony proceeded, but the congregation and the crowd at the door had grown distracted; the organist made a number of false starts and, to Pavana, the whole ceremony seemed furtive and rushed. The minister was forced to raise his papery voice above the loud whispering and throat clearings. The groom had lost his impressive self-confidence, smiling and frowning alternately, glancing nervously to the rear of the church, fearful perhaps that Miss Junie Silver would return.

At last it was over. The bride's smile was a grimace of pain. As the couple left the cathedral, hands clasped tightly together, the old bells pealed in a prolonged and clangorous joyfulness, as if determined, Pavana thought, to reach Miss Junie Silver's ears wherever she was.

As the bride and groom walked slowly through the crush of well-wishers and curious onlookers, tears were bright in the bride's terrified and angry eyes, and the groom looked fearful and embarrassed. He ran his finger beneath his shirt collar as if it was strangling him, while his eyes examined the faces in the crowd lining the pathway from the door of the cathedral to the street, as if he knew Miss Junie Silver had not really gone away.

Pavana, following the groom's gaze, saw her standing quietly beside a church attendant, just outside the gates of the church. She was still holding her baby, as a child would clutch a doll, tightly against her chest. The very instant Mr Edward Kelly's eyes met hers, Miss Junie Silver stabbed her baby through the throat with a pair of scissors. It took a long while for the church attendant to wrench the baby from her arms, and by the time he did so the infant was dead.

When the ambulance and the police van arrived, Miss Junie Silver was still standing there quietly beside the attendant. She held the scissors loosely in one hand, and with the other tried futilely to wipe the blood spilling from her baby's throat.

Her heart thudding wildly, Pavana walked silently home with Miss Erline, who staggered occasionally as if she would fall. Once they reached the garden, Pavana, tears rolling down her cheeks, hastily emptied the buckets of water on to the ground, averting her gaze from the scattered rose petals reddening the white shell-sand. They rolled up the balls of twine and wire and hung them carefully on nails in the house posts. Pavana covered the drums of water with sheets of zinc, and picked up her book from the hammock before climbing over the fence into her own yard. Miss Erline followed her to the fenceside.

'These things happen in life,' she said.

'I know,' Pavana replied, the body of Miss Junie Silver's baby vivid in her mind, blotting everything else out.

'But I must say I am sorry we were there to witness it. Every day women in this town have babies for men who don't marry them, but they don't kill their babies. They keep their head. Something is wrong with Miss Junie Silver, do you understand me, Pavana?'

'Yes, Miss Erline.'

'And people like Miss Junie Silver, well, sometimes they get fixed on an idea. The baby may not be Mr Edward Kelly's at all, now that I think about it.'

'Yes, Miss Erline.'

'Although I wouldn't be at all surprised if Mr Kelly had been kind to her. Many people mistake kindness for love, did you know? And Mr Kelly is a decent, upstanding man, a fine Creole, well respected in the service and by everyone. And the bride's father, he's in the service as well. They come from a long line of people in the service. Fine people all.'

'Yes, Miss Erline,' Pavana said, gripping the top of the zinc fence. The setting sun flooded the pale evening sky with a harsh light, almost the colour of blood. No wind blew through the dark green leaves of the mango trees and the coconut palms were motionless, as if standing to attention. Her palms felt moist and sticky. She could hardly breathe.

'You forgot your flowers,' Miss Erline said, giving Pavana the posy of rosebuds she was squeezing so tightly in one gnarled hand. 'I would have loved to have that poor little baby,' she continued. 'Isn't that always the way?'

'I know, Miss Erline, thank you,' Pavana said. 'I'd best go in now.'

On the back veranda of her own home, Pavana quietly opened the garbage can and set the posy, tied with narrow red ribbons, gently inside among the chicken bones, fish skeletons, plantain skins and coconut trash.

Each day in her neighbourhood brought a succession of sad and tragic stories, and after a few months the wedding, Miss Junie Silver and the

13

dead baby gradually faded from her mind. Nevertheless, it was a very long time before she and Miss Erline even considered returning to the arched doorway of the Anglican cathedral to watch any more weddings or funerals, no matter how grand or how momentous.

'Did they ever have any children?'

'Who?' Mr Grant asked, busy with his packages and briefcase.

'Mr Edward Kelly and Miss Sylvia Johnson.'

'Oh, yes, they have a fine son. In the public service like his father.' Mr Grant closed his briefcase with a final click.

'And Miss Junie Silver?'

'Died some years ago, I believe. Ate a quantity of rat poison, so I was told. Although, our institutions being what they are, I would not be in the least surprised.'

'How awful,' Pavana said looking at Lisa and Eric sleeping beside her. Living away from home for such a long time, Pavana had romanticized certain aspects of life in Belize, not only to herself but to her children. It was only in recent months that she had allowed herself to remember some of the horror, cruelty and sadness she had witnessed as a child on Kiskadee Avenue.

'Your children must be very tired,' Mr Grant said, observing Pavana's concerned look towards Lisa and Eric.

'Oh, yes, it's been a long journey in one way and another. We left my friend's home before five o'clock this morning to reach Green Bay in time for the seven o'clock flight to Chicago. We took another plane to Miami, got on this one, and here we are.'

'You have fine-looking children, Pavana,' Mr Grant said, 'and they look exactly like you did at their age.'

'That's what everyone tells me. When they were babies, I was always so relieved to be able to tell them apart. I've been lucky.'

'Indeed,' Mr Grant said. 'Not married yet, I suppose?'

'Not yet.'

'Can't understand why not,' Mr Grant said, watching Pavana as she bent over to pick up two crayons from the floor. She put each one carefully in the box, closed it, laughed, but did not reply.

'My goodness, you're not mashed up yet. Far from it. You look younger than your years. Too busy travelling about, I suppose?'

'That's probably it,' Pavana said. She waited anxiously for Mr Grant to ask the obvious question about the children, which, as an old friend, he was entitled to do. But he didn't, and she smiled at him, grateful for his attempt at gallantry.

Chapter 4

Although it was probably not what Julian Carlisle, in the latter days before her eventual departure from East Africa, would have called a 'worthwhile value', Pavana felt momentarily cheered by Mr Grant's backhanded compliment. Maintaining a relatively youthful appearance had not been so very difficult, preserved as she had been for two years in the materially comfortable life as Julian's administrative assistant, on the periphery of the aided development community. The stresses and strains which beleaguered the overseas employees of these agencies were legendary. Every now and then someone had to be evacuated 'in a strait-jacket', or was 're-assigned' or left the country suddenly for medical or other reasons cloaked in numerous imaginative euphemisms.

Pavana's way of coping was to swim, with Lisa and Eric, several times each week in the pool at the International Club, or to play badminton with them on weekends in the gymnasium of the International School. These activities did help to offset the adverse effects of her essentially sedentary occupation, and the debilitating consequences to mind and body of lavish dinner parties, receptions and picnics, which were as much an integral part of the aided development activities as projects, reports and meetings – cynics often said they were the most important part.

On one occasion, Lisa and Eric had been given small singing parts in *Joseph and His Technicolor Dreamcoat*. Pavana had sat with Julian on metal folding chairs to the rear of the open-air theatre at the club. Overhead the sky was bright with stars, and a light, gentle wind cooled the perspiration on her forehead. As the curtain went up and the small orchestra began playing the overture, she forgot the last-minute chaos of getting the children ready and to the theatre on time. She gave herself up to the enchantment of the music, and to Julian's comforting presence. The giant old trees, growing on the perimeters of the concrete floor of the theatre, seemed to hold those few hours in a protective embrace.

'I wish old Basil was here,' Julian whispered against her ear. 'We could pretend we were a real family then, couldn't we?'

Pavana nodded, squeezed his hand and met his gaze, which was sombre and thoughtful. There were deep furrows in his cheeks, and his face was drawn as he observed the young people on the stage. It had been thoughtless of her to invite him.

'I'm sure Dora will send him next summer. She's promised.'

'I wish I could be sure of that,' Julian replied, uncapping his silver whisky flask. His eyes were a clear, sparkling grey, startling against his deep olive complexion which had tints of copper in it, and his curly light brown hair was trimmed close to his head. Of average height and slender build, in dark trousers and a white shirt open at the neck, he looked like what he was, the deputy resident representative of United World, a non-government agency involved with refugee programmes in East Africa.

Even as the audience rose to its feet at the end of the last act, clapping and shouting 'Encore, encore', Pavana felt the onset of the immobilizing fears which, more frequently of late, caused her to walk up and down her bedroom unable to sleep. Her eyes filled with tears as she watched Lisa and Eric waving their black berets at the cheering audience. Beside her, Julian, clapping enthusiastically, looked a lot older than forty-one; his smile, usually warm and wide, revealing front teeth that overlapped slightly at the edges, was strained and she knew that he must long to weep.

Sometimes, in that alien, arid environment, particularly when Julian was away, she too, felt like hell, anxious over irreversible decisions she had made, by the consequences of choice, of past actions. She had a growing sense that somewhere in her life she had unwittingly wandered down an interminable side road, which had brought her to the very end of the earth.

Even so, there were many compensations to being a part of the aided development set, even if peripherally, as Julian often reminded her. It was also quite possible, had she been able to overcome certain inconvenient scruples and a great deal of false pride, that she and Julian could have lived quite amicably together. They could have looked forward to 'home' leaves in Julian's flat overlooking the Sussex Downs, near Ovingdean, a few miles from the institute where Julian had received part of his training in international development. He would cheerfully, even lovingly, have assisted her in carrying the burden of her responsibility for Lisa and Eric.

But she had known Julian for too long not to realize that she would be taking advantage of his temporary vulnerability. Because their friendship had always been based on mutual consolation, one shoring up the other in time of need, she understood that the offer had been another rescue attempt, like the job offer which had taken her away from economic difficulties and the dull routine of her life in London to a relatively glamorous, well-paid job in East Africa. It was just Julian manifesting his basically humanitarian instincts.

So, about seven months before, she had left their relationship 'suspended' – Julian's term – there on the sand dunes of Mosque Bay. They'd gone there, as they did most Fridays, the Moslem holiday, on a picnic with friends.

Even now she could see the red, blue and green picnic umbrellas staggering in the strong winds from the Indian Ocean, see the shimmer of iridescent sand like bottled glitter clinging to the palms of Eric's hands and on the bottoms of Lisa's feet, its shine reminding her of incongruously painted faces in carnival parades, of ancient school entertainments, of circus clowns and of the burlesque.

The burning sunlight fell heavily on her neck and shoulders and she drew aimless patterns on the sand, longing for sunset, wondering why coconut trees did not grow on that shoreline as they did on almost every other beach she had ever known. Julian yawned, stretched his slim frame full length on the sand, and pulled his cloth hat further over his face. He could never, it seemed, get enough sunshine, and nearly always had a drink shortly before nightfall 'to ease the transition' he said.

'It's difficult for people with different manners and habits to live together,' she'd said a while before, quoting from a book they'd both read. 'At least not very comfortably, for any length of time.'

'Aha,' he'd replied, his voice muffled, 'But you've taken that out of context. That book was written nearly fifty years ago. Different cultures, maybe, but we don't have different manners and habits, anyway not so much that they would have mattered after a while.'

Of course they already had, but Julian was eternally optimistic and would never admit it. He certainly had not asked her to change, but during the months she worked with him, trying to fit in, she thought her personality altered in ways she found uncomfortable. On several occasions Pavana had caught herself lapsing from her regular way of speaking into a ludicrous imitation of others. She developed a jarring inaccuracy of accent and heard herself saying to Julian's professional acquaintances, '*Do* stop by for tea,' and, when they arrived, busied herself with a teapot, cosy and biscuits, asking, 'One lump or two?'

It hadn't stopped there. During tea, on being questioned about Julian's whereabouts, she replied, 'on safari': legitimate, everyday words in the lexicon of Julian's friends and acquaintances, many of whom considered themselves 'old Africa hands'. But words that conjured up in her mind the most unfortunate images of photograph albums, with faded pictures of helmeted 'great white hunters', their booted feet resting lightly on the still warm, she imagined, carcasses of lions or elephants. Words that in no way conveyed the seriousness and dedication with which Julian and others worked to assist the refugees.

Once, on a field trip with Julian to a dismal, horrifying refugee camp, devoid of the most basic amenities, she leaned against the Land Rover waiting for Julian, who was huddled with a group of officials discussing an outbreak of cholera in the camp. She had observed with morbid curiosity the funeral rites for a two-year-old child who, from a distance, appeared to be only the size of a six-month-old baby. As the refugees crowded around the grave, she realized that in many ways she herself was a displaced person, her uprootedness disguised by the economic freedom to travel her education had bought.

She'd used the word 'mosquito' all her life with no difficulty and had never felt the slightest urge to contract it into an affectionate diminutive. But she'd started using the word 'mozzie'.

'Please shut the screen door,' she'd call to Lisa and Eric. 'Lots of mozzies out this evening.'

Like the word 'safari', the diminutive 'mozzies' immediately brought to her mind the image of a long line of black bearers with mosquito nets, an essential item no doubt in the camping gear they carried on their heads, trudging through the long golden grasses of an East African savannah.

Apart from anything else, she'd always valued her individuality and had an absolute distaste for the poseur. Therefore she was appalled to find how easily, under the stress of trying to make herself acceptable and to network for her own professional advancement, she was beginning to lose a sense of balance, a sense of identity, entering an altogether bizarre dimension, that of caricature and the burlesque.

Chapter 5

A cold wave curled around Julian's feet and he sat up, brushing the sand from his shoulders and arms. Dropping his sun hat into his duffle bag, he took out his pipe and asked, 'Do you seriously think that you'll be able to adjust to life in Belize, Pavana? What has it been? Fifteen years or so, except for the occasional holiday?' He crossed his legs and observed her thoughtfully through the smoke drifting across his face.

She didn't reply immediately, listening to the surf droning like distant war planes over the reef; to the optimistic laughter of their friends gathered around the makeshift buffet tables; and to the hollow clanking of a bell, bone against metal, as a camel train moved across the red, undulating sand dunes, towards the nearest watering hole. She followed the progress of an uprooted thorn bush tumbling along the sand as though pushed by invisible hands rather than by the wind. Julian had not posed his question idly, and so it was difficult to frame an answer. There were so many conflicting emotions, successfully ignored for years, stirring urgently within her and demanding recognition, resolution.

For the most part she had enjoyed living and working in Somalia, asking for little more than the opportunity to observe and marvel at the differing rituals and traditions by which people charted their days and nights, or marked the changing seasons of their lives. But, after that disastrous dinner party several weekends before, held on Julian's spacious patio, she had begun in earnest to question the choices she had made so far in her life, and which had brought her so far from home.

That night she had grown sharply defensive, perhaps inappropriately so, and had 'over-reacted', Julian said and, although he denied it, caused him embarrassment. She had vehemently objected when his

19

regional director had referred to certain national counterparts as 'like children' who were incapable of assuming the burden of their country's responsibilities. That evening she had also lost the possibility of a two-year contract as a consultant to a women's organization in the country, a job which at the time seemed attractive, one she felt reasonably sure she could do, and for which Julian had encouraged her to apply.

Lying there on the beach at Mosque Bay, Pavana finally decided that a simple, direct reply to Julian's question was probably the best she could do.

'I'd like to try, Julian. Most likely I'll be able to get some kind of teaching job.' She kept her eyes down, replaiting the fraying ends of her hair.

Julian snorted. On the verge of anger, he jumped to his feet and carried their bags further up the sand dunes. Pavana followed, her arms filled with wet towels and the two thermos bottles, the remains of coffee and lemonade sloshing about in them as she climbed the sand dunes behind Julian, noticing the wet tendrils of hair on his legs, the dark blue swimming trunks trimmed with white hugging his slim hips.

As they settled down again, Julian asked, 'Are you sure it's not disappointment over losing the consultancy? These things happen regularly in this business. Surely you know that. There'll be other opportunities, better ones most likely.'

'It's only partly that, Ju. I have this uneasy feeling that the way I behaved when Harry Hawkins was here probably cost you the pro-motion you deserve. The consultancy would have been great, but I'm beginning to see I probably wasn't the right person for the job in any case.'

'You did shake him up a bit, I must say. But I'm not overly ambitious as you know, and think of all the other occassions when we've made an excellent team.'

'I know, and I'll miss you very much, and my job. But maybe it's time I faced up to my own environment, don't you think? You'll probably laugh, but I do feel some resurgence of . . . I hate to use the word . . . patriotism in these nationalistic times at home. I wish you wouldn't laugh like that. Julian, it – '

'Gets on your wick, all right, I won't. But it's a bit late for all that, I should imagine, and hopelessly romantic as well. *I* don't fit very well into English life for any length of time any more, if I ever really did.'

20

'That's probably because your mother was a Belizean.'

'Oh, I don't know about that. It's a common side effect of the life we lead overseas. We become accustomed to the freedom . . . from a number of constraints we would be subjected to at home.

'Besides, Pavana, my mother wasn't a Belizean, in the sense you mean. Not by a long shot. Mother was a British Honduran, with all the values, attitudes and traditions that implies. She was quite content living as the wife of a policeman in an English village. She travelled to England as a nurse, during the Second World War and felt she had gone home. She never returned to Belize, nor ever wanted to go, not so far as I know anyway.'

'That sounds strange to me, do you know that, Julian?'

'Perfectly natural, as a matter of fact, considering the times in which she lived.'

'Downright strange,' she said, peering down into his face, surprising a tender look in his eyes and a softness about his lips which had been absent lately. He lay stomach-down on the sand, his chin on one arm, looking out across the waves.

'In any case, Julian, once your difficulties with Dora are resolved, perhaps we can get together again.'

'Oh, but we certainly must,' he said, jumping to his feet.

'Are you avoiding the subject, Julian?'

'Don't be silly, of course I'm not. Shall we do our usual mile?'

'Well, all right,' Pavana said, wrapping a *kanga* around her swimsuit.

Eric and Lisa had left the water and were playing volleyball with a number of other young people on the ridges of sand piled up by the wind.

'Soon be back,' Pavana called up to them.

Strolling along the beach, they stopped now and then to pick up the thin, brittle shells abandoned by sea urchins for Julian's collection, which he displayed on coffee tables in giant, circular glass jars. The sky had clouded over and a strong wind was blowing from the ocean. After months of dry weather, it was hard to believe that the few rainy weeks of the year had finally arrived. There had actually been a thunderstorm the evening before, and now they walked through tangles of exquisite, delicately coloured reef flowers of green, tangerine and brown, torn from their beds by the roughness of the currents. Julian squeezed her hand tightly.

21

'I'm sorry the problems we've both been having are affecting our relationship. I had great hopes we'd surmount them somehow.'

'I suppose we will, eventually. It's just that I find myself these days increasingly defensive on behalf of the developing countries, and who's to say they need or want my defence? Most are probably quite content being on the dole, so to speak, or consider aid their just desserts after centuries of exploitation by others, or some such. I can't tell any more.'

'So you're chucking all this up for a teaching job, are you?'

'Something like that. I loathe the fact that the realities are such that our begging bowls are always to hand.'

'And you feel teaching will remove you from these realities?' There was a hint of amusement in his voice.

'Not altogether, of course, but maybe I'll begin to have more self-respect again. I'll feel less like an aggressor each time I open my mouth, and less like a victim when I keep it closed. It's a place to start, in any case.'

For a moment, Pavana had a vivid image of Harry Hawkins, his mouth slightly open, his bald head shining, his massive face an ugly purple, as she'd asked, 'Why should people in the developing countries – odd term, that – try to be self-reliant, or pay any attention to community leaders who try to point the way towards self-reliance, when agencies like United World are only too pleased to receive proposals for money, goods and services? Sometimes I think these so-called aided development programmes are diabolical schemes to keep us in our place.'

Pavana shuddered, remembering how much courage it had taken for Julian to stand at the wide veranda doors of his villa on the night of the dinner party in honour of Harry Hawkins. Julian didn't as a rule enjoy large parties but, when acting as representative as he did several times a year, he performed his duties with style and grace. Informally dressed in a white shirt, tucked into dark, baggy trousers, and black, handmade leather shoes, he greeted his guests with a shy smile, his grey eyes twinkling behind round, silver-rimmed glasses.

The United World flag, on a pole near the high, white-washed compound walls, shimmered in the spotlight. From the broad veranda, where the guests assembled for dinner, there was a magnificent view during the daytime, across the rose-coloured rooftops of other white-washed villas and of the thundering ocean many feet below.

'Dora always maintained that I was an absolute fool not to do what I needed to do to ensure my promotion. She saw me as weak and terribly doveish.'

'I hope you didn't take that "weak and doveish" slander to heart, did you?'

'I must confess I am beginning to seriously think about it.'

'And?'

'There may be some truth in what she said. I've never objected to being passed over.'

'But still, Ju . . .'

'It's all so much water under the bridge anyhow. My commitment is such that I've learnt to live with the uncertainties and risks of being a development professional, for what that's worth.'

'Then you're not disappointed, I mean about Hawkins's cable that someone else will be res. rep. here?'

'Of course I'm disappointed, but not surprised. And don't feel that it had anything to do with you. It's partly because I loathe the game-playing as much as you do. And it shows.'

'But aren't there goals you want to reach, ideas you want to implement? You talk and write about them all the time.'

'Certainly. But not at any cost.'

'I see,' Pavana said, watching Julian heaving chunks of rock far out into the ocean. 'I feel better about old Harry the Hawk, then . . . if you really and truly feel that way.'

'Oh, I do. In my own way I do try to project overseas the best development concepts I know, but somehow word has got round at headquarters that I'm a nay-sayer, a doom and gloom man, not a team player.'

'Do you know something, Julian? I've never listed my values, by these I live, by these I die type of thing. They sort of crop up when the need arises, surprising me sometimes.'

'You should examine what you do value, at least every now and then, to make sure they're still valid, not based on nurture, religion and all that. I've chucked out quite a few of mine over the years as being totally unserviceable.'

'It's funny . . . a lot of people, myself included, find development attractive but disturbing at the same time, you know what I mean? At home I'll try to discover what those values, attitudes, traditions and so on are that keep us "developing" but never "developed".'

Julian laughed. 'That'll be the discovery of the century! I'll visit Belize, shall I? Then you can demonstrate your findings. It might be instructive – fun, too. Besides, it is strange that I've never even thought to visit the country in which my mother was born.'

'I hope you really do visit me.'

'You have my word,' Julian said. 'And don't worry about Hawkins, we're old sparring partners. I'm not easily shaken off, as he well knows.'

They scrambled several feet up the sand dunes to get away from the tide dashing inland. Up and down the beach, everyone else was doing the same, carrying their chairs, baskets of food and wet towels. Pavana felt a sudden urgency to reach their friends and acquaintances, to sit with Eric, Lisa and Julian around the barbecue fire, to watch the sun sink slowly behind the red sand dunes, to listen to their voices mingling with the roar of the darkening waves pounding inland, over the rocks until the white sandy beach was only a memory.

'Imagine, Ju, this may be my last picnic at Mosque Bay. It's hard to believe. I'll miss all that,' she said gesturing towards the group sitting on the sand dunes, but meaning much more.

'I expect you will,' he replied. 'You needn't go. You're still employed.'

'Perhaps, after all, I am more a part of this world than I ever realized. I have this dreadful feeling of nostalgia, of loss.'

For a moment, Julian watched as she retied the wet, floral *kanga*. As she knotted it around her neck, he said, 'Dora and I will resolve our difficulties one of these days. In the meantime, we could combine our households. Tandem couples are quite the thing these days . . .'

'Lisa and Eric might not understand. Anyhow, I thought we'd agreed that since there isn't a grand passion between us, we'd see what the future brings?'

'Ah, but who knows? A grand passion might develop. I've heard of such happenings. And goodness, look at all the years of friendship we've got between us. Those should count for something in my view. I expect Lisa and Eric would love it. Basil, too.'

'I'd better not,' Pavana said. 'Although it is a tempting idea. Sorry, Ju Ju, it's probably one of my unserviceable values rearing its unexpected head. I'll live to rue the day, I'm sure.'

When they were a few yards from the group around the barbecue fire, Julian said, 'You're bound to bump into old Alex Abrams while you're in Belize. Do you have any idea what he's doing these days? Still on the fringes of the political world there, I suppose. There was a grand passion between the two of you in the old days. I've often wondered whether you . . .'

'The passion was all on my side, Julian, you know that very well.'

'Still, you must have some sort of situation to resolve there, haven't you?'

'In some ways I have, in other ways I hope I haven't,' Pavana said.

'Anyway, we're getting awfully gloomy and it *is* your last weekend. It's not as if we're irrevocably cutting ties and all that. Why don't we suspend this discussion until my visit to Belize?'

'That's if old Harry Hawkins doesn't post you to Nepal as res. rep. or to some other part of the world you couldn't possibly refuse.'

'Nepal would be interesting, I must say,' Julian laughed. 'And hard to resist. Unlikely, however, so watch out for me.'

Their arms around each other, they staggered against the stiff wind from the ocean towards Lisa, Eric and the friends Pavana had made, in Julian's world, laughing and talking around the fire on the sand dunes.

Chapter 6

'The cayes, Mummy, the cayes,' Eric said, shaking Pavana's arm. 'Land ahoy, heigh ho!' He reached for his large yellow goggles, propping them on top of his short, curly hair. Putting his driver's manual into the backpack under his feet, he leaned forward in his seat all set to enjoy his turn at the aeroplane window.

As a child, she had spent many holidays on several of those islands where coconut trees grew so luxuriantly. Before it was quite light in the mornings she would rush outdoors, shouting in gleeful anticipation, headlong and unafraid, across the sand towards the sea, her voice drowned by the surf roaring over the reef. As she ran, the bellowing wind thrashed the palm fronds, tore her hair from its plait, propelling her along, arms outstretched, to greet the cool, stinging slap of an incoming wave. In the mornings then, when she'd awakened from sleep, the briny taste on her lips and the burning sensation in her eyes had been only from the strong winds of December and from the saltiness of the sea.

'I do wish you wouldn't say that all the time, Eric,' Lisa said, settling herself in the seat beside Pavana. She opened a pocket-sized book of crossword puzzles, and hunted in the seat for a pencil.

'Say what all the time?'

'*Heigh ho*. It's boring. And you are never going to wear those goggles in the airport, are you, Eric? Mummy, tell him he can't.'

'And why not, Lisa Leslie, give me one reason why not, heigh ho?'

'It's embarrassing, that's why not. People will stare at us.'

'And how about you with those earphones on your head, all the time? You'll wear out your ear drums, Mummy said so.'

'Earphones are different, Eric. They're allowed, aren't they, Mummy?'

'Well then, I'm wearing my goggles and that's that, heigh ho.'

Pavana stared at the twins until their eyes reluctantly met her own. The look was one usually guaranteed to quell almost any public squabble. She often wished it worked as well when they were at home. Remembering the lovely afternoon they had spent with Gail at the shopping plaza, where the twins had made their purchases, Pavana said, 'Goggles and earphones are both all right so long as no noise comes from either.'

Pressing an elastic band urgently into Pavana's hand, Lisa rolled her eyes in Mr Grant's direction and whispered, 'Isn't he ever boring, Mummy?'

'Not really,' Pavana whispered back, twisting the band expertly around Lisa's thick brown plaits, bunched together at the nape of her neck.

Pavana kept her frown in place until the twins had settled down again. Watching the shifting expressions on their faces turned towards the window, and as occasionally they asked each other a question or exchanged information, Pavana felt a familiar surge of love and pride in them; it made her want to hug them close as she used to when they were younger, but she restrained herself; public displays of affection, of late, were also 'embarrassing' to both of them.

Aside from the recurring uneasiness about her imminent change of occupation, and the rash promise she had given, years before, to Lisa and Eric, Pavana was basically more at ease with herself than she had

26

been for any number of years. Her new job, with its challenges, broader opportunities and a salary almost twice what she was now earning, was crucial to all they hoped to achieve as a family. And if she could only keep her nerve, in two years or so the plans she had discussed with Gail and her husband Robert would be well under way.

'The economy is in an absolute shambles, as usual,' Mr Grant was saying, 'The price of sugar on the world market, you know?'

Pavana nodded. She thought of the trucks loaded with the long, slender, brown stalks of cane, rolling along the Northern Highway to the factories; and of the plight of many cane farmers whose livelihood was dependent on that source of income.

'And you've heard about our secret crop, of course?'

'Marijuana? Oh, yes, of course. I did hear that a number of people have grown suddenly wealthy in recent years. Is it really true that light aircraft use the highway as a landing strip?'

'Regularly, so I've been told. It's our biggest export item nowadays, apparently. The profit is bigger than our national budget, so I understand.' Mr Grant paused to accept a glass of water from the air hostess. He lowered his voice.

'High level people are involved, so I've heard. But the trade touches many thousands of people. Hard to see what the outcome will be. As I've said, we're facing serious problems this Independence Year. Not the best time for . . .'

'I really do appreciate your advice, Mr Grant,' Pavana interrupted, staring through the window at the dense green bush over which the aeroplane was now flying.

Scattered widely over the small, sparsely populated country were villages with names like Double Head Cabbage, Crooked Tree, Bullet Tree Falls, Never Delay, More Tomorrow, San Narciso, San Antonio, Hopkins, Chan Chen, Crique Sarco, Sarteneja and Monkey River, in some of which she would probably be working. Pavana wondered how much, with no technical training, she could really contribute in the face of the overwhelming problems under which the country laboured.

With Mr Grant clearing his throat, blowing his nose and shifting his bulk uneasily in the seat beside her, doubts about her decision and its possible consequences threatened to spread through her mind like the roots of those casurina trees which grow in ever-widening circles,

27

sucking the nourishment from the ground; underneath their seductively sighing branches only the hardiest plants can grow.

Pavana continued to gaze resolutely through the window. As she watched, her thoughts chaotic and her emotions mixed, the plane flew lower over the rooftops of Belize City, a town of about 50,000 people and until a few years before the country's capital city. The overcoat was beginning to feel unbearably hot and heavy on her lap, but there was little she could do except hold it there. The overhead compartments were crammed with people's purchases.

She had returned home only when she had become fairly well convinced that the risk to the children's emotional stability, and to her own, was negligible. She felt reasonably sure that this was still true but, with the events of the past weeks still vivid in her mind, she couldn't help but wonder whether she was now jeopardizing that emotional stability, which for years she'd sacrificed to achieve and maintain.

'Try *grip*,' Eric was saying, as he frowned at the grubby page with numerous erasures which Lisa proferred. About the same height, they still preferred wearing jeans, sneakers and the first polo shirts that came to hand in the mornings.

'That's only four letters, Eric. Do try.'

'*Grasp*, then,' Eric said.

'That's it!' Lisa said, as frowning with concentration she swiftly pencilled in the word.

'You really should bring your dictionary along,' Eric said, returning to his book.

'It's too big for my backpack, you know that.'

'Maybe Mummy and I can get you a smaller one, as a birthday gift.'

There was a pause as the twins looked at each other, before glancing at Pavana and then turning away.

Lisa and Eric were greatly looking forward to meeting their father, and often discussed it with each other at mealtimes or in the privacy of their bedrooms. Pavana seldom joined in these discussions any more. She had begun to feel inexpressibly relieved that they were old enough, and close enough most of the time, to carry on these discussions between themselves. She had already told them all she felt she possibly could, over the years, and given the circumstances they were as well prepared as two young people could be. But Pavana was uncertain about the thoroughness of her own preparation; it was time she gave some thought to that.

She hardly noticed when the aircraft landed. As it came to a stop on the runway she and the children joined the line of disembarking passengers crowding into the aisle.

'There may still be a bit of a wait,' Mr Grant said. 'The delegation, you know.'

'We might as well be ready,' Pavana said, taking the backpacks and the overcoat which he passed to her from her seat.

Passengers en route to Central American countries further south peered curiously out of the windows at a large crowd of cheering people massed to the rear of the terminal building, a few minutes' walk from the aircraft.

Chapter 7

As they emerged from the aircraft into the Belizean sunlight, Pavana observed the returning delegation of ministers moving among enthusiastic government officials and party members waiting to welcome them home. Overhead the sky was the palest blue, and clouds without a hint of grey moved about in the most desultory fashion. Harrier jets, property of the Royal Air Force, thundered briefly through the air on routine practice manoeuvres. The wind whipped strands of hair about her face, which in spite of all her mental preparation had gone cold and tense.

The roar of the crowd was long and continuous. She scanned the group of officials quickly, searching for a familiar figure, and sure enough there was Alex Abrams striding across the tarmac. Party flags, green and yellow, fluttered high over several hundred heads as he advanced to hug and shake hands with the returning ministers before turning to wave both hands to the crowd who shouted their approval.

Pavana, flanked by Lisa and Eric, walked in a huddle of other passengers moving briskly towards the airport terminal, built like a large bungalow except for the observation tower on the roof. To her left

Mr Grant, burdened with his packages, limped his way slowly across the tarmac, his jowly face sombre and in complete contrast to the expressions of triumphant joy on the faces of the people surrounding the delegation. She read the placards held high above the heads of party supporters:

'Our prayers are answered.'

'All our territory intact.'

'Safe and secure Independence for Belize.'

Alex stood in the forefront of the crowd, six feet tall, slender, immaculately groomed. The bald patch, like a monk's tonsure in the very centre of his head, was not something she remembered, but his large eyes under thick eyebrows seemed just as intense, just as sincere, and his smile, winning, confident, never left his face as he paused to greet party men and women who dipped the giant flags, slowly, solemnly over his head.

It was a measure of the political climate, Pavana reflected, that she and Alex who had known each other so well in the past, could be at home in a country of about 165,000 people and make no attempt to contact each other. Alex's political allegiances had shifted since those early days, and it was entirely possible that in the next elections he would seek political office under the ruling party which was courting him as assiduously as he courted them.

Rumours about his political activities drifted to Pavana almost daily, and his official duties as special adviser to a cabinet minister were reported regularly on the radio and in certain newspapers, even when, as Pavana's father was fond of remarking to her mother, 'He accompanies his minister to declare open an out-house at Pull Trousers Creek.'

Lisa and Eric were already drenched in sweat as they stood with Pavana in the long line at the immigration desk. Still to come was the inspection of their luggage by customs officials before they could leave the airport. Pavana's short-sleeved white shirt clung to her back, and like the twins, fidgeting beside her, she was longing to get home, to shower, and to sit for a while on the veranda where it was shady, cool and soothing to the nerves. As she removed the passports from an inside pocket of the bulky overcoat, she glanced at her watch; it was nearly five o'clock already.

She recalled the November evening in London, many years before when Alex had given her the watch. It had been her birthday that Friday, several weeks before the start of the Christmas holidays. Gail and a few of their mutual friends had thought to give her a birthday surprise. When Alex arrived late to join them at a small café near the polytechnic where Pavana studied, four small tables had been pushed together and the dingy tablecloths made festive with flowers, a cake and a number of gaily wrapped gifts, including a bottle of champagne which Julian and his fiancée Dora had brought.

Dora was taller than Julian, with long, straight blonde hair, caught at the side with golden-coloured barettes. Her eyes were deep blue, her lashes long and dark. Although Dora's face was alight with laughter, her high cheekbones pink with mirth, there was a glint of real annoyance in her eyes as she fussed with the shower of silver ribbons tied around the neck of the bottle.

'The champagne's one thing, but he dragged me all over the West End to find just the right ribbon. Even then, it was half an hour before it was tied to his satisfaction.'

'And a good job you made of it, too,' Julian said, smiling fondly at her, running his hand over her hair which fell below her waist.

Moria, exclaiming over the thick cluster of diamonds in Dora's ring, broke off suddenly to call, 'Where the hell were you, Alex? At this rate we'll be here all night, and we're supposed to be going out later, aren't we? I have a good mind not to go with you after all!'

Moria's voice tinkled like a small bell in the café, causing people to glance at Alex as he made his way towards them, his grin lopsided, embarrassed.

'The meeting lasted much longer than I expected,' Alex said, kissing Moria on the top of her head, which made her smile, and seating himself on a chair beside Pavana. 'Sorry I'm late.'

Flicking her lighter, Moria lit the twenty-one candles on the cake Gail held towards her. Moria and Pavana had become more friendly of late, although a friendship with Moria had seemed most unlikely when they'd first met.

She looked very much like Alex: the same narrow face, extraordinarily large, bright, expressive dark eyes, and black hair curling round her face. Like his, her nose had a slight hook. That evening she wore a tangerine caftan, hand-embroidered around the neckline and sleeves. A quantity of what appeared to be tarnished, antique silver bracelets

31

jangled each time she moved her arms, but the bracelets may not all have been silver. Moria was very clever about money, jewellery and clothes.

Surprisingly, Moria was the one who began the birthday song, joined by the others in a raucous chorus. She was extremely popular with men, not so much because she was intelligent, pretty and charming, all of which she was; but because she maintained a curious reserve in all her friendships and, so far as Pavana knew, had never formed any close relationships with any of her male friends, treating each one more or less the same. Moria always had more invitations to parties, dinners, trips and sporting events than she could handle.

As Pavana blew out the candles, she caught Moria looking venomously at Alex, who seemed to be silently pleading with her about something that had nothing to do with his being late for the birthday celebration.

Dressed in a dark blue suit, white shirt and dark blue tie, Alex was freshly shaven, his hair and beard newly trimmed. He looked formally elegant among the more casually dressed men at the tables. Although his face wore a look of chagrin each time he met Moria's eyes, he also seemed secretly excited, distracted, anxious to be gone.

Pavana immediately dismissed the thought that the care he had taken with his appearance had anything to do with her birthday. His increasing discomfiture did seem to have something to do, however, with the fact that what he had imagined would be a brief, private occasion had turned into a larger gathering than he had anticipated.

'Look, Pavana,' he said, shielding his face with one hand as though the dim overhead light bothered his eyes. 'There is something I wanted to discuss with you, but I don't think it will be possible this evening.' He glanced at his watch, then at Moria, whose eyes were fastened on his face. He dropped his neatly wrapped gift casually in among the others. 'Happy birthday, Pavana. A thousand more.' He kissed her lightly on one cheek.

Pavana knew that she was being stupidly sentimental, but it hurt her very much that Alex had not felt it important to tie a ribbon around the gift he had given to her.

'The party was a surprise for me, too, Alex. Perhaps we can talk later this evening or tomorrow?'

'I'll be tied up for the next few days,' he said, shifting his gaze to the crowded sidewalk outside the café. 'But I'll be in touch as soon as I can. We must talk, you and I.'

'I'll look forward to that,' Pavana said, trying to sound as though she believed he really would call. 'How is Helga?' she asked, wondering how she could bring herself to ask such a question, but anything seemed better than silence between them.

'You know Helga, always busy with one project or another. Her mother arrived yesterday for a visit. Moria and I promised to go out to dinner with them. Tomorrow we're going to the theatre, which is why . . .'

'That's nice for you,' Pavana interrupted. 'I know you'll call when you get the time.' She chose her words carefully, hoping he would meet her eyes, but now he seemed to have forgotten whatever it was he had hoped to be able to say. He was smiling faintly as he listened to Stoner Bennett's half-humorous complaints about one of the students with whom he shared an unfurnished flat.

'And so I told him, I said, Dulipji, my son, it's been a few years. You must treat the entire thing as a lesson. The next time the Chinese invade, remember my advice, it's gunpowder not curry you need to be using. Joking, you understand? But the fellow he packed his goods in a hurry and walked through the door. Kindness is expensive, believe me. I've been left with this month's rent to pay.'

There was a great deal of laughter at Stoner's expense, and nobody laughed louder than Stoner himself, who pulled the African cap he always wore even lower over his jutting forehead, causing wrinkled flesh to form above bright, elongated eyes, which narrowed further as he turned his thin body in his chair to glance at Alex. So far, Stoner had roomed with a Nigerian, a Trinidadian and a Jamaican, and now his Indian friend had gone the way of the others.

'Are you quite sure you didn't throw his luggage through the door, the poor bastard?' Julian asked.

As Stoner had actually done this to another student a few months before, there was more laughter, drowning Stoner's high-pitched voice, protesting, explaining.

Alex smiled, but remained detached from the camaraderie he had for several years fostered among most of them. Another round of drinks was brought to the tables, and Gail called, 'Speech, Pavana, speech!'

As she thanked everyone for their kindness, Alex gave her sidelong

33

glances, smiling in a way that was not particularly friendly, as if to say, 'You're loving all of this, aren't you?'

She'd felt on the defensive then, and wanted to ask him, 'Why shouldn't I enjoy this? And what is it about me exactly that you disapprove of so?'

Perhaps that afternoon she had extended her remarks longer than she would otherwise have done. It was very puzzling to her that the more confident she became, the more she developed her abilities, the more adept she became at social skills, the more distant Alex became. Puzzling, because when she'd first arrived in London he had gone to great lengths to protect her, to bring her along. He had encouraged her to develop abilities she had not known she possessed.

Now whenever she told a story that made the group laugh, or talked about her interviews for the polytechnic newspaper, or spoke out on any issue of importance to her, he didn't seem at all impressed, only impatient for her to be finished. And since Alex formed the bulk of her private audience, or at least he used to do, his growing lack of interest hurt.

Moria and Alex left the party early, and pride kept Pavana glued to her seat, although she longed to follow casually after them, as she used to do not so very long before.

The watch, attached to a very narrow, silver bangle, still clasped her wrist like a small *abrazo*, even after all that had happened. She'd worn it deliberately, every day, as a reminder of what she called in her more cynical moments her 'age of belief'. The mechanism of the watch was simple, and it only required rewinding once a day, and occasional cleaning. It had kept good time over the years but seemed unassuming now, old-fashioned, alongside digital watches, or those that were really miniaturized computers, storing calendars, calculators, timers and who could guess what else. Even in the latter days of that age Pavana had clung to the belief that her companions were as dedicated to the development of the Caribbean region as they said they were, and she had little doubt that in the early and middle periods of the age they had been.

She had observed her student friends and acquaintances during those years abroad: Alex in their midst, talking and planning, in houses, bedsitting rooms and flats; writing petitions, taking part in demonstrations, making speeches in parks, at conferences, at parties. They'd convinced her, and many others, that they were a new breed in the Caribbean; that they would attempt to create an economically viable, progressive, creative and just society, a society that would offer the possibility of participation for everyone, and that elections would be free and fair.

A large number had really tried, but too many had been pressured not only out of governments but permanently out of their countries, often by forces they could guess at but could seldom prove.

It was hard now to watch, in Belize at any rate, a remnant of that London group, irrespective of political persuasion, effectively implementing a policy of rewarding their friends and punishing their enemies. Surely only mad persons made a habit of grasping for political power, holding on to political power, for its own sake, at any cost; not those whom one had admired and loved, not those among whom one has lived, not those for whose professed ideals one has worked.

Chapter 8

But in those London days how much could she have known, as she'd joyfully enlisted as a foot soldier, labouring on the fringes of the set Alex and Moria attracted so easily to themselves? She had been so flattered, so astonished, so delighted to find herself included in a 'group'; she, who through some curious quality within herself had always found it difficult to sustain being on the inside of any circle.

How grateful she had been to be a part of that company, to observe them through their days and nights, how charmed, how fascinated, how devoted to Alex, who had taken great pains in guiding her, smoothing out what he saw as rough edges, correcting her pronunciation of certain words.

'Don't pronounce the word "war", Pavana, as if it had an "r" on the end, even though of course it does. Say "wa" as in water.'

He protected her, so it had seemed, from the spontaneous convulsions of laughter and barbed comments – which always passed for humour – of a number of Caribbean types in their larger group, and of Moria, who had been embarrassed by Pavana's inclusion and later resentful of the protective way in which Alex sometimes came to her defence.

Stoner Bennett, a perpetual student, was forever staging farewell parties for his imminent departure from London. To these, people brought food and drink, some of which Stoner squirrelled away to sustain him during his 'meagre season' as he called those days when no money was forthcoming from his usual sources. People grumbled, but went anyway. Stoner's parties, they told each other, were always great fun.

'I'll never forget the first time I saw you, Pavana,' Moria said one evening at another of Stoner's bogus farewell parties, in the huge, unfurnished flat in Bayswater he was then sharing with several West Indian students. 'On your way to mass that first Sunday you arrived, when you and Gail lived in Alex's bedsitting house? Remember? You had on a little white straw hat with a brim. Did you buy it at Rita's Fancy Shoppe on Albert Street at home? The veiling was over your face and you wore white cotton gloves! You must have been freezing cold!'

Her innocent, bubbling delight in telling this story had drawn a few people around the pile of cushions on which she sat, legs crossed, in a corner of the room. 'With your black skin and skinny frame, you looked quite the little monkey, so cute.'

She had said later, as they sat together on the stained, musty, mustard-coloured carpet, plates of steaming hot curry and rice on their laps, 'It was only a joke, Alex, for God's sake, everybody is so sensitive these days. At home people call each other black monkey all the time. What's the problem? Has the fashion changed while I wasn't looking?'

The music and noise had risen to almost deafening proportions, and even though it was nearly midnight people were still arriving, some from other parties, others with bottles of liquor or containers of food. All-night parties, particularly on weekends, were a routine occurrence in the city, where no buses or trains were available after midnight. Once the initial novelty had worn off, Pavana had grown to detest these all-night bacchanals, and attended them now only because it gave her a chance to be near Alex. He was on familiar terms with most the guests, many of whom he met at the university, law inns, students' unions or at meetings of one sort or another.

'Pavana may have looked like a monkey to you, Moria, but have you ever considered that you act like an ape sometimes, adopting manners, speech, behaviour and dress you consider stylish, with little idea of their origins and what they mean, exactly?'

'Cutting, Alex Abrams, chief ape, very cutting. I've already said I'm sorry, what more can I do? Everyone around here makes jokes about everybody else. I was just dancing with that Jamaican over there, and do you know what he asked me? He said, "You people still living up in trees over there in B. H.?" I didn't get offended, it was a joke, conversation, so I laughed and asked if he'd heard the one about London on the Thames, Paris on the Seine, and Kingston on the Sandy Gully! We curled up laughing. At the rate you two are going, paranoia may soon be classified as the number one Belizean disease.'

'Awareness is the thing, Moria. I trust insensitivity will never make me unthinkingly cruel, whatever else it does to us all.'

'Hoo, hoo, listen to the man talk. You can get right down off your rostrum, Alex Abrams. He's nothing but an ol' hypocrite, Pavana, you take it from me. At least people see and hear me when I talk. Don't let me open my mouth here at the people's good party.'

She got to her feet, plunking her half-eaten plate of food on a nearby table. As she was about to move towards the Jamaican beckoning to her from the bar across the room, Alex stretched out his hand and held on to her wrist.

'Let's dance,' he said, 'I want to have a serious talk with you, Moria. Soon be back, Pavana.'

They'd linked fingers, squeezing into the mass of bodies. The room suddenly seemed small, claustrophobic; and she had felt oddly jealous. Perhaps it was the way Moria's head rested familiarly below Alex's shoulders. Or was it because Alex propped his chin on top of her head, his arm curved with infinite tenderness around the very slender waist? Although they quarrelled a lot, Alex and Moria truly cared about each other. Their closeness should not have seemed strange to Pavana, knowing, as Alex had told her, the manner in which they had been raised.

It must have been an isolated life for the two light-skinned Creole children, whose parents had developed for themselves, through love of the land and unremitting labour, a citrus estate in the Stann Creek Valley, a more than three-hour drive to the south of Belize City. In those orchards, fragrant with orange blossoms, Alex and Moria grew, running up and down the hilsides, playing in the cold, rapidly flowing streams, helping at harvest time to fill boxes and sacks with fruit piled in golden mounds under the low branches of the orange trees.

Pavana felt nauseated from the peppery curry and rice she had eaten far too quickly, and from the wine which was making her melancholy. Perhaps there was someplace she could lie down and go to sleep. Each of the rooms was packed with Stoner's friends and with gatecrashers; but first the kitchen. She could see it from where she sat. Picking up her plate and utensils, she padded on stockinged feet down the corridor towards it.

Leaning against the counter, dressed in an orange, green and yellow striped Nigerian *agbada*, with a matching cap perched comically on his forehead, was Stoner. He stood with a group of men and women wearing various types of African clothing. Some of the men wore their hair in dreadlocks, which made one man in particular look positively leonine and dangerous; a few of the women wore theirs in tiny plaits which stood up like sticks all over their heads. Two other women with longer hair had decorated their multiplicity of plaits with multi-coloured beads, which rattled ominously as they swung their heads from side to side.

They eyed the front of Pavana's hair, cut short, straightened and curled, the plait down her back, the grey pullover sweater, the string of graded fake pearls and the baggy ankle-length maroon skirt; and as she shoved the greasy plates on to the counter, crowded with dozens of dirty dishes, glasses and utensils, she said, 'Hi,' and the leonine man replied, 'Rasta-far-I.'

'Enjoying yourself, Anna Banana?' Stoner asked.

'So, so, Stoney. Yourself?'

He lounged against the counter eating his curry and rice with his fingers, which he'd told her he did to show solidarity with the masses. He chewed the bones to splinters before spitting the residue into an almost overflowing garbage container near his feet.

'I live in hope,' he replied, wiping his sticky fingers on a grimy dish towel and grinning at her through his overgrown moustache and beard. 'Want to dance?' He had widely spaced teeth and a broad nose, and because he wasn't very tall resembled, at a distance, a teenager of about eighteen or nineteen. But Pavana felt sure he was about Alex's age, twenty-four, or perhaps a year older. She had never asked Stoner his age directly, because from experience she knew Stoner was bound to give her some old-talk about 'age being relative', or that he'd 'lost his age paper'. For Stoner, it was quite obvious, had absolutely no intention of growing old if he could help it and steered clear of any talk about age. He was fond of saying, especially after he had been drinking for a while, 'My childhood is just beginning. Playing is fun.'

'To tell you the truth, Stoner, I feel a little upset. It's the curry.'

'It's not the curry *per se*, Pavana. It's because it's curried goat and at home people don't eat goat as a rule, *ergo* you feel sick. That's known as a dietary prejudice and you should rid yourself of it.'

He waved his arm and the sleeve of his *agbada* flapped against her face.

'What will you do when you go to Africa and people offer you camel milk to drink, or fried insects to eat? What will you do, Anna Banana, refuse the brethren and sistren?'

'But you're the one wanting to go to Africa, Stoner, not me. When I finish at the poly, I'm going home. I'll be waiting right there to watch you educate and uplift the masses at those giant people's rallies you guys are planning.'

'It's not a joke, Pavana. You should try to broaden your horizons a little, eat different kinds of food, meet different kinds of people, it's part of your education.'

'But I try to do that all the time, Stoney,' she replied, following him through the crowd outside the kitchen door.

He led her to the opposite end of the corridor, raising her consciousness about the dietary differences and similarities between Africa and the Caribbean. He opened a door to a room which looked as if it had once been a storeroom.

'You can sleep on that,' he said, referring to a camp bed against one wall.

'I'm grateful, Stoner,' Pavana replied.

The floor was littered with books, magazines and pamphlets, all of them in one way or another connected with the Black Power movement in the United States or with apartheid in South Africa. There were blown-up prints of Fidel Castro and Che Guevara on the walls. Stoner no longer attended any university or college. He was educating himself, he said, and took great pride in confounding his friends with his knowledge of little-known facts on widely discussed subjects and personalities.

'Is this your room then, Stoner?' she asked, thinking of the flat's three spacious bedrooms.

'Yeah, I hang out here off and on,' he said. 'Must pay the rent, you know. Besides, the living-room and kitchen are always available if I need more space for my work.'

'Are you working on something now then, Stoner?'

'In Asia,' he said, ignoring her question, removing papers, books and pamphlets from the army blanket on the bed, 'poor people eat whatever comes to hand, not like some of us in Belize, who can always catch a fish or get a bit of game, or beg a plate of food off a relative. Asians can't afford to pick and choose like we can.'

'I thought we were discussing Africa, Stoner.'

'I was speaking about oppressed brothers and sisters in general, Pavana,' he said, shoving an armful of clothing into a chest of drawers. She lay down on the narrow cot and pulled the blanket up to her chin.

'Yes, of course, Stoner.'

'Take India, for example . . .' Stoner said, sitting on the floor beside the camp bed, leaning his body against the wall as if he intended to remain there talking all night. Pavana could smell the curry on his breath.

'In a place like Delhi . . .'

'Bennett! You in there, Stoner Bennett?' One of Stoner's pseudo-Rastafarian friends blocked the light in the doorway. It was the leonine man, who glanced from Pavana's face to Stoner's.

'Fellow in the kitchen wanting that jug of wine he brought, Stoner. Fellow acting really ugly, I'm telling you. Hurry up, man.' He winked at Pavana as he closed the door behind them. She could hear Stoner's protesting voice lingering in the corridor.

Pavana locked the door quietly, relieved to be away from the noise, the need to smile, to listen, to make conversation, to be clasped, or having to repel some sweaty, temporary, unwanted embrace. She had trailed behind Alex and Moria for three nights in a row. It was now nearly Monday morning, and she felt disgusted with herself for continuing to play the role she had allowed Alex, Moria and even Stoner to foist upon her.

Alex did not attend parties and functions merely for the pleasure of it. He used the occasions, when Belizeans, West Indians and other nationalities gathered, to exchange information about what was happening in the Caribbean and in other countries. At most parties he sat or stood with groups of people talking politics until the parties ended, dancing occasionally with Moria, herself, other women he knew, and many that he didn't.

Earlier that evening, she had listened to Moria's remarks with a detachment which surprised her. Moria might have been talking about someone else; which, in a way, she was. Pavana had changed a lot since she'd first arrived two years before. Moria's remarks, in spite of Alex's attempt at a defence, emphasized Alex's change of attitude towards her, now that she could no longer sustain the role of *ingénue* nor cared to do so. Tonight she was along for the ride and would jump off as soon as she recognized her stop. After tonight she would try to see Alex and Moria as rarely as possible, if ever.

Pavana understood Alex far better now, knew his weaknesses, conceits and deceits as he knew all hers; and she had let him know she knew, which had been a tactical error, but which she could no more help than breathing, or thought she couldn't. Pointing out a person's flaws does not necessarily help that person to change, especially if the person feels superior and perfect in the first place.

It was only lowly types like herself, Pavana thought, who were susceptible to other people's criticisms, and would forthwith set out to 'improve' themselves. And 'heroes' do need *ingénues*; she understood that he was moving on, knew he had no intention now of breaking off his relationship with Helga as, in the earlier days, he had said he would do. Only last weekend Gail had met them having dinner together in one of the expensive restaurants off Oxford Street.

'You won't believe this, Pavana,' Gail had said, 'but Alex didn't look in the least bit fazed or embarrassed to see me. There were about eight or ten people at the table, everybody dressed *up*, like the proverbial puss backfoot!'

'Was Moria there, too?'

'There! She was the very life and soul, resplendent in black and gold. I think she'd been to the hairdresser. They waved briefly, she, Alex and Helga, and that, Pavana, my love, was that.'

'Who else was there? English people?'

'Definitely not English. I heard Spanish, so maybe they were from Spain, Cuba, Argentina, Mexico, who knows? They looked moneyed,

41

anyhow. Lots of true gold, flashing rings and expensive perfume. Lots of
I bow to you, and you bow to me, too.'

'Not Guatemalan?' Pavana ventured.

Gail paused, pulling hair from her brush, dropping it bit by bit into
the wastebasket near the dressing table. She looked at Pavana sprawled
horizontally across the bed.

'I never thought to think that, but they might have been. So what are
you trying to say?'

'Nothing,' Pavana said, 'It just goes to show . . .'

'What?'

'That they have a lot of different kinds of friends!'

'Well, don't shout at *me*,' Gail said, raising her voice.

'I *wasn't* shouting at you. Tell me about Helga again, did she really
have her hair in a bouffant?'

There had been no point in hiding from Gail how upset she had been,
particularly as Alex had told her he would be studying for his exams all
that weekend. He had also never invited her out to such an expensive
restaurant; had often claimed to be short of money, and Pavana had
shared her own small allowance with him on more occasions that she
cared to remember.

The banging of the front door of Stoner's flat awakened her the
following morning, and she opened her eyes to meet the disapproving
gaze of a Black Power militant seated in a throne-like cane chair, a beret
on his head and a rifle clasped in his arms. She gave the poster on the
ceiling a friendly little salute before stumbling down the corridor
towards the bathroom which was filthy and stank to high heaven. The
floor was wet and slippery, covered with bits of tissue paper. She was
definitely going to throw up. She felt so ill. 'This is it,' she resolved. From
today she had to take charge of her life again. She would go to the doctor,
buckle down to her studies, and let Alex and Moria fall off the edge.

On her return journey along the corridor, she peered into the living-
room which reeked of stale liquor, food and cigarette smoke. Stoner,
Moria and Alex were in the middle of a group of people drinking coffee
and talking animatedly. They had probably stayed up the entire night.
Once Alex dropped Pavana off at her flat later than morning, he would
most likely go straight to Helga's where he could be sure of a hot lunch,
beautifully served. Pavana sat with the group on the carpet for a short
while before slipping unnoticed out of the room. She retrieved her coat,

42

gloves and hat, put on her boots, and let the heavy door click gently shut behind her.

She stood on the steps for a minute in the early-morning air feeling slightly dizzy, low and of no account. Slowly she forced her fingers into her gloves and then started to walk towards the underground station. People were hurrying to work, to the shops, to schools, to colleges, to universities. If she caught a train very soon, she could still make it to the flat, change, grab her books and arrive at the polytechnic for her nine o'clock class.

Still she hesitated, tempted to go back inside, willing Alex to miss her, to come looking for her. But the door remained closed. Perhaps for Moria and himself the party would never end; perhaps they would play for ever. She forced herself to walk down the stone steps and into the street. She walked faster, filling her lungs with the chilly air. It was strange, but London continued to smell most peculiar, with upsetting scents she had never noticed before.

Chapter 9

Nearly three hours after their arrival at the Belize International Airport, Pavana, Lisa and Eric were finally free to leave the customs and immigration building. British Harrier jets continued to zoom through the sunny sky. A Union Jack flew side by side with the green and yellow flag of the ruling party.

Jennifer and Morris Burns, the young couple from whom Pavana rented an upstairs apartment, were waiting for them outside the wooden doors. Morris was of medium height, brown, rotund, with a resounding laugh, while Jennifer was petite, pretty, pale-skinned, with a mane of copper-coloured hair streaked with grey. Both pairs of brown eyes held the slightly anxious expression of ambitious entrepreneurs, in their mid-thirties, beginning to wonder for the first time whether or not their enterprise would succeed.

The twins uttered shrieks of delighted surprise as Morris and Jennifer hugged each child in turn.

'Thanks a lot for coming to meet us,' Pavana said, following Lisa and Eric into the rear seat of the station wagon.

'Cho, man, don't mention it,' Jen said. 'You'd do the same for us.'

'Thought we'd save you the taxi fare,' Morris said. 'How did things go?'

'Fine,' Pavana replied. 'Gail sends her regards, by the way. We really had a lovely time.'

'That's nice,' Jen said. 'It's hard to believe that we haven't seen Gail since she left for London all those years ago. And, of course, we don't know Robert at all.'

As he swung the car on to the road to Belize City, Morris asked, 'Do you suppose they'll ever return to live permanently in Belize?'

'I very much doubt it, although they talk about it from time to time. Gail has this terrible phobia about canals. She told me she still has nightmares, sometimes, of drowning in excrement.'

'Isn't that what happened to her dad?' Jen asked. 'I remember the story now. He'd gone to the lavatory before daylight and fell off the bridge over one of the canals. Heart attack, I believe it was.'

'Mmm,' Pavana said. 'And, of course, Robert always says he wouldn't be able to earn enough in Belize to live the way they want to live.'

'Can't fault him there,' Morris said. 'Jen and I are just about breaking even these days, and we don't have any children.'

'You have *us*,' Lisa said.

'Ah, yes,' Morris replied, peering at the twins through the rear-view mirror. 'Still love me?'

'We do,' Lisa replied, 'except Eric doesn't want to say.'

'Glad to hear it,' Morris said. 'We're going to have a wonderful time one of these weekends when Jen and I don't have any tours on. We'll go to the caye – swim, dive, fish, what do you say to that, Eric?'

'Sounds good to me,' Eric said, smiling broadly, holding his new goggles tightly in his hands.

Hunched behind the wheel, Morris drove with the expertise of long practice along the narrow, curving road leading to Belize City. Along the nine-mile route, Pavana noted that the flamboyant trees, which only flower for a few months in the year, had already begun their transformation, creating orange-red splashes against the darker green leaves of mango trees and mangrove bordering the river.

44

The car sped past houses almost hidden by overgrown hibiscus hedges, covered with scarlet flowers, and by bougainvillaea vines trembling under the weight of red, white or purple blossoms. Coconut trees lined the roadside for part of the way, their branches a shining yellow-green in the late afternoon sunshine.

'You'll be surprised, Pavana, at the number of things that have happened here in the week you've been gone,' Jen said, as Morris slowed the car at the crossroads which marked the entry into the city.

'I heard a bit about it on the plane, Jen. Belize, Britain and Guatemala are finally reaching some sort of agreement? That's really remarkable, isn't it?'

'I don't know about that,' Morris grumbled, turning left on to Princess Margaret Drive. 'I foresee lots of trouble.'

'People don't trust this agenda at all,' Jen said. 'They are calling it a snake with sixteen heads, and that's mild to some of the other names I've heard.'

'As bad as that, eh?'

'Worse,' Morris replied. 'And it's bad for business. People walking about with machetes and things.'

'It sounds terrible,' Pavana said, glancing at Lisa and Eric, perched on the edge of the seat, listening intently to the conversation.

'More than terrible,' Jen said, tapping on the handle of the car with her long fingernails, painted a brilliant red. 'I've had two groups of tourists cancel their trips to Xunantunich today. Who knows what tomorrow will bring?'

'What a blow. I'm very sorry,' Pavana said, as Morris turned the car into Sapodilla Street on which their home was located. As the car tyres crunched over gravel and bounced in and out of potholes, Pavana noticed that the customary sounds of the neighbourhood were unnaturally muted for the time of the day. It was as if the residents had only just discovered that they were in the grip of a fatal epidemic.

For the past three days, according to Jen and Morris, groups all over the country had begun to huddle at street corners, at fencesides, in town centres and village parks and on the beaches of the islands offshore, in various stages of uncertainty, disbelief and shock.

'Each rumour is more fantastic than the last,' Morris said, closing and bolting the iron gate.

'You're having tea with us, OK?' Jen said, as she helped Lisa to lug

45

one of the suitcases up the stairs. 'We're not often home at this time of the day, so we must take full advantage of the occasion.'

'That's kind of you,' Pavana replied. 'But . . .'

'Not at all,' Morris said. 'It's self-preservation. I'm watching my figure.' He executed a mock pirouette, one hand waving delicately in the air, the other placed lightly on his stomach.

The twins were screeching with delight.

'Again, Uncle Morris,' Lisa said. 'Do that again.'

'Only,' Morris said, narrowing his eyes craftily, 'if you, Eric and your Mom agree to come to tea. Somebody must save me from the coconut pie.'

'Don't say we're tired, Mom, we're not,' Eric called from the upstairs doorway.

'You're on!' Pavana laughed, thinking how luxurious it felt not having to prepare a meal for themselves on their first evening back.

After they'd eaten, and the twins had departed to visit friends further down the street, Pavana sat with Jen and Morris in low, wooden chairs on the screened-in patio of their ground-floor apartment, furnished like a room with ceiling-to-floor curtains, drawn back to let in the night air.

As she listened to their animated account of the past few days, it seemed to Pavana that 1981 was turning out to be a year Belizeans were unlikely to forget in a hurry.

'Well, m'dear, somebody,' Morris said, lighting a cigarette, 'heard from somebody else that an agreement had been signed. You know how we love a rumour.'

'And if it's not so, it's nearly so, which is almost as good,' Jen said, 'and things just took off from there.'

It was quite true, Pavana reflected, that Belizeans enjoyed discussing and dissecting almost any kind of rumour, but not those connected with Guatemala and its alleged claim to Belize. Those kinds of rumours gave them 'palpitations of the heart, high blood pressure and shortage of breath', as Jen, tinkling the ice in her glass, was quick to point out.

The unexpected and unsettling rumours started, apparently, on Wednesday 11 March. There was little panic at first. Time and increasing political experience had taught Belizeans to sift, evaluate and wait. And so although they cautiously discussed this first rumour, nobody was prepared to be considered so simple-minded as to believe that other Belizeans would sign any document, no matter how tentative, to discuss, for example, allowing Guatemala the 'use and enjoyment' of the Ranguana and Sapodilla Cayes, coral islands many miles south of Belize City.

When the rumours began – some said they were started by the hopelessly ineffectual, at the time, opposition party and in 'other circles' opposed to the government – a large number of citizens had no idea that the country owned any coral islands by those names.

'It is so when you are a colony,' they muttered in pathetic tones to relatives and friends. 'Your own riches you don't know.'

Still, what had not been known before swiftly became beside the point. Now they knew, and they did not even like to consider the idea of Guatemalans 'using and enjoying' those cayes on any official basis. Belizeans had lived with the threat of a 'Guatemalan takeover' for so long that it was quite easy for them to instantly hear the clump, clump, scrape, scrape of soldiers' boots, see the guns, feel the bullets and watch their homes burst into flames.

And then, Jen reported, another day of uncertainty, just as they were about to dismiss the unlikely rumours as another example of the vicious and devious lengths to which opposition elements were prepared to go in their greedy quest for power, another item from the rumoured agenda was brought to their tables, almost causing them to choke on their rice and beans, tortillas, hicatee, gibnut, crayfish or cassava, depending on where they lived in the country.

'Oil pipes from Guatemala across Belize?' they asked, their voices rising in incredulity.

'Through whose land?'

'Into whose plantation? Which *milpa*?'

'Well, not in this one. I practically forced my poor Tío Joe, who doesn't even believe in this new politics, to plant those *poco tiempo* palm trees at the front gate, to try and make our yard look like something for this so-called independence, which for sure is coming, but only the sweet Jesus knows when. How will I explain this to Tío Joe? He ran away from Guatemala. And tell me, *Señora*, how much does independence cost nowadays?'

There was at least one topic on which people were able to agree. They were hard put to remember when the month of March, one of the loveliest months of the year, had opened with such consistently promising signals of even more glorious weather to come. Sweet breezes

47

blew with rasping chuckles through the green and gold branches of coconut trees swaying to and fro under an almost cloudless sky. The sun, at its most deceptive, shone benevolently down on a sea that was a clear, brilliant emerald in shallower waters and the purest lapis lazuli beyond the reefs.

The rumours intensified shortly before nightfall on Thursday evening, that time of day when people sit on their verandas in soft and mellow moods, eager to enjoy the country's annual picture show and to listen to the laughter of young children racketing about yards, streets, alleyways and playing fields. It was that time of the year when the luckier families excitedly contemplated trips upriver to the bush, the lagoons, the mountains or to the offshore cayes.

'But is this agenda serious? Do you suppose it's true? How can we discuss giving away miles of seabed we don't yet own? Supposing we find oil down there, if and when we get it? Or an ancient wreck filled with buccaneer gold?'

Whether the rumoured contents of the agenda were true or false, and no matter in which political camp they were entrenched, Belizeans understood their duty. Proposals on this very issue had been drafted before. They considered themselves extremely fortunate, all things considered, for rumour had it that this was only an agenda for future discussion. There was time to write or telephone friends and relatives abroad, who in turn would consult the international community for advice on their predicament.

In the meantime, in all camps up and down the country, from the Rio Hondo in the north on the Mexican border to the Sarstoon River in the south, bordering Guatemala, all citizens – whether they were Maya, Creole, Mestizo, Garinagu, East Indian, Chinese, Mennonite or members of other ethnic groups – called a temporary halt to most overt hostilities. This was the first attempt to end the dispute between Guatemala and Britain in which Belizeans were directly involved. So, abandoning the seductive fantasies of March, they turned their attention to studying 'the situation' which had been a part of the Belizean reality for over a hundred years.

While hoping for the best, Belizeans prepared for the worst as they did in all national crises, which included economic difficulties, hurricanes, independence-to-come, draft proposals, and now an agenda for discussion. Although all camps ceased hostilities, no camp became inactive. In some, the faithful of the ruling party organized themselves to give a reasonable show of support to the returning delegation. In opposition groups, meetings took place where it was decided that if the rumours were true, the government would be pressured into holding a referendum on the agenda by any means necessary.

Chapter 10

As the screen door slammed shut behind them, Pavana inhaled a breath of jasmine growing in giant clay pots on either side of the doorway. Morris yawned, looking up at the sky crowded with stars.

'What a day, boy, what a day,' he said sleepily.

'An almost perfect night, eh?' Jen asked, as they reached the bottom of the stairs. 'Lucky thing you aren't taking that job, Pavana. Who knows what is going to happen?'

'I am, you know, Jen, taking the job, I mean. At this stage, I don't think I can afford not to . . .'

'After all that brouhaha in the cabinet?' Morris asked. 'Better you than me, m'son.'

'It's a challenge, something needed, useful. Then the salary is almost twice what I'm earning now, plus other benefits like a gratuity or a pension eventually, maybe.'

'I can see where you have to look to your future, what with the twins' education and all that . . .' Morris said, chewing on his underlip.

'Sure, she does,' Jen said. 'Besides, cabinet brouhahas are routine, a dime a dozen, eh, Morris?'

'Eh? Oh, m'lord, yes, hear about them all the time.'

'Well, I certainly hope that they are . . .' Pavana said. 'Routine, I mean. Goodnight, you two, thanks for everything.'

Later that evening, as she, Lisa and Eric unpacked, watered the veranda plants, talked and got ready for bed, Pavana reflected that if people had not been leaving the country in such large numbers, among them qualified, experienced bureaucrats, she would probably not have had the slightest idea that a position such as the one for which she had been encouraged to apply was open in the ministry.

As a teacher in a private girls' school, she did not ordinarily meet many bureaucrats and the invitation to attend the dinner meeting, where the offer was made, had come about in a circuitous manner.

She had been sitting in the school library one Friday morning early in January, during a free period, correcting a stack of test papers overdue for return to the students in her literature class. At the same table sat Vicky Shields, a 22-year-old Peace Corps volunteer. Short and plump, Vicky had heavy, black hair scraped to the top of her head and secured there by a number of hairpins. She had a habit of removing the pins, massaging her scalp and then putting the whole lot up again. She was doing that now, frustration in every emphatic shake of her head. Catching Pavana's glance, she whispered, 'Ooooo! This stuff is driving me right out of my tiny mind!' She flicked a finger disgustedly at the textbook and moved her chair nearer to Pavana's.

'I came to Belize to work with the people, not to teach English! I have half a mind to chuck it in June.'

Vicky had great ambitions to make international development work a career: today Belize, in the next year or so maybe India or Bangladesh.

'My goodness, Pavana,' she often said, 'there's so much to see and *do* in the world. I refuse, but utterly, to spend any of my days baking and serving yummies to the after-church crowd on Sundays. We do that in our church basement to raise money for the starving millions in India and Africa.'

Instead of the 'hands-on' rural experiences she expected to have, Vicky had been asked to teach English language at Sacred Heart, a 'ho hum' city job which she detested because it frequently involved studying pages of grammar during her free time, before she felt confident to enter the classroom to work with students whose grammar was often weak.

'Aren't your students the people, too?' Pavana asked, amused at the indignation on Vicky's red face. She had grown up on a small dairy farm in Wisconsin, not far from the town in which Gail and Robert lived, and Pavana somehow felt responsible for her welfare.

'But these students are not the kind of people I want to work with. I want to be out there, you know, in the villages helping to organize community projects, women's groups, community theatres, things like that. I could be teaching grammar at home, and may God always forbid it.'

'Ah so!' Pavana teased, using one of Vicky's current expressions. 'A regular change-agent, are you? It's a dangerous occupation, and an ungrateful one. In any case, you've only been here eight months, Vicky. Maybe you'll get your moment in the sun yet. This is the veritable land of opportunity, don't you know, particularly for the aided development set.'

Vicky leaned an elbow on the table, her grey-green eyes wide with excitement.

'I may get a chance to work with an honest-to-God development project yet! I may even get to go and live in a village. How about that, eh?'

'Really?' Pavana asked, wondering what the land of opportunity had thrown up this time to wipe the 'ho hums' off Vicky's pretty face.

'Well, only a small chance, if I can make the right connections in the ministry.'

She lowered her voice, conscious of the students staring at them from nearby tables and of the librarian, scowling at the whispering students, in a cubicle near the doorway.

'You've heard of Jackie Lee Baines, haven't you?'

'No,' Pavana said.

'You haven't? Where in the name of God do you live?'

'Good question,' Pavana said, looking at her thoughtfully, wondering where in the name of God she did live. The beaches of East Africa? Primrose Hill? The past in general?

'I can't believe you've never heard of Jackie Lee. She's a real mover in this country. You should meet her. She's travelled around quite a bit, like you have.'

'What does she do?'

'She's a UN consultant for their women's programmes. She can whip up a project proposal for vast sums, overnight, and she gets the money straightaway. She's just obtained thousands for the Ministry of Community Development to establish a Women's Unit in their Social Development Department.'

'A mover, as you've said.'

'Everyone says she'll be a regional representative very soon, and she's only about thirty-five. I should be so lucky.' She turned a gloomy glance towards her papers and books at the end of the mahogany table.

'Well, not to worry, Vicky, you've still got about twelve years to go,' Pavana said, retrieving her red marking pen which had fallen to the floor. She held it, hovering pointedly, over the stack of papers before her.

'Jackie Lee says that the whole point of the unit is to upgrade the status of women through . . .

'Education, training, advocacy work, research, reviewing the laws, etcetera,' Pavana said.

'You do know something about it!'

'Not about the Belize programme, but I once applied for a consultancy to help with the research and writing of one of the basic documents, the situation of women in . . .'

'Did you get it?' Vicky asked eagerly.

'No.'

'Nuts! What a pity.' She looked reflective. 'But isn't it an exciting idea? Jackie Lee says the plan is to start out as a unit, and then get that upgraded to a department bringing in other units like home economics and income generating. Boy, oh boy, would I love to run a programme like that.'

As Vicky talked Pavana fidgeted impatiently, praying that the recital of Jackie Lee's undoubtedly well-deserved successes would soon reach its conclusion.

The table at which they sat faced Orchid Street, and a vacant wooden house where an old school friend had once lived. A part of the roof had blown away, the panes in most of the windows were broken, many of its shutters hung loosely on rusted hinges and the doors had been boarded up to discourage intruders. Bits of masonry from the broken pathway to the house were piled outside the gate. Some years before, a hurricane had extensively damaged the house and it had remained unrepaired ever since that time.

It pained her to see bushes, weeds and vines choking the flowering plants and trees which had made the garden such a delightful place in which to play all those years ago. After graduation her friend had gone to live abroad, but Pavana still had a clear mental picture of the way the house had looked then, of the class parties that had been held there, and of the friendly, cosmopolitan family that had been its occupants.

Among the books and papers on the library table, Pavana had a notebook containing estimates from several contractors. During spare moments in the working week she pored over the alarming figures, trying to decide whether or not it would be possible for her to obtain a loan to purchase and restore the house on Orchid Street, which she wanted to turn into a small hotel. She planned to call it 'The Belizean Heritage Inn'. In the notebook she also had pages of carefully ruled drawings of each of the twelve rooms in the house, of the passageways, the old-fashioned kitchen with its ample storerooms, and the unusually large living-room with polished pinewood floors and doors leading into the garden.

Her savings from those more lucrative days as Julian's administrative assistant had been carefully hoarded, but even with a loan it was still far from enough to purchase the house and restore it to its former comfort and attractiveness. Lisa and Eric were very excited by the idea of helping to run an inn, which Pavana believed with hard work and good management would enable her to finance the twins' further education. As she looked at the house across the street Pavana sighed regretfully; she could see no way, on her present salary, of raising the money for a down payment on the house. She was startled when Vicky, raising her voice slightly, said, 'Well, what do you think my chances would be?'

'Chances for what, Vicky?'

'Getting an assignment with the new Women's Unit, maybe down south in one of the villages?'

'Good, I expect, especially if Jackie Lee puts in a word for you, and if you're sure that's what you want to do.'

'Oh, I'm sure, very sure. Sometimes I feel a bit trapped here, you know; I like to get outdoors, meet people, move around the countryside. Don't you feel that way sometimes?'

'Oh, I suppose,' Pavana said. 'But on the whole I enjoy it. Besides, I do have two young people to support.'

'Some support that is,' Vicky said. 'Do you know what's surprising about you, Pavana?'

'What?'

'Well, it's surprising that you're not more involved in community activities. You don't even seem all that interested.'

'You mustn't think that, Vicky. It's just that . . .'

'If I were you, I'd be out there in the thick of things, encouraging people, sharing my experiences, instead of . . .'

'Correcting papers, reading books, gazing through the window?'

'Exactly. Don't you miss the action?'

'Action?'

'Don't you feel that your experiences overseas are being wasted?'

'Who wants to know? Besides, you'd be surprised at how much of my limited experiences I do try to share with the students.' She smiled at Vicky's expression, which was still puzzled and disappointed at her seeming lack of interest.

'I really do hope you get a chance to work with the new Women's Unit, Vicky. I know you'd make an excellent member of the team. Don't worry about me, OK? This job is exactly what I need at this time.'

'So many people in Belize seem to do that – stay detached, heads way down, I mean, fearful of involvement.'

'I expect they have very good reasons for doing so if they do, Vicky.' Pavana looked surreptitiously at her watch. She had so much to do before . . .

'I wonder what's going to happen to this country?'

'Vicky, I wonder the same thing, every day. Look, I don't mean to rush you, but it's nearly time for the bell.'

'Is it? Oh my God, and I haven't finished ploughing through that exercise. Talk to you later.'

Pavana tapped her pen on the papers before her, thinking about what Vicky had said. In spite of what she believed, Pavana was very interested in the stories Vicky told about the activities of the various volunteers who worked in the government ministries. It must have been through her volunteer friends that she'd met Jackie Lee Baines, and had become so familiar with the Ministry of Community Development.

Apart from her aspirations to join the international development set, Vicky had been, when she'd first arrived, a keen amateur archaeologist. With other volunteers, she had spent many of those earlier weekends clambering up and down the limestone steps of the Mayan ruins in various parts of the country. These expeditions had enabled Vicky to visit some of the more remote villages, and she returned to school with plans and schemes 'to improve the quality of village life'.

To Vicky, who always included some self-deprecating story about her own miserable performance on these expeditions, it was all a grand adventure out there, the last frontier, with chances to make one's mark, for heroism and derring-do.

54

As the bell rang, Vicky hissed, 'I've just had the best idea, Pavana! Why don't you come to the meeting with me?'

'Which meeting, Vicky?'

'At Jackie Lee's house to meet with people from the ministry. It may be my big chance!' She looked reproachfully at Pavana, 'Weren't you listening?'

'When is it?'

'Tomorrow afternoon, in Belmopan.'

'Belmopan on a Saturday! I couldn't, Vicky. I'm sorry.'

'Oh, please, Pavana. I'll feel awkward going by myself, and Jackie Lee did say I could bring a friend.'

'I don't know, Vicky. I have lots of chores on a Saturday, and I was hoping to finish correcting these by Monday.'

Vicky reddened with embarrassment.

'To be truthful, Pavana,' she said, 'I thought that my going with a Belizean might give me more credibility with the powers-that-be in the Ministry. Who knows, you might be able to introduce me to a few of them.'

'You're devious, Vicky!'

'I know,' she said humbly. 'Will you go?'

'Oh . . . all right,' Pavana said reluctantly. 'I wouldn't like to thwart the efforts of a future Mother Teresa. But don't count on any introductions.'

Chapter 11

Keeping her promise to Vicky had turned out to be more of a sacrifice than Pavana had bargained for. About twenty people had gathered for the meeting, which was being held in the shadow of Jackie Lee's bungalow. The group seemed mostly composed of bureaucrats, representatives of non-government organizations, and volunteer community workers who were listening to Mrs Elrington as she outlined a proposed workshop on women and development issues which was to be held in Boom, a village about a twenty-mile drive from Belize City.

As Mrs Elrington concluded her presentation and the discussion began, Pavana slipped away from the meeting and went to the telephone on a table near the doorway of the bungalow. Jen answered at the first ring.

'They're next door, playing basketball,' she said. 'Don't worry, Pavana. I can see and hear them. We'll eat in a little while and then watch a film.'

'Thanks, Jen,' Pavana said, remembering that it was one she and the twins had planned to watch together with Jen and Morris. 'Why do I always do this?' she asked herself. 'Why?'

Many of the participants, who had valid excuses, arrived late so it was nearer three o'clock when the meeting started rather than one o'clock as originally scheduled. A sporty informality seemed, on the surface, to be the chief characteristic of the group sitting on the grass, listening with absorbed attention as Mrs Elrington, Jackie Lee Baines at her side, answered the questions that were being put to her. Mrs Elrington was dressed in a brown skirt and a tan blouse. A number of other people wore jeans, or gaily coloured skirts, shirts or headties.

As Pavana rejoined the group, Mrs Elrington was saying, 'I must admit that our programme has been slow getting off the ground. The Decade for Women opened in 1975. However, we have held a number of very successful workshops, ploughing the field so to speak.'

In the pause, a wave of murmuring swept across the group.

Nearly six feet tall, Mrs Elrington was slender, brown-skinned and about 50 years of age. She seemed to be highly regarded in the community, and had become a head of department through hard work and dedication to service. During her lifetime of work she had endured a number of bitter personal blows and disappointments, but she had not caved in, nor had she become cynical – at least not so that it showed. She held up her hand, and the murmuring subsided.

'Jackie Lee has reminded me, but I did intend to mention that a director for the unit will be appointed, we hope, before the Boom workshop.'

The murmuring started up again, and a heavy-set, middle-aged woman, white curly hair blowing in the wind, was prodded to her feet by the people around her. She rose with some difficulty, as though her legs were cramped. Fiddling nervously with the handles of her glasses she

said, 'Excuse me, Mrs Elrington, but some of the people here understood that a director had already been selected?'

Vicky leaned over to murmur into Pavana's ear. 'That's the head of
the Home Economics Unit, all her life in the service too.'

'Oh ho,' Pavana said under her breath gazing speculatively at the
woman who was turning sideways as if for confirmation from other
members of the group.

'Thank you for that reminder, Mrs Carillo. I should have mentioned
of course that the person we had in mind decided not to accept the
position after all. A pity, but there it is. You have a question, Brenda?'

Apart from Mrs Elrington, Brenda Kirkwood was one of the few
people at the meeting Pavana had met before. Of medium height,
shapely and attractive, she had a habit of biting her lips as if to control
wild amusement at something funny only she could see, then suddenly
letting them go, revealing a dazzling smile that was completely winning.
Of course winning 'any old-who' as Vicky would say, was not Brenda's
aim.

She had ready eyes – large, a golden-yellow in colour – for those it was
important, useful, smart, to cultivate, and for those she thought she
could safely ignore. Her voice was lovely too: educated, well modulated,
clearly tuned to reasonableness at all times. Brenda gave the impression
of being a broad-minded individual fastened to no fixed position, open
always to compromise.

'Surely,' her unheard chuckle seemed to say, 'there must be *some*thing
we can do?'

It was a voice eminently suited to boardrooms and to meetings, and
she was using it now to full effect.

'I'm not thinking of myself, you understand, Mrs Elrington. In fact
you, Jackie Lee and the ministry should be congratulated for overcoming the many obstacles to establishing the Women's Unit in Belize.'

There was loud applause at this point, during which Mrs Elrington
and Jackie Lee looked suitably modest and grateful for this acknowl-
edgement of their work.

'However, as I said before, these are questions that are being asked
here this afternoon, and it would . . .'

'Yes, certainly, certainly,' Mrs Elrington said, 'particularly as we do
have a large number of applications on file. No, we will not be

advertising the position again, although we will be conducting interviews.' As Mrs Elrington continued to answer questions, Vicky whispered, 'Kirkwood has applied for the job. I heard Jackie Lee talking to
her about it on the telephone several weeks ago.'

'Why hasn't she been appointed, then?'

Vicky shrugged. 'Maybe Mrs Elrington is her obstacle.'

'Do you know why?'

'Not a clue,' Vicky whispered, as Mrs Elrington raised her voice
above the general discussion.

'If there are no more questions, and since we have already formed our
committees, I don't think there is very much more we can do today.' She
smiled cheerfully as she placed her files in the battered briefcase she
carried like a baby in her arms. 'I must thank you, Jackie Lee, on behalf
of everyone for all you have done, and for providing us with this lovely
setting for our meeting, and food as well!' Mrs Elrington sniffed the air
appreciatively.

'But I love having you all here,' Jackie Lee said, springing to her feet.
'We should get together more often. Let's go indoors, please. The food is
ready.' She wore a tiny, faded triangular scarf over thin, waist-length
hair, and her peasant skirt swung around her bare feet as she led the
group into the living-room. 'Make yourself comfortable,' she called,
before joining her helper in the kitchen.

A leftover sixties child, Pavana thought, and immediately felt sorry
for feeling so meanspirited. You're jealous, Pavana Leslie, because she's
competent, committed and successful. Make an effort.

Inside the bungalow, people sat on the high, rectangular floor
cushions ranged along the walls on which hung rubbings, at eye level,
from the carvings found on the Mayan ruins, and a great variety of local
paintings, baskets and framed embroidery. In several corners of the
four-roomed house were enormous clay water jugs, filled with armfuls of
the beige-coloured, reed-like grasses with feathery heads that grew at
certain seasons along the highway to Belmopan.

From where she sat, near an archway, Pavana could see the buffet
table covered with a purple and white batik tablecloth. Matching
curtains puffed like sails at the windows and, as the evening darkened,
Jackie Lee flitted around the room lighting hurricane lanterns which she
hung on ceiling hooks. The aroma of *relleno*, a thick black soup, and of

baking corn tortillas filled the room, and Vicky, who had also taken off her shoes, came over and sat down, her face pink with pleasure and satisfaction.

'Isn't this just the way?' she asked, picking up a handful of salted plantain chips from a calabash on the floor.

'Quite,' Pavana replied, sipping her tepid papaya juice and listening to the voices of Mrs Elrington, Mrs Carillo, Brenda and a few others who had formed a group in the centre of the room.

Shortly after Pavana had returned to Belize, she had met Brenda Kirkwood through a member of a newly formed, non-government women and development group. The group had asked Pavana to help write, on a voluntary basis, a project proposal to obtain funding through an outside agency.

Pavana had not been able to participate in the writing of the proposal because she had already accepted a heavy teaching load, and had been anxiously trying to reorient herself before making too many commitments.

From her work with Julian, she knew it would be an all-absorbing, extremely time-consuming job, and one which would force her to take a stand on certain issues about which, at that time, she was still undecided.

Brenda Kirkwood, now chatting animatedly with a group near the doorway, ignored Pavana, barely acknowledging her greeting. It was as if they had never met. All of a sudden Pavana felt completely out of her element, and longed to get home to Lisa and Eric. She looked at her watch, her fingers tingling with memory as she traced the grooves and curlicues on the silver bangle. Seven o'clock! It felt like nearly midnight.

Vicky was nudging her arm. 'Mrs Elrington is signalling to us, Pavana. Let's go sit with her,' she said enthusiastically, determined not to waste a precious moment. 'I do think she's a great woman. She's asked me to help Mrs Carillo to contact the leaders of the women's groups for the workshop. I'm on Mrs Carillo's committee. *In*, you understand,' she hissed, squeezing Pavana's arm.

'There you go, Vicky girl,' Pavana said, laughing, in spite of herself. 'Next stop Calcutta.'

'Ah, Pavana, my dear,' Mrs Elrington said, 'do sit down. You too, Vicky. Pavana, this is Jackie Lee Baines from the United States. Jackie, this is Pavana Leslie, a teacher at Sacred Heart. I've known her family for many years. And, Pavana, this is Mrs Carillo.'

'How do you do,' Mrs Carillo said, extending a limp hand to Pavana, who sat silently while Mrs Carillo selected a tortilla and dunked it into the *relleno*, scooping bits of chicken and boiled egg into her tiny mouth. Her hands were shaking, and she seemed greatly agitated. Pavana glanced at her face thoughtfully, and then looked at Brenda Kirkwood, still standing at the doorway. Lo, the winning smile was absent, and she immediately turned away, but not before Pavana had seen the distinctly displeased expression on her face as she looked at Mrs Elrington.

'Delighted you could join us, Pavana,' Jackie Lee was saying. 'Mrs Elrington has told me a lot about your background, and Vicky here has been singing your praises every time I meet her. You should get involved. Are you on any of the committees?'

Pavana cleared her throat.

'Not yet,' she said, but Jackie Lee's eyes had flickered to Pavana's face only briefly before sliding around the room.

A current of distinct animosity had passed between Jackie Lee and herself. At first, Pavana was puzzled as to why this should be so. It took her only a minute, in her own case, to recognize why. She had met this type of person many times in the past, the international development worker with an eye on the main chance, who really saw a person only in terms of her status in the community. The sort who had no time for the cultivation of friendships with nationals unless they were potentially useful in furthering their goals and careers.

'Excuse me for a moment, will you?' Jackie Lee said, grinding out her cigarette in the huge scalloped seashell she used as an ashtray, 'but I must have a word with Brenda before she leaves.'

'But of course,' Pavana said, astonished to find an echoing animosity in Jackie Lee's eyes before she dropped them, picked up the shell and sauntered towards Brenda at the doorway. Their heads were close together as they talked.

'Would you like a little more *relleno*, Mrs Elrington? It's quite good, isn't it?' Mrs Carillo was asking. Her voice was subdued, almost fawning, although there was not a hint of friendliness on her pale face.

Vicky, who missed very little, rolled her eyes at Pavana.

'Mmmm. Yes, that was good,' Mrs Elrington said, dabbing at her lips with a paper napkin. 'But I can get it myself, thank you, Rosalie.'

'Oh no, let me,' Mrs Carillo said. 'I'm getting some for myself.'

'Well, in that case, thank you,' Mrs Elrington said, giving her the bowl.

'Now, Pavana,' Mrs Elrington said, lowering her voice. 'You can't imagine how thrilled I was to see you at the meeting this afternoon. It's given me the most wonderful idea.'

'Really? What idea is that, Mrs Elrington?' Pavana asked, turning to signal to Vicky that they should soon be leaving. But Vicky had followed Mrs Carillo to the buffet table.

'Well, as you heard this afternoon, we've been trying to find suitable applicants for the position of director. But it's been so difficult to find the right people. Public service jobs are not very popular at this time.'

'I can well understand that,' Pavana said, taking a sip of papaya juice to soothe her throat which was burning from the peppery hot *relleno*.

'I was hoping you'd be interested in applying.' Mrs Elrington was smiling at her in great triumph, as if she stood on a high hill surveying conquered territory.

'Oh, but I couldn't,' Pavana said, coughing a little. She cleared her throat. It was difficult to explain in the face of Mrs Elrington's elation. 'I mean, surely you'd need an experienced bureaucrat, or someone already working with women and development issues, who could . . .'

'That's exactly what I don't need,' Mrs Elrington said, with an air of someone who had mapped out the territory beforehand and was determined to avoid being led through a swamp. 'You have exactly the kind of qualifications we are looking for . . . a fresh, even creative approach, your overseas experiences, teaching background . . .'

'It's kind of you to think of asking me, Mrs Elrington, but I am sure I am not the kind of person you need. Thanks all the same, though.'

Pavana watched Mrs Carillo and Vicky walking carefully back to their seats, the bowls of soup balanced carefully in their hands.

'Look, Pavana,' Mrs Elrington said, 'I really urge you to consider the position. The initial contract is for two years, and the salary is more than double what you must be earning now. Jobs like these don't often come our way.'

'I agree that it sounds like a most unusual opportunity for somebody,' Pavana said, thinking about the house on Orchid Street.

61

'Don't give me your final answer now, Pavana. Think about it and let me know by Monday morning. I don't mind confessing to you that I'm really desperate to fill this position as soon as possible. We're already way behind schedule.'

'I'll think about it then, and let you know,' Pavana promised.

'I'd be grateful, very grateful,' Mrs Elrington said, accepting the bowl of *relleno* from Mrs Carillo. 'Oh, and Pavana, did you drive to Belmopan?'

'Yes,' Pavana said. 'Vicky and I came together. Do you need a ride to Belize City?'

'Both Jackie Lee and I do, if you have space, that is.'

'Oh, certainly,' Pavana said. 'It's the least I can do.'

'It'll give us all a chance to discuss the unit and what we hope to achieve during the next few years.'

After dinner was over, and Vicky and Pavana were walking across the gravelled driveway towards the Land Rover, Pavana told Vicky about Mrs Elrington's suggestion.

'You will, won't you? Come on, Pavana, I'd walk a million miles for a job like that. So would most of those women at the meeting.'

'Something doesn't feel right, Vicky, although the salary is excellent. When you come to think of it, I really don't know too much about the issues.'

'But who does?' Vicky asked, a reckless gleam in her eyes. 'It's all new. Risk it! Apply, Pavana, apply. Wouldn't it be a riot if we both ended up in the same ministry?'

'Absolutely,' Pavana said. 'I suppose I do have some experience that might be useful.'

'As much as anyone else, anyway, from what I've heard,' Vicky squeaked in her ear. 'The Decade for Women won't last for ever. Apply.'

'You know, Vicky, I just might, although I'll need to discuss things thoroughly with Eric and Lisa. It'll involve so many changes in our home life.'

'I know your kids. They can handle it.'

'I hope so,' Pavana said, smiling cautiously at Jackie Lee who was climbing into the rear of the vehicle. As Mrs Elrington slammed the door shut and Pavana drove the jeep out of Jackie Lee's garden and into Toucan Street, Jackie said, 'What are we going to do, Cora, about finding a director for the unit? I was thinking of someone who might be exactly . . .'

'I've got the most wonderful idea, Jackie Lee,' Mrs Elrington said.

Vicky looked at Pavana and smiled beatifically.

Chapter 12

In the kitchen Pavana listened to a repeat of an earlier broadcast, which confirmed that an agenda, for later discussions with Guatemala, had been signed in London. As the broadcast came to an end she switched off the radio. The afternoon sunshine glinted through the vacant eyes of a giant African mask, positioned near the top of the high kitchen window, and a steady stream of light poured through the huge, thick lips carved into a gruesome grin.

'And well might *you* smirk,' Pavana muttered, rinsing the seasoning from her hands before shoving the roast into the oven.

When the details of the agenda had first been broadcast, on Monday l6 March, the entire population had seemed immobilized, aghast that the earlier rumours had proved to be accurate. But their recovery had been swift. It was now Wednesday and already angry groups of people, opposed to the agenda or certain items in it, were marching through the streets and picketing government buildings. A number of voices spoke up, supporting the agenda, arguing that it was a small price to pay for a 'secure' independence, but these 'heretics' were dismissed as being under the influence of foreign propaganda. But it was when the citizens heard other voices suggesting that all, or part, of Toledo, the southern district bordering Guatemala, might have to be sacrificed, that they decided, 'Enough is enough,' and shouted with one voice, 'Not a square inch.'

At the end of the school day, according to a well-established routine, Pavana, Lisa and Eric met near their battered Land Rover parked in the shadow of the school building, outside Pavana's classroom. As they threw their backpacks into the rear, she said, 'The country is in a crisis. Perhaps we should go straight home today, eh?'

'I don't mind,' Eric said. 'But I did miss my lesson last week because of the baseball finals. If I miss again, Sister Marguerite won't let me take my exams. She's warned me several times. She says I have to choose between baseball and piano, which is unfair. Of course,' he added wistfully, 'I could drop piano, and take it up again, maybe next year?'

'We've discussed that, Eric,' Pavana said. 'How about you, Lisa?'

'I'd better get right over there. They're going to measure for costumes today. If I'm not there, I might even lose my place in the show. You know what Señora Vega is like.'

'That's settled then,' Pavana said, 'But don't walk home today. I'll pick you both up after my meeting. Got that?'

'Got it,' they replied together, scowling as she drove through the school gates. They both, naturally, preferred strolling home with their friends, stopping to buy frozen ices or cold drinks, before continuing on their way.

Pavana felt uneasy about her appointment with Mrs Elrington scheduled for four o'clock. Two weeks after the Belmopan meeting, she had applied for the job. The interview, by a panel of three persons, had taken place fairly soon. Mrs Elrington had called her several days later to say that although she was having great difficulty in getting the appointment approved by the cabinet, she was confident that it would be in the end, particularly as she had the backing of the panel.

Within a few days, the letter of appointment had indeed arrived, and Pavana turned in her notice at Sacred Heart. However, she agreed to continue teaching, on a part-time basis, three literature classes each week, until a replacement could be found.

To her surprise and dismay, on the Monday following their return from the visit to Gail and her family, Mrs Elrington telephoned to say that the letter of appointment was not 'quite official'.

'There's been a misunderstanding,' she'd said. 'Could you come in on Wednesday to discuss your contract? By then I should have everything squared away.'

Pavana stood, shredding callaloo and lettuce, at the breakfast counter which divided the kitchen from the large, sunny living-room. School books and papers were scattered over the dining table and chairs, set between two windows overlooking the street. Growing on either side of the garden gate were twin royal palms, framed by sliding glass doors, leading on to the screened veranda, with its view down the lane to the sea. On the right wall, above the shabby, comfortable cane sofa, with its sky blue cushions, was a picture painted by Gail during their student days.

Of all Gail's paintings that Pavana had seen it was the one she liked best. It depicted a ramshackle neighbourhood, like the one in which Pavana had lived as a young girl. The weatherbeaten houses on stilts were set among coconut trees, tossing their fronds in the wind. Overhead storm clouds dominated the sky, suggesting a week of rain and flooded streets, and in the background the sea glimmered in the fading light. As she watched, Pavana could almost hear the croaking of frogs and the screaming of crickets.

One morning during her visit, she had watched Gail working in her own bright kitchen, with its view of the frozen river lined with leafless birch trees. As she prepared coffee for them both, Pavana stood at the window looking out at the exquisite, but bleak, winter landscape etched in grey, black and white, except for the evergreen trees that grew everywhere.

'Isn't it difficult remembering in the middle of all this snow and ice?' she'd asked Gail, referring to the almost completed painting of a tropical river in flood.

'How can I forget, is more the question. Besides, whenever I'm really working,' she looked at Pavana with a smile, 'I don't usually notice what's outside.'

'It fades away, huh?' Pavana asked, putting the mugs on the table. She peered over Gail's shoulder, impressed with the eerie quality of the riverbanks. One expected to see the snout of an alligator or the forked tongue of a snake, or to watch the gulping throat of an iguana, to hear the zing of mosquitoes, or feel the bite of the dreaded fire ants.

'Something like that. What's the matter? Are you thinking of taking up painting as well as becoming a bureaucrat?'

'Not at all,' Pavana said, averting her eyes to the window. Church spires peered above the huge trees in the park opposite, and a few people were ice-fishing on the frozen river.

'I wouldn't worry. It all sounds very exciting to me. And besides, here's a chance to put your hands where your mouth has always been. Haven't you been saying since the old London days that the lives of women have improved very little in spite of all the sweat and money they've put into the total independence effort?'

65

'That's all very well, Gail. It's just that I had no idea the job was going to be so controversial, so public. Mrs Elrington couldn't tell me very much but she did say there was quite a furore.

'Women with UN money to spend on issues of concern to them is a new concept at home. It's bound to attract a lot of attention at first, or until the funding runs out . . . But so what? You haven't got anything to hide, have you?'

Pavana had looked at Gail for a moment, laughed and said, 'Haven't we all?'

Gail hadn't taken her up on that point. Instead she'd said, 'In any case you now have your letter of appointment, and I would make sure to use it well if I were you.'

There had been other opportunities, during the days she spent with Gail, when Pavana could have discussed with her the promise she had made to the twins. On visits to the local library, for example, where several of Gail's paintings were displayed in the spacious foyer, on walks with the children through parks, in restaurants and shops.

Gail was not at all 'the artist' in temperament. In everyday matters, and in crises, she was practical, reliable, responsible, perhaps even a little intolerant of 'fears and fancies' unless confronted with solid reasons for their existence. Gail would have understood and perhaps even offered her sensible advice. She probably would have said, 'Good God, Pavana, I can't believe this. Pick up the telephone, call the man, say what you have to say and put the telephone down.'

Pavana scraped the vegetable scraps, and Gail's hypothetical suggestion, into the garbage and replaced the lid.

'I'll write him a note,' she promised herself. 'I'll invite him to lunch, or something. But not now. I'll wait until this crisis is over.'

Rinsing the lettuce leaves under the tap, Pavana noted with a mixture of amusement and concern the street lamp at the corner of the lane leading to the sea, which burned by night and by day in sunshine and in rain. During windy or stormy weather the shades clattered against the bulb, but it continued to shine brightly, except during the frequent blackouts that incensed the residents of the city.

Every now and then a worker from the Electricity Board climbed the post and fiddled with the lines and tubes, but as yet nobody had figured out a way to switch the light off during the daylight hours. The high cost of living, including the price of electricity, was an unfailing source of conversation in the neighbourhood, once the residents had exhausted themselves bewailing the deteriorating living conditions in the older parts of the city.

Before leaving the house, Pavana tilted the louvres of the windows in the brash face of the March wind breezing with typical insouciance through the three bedrooms facing south. It didn't look like rain, but in Belize one could never really tell.

The houses on both sides of Sapodilla Street were all less than twenty-five years old, except for one older, decaying wooden house across the street. Only a middle-aged, eccentric caretaker lived there, an angular man who camped in a small room beneath the house, which had been the first one built in the area. The neighbourhood was terrified of him as he had been known to fire his blunderbuss at anyone who set foot on the property he guarded.

On humid Sunday afternoons, when Belizeans from the centre of the city walked to the sea, bordering Caribbean Shores, to get away from the heat, dust and dirt, they took great care to walk on the opposite side of his street. From this safe distance, children and adults teased him unmercifully, hoping to enliven a boring interlude with a display of temper and for the excitement of seeing him brandish his ancient gun in the air, as he was sometimes known to do. Generally, though, he took little notice of them but continued swinging his machete at the almost uncontrollable wild grass and weeds growing in the neglected garden of a home that must once have been well loved and maintained.

He was known as 'Red Man', although he was black, because he suffered from hallucinations. Occasionally he would climb the back steps of neighbouring kitchens to describe in his gruff voice the horrifying Red Man that had returned to hang in his doorway, blocking his entrance to the room, preventing him from eating or sleeping, and would 'Miss Jennifer, and Miss Pavana, please come over and see'.

Pavana, Jen and the children had several times visited Red Man's little room, cluttered with the debris of his sad life, but as they were unable to see the phantom which plagued his existence Red Man had lost faith in them and had turned to others in the neighbourhood, hoping to find someone who 'could see'.

As the Land Rover bounced in and out of the potholes along Newtown

Barracks, a road following the sea, Pavana spied Red Man in the distance. His head was tied with a bright red and blue bandana. All his belongings were in an old bedsheet which he carried on one shoulder; his blunderbuss was slung over the other. He, too, was going to town.

Chapter 13

Pavana's heart was beating rapidly, that humid Wednesday afternoon, as she drove the Land Rover slowly down the south-side approach of the Swing Bridge spanning Haulover Creek flowing sluggishly to the sea. She scanned the street in dismay. All around her was evidence of the continuing unrest in the city and country. Shop windows were broken and empty or boarded up. Roving bands of young people taunted the police and soldiers. She ducked her head instinctively as a bottle flew through the air, bouncing off the bonnet of the Land Rover before splintering on the street.

As she inched her way along, the crowds continued to grow larger. People carried banners and placards, the bells from a nearby church began to peal, and angry voices drowned out the voice of the speaker at a public meeting in Independence Park, in the centre of town.

Turning left off Albert Street, she eased the Land Rover into Church Street, a depressed area where in more normal times drunks lounged in front of bars. She misjudged the distance between the Land Rover and the makeshift stalls on the corner of the street. The fenders grazed a stall and it crashed to the ground. Limes, oranges and other fruit rolled into the street and into the drain. Swiftly she parked the car on the opposite side of the road.

'By rights I should call the police,' the vendor was shouting at her.

Picking her way gingerly through the glass and debris littering the street, Pavana helped the scrawny woman set the stall upright. Together they collected the fruit scattered in several directions. The smell of squashed oranges and limes filled her nostrils.

'So sorry, ma'am, so sorry,' Pavana kept repeating, picking up the vendor's straw hat which had fallen to the ground. The woman jammed the hat on to her head, covered with a tattered and grimy scarf.

'Give me a few dollars and forget the whole thing,' the vendor said, watching the tears rolling down Pavana's face. 'Seems you have worries of your own. Those I know about. Five small pickneys and my man gone.'

Pavana gave her the money. As she left the stall, the woman was shouting at the crowds milling up and down the street, 'Get your limes right here, fresh limes, green limes, yellow limes, limes, sourer than my life.'

Scanning the front of the buildings, Pavana located a weathered three-storey wooden house with the sign Ministry of Community Development. As she climbed the stairs she felt the anger, which she had suppressed for days, beginning to rise within her, echoing the anger raging in the streets below.

On the veranda men and women stood waiting, she supposed for social welfare payments, their faces sombre as if they felt extremely ill and feared the office would close before it was their turn to see a doctor. Pavana followed the receptionist, an overdressed young woman with a disconcerting air of disinterest, to a room outside Mrs Elrington's office. The receptionist pointed to a bench on which she could sit facing a number of desks, two of which were occupied by men who, Pavana guessed, must be social welfare officers. They were deep in conversation as Pavana sat down, away from the door, and nearer a dirty, broken window overlooking dilapidated buildings housing bars, warehouses and offices. In the distance, above the noise of the crowded streets, she heard faintly the music of a marching band.

One of the officers ran a finger around his shirt collar, black with the dirt of many days. His eyes were bloodshot and his fingers shook as he lighted a cigarette, inhaling deeply.

'And then Tony, boy,' he said, 'the road from Belize City to the Guatemalan border is to be improved, and Guatemala is to have freedom of transit across Belize to the sea. Which sounds worrisome, if you ask my opinion.'

'Which nobody did, Paulie, my son,' Tony replied. He scratched his head with a grimy fingernail almost half an inch long. 'What worries me are these areas of mutual development we're supposed to explore together. What do you suppose those could be?' He stretched unusually

69

long legs out under the desk, nodding in a friendly manner to Pavana who had begun to feel as ill as the people outside on the veranda appeared to be.

'We're not likely to know, not now anyway.'

'What else do we get?'

'Let's see here,' Paul replied, scanning the sheets of paper on the desk in front of him. 'Guatemala will recognize us as an independent state and we'll have similar freeport facilities, but not too much else as far as I can see.'

'Sounds like they are asking us to pay a bill we don't owe, eh?' Tony asked, wiping his black face with a handkerchief, '*Serioso*, no?'

'Very *muy*,' Paul said, blinking several times, his pale brown skin shiny with perspiration in spite of the noisy fan, encrusted with years of dust, swilling the musty air around the room.

'It's our duty to advise people, if they ask,' he said.

'And we have to advise against it, if they ask, right?'

'Exactly right, Tony my boy,' Paul said, getting slowly to his feet and brushing cigarette ash off the front of his shirt. He walked to the door and called to the receptionist.

'You can send the first person in now, Miss Campbell.' As the receptionist brought in an elderly man, unsteady on his legs, she said, 'Mrs Elrington will see you now, Miss Leslie.'

Pavana followed the receptionist into a small room at the rear of the building. As she entered, Mrs Elrington said, 'Congratulations, Pavana, the job *is* yours . . . if you still want it, that is. Do sit down.'

Pavana sat on one of the chairs facing Mrs Elrington's desk, noticing that her air of triumph had gone. She looked extremely distraught, taking frequent sips of water from the glass at her elbow.

'I'm so glad,' Pavana said, continuing to feel uneasy. 'I couldn't understand what was going on.'

'It's a good thing I had the foresight to send you a letter of appointment, otherwise . . .' She paused, and then asked, leafing through the papers on her desk, 'You haven't ever been involved in party politics, have you?'

'I'm not a card-carrying member of any political party, if that's what you mean, and I haven't been actively involved in any campaigns or things of that sort. Of course, I am interested in party politics as everyone has to be.'

'That's exactly what I told Minister Galvez, who is extremely upset at cabinet's reaction to your appointment. He feels I've let him down, can you imagine?'

'I was surprised to learn that this kind of job is discussed at cabinet level,' Pavana said. 'Of course I have no experience in the bureaucracy.'

'Oh, yes, cabinet now reviews nearly all appointments of this kind.' Her voice, normally soft and enthusiastic, sounded harsh. 'Of course, they do . . . tend to select party affiliates, so I try to get around this in any way I can.'

'I see,' Pavana said, alert now for every nuance.

'There are several other units in my department,' she said. 'I've always, until recently, had the final word on the people appointed to head them.'

Mrs Elrington looked down at the contract before her. She seemed to have forgotten that Pavana was in the room as she ran her pen through several lines on the typewritten pages. It was obvious from the stern cast to her strong face that she was waging an internal battle, or rehearsing a recently ended one. Pavana waited to see whether Mrs Elrington had won or lost.

Pavana glanced at the plastic flowers in a small plastic green tub on the desk, at the framed quotations on the walls, at the peeling green linoleum on the sloping floor, at the bookcases piled with dusty pink files, at the straight-backed chairs, and finally through the window.

In the yard next door a mother was bathing a little boy in a bathpan set near a leaning water vat. The yard was filled with broken boards and bits of rusting machinery. Pavana felt like a very lucky person at that moment. 'How much is enough?' was a question she had often heard Julian ask at conferences and meetings.

As Mrs Elrington looked up, Pavana asked, 'What were their objections?'

Mrs Elrington cleared her throat, 'Well, your family background was mentioned, and it seems that they had heard from someone, and believed, that your appointment was decided upon before the interview, which they felt was held only to uphold the letter of the law. I am afraid some of the other applicants feel that way too.'

'I see,' Pavana said, thinking of Brenda Kirkwood.

'Perhaps you don't. It is quite common practice for departments to

71

have a candidate they prefer before the interviews are held. Cabinet knows this very well. They make a regular practice of it, in fact.'

'Will I be able to work effectively if the politicians are opposed to my appointment?'

'That depends. It won't be easy, and not all of them are, obviously. One or two, including Minister Galvez, supported your appointment based on my recommendations. An adviser, Mr Alex Abrams, was asked for his view and, I understand, he spoke up on your behalf.'

Pavana left the window and went to sit on the chair to the left of Mrs Elrington's desk. Her legs felt as wobbly as those of the old gentleman she had seen earlier.

'Do you know what, exactly, it is that the others have against you?'

'Not really, except that my family is considered to be supporters of the opposition, but you know that. As a trainee journalist, I must have been eighteen or so then, I wrote a profile about one of the ministers, a hodgepodge of what was already a matter of public record, but it was published. Apart from that I don't know of anything else that I have done personally.'

'Oh dear, that's enough. Something like that could do it – brand you, if you know what I mean. I gather it wasn't particularly flattering? Yes. Well. I am sorry we didn't discuss these things more fully before, but I underestimated the paranoia of these times.'

'I had no idea that the director of the unit should be a political appointment. If that is the case . . .'

'In some countries it is, I gather. But it doesn't have to be, and it is my profound belief that it shouldn't be. In our earlier discussions you said you believed that the unit should be run for the benefit of everyone, which seems fairly obvious, but . . .'

'It helps to have the support of the politicians, doesn't it?'

'Well, yes. However, I have no intention of allowing the unit to be used as a political mobilization arm of the government. In one way or another, most of us in the service must work at times without personal political support. It makes a difficult job a hundred times worse, but I hope you will think in terms of the contribution you can make to Belize as director of the unit.'

'I have thought about it, and have asked the advice of several people. However, the more I think about it, the more I feel that it is worthwhile doing.'

'Delighted you still feel that way,' Mrs Elrington said, keeping her eyes on the papers before her. She folded her arms on the desk.

'It is essential that people understand what the unit is all about, particularly those people who might feel uneasy or threatened at the start.'

'I believed we discussed starting a public education programme on the radio?'

'We did. And I would want to get that started almost immediately.'

As Mrs Elrington talked, Pavana reflected that she appeared to be a woman of amazing strength and courage. And Pavana resolved to try and be more like her. Mrs Elrington, it seemed, had never had the luxury of running away from her problems, or if she had, she'd never chosen that option.

After fifteen years of marriage, her husband died in an accident, suffocating beneath tons of brown sugar when a chute broke loose in the factory where he worked. She had been left with four children to raise.

'There are other things to consider,' Mrs Elrington said, her eyes apologetic, embarrassed.

'What are those?' Pavana asked, trying to stifle the apprehension within her. In the yard below, the mother was throwing a bucket of water over another little boy. This one was screaming at the top of his lungs.

'Cabinet has decided that your salary must be the same as any other public service officer of your qualifications, experience and age. Which means, Pavana, that you will not be earning very much more than you do at the moment.'

Pavana gazed at her, horrified.

She would lose the long vacations. The hours worked would be much longer; she would sometimes have to work on the weekends and she would not be able to employ a household helper as she had planned. She would be upsetting the lives of Lisa and Eric with very little to show for it.

'Good God,' Pavana said, feeling as if she'd been punched in the stomach, which in a way she had been. She looked at Mrs Elrington with new eyes now, noticed the grim look on her face, the bared teeth which passed for a smile. Surely she must have known this would be the outcome?

'So,' she said, dropping her eyes – to hide *what* Pavana could not even begin to guess, 'as the old saying goes, you won't be doing well, while you're doing good.'

Pavana had never noticed before how much white there was around her eyes, nor the tautness of the skin on her bony face, nor the faint line of white at the roots of her hair, nor her hands which looked as if they could lift two or three hundred pounds of weight and carry her battered briefcase as well. Had Jackie Lee and herself been through this process before? She remembered the unknown candidate who had refused the position.

'I'm afraid it gets worse,' Mrs Elrington said.

'Oh?' Pavana said, rapidly losing interest, feeling in limbo, wondering if the personnel officer at Sacred Heart would agree to have her back as a full-time teacher. Pavana doubted it, but she would have to give it a try.

'I feel very badly about this, Pavana, but you will also not be able to represent government overseas. I had hoped they would at least allow you to attend conferences, workshops, meetings and so on in the region, so that you could gain experience and establish a network of support for the unit.'

'They certainly are trying to discourage me, aren't they?' Pavana said, trying to smile.

'I'm afraid they are,' Mrs Elrington said, her face set in even harsher lines. 'Your contract has been reduced to one year.'

'I'm sorry, Mrs Elrington,' Pavana said, getting slowly to her feet. 'Thank you very much, but I can't see this working out. From what I've gathered, politicians can make one's life and work impossible if they choose, and it seems they have chosen.'

'There it is,' Mrs Elrington said. 'It's a defeat for both of us. I would go so far as to say for Belizean women in general, but perhaps I exaggerate.'

'Perhaps,' Pavana said, hoping if she said as little as possible, the meeting would end sooner. She needed to pick up Eric and Lisa, get home, think, and then act very quickly if she was to save her job at Sacred Heart.

'I have a suspicion, more than a suspicion, that the cabinet does not want the unit to be established at all.' Mrs Elrington was glaring at her as if she expected Pavana to give her an immediate explanation for the cabinet's decisions.

'I am sure they were aware of the unit's objectives when they signed the agreement to accept the funding . . . ah, I see,' Pavana said.

'I hope you do, Pavana,' Mrs Elrington said sternly. 'I hope you do.'

'I wish I could help, Mrs Elrington, but I can't. I hope you understand.'

'Oh, I understand completely,' Mrs Elrington said. 'Neither the permanent secretary nor the minister is expecting that you will accept this job. Then, as a head of household, you do have your responsibilities to consider.'

'Thanks anyhow, Mrs Elrington, but you do see that it would be like trying to walk uphill, a bundle of firewood on my head, a baby on my hip, pregnant with another, and a bucket of water in my hand!'

'Precisely,' Mrs Elrington said, tapping a letter opener on the contract on the desk.

'It's absurd,' Pavana said, forcing a smile to her lips. But Mrs Elrington made no attempt to do the same. She looked very sad, and very disappointed.

'Did you manage to salvage anything?' Pavana asked, thinking of the unknown candidate who had refused the job. Some women were *so* smart. They did the practical, sensible thing and opened the plughole on the rest. Pavana's eyes strayed to the misery of the yard below Mrs Elrington's window.

'We will be getting very nice offices here in Belize City, and I managed to hold on to the vehicle, brand-new, by the way, but not much else, I'm afraid.'

'What about your other candidates?'

'We do have a few, but none with your experience and skills. We'll have to re-advertise the position, which will set us back another six months. It's taken us two years to get to this point.'

Pavana hesitated, understanding fully that there would be little to be personally gained from taking the job. She struggled against committing herself to the unit, but heard herself saying, 'I'll take the job, Mrs Elrington. It's only for a year, isn't it? The unit does need to be established, that I know.'

Mrs Elrington smiled, on top of her high hill again.

'I knew you would, Pavana, something told me you would! Will I have a surprise for Minister Galvez and PS Kelly at the meeting tomorrow! I can't wait to see their faces when I tell them. I wouldn't be at all surprised if they aren't lining up their own candidates at this very minute.'

She pushed the contract across the table for Pavana to read and sign.

'There's one other thing,' she said, and added quickly as she noticed Pavana's expression of alarm, 'it's nothing serious, but you will need to travel to Belmopan twice a week for meetings and so on. Will that be a problem?'

'Everything about this job seems to be a problem,' Pavana said, 'but I'll try to find a way.'

'I'll help you all I can,' Mrs Elrington said, as she walked with Pavana to the stairs leading to the street. In the distance they could hear voices chanting. 'No agenda. No agenda.'

'The situation is getting much worse, isn't it? There are rumours that the public service may go on strike. We are not too popular with the politicians at the moment.'

'So I'm to get right on with the job, am I?' Pavana asked.

'Oh my, yes. You're on board. Go into the office as soon as you can, read the files, get organized. I'll arrange a meeting for us with Elsie Rodriquez at Radio Belize for a start.'

'That sounds great,' Pavana said. And it did. Instead of feeling depressed or resentful, she felt exhilarated, anxious to begin. Strange, she thought, pausing for a moment on the landing. And to think, Alex had supported her appointment!

She looked up to find Mrs Elrington observing her from the veranda.

'My regards to your family, Pavana.'

'Thanks,' Pavana said, hurrying down the stairway. It was time to pick up Lisa and Eric. She had so much to tell them.

Chapter 14

The fury in the streets had intensified to such an extent that the vendors had shrouded their ramshackle stands in sheets of gaudy plastic and gone to ground. To Pavana's left, huge puffs of black smoke billowed from fires burning on the narrow bridge spanning the filthy, sluggish canal in which Gail's father had drowned. Looters, yelling in maniacal triumph, rushed past where she stood, their arms loaded with appliances, bolts of cloth, food and anything else they had been able to grab and carry. The Land Rover, its tyres flat, stood conspicuously upright between two overturned cars surrounded by sharpened fence palings with rusted nails. She was left with no choice but to leave it where it was until the following day.

Manoeuvring her way cautiously towards Albert Street, Pavana found that her brief feeling of euphoria had vanished, to be replaced by a nagging sense that Mrs Elrington had pitched her a ball with a wicked curve, and impulsively she had swung at it instead of sidestepping and letting it fly past.

She had little doubt that she would reach the dancing school before Lisa's class ended, but would they be able to find a taxi and reach Eric before he became impatient and started for home? Sweat poured down her face as, scarcely daring to breath, Pavana made her way inch by slow inch through the frenzied, angry mob, and cheering battalions of neatly dressed high-school boys hurling rocks, bottles and sticks at shop and store windows up and down the city's main thoroughfare. Tear gas lingering in the air irritated her eyes, causing them to blur and water. The screaming sirens of police cars and the incessantly clanging bells of the firetrucks aroused within her alarm and foreboding such as she had rarely known.

'Keep them safe, dear God,' she whispered. 'Keep them safe.'

The crowds, hundreds deep, milled in and around Independence Park. In more normal times, the park was a refuge for market vendors, homeless people and melancholy drunks, their bleary eyes scanning the busy thoroughfares, on the constant lookout for the source of another drink. At night the park people slept fitfully, beneath naked lightbulbs, on concrete benches scattered in the vicinity of a depressingly ugly, crudely built fountain.

This two-tiered monstrosity had long ago ceased to emit even the occasional trickle of water, a situation lamented by the park's residents who had found it a valued convenience for washing themselves and their garments, drying the latter on the lower branches of the luxuriant flamboyants planted around the small plot of ground. Perhaps, for some, it was as good a place to pretend that time had ceased to be relevant, for the four-sided face of the clock on the roof of the courthouse opposite the park had indicated for years that the time was other than it was commonly thought to be. But then perhaps this was also true in other parts of the city, where the public clocks seldom if ever told the correct time.

Pavana used the narrow, broken sidewalk rimming the park as a guide. Squeezing her way through the crowd, she tried to become one with it, surging when it surged, retreating as it retreated from tear gas, smoke bombs, water hoses and the flailing batons of the riot squad. Around her, sweating, angry rioters, gone beyond fear, wielded broken handrails, bits of masonry and jagged glass. Beyond the courthouse was the Foreshore, a street running parallel to the sea. If only she could reach the sea. Another frantic surge of the crowd shoved her against a tree trunk nearer the centre of the park. The rough bark peeled skin from her forehead and blood trickled down her cheek.

She held tightly on to a jutting branch, willing herself not to panic, not to allow herself to be swept into the all-too-familiar caverns of anxiety by unfounded fears for Eric's safety. He was quite sensible, and would wait for Lisa and herself no matter how late it was. Keep your eyes open, she commanded herself, watch for a break in the crowd, get across Regent Street, then keep moving until you reach the Foreshore.

On a makeshift platform in the park, several men were burning the yellow and green flag of the ruling party, while others burnt their voter-registration cards to demonstrate their contempt for the electoral process. Someone was bellowing over a loudspeaker.

'March to the Swing Bridge. Sit on the bridge! Block traffic, bring them to their knees. Let's march. Let's march.'

Around her the crowd took up the chant and, as she continued holding fiercely on to the tree branch, the people pressing against her back took up the chant, drowning out every other thought.

'Block the agenda! Block the agenda!'

Then a sudden relief as the crowd, shuffling in a rough march, began streaming from the park on their way to the bridge connecting the north of the city to the south. Pavana let go of the branch, weaving her way in and out between the demonstrators until she was safely across Regent Street. She raced down the short and narrow lane between the courthouse and the Treasury Department, resisting an almost over-whelming urge to lean against the whitewashed walls of the courthouse wall and retch like the poor drunks she had so often observed on her weekly shopping trips to the centre of the town. At the Foreshore, lightheaded with relief, she inhaled great gulps of air, lifting her face to the uncompromising wind, wincing as the salty air stung the bruise on her forehead.

Far away, Pavana heard again the faint music of a marching band. The heel of her left shoe had been lost somewhere between Albert Street and the park, so she was forced to teeter along the seawall as swiftly as she could towards Prince's Lane, where the dancing school was located. She walked as she had as a young girl, allowing her eyes to follow the gulls swooping over the sea, gazing at the customs house, and the lighthouse on the opposite shore of the wide creek mouth.

A sudden surge of the waves dashing over the wall soaked her shoes and the hem of her skirt. Floating in the choppy waves, bouncing over the wall, were dead fish, rotting vegetables, a cow's head, an old shoe and other debris from the market and the town. The shoe, its leather sole skinned back, resembled a toothless mouth opened hideously in raucous laughter.

Everything is going to be just fine, she told herself, stepping down into the street to avoid the water rushing through a huge gap in the crumbling wall. Just fine, she repeated over and over, just fine. It was suddenly late afternoon, and the last lingering streaks of golden sunshine suffused the clouds and sky.

Boys and girls ran up and down the Foreshore and Prince's Lane, still flying their kites in the rapidly fading light. As she entered the lane a young boy, about Eric's age, brushed past her, groaning as the string of his lovely singer kite broke. It staggered backwards over the zinc rooftops and coconut trees before disappearing from view. She watched with sympathy as he tore barefooted down the lane towards Regent Street, intent on its recovery.

Many of the houses on Prince's Lane, like so many others in the centre of the city, were dilapidated. On some verandas, laundry dried on drooping clothes lines, the yards were swampy, and there were some in which sour grass grew as high as bushes. Uncollected garbage, swarming with flies, spilled into the lane. The shallow, narrow drains, uncleared for weeks, overflowed with stinking water, green with morass.

Stepping gingerly on to the boards laid across the overflowing drain, Pavana climbed the few rickety stairs to the veranda of the dancing school, an old shingled house formerly as fine as some of those on the Foreshore, beaten featureless now by weather and by the onset of hard times in Señora Vega's life. The melancholy strains of *Giselle* poured out

79

from the first floor, spilling into the lane, colliding with popular music from radios turned up full blast.

In the brief pause, Pavana heard the drums of the marching band and the shouts of the crowd which seemed nearer now. Blocking the doorway were three young boys, pockets bulging with marbles, clicking and rattling as they gyrated their arms and legs aping the dancers. Señora Vega, a petite woman in her early forties, opened the door to Pavana, allowing her to slip through before closing it gently in the boys' faces.

As she made her way to the telephone, in an adjoining room which served as an office as well as a sitting-room, Pavana caught a glimpse of Lisa's shining, absorbed face as she once more took up her position in the group behind the lead dancer, a slender brown girl, ethereal in looks, gliding across the uneven floorboards.

Watching the dancers moving across the floor of the drab room, Pavana understood why Lisa did not often willingly stay away from her lessons at the dancing school, where Señora Vega, unbowed by a capricious fate which had dismantled most of the accoutrements of a once comfortable life, drew remarkable performances from even her most awkward students. As Señora Vega's husky voice rose above the music, exhorting and instructing, Pavana strained to hear Sister Marguerite's reassurances at the other end of the line. Yes, she knew all about the disturbances. Pavana was not to worry about Eric. She would make certain that he waited until she arrived.

Relieved, Pavana washed her face in a nearby bathroom, dabbing gently at her forehead where the bump had swollen to the size of a small guava. Her blouse was torn at the shoulder and her head ached. Not having the Land Rover was such a blow, today of all days, and walking around with one shoe heel missing depressed her further.

She had to will herself to open the door quietly and step into the large room where the students were still moving back and forth across the floor to the haunting themes of the disorienting music. Her eyes continued to burn and water as she made her way to the outside door.

In the yard she joined a group of teenagers, who, finished for the day, stood against the fence, hastily pulling school uniforms over their black leotards and tights. Pavana recognized a number of the young women as students of Sacred Heart Academy. Almost immediately the marching band turned into the lane, and the music of *Giselle* was drowned out by the clashing of cymbals, the beat of drums and the shouts of people lining the street, baiting the marching crowd waving placards which read:

'Support the heads of agreement.'

'Independence for Belize.'

'All our territory intact.'

A mad man capered and danced at the head of the band. Surprised, Pavana saw that it was Red Man, dressed as she had seen him earlier that afternoon in his red bandana, his bundle on his back and his trousers held around his waist with a piece of fraying rope. He brandished his blunderbuss menacingly, whirling like a dervish, before sashaying back and forth across the street, dipping and swaying, staggering back, moving forward, lost in his own world, the blaring brass band his only guide.

In the rear of a pick-up truck moving slowly behind the marchers stood a rotund, middle-aged politician, his dark skin dripping with sweat. He waved his pudgy arms continuously to the right and left, in spite of boos and jeers from verandas and windows of the houses, and from the streetside crowd of predominantly young people who were closing in on the marchers.

As the truck drew nearer to where Pavana stood, she saw with further surprise that one of the men standing in the truck with the minister was Alex Abrams. His smile looked forced, even in the fading light, and every now and then he ran his hand over the bald spot on his head or fingered his beard. The teenagers beside her were screaming, 'Sell out! Sell out! Sell out!'

As he glanced towards the dancing school, where more students, Lisa among them, were spilling into the yard taking up the chant, Pavana saw him look towards the students, then look again, his surprise visible as his eyes met her own. Alex was on trial, Pavana saw that at once. Going out among the people, to try and convince them that the heads of agreement was really a breakthrough in trying to resolve the Anglo-Guatemalan dispute over Belize, was his ultimate test by the ruling party, which, like the opposition party, seemed to value unquestioning loyalty above all other qualities.

The boyish features she had loved had wizened into a face that in the last light of day seemed weasel-like, cunning and corrupt. But his enormous black eyes were still luminous, and she knew the brush of his long lashes against her cheek, and had often kissed the hook of his huge nose, even more prominent now in a face that was haggard with strain. As the truck continued on its way towards the Foreshore, Alex gave Pavana a brief salute of recognition. She hesitated, then she lifted her hand, saluting him briefly in return.

'For his support,' she told herself, 'For the children,' and then, more honestly, 'For old times' sake.'

The noise from the band had reached deafening proportions, and the angry, chanting crowd, led by militant teenagers, had brought the march to a complete standstill. As Pavana watched, she saw Alex staggering backwards into the group of men surrounding the minister. At first she thought he had lost his balance when the truck jerked forward, but as the chanting of the crowd changed to screams of terror, Pavana realized that Alex had been hurt. The dancers shouting to each other confirmed Pavana's fears.

'Abrams got shot. Somebody shot Abrams.'

Slipping through the gate, Pavana pushed her way through the panic-stricken mass of people struggling to get out of the lane. A few policemen flailed their batons ineffectually, linking hands to form a cordon across the street between the crowd and the truck. She caught a glimpse of Alex slumped in the arms of two bodyguards, his eyes shut, his face contorted with pain, his white shirt awash with blood. The driver pressed the horn in a continuous blast, careering the truck recklessly through the mass of people, beyond the police cordon, who were scattering in several directions.

The jostling crowd cut off her view of the truck and she remained in the middle of that throng of people, breathing heavily as though she had run a great distance, all her senses concentrating on the horn, blasting insistently as it sped along the Foreshore towards the hospital. The policemen relaxed their stance and, although she knew it was a futile gesture, she found herself moving in the direction the truck had taken. Then she stopped abruptly, remembering that Lisa was waiting for her.

Astonished at the strength of the old emotions aroused within her, Pavana walked slowly through the rapidly thinning crowd towards the dancing school, where she could see Lisa on the veranda with Señora Vega and other dancers, chattering excitedly as they gesticulated towards the street. In the drain were the remains of a soggy kite, its red dye mingling with the bilious green of the morass.

'Oh, Alex,' she murmured out loud. 'Oh, Alex.' For she was back in London, and they were walking together towards Lord's Cricket Ground, he excited and elated because he knew the West Indies were going to win, she caught up by his enthusiasm, delighted that she was going to be with Alex for an entire afternoon. For that she was willing to endure the cold winds of an English summer day.

Pavana, seeing Lisa's vigorous wave, quickened her pace, even more anxious now to call a taxi and get the children home. When she was a few yards from the gate of the dancing school, someone in the dwindling crowd gave her plait a sharp tug which hurt the base of her scalp. Expecting to see one of the mischievous boys who were still running up and down, Pavana swung round, scowling fiercely. Then she stopped abruptly, peering uncertainly at the man behind her.

'Stoner Bennett?' she asked, her shock at seeing him turning swiftly to anger. 'Why did you do that? You nearly scared the living daylights out of me! Don't you ever do that again!'

Stoner laughed, throwing an arm around her shoulders as though he did this every day of the week.

'Poor old Anna Banana,' he said. 'I've never met you when you weren't on the run.'

Chapter 15

Shrugging his arm off her shoulders, Pavana looked with apprehension into his face. Over the years, she had sometimes read of Stoner's travels in the newspapers. But her last memory of actually seeing Stoner Bennett was about the time he had become one of the drifters on the fringes of West Indian student life in London. She shouldn't have been surprised to see him, because on the streets of Belize City, as in other small towns, it is an almost everyday occurrence to bump into friends and acquaintances home on a visit, or others who had returned home to see if they could stay. It was also possible to meet, although with much less frequency, those who had been forced to return by the authorities in other countries.

Perhaps her surprise, and apprehension, was due to the fact that the little she had read about Stoner and his activities did not lead her to believe that he would return home willingly, even on a visit. But here he now was, steering her firmly by the elbow, decked out in a safari suit that was slightly too elegant. He looked expensive and cool, his aftershave wafting towards her nostrils, causing her stomach, already churning with anxiety, to feel increasingly queasy.

The colour of Stoner's suit was a grassy green with an off-putting sheen to it, not a shade nor material usually favoured by the intellectuals and pseudo-intellectuals in town, nor the Caribbean for that matter. This type of suit was a statement, since jackets and ties were 'too European' and *quayabreras*, at least in Belize, at the time, 'too Latin'. Stoner had always aspired to that class, hung around them, a fixer, the kind of person who could be depended upon to do the dirty work which everybody else was too respectable to do. As far as she could recall, he had never seemed able to actually buckle down and pursue a specific line of study for any length of time. But maybe by now he had. Who could tell?

She was amazed at the tautness of his body. He looked muscled, fit, in training, not scrawny and undersized as he had appeared to her at his Bayswater flat all those years ago. Glancing towards the dancing school, Pavana saw with relief that Lisa, the other dancers and Señora Vega were no longer on the veranda. Stoner stood in front of the gate effectively preventing her from entering, his arms stretched along the pointed palings.

'It's still the same, isn't it, Pavana? It beats me why you should still care after all this time . . . with grey in your hair and all? Anyway, it was only a flesh wound, he's not going to die, believe me.' He spat into the drain.

'How do you know, Stoney Bennett?' She looked at him accusingly. There was a scar on his face from his left eye to the middle of his cheek, which had not been there before. He shrugged his shoulders.

'That's what I heard,' he said, looking her fully in the eyes, smiling all the while, as though he was trying to put her at ease. 'From an impeccable source.'

'And what are you doing at home? The last I read you were in Africa, reclaiming your cultural heritage,' Pavana said, still angry at the shocking way he had chosen to make his presence known to her.

'I've been home a lot longer than you have. And don't go looking at me so suspiciously. I didn't touch a hair on Abrams' head.' He paused, then asked, 'Why are *you* home? Don't tell me,' he said, shading his eyes in mock horror, 'I think I can guess but I really couldn't bear to hear it.'

'Aren't you afraid of talking with brainwashed colonial lackeys like myself? After all, I just might contaminate the purity of your spiritual rebirth. But perhaps all that was simply rhetoric, guaranteed to make newspaper headlines, eh? Or were you pitched out of Africa, the homeland of us slaves?'

'I was fighting for a cause, Pavana, the overthrow of an oppressive regime. We weren't successful, but at least I tried. In addition, I did get an excellent political education along the way.'

'Which you're passing on to the Belizean brothers, no doubt?'

'And my Belizean sisters. On the subject of the sisters, Pavana, I hear you are about to take a certain job to do with the education of the sisters, which is good, surprising to me as it is. But you are on the wrong side at the wrong time.'

'The unit is a government agency. It is supposed to be of service to everyone, particularly women, and I will try to run it that way, no matter which political party is in power.'

'You always did have good intentions, Pavana, but that one is as romantic and unrealistic as any I've heard, particularly now.'

Pavana's scalp still tingled from Stoner's sharp pull on her plait. But there was little to be gained by any further wrangling with him. The point was to get Lisa and Eric home as soon as possible. She couldn't understand why he continued to block the gate. Had he gone the way of Red Man? She watched as he lit a cigarette, cupping the flame in his hands.

'Stoner?' she said, mustering as friendly a tone of voice as she could manage, 'could you give us a ride? I had to abandon my transport on Albert Street, and . . .'

Stoner laughed as if he'd suddenly thought of a private joke.

'I don't own a car, Pavana. It wouldn't be good for my image. I live near the old burial vault, and my neighbours are mostly criminals and drug addicts. So now you know.'

'But, of course,' Pavana said, trying to put a laugh into her voice. 'A man of the people ever since the old London days. How could I have forgotten?'

85

'I hear,' he said, his voice barely audible, 'that you're taking that job to try and play ball in the power league. But something tells me that you may be changing your coat, becoming a camp follower for the sake of an old love.'

'Stoner,' Pavana said, bracing herself, 'why this sudden interest in my activities? I have no intentions of taking sides publicly nor allowing my private opinions to dictate any decisions I make at the unit, not any more than I can help in any case.'

'But your new job involves the mobilization of women on behalf of the current politicians. That's how they will see it. On the other hand, you'll have trouble with a lot of the bureaucrats who won't do much from here on to prop up the government. To put it bluntly, they don't want you there, and we need your help.'

Pavana stared at him, completely taken aback.

'Who's we, Stoner?'

'The action committee. We've joined the public servants, the opposition and other concerned citizens in rejecting the agenda by any means necessary.'

'Look, Stoner, if you are asking me to become involved, just don't, because I won't.'

'But I am asking you. I wouldn't expect you to do anything big and bad and bold, believe me. I remember your timidity and inhibitions of old. Alex keeps dodging me, refusing to see me. I've tried to get hold of him every day since that agenda was made public.'

'So?'

'I want you to use your influence to arrange a meeting between Alex and myself. I need to know quickly whether the cabinet has any intentions of agreeing to a referendum on this agenda or not.'

'My influence with Alex! My God, Stoner Bennett, who is being romantic and unrealistic now? I haven't spoken with Alex Abrams for years, and whatever gave you the impression that he would consent to discuss cabinet decisions with me?'

'Because I learnt from some of my colleagues in the public service that he supported your appointment, and because I remember . . . quite a few things about your old relationship with Alex.'

'But that's a whole other thing, Stoner, it's . . .'

'Is it, Pavana? I've been doing a little scouting around and it's public

86

knowledge that you have two children attending Sacred Heart Academy. I've also been doing a little counting, and unless you can come up with another explanation, I can only conclude that Alex is their father.'

Pavana didn't reply. She averted her eyes to the doorway of the dancing school where Lisa had appeared, pointing to her watch, semaphoring with exaggerated gestures behind Stoner's back.

He clasped her wrist gently but firmly, as though they were lovers, prolonging a *tête à tête*.

'Isn't he, Pavana?' he repeated.

She fought to control a blazing anger threatening to push her over the edge into futile violence. She wanted to rake the skin off his face, to bash his head against the fence until he let her go. How dared he? What gave him the right? And yet, hadn't that been one of her primary motivations for returning home, to cleanse herself of subterfuge and secrecy? But even in her most pessimistic scenarios for doing so, she could never have imagined that Stoner would be the one who would drag her to the brink.

'Yes,' Pavana whispered. 'But . . .' She couldn't say the words.

'But what, Pavana? But what?' Why was he shouting? Why was he so angry?

'He doesn't know that, Stoner.'

'Jesus,' Stoner said and fell silent. His face became sombre, and for a minute she thought she saw a glint of tears in his eyes, but he cupped his hands to light another cigarette and when she looked again they were gone. 'Quite the little Brownie, aren't you? Was it the famous Belizean false pride or was it revenge?'

Pavana did not reply. She had said what she had been forced to say, but her motivations were none of his business.

'You're inflicting great psychological damage on your children, Pavana,' Stoner said, deliberately twisting the knife. 'I can speak from experience,' he added, injecting a false sternness into his voice. 'I don't really know who my father is, either.'

'That's one of the reasons I came home, Stoner, to tell Alex and arrange for them to meet him. But it all has to be handled very carefully, surely you can understand that. I need to wait until this crisis is over.'

'Much as I'd like to sympathize, that will be too late for the committee's purposes. The newspapers might well be interested in an anonymous letter concerning our mutual experiences in London, personal and political. It wouldn't be nice for your children to learn who their father is from our political rags.'

'You wouldn't, Stoner, you couldn't. The three of us were friends for years. How can you forget all that?'

'Oh, I haven't forgotten, believe me, but you and Alex did. Have you, for instance, given me one single thought from then until now? Of course not. So don't try to play the old nostalgia game with me, Pavana. I want you to remind Alex that I know why he manoeuvred me out of our group in London, and tell him I still have a copy of that memo he tore up. I'll use it if he continues to refuse to meet with members of our committee.'

'Alex denied he shoved you out, Stoner, and the group began questioning your source of funds. They pressured Alex into asking for your resignation. Especially after you attacked him in the hall, the night he was elected president instead of you.'

'He didn't deserve to be president.'

'Why didn't you explain your reasons to the members? I never understood why you didn't.'

'I had my reasons – besides who would believe my story against the spinmaster's? Alex would have invented a plausible explanation. And that memo didn't mean much then but it certainly does now to an aspiring politician.

'And for your information he certainly didn't question the source of my funds when he needed them for his own use. When I look back now, I realize that most of that bunch were extravagant, lazy, sleeping by day and partying by night.

'I worked nights in the post office and in factories to earn money, so I could live in a fancy flat and fool myself that you all were my friends, in case you're interested, while the rest of you were waiting for bank drafts from home.

'I only lent him my savings because I guessed from what he said that *you* were in some kind of trouble. And I gave it without question, because believe it or not I cared about you and Alex. I didn't know then what the unnamed trouble was, but I certainly know now.'

'I had no idea, Stoner, no idea,' Pavana said, hugging her bruised body. She felt so chilly. Alex had borrowed the money for her abortion from Stoner. She could hardly believe it. And in the end, what had she used it for? Bassinets for her babies, talcum powder, diapers, pins and booties.

She looked at Stoner's face, angry, hurt, the feelings of rejection naked in his eyes. Stoner would show no mercy, and she couldn't expect any.

'How could you? You were too busy in those days performing rituals and obeisances to God Alex.'

Pavana remained silent, on guard, watching Stoner's eyes as he cornered his quarry.

'In my strange way, Pavana, I still believe in the rhetoric we spouted at those dinner parties, and although I can understand why he would, politics being what it is, I can't quite accept that Alex has become entirely cynical and self-serving, can you?'

Pavana shrugged, pressing her lips together, they were quivering so much.

'Did he ever repay you the money?'

'Oh, he did, but that's not the point in any case. But how do you think I felt when I heard about his fine wedding, to which I was not invited, and about the trip across the Atlantic on the *Queen Elizabeth*?'

'It was a small wedding, I understand.'

'Still, it made me think, Pavana, made me come to terms with a lot of things I'd refused to face before.'

She nodded, wanting only to crawl into her bed and pull the sheet over her head, and cower there. Stoner was silent for a minute. Then he ground out his cigarette with his heel.

'Of course, I can't force you to help, to do what you can, and I hate to threaten people like you, I really do. If you decide you can't or won't, I'll pretend we never had this talk, that's a promise. But I'd really like to see Alex's face when you tell him what you didn't do with my loan.'

In that instant, Pavana's heart flooded with relief. She'd been given a reprieve, she could follow her original plan. Stoner would keep his promise, she knew that, 'Oh, Stoner,' she began, and then at the look of deep disappointment and disrespect on his face she stopped. He had obviously hoped against hope that she would help him. She looked up and down the street, thinking of the battling crowds earlier in the afternoon, of the twins, of Alex, of Belize.

'But even if I do try, Stoner, how will it all help?'

'We don't know that it will, Pavana, but it has to be explored.'

'All right, I'll try, but I need time to sort all this out. It's been quite a

89

shocking day for me, in one way and another. For most people, I expect.'
Her meeting that afternoon, with Mrs Elrington, seemed to have
happened on a faraway day and to a self other than the one coming into
being as she listened to Stoner's voice.

'Time is short, Pavana. Today is already Wednesday, and the Public
Service Union plans to hold an open meeting on Monday night to decide
whether or not to strike. I need to get advance warning to the action
committee executive so that they can mobilize the brothers and sisters to
support the union, if they call for a countrywide strike.'

'How will I find you?' She knew without asking that Stoner didn't
have a telephone, and would be reluctant to give her his address. It was
quite likely that he didn't sleep in the same place two nights in a row.

'Let Alex worry about that. He's got hordes of minions. He'll know
how to make contact, if he wants to.'

'All right. And Stoner, what was in that memo?' Was she hoarse? Her
voice sounded so peculiar, harsh and rasping.

'Still anxious about him and his wretched rise to fame and glory,
aren't you? Well, you're going to see Alex soon, ask him,' and he strode
abruptly down Prince's Lane with the quick, anxious steps she remembered, his head bent, shoulders hunched, his hands stuffed deep into his
pockets.

Stoner had perhaps met her that evening by chance, but it was
obviously a chance he'd been actively seeking. The camaraderie she had
chosen to remember of their years in London seemed to mean very little
to Stoner now. He focused on other, bitter memories, other motivations
that burnt so strongly that even at a distance she could almost imagine
she felt the intensity communicating itself to her.

As she watched Lisa run down the veranda steps, her bag over one
shoulder, Pavana wondered whether, in the end, Stoner would receive
any lasting recognition by the committee he was presently serving with
the same commitment as he had served their students' group in London.
She doubted it. There was a proclivity to violence in Stoner's character
that seemed to preclude it.

'I must find a way to see Alex,' Pavana said to herself, trying to buoy
up her courage, not only for herself, and the childen, but also for Stoner
who had, years ago, proved himself a better friend to her than she had
ever been to him. It was a debt she owed; and, when all was said and

done, Alex had been his hero too. And she thought she understood, as well as most people, how difficult it was to let go of ambitions wrought in youth, to set fire to unserviceable lifescripts; and the strength and discipline required to resist the lure of a primary, if ancient, love.

Chapter 16

The lights had gone out all over the neighbourhood and the garden, in which she usually took such pleasure, seemed menacing, alien, and her stomach burned with an unaccustomed acidity. Somewhere a generator roared into life, and to her left a mass of thick, black smoke rose ever higher, blotting out the starlit sky. In the centre of the city, which they had left over five hours before, the demonstrators were continuing their violent protests and she had no doubt that Stoner was still among them.

It was long after midnight before Lisa and Eric tumbled into bed, disoriented and shocked by the events of the evening, and a while after that before a power failure silenced Eric's tape recorder. But in her mind, as she sat there huddled in the low, slatted wooden chair, the soaring notes of the pan flutes played continuously, telling their story of sadness, of mourning, and of internal distress.

'Who was that man you were talking with for such a long time, Mom?' Lisa had asked in the taxi. 'You stood there for ever. I was so embarrassed.'

'I am very sorry, Lisa,' Pavana said, as the taxi, reeking of stale smoke and the scent of countless bodies, sped along Princess Margaret Drive.

Turning her face away from the children's eyes, she peered through the cracked window glass as they drove past the National Stadium, another misnomer. The drains bordering its chain-link fence were choked with overgrown, razor-edged weeds. She caught a glimpse of the ramshackle viewing stand where as a girl she would sometimes sit with her dad watching the horse races at Eastertime. To its rear, near the sea, was the dreary municipal airport where light planes, commercial and private, took off for the coral islands or for the country's interior.

'Is he your boyfriend?' Lisa persisted, as the taxi neared Sapodilla

Street. Pavana watched the waves bouncing over the seawall, soaking the sandy area where during the early evenings children ran shrieking up and down the sandhills, and where at night it served as a trysting place for lovers.

'Don't be so idiotic, Lisa,' Eric said impatiently. 'Uncle Julian is.' He placed his hand around her neck. 'Who were you talking to, then, Mom? Who?'

'Oh, just someone I knew in London but that was a long time ago, before you were born.' She thought briefly about Julian. She hadn't received a letter from him in months. By now he'd probably forgotten about his promise to visit.

'But why did you have to talk to him for so long, then? Sister Marguerite was quite annoyed when you didn't pick me up at seven, as you said you would. She said ten rosaries, I counted.'

'We'll talk about it all, tomorrow, all right? I don't feel at all well just now.'

'But . . .'

'Eric,' Pavana interrupted, 'and you, too, Lisa. I will discuss it with you tomorrow. As soon as we get home, we'll eat and then get to bed.'

'I've got homework,' Lisa muttered.

'Me, too, lots,' Eric said.

'I'll wake you early so you can do it. Let's not fuss any more, all right? It couldn't be helped, and I really don't feel at all well. In fact . . .'

'Is the Land Rover really wrecked?' Eric asked.

'I don't know, Eric, I don't know. But we'll just have to take care of that tomorrow.'

'Tomorrow! Tomorrow! Everything is always tomorrow! I'm sick of it,' Lisa said, on the verge of tears.

'That's enough now, from both of you. I really am very sorry.'

Lisa and Eric were silent until the taxi drew up before their gate. They watched Pavana's hands trembling violently as she scrabbled in her bag and placed the fare in the driver's outstretched hand. Instead of rushing up stairs as was their custom, Lisa and Eric stood side by side on the driveway while she wrestled with the rusty bolt on the gate, pinching her finger in the process.

'Damn,' she said, sucking at the blood on her finger. The outdoor lights made the silver bracelet of her watch shine whitely. My God, Pavana, she said to herself, wrenching it from her wrist, and slipping it into a pocket. There's none like an old fool indeed, except perhaps a romantic old fool like yourself. The downstairs apartment was dark, except for a light in the kitchen.

'Did someone tear your sleeve?' Eric asked.

'I tore it on a tree in the park, I think. I can't really remember, except I was quite frightened in that huge crowd.'

'It must have been awful,' he replied.

'It was,' Pavana said.

'It wasn't even worth your while, was it?' Lisa whispered as they crept quietly up the stairs, stepping on the shadows of the flamboyant tree, its branches scraping and rustling in the gentle breezes of the night. 'Standing there with him for so long. Was he trying to invite you out?'

'No.'

'Then what were you saying to him? You looked angry and very upset. Was it about the shooting?'

'That, and about the time we spent in London.' Pavana wanted so much to hug them, to feel their comforting arms around her body, to weep, unburden herself to them. She wanted to say, that was him, your father who was shot, that was Alex. Control, she cautioned herself, control, don't make everything worse. Do not over-react, for God almighty's sake. You'll lose them, as well, if you're not careful.

'London, Mom? At a time like that? You should have excused yourself. You are far too polite.'

'I probably should have done.'

'And you've been crying,' Eric said, turning on the hall light and peering anxiously into her face. 'Did he hurt you?'

'Not really. Come on now,' she said, forcing briskness into her voice. 'Let's do what we have to do, and then let's get to bed.' She was tempted to say, 'Things will seem better tomorrow,' but she choked the words back just in time. One look at the twins' faces showed her a maturity she'd never noticed before. They knew she was far from being her usual self, and that something was terribly wrong.

'How did the lessons go, Eric?'

'So, so. Sister Marguerite and I kept rushing to the window to watch people marching in the street. Do you think we could get a piano?'

'A second-hand one, maybe. We should advertise. Your dancing has improved, Lisa. I watched you for a bit.'

Pavana moved purposefully towards the kitchen, the twins following

93

closely on her heels. There was a clatter of plates as Eric placed them on the tablemats. Lisa plunked ice cubes one by one into the jug of limeade, stirring the drink loudly with a long spoon. Their spirits seemed to have revived somewhat.

As Pavana turned on the oven to heat up the roast, she glanced through the glass doors leading towards the veranda. The fronds of the twin royal palms at the gate moved gently back and forth. She wondered if Alex too was looking out on the night. How badly was he hurt? In the past, she had spent thousands of minutes, at odd times and in various places, trying to imagine what he was doing at a particular moment. She felt a ridiculous impulse to go immediately to the hospital, if that was where he was, to tell him all that Stoner had said.

But there was a cold and arrogant side to Alex's personality of which she had many times been deathly afraid. She had felt its whiplash, the sting of his withdrawal, and she had chosen in those final weeks to stand back, to protect herself from further humiliation, from another rejection. Nevertheless, she would have to dredge up the courage from somewhere to try and speak with him very soon. Pavana had always felt it difficult to let down her guard completely with the men she really cared about. Alex had broken through her defences, but over the years she had built them up again and she wondered whether she would be able to adequately explain to him her twin mission.

'Mom?' Lisa said, '*did* you hear me?'

'What did you say, Lisa?'

'That I probably would have been asked to dance a solo except I was so nervous at the tryouts.'

'I'm sure you'll get a solo next time,' Eric said loyally.

'So am I, Lisa,' Pavana said. 'You're good, and you work so hard.'

'I want to study in London, like you did. I miss it sometimes.'

'Things were a lot different when I was your age. You have everything to stay here for these days. I'd love to see you choreograph another local ballet. That market scene you did with your class last term was hilarious, well done, almost professional.'

'Don't you want us to go back to London then, Mom?' Eric asked. 'What about university and stuff?'

'Well, of course, if you get the chance, and we can afford it, why not? But that's still some time in the future. You might want to go somewhere else by then.'

'Maybe,' Lisa said, pouring limeade carefully into the glasses. 'And I'm so glad Mr Abrams wasn't badly hurt. He wasn't, was he? He seems like a really nice person.'

'Really cool,' Eric said. 'I like his jokes. You can have a real conversation with him.'

Pavana paused in the act of removing the roast from the oven. Her hands had begun their uncontrollable trembling again and she didn't trust her ability to carry the glass dish to the counter.

'Do you know him?' she asked, realizing it was a stupid question.

'We both do,' Lisa said. 'We met him when he gave a talk during Children's Week. He was deputizing for a minister who was out of the country.'

This was it, she had to tell them now. She removed the roast and took it to the counter, and as Eric picked up the electric knife to slice it, Lisa continued.

'After his talk, our class did that same market ballet in his honour. He enjoyed it very much. After the programme he complimented me on my dancing, and said I should continue to work hard at it and apply to the government for a scholarship.'

'It was very good of him to take the time to be so encouraging,' Pavana said.

'He talked to me, too,' Eric said, above the whine of the knife. 'He asked me my name, and said I reminded him of someone.'

'He seemed really interested in Eric and me. He talked to us the longest.'

'I have no doubt that he was sincere,' Pavana said, 'but politicians have a lot of people to please.' She opened a cupboard and poured some gin into her glass of limeade.

'I know, but it was nice of him to say that if he was still around he would advise his minister to endorse my application. We are as out as out can be with the government, aren't we? Will you be working with him in your new job?'

'No,' Pavana said, drinking too quickly. Her throat was parched and her stomach quivered so much she knew she would be unable to eat. 'Alex does like to help young people improve themselves,' she said. 'You mustn't read anything else into it.'

'Why should I?' Lisa asked, looking as if greatly surprised at Pavana. 'Anyway, I am very glad he wasn't killed.'

'Oh, so am I,' Eric said fervently, chewing on a slice of beef. As Lisa ladled a spoonful of rice on to Pavana's plate, she finished her drink, set the glass carefully down and said, 'I'm glad you feel that way about him.' The tears were pouring down her face now, and the gin made her lightheaded. Eric and Lisa were staring at her in dismay, watching her struggling to speak, but the words came out quite easily after all.

'He doesn't know it, of course, but Alex Abrams is your father.'

She braced herself for their questions, but there were none. Lisa's lips quivered as she chewed on her food. Eric pushed his plate away and leaned his head on his elbows.

Pavana babbled on, 'I plan to tell him very soon, and arrange for him to meet with you, and . . .'

'I don't want to meet him now,' Eric said. 'I'd feel too embarrassed, Mom.'

'Neither do I,' Lisa said. 'It's all different from what we thought, imagined, I mean . . .'

'Oh but you must,' Pavana said, 'I promised . . . for your birth-day . . .'

'We don't want to, don't need to now. We've met him, anyway,' Eric shouted. 'Lisa's told you.'

'That's right, Mom, I did,' Lisa said.

There was no reaching them. Eric pushed a cassette into his tape recorder and the pan flutes erected a wall of wailing music between them, a wall that grew higher and higher as they cleared the table before disappearing into their rooms to prepare for bed.

Did the music remind them, as it did her, of happier days driving with Julian through the gameparks in East Africa? She remembered how the children had been then, with such a trusting sweetness in their eyes. Their faces glided across her memory in the soft rainbow colours of her love, the terrible innocence of their smiles, and their unconditional, unquestioning love for Julian and herself. She felt totally devastated when she contrasted those days with tonight, their tight control, the eyes which refused to meet hers, the pinched look around the mouths. They had aged considerably in twenty-four hours.

Pavana washed the dishes, dried them, put away the food, swept the floor, emptied the garbage, hoping against hope that they would return to the kitchen and ask her those questions she now longed to answer. But they didn't, and finally she had changed into her pyjamas and had come to sit here on the veranda. It was nearing two a.m., and she doubted now she could sleep. She was glad of the dark, for as she stared steadily at the myriad flickerings of the candle in its holder of fretted brass, she felt her face muscles slacken, though the discs in her neck still ached unceasingly. She leaned her head back against the chair, allowing her mind to wander to those earlier months in London, long ago.

Chapter 17

On her third morning there, that faraway winter, in 1967, she had stood peering in dismay through the grimy windowpanes at a snow-filled avenue in Maida Vale. The excitement of arrival had begun to dissipate the moment she entered the hallway of the bedsitting house, where furniture polish, or perhaps it had been floor wax, waged an almost palpable battle with disinfectant, underarm stench and an odour that reminded her of soured red kidney beans. Permeating it all that afternoon had been the smell of fresh food being cooked with unfamiliar spices, seeping beneath the doorways of a dozen or more rooms, occupied by almost as many nationalities.

Number ten, the room which Gail had agreed to share with her until they could afford a proper flat, was on the third floor of the tall, narrow house, in a row of almost identical houses built in some bygone age on both sides of the avenue. In one corner of the room was a basin, where presumably one was expected to wash oneself as well as the dishes, a situation which most Belizeans she knew would have scornfully dismissed as 'nasty foreign habits'. But that is exactly what she had had to do that morning when the water heater in the house's one bathroom, rank with the smell of strange bodies, exploded inexplicably, scaring her half to death and scattering soot everywhere.

Terrified, convinced she had done some irreparable damage, she had rushed up the stairs from the landing on which the bathroom was situated. Gail had, of course, left hours before for her art classes. Once Pavana's heartbeats subsided, she took herself in hand, did the best she could at the basin, dressed and prepared to beard the housekeeper or her assistant in their basement lair, off limits to the run-of-the-mill occupants of the bedsitting house like Gail and herself.

'Only the privileged few are invited down there, my dear child,' Gail had said, indicating the closed door under the stairs which led to the basement. 'Ever since I've been here, it's been the scene of the most mysterious comings and goings, bearded university types and the like who mutter sweet nothings to each other in the hallway. A most conspiratorial bunch, very much of the Fidel-Che ilk, *and* their consorts, of course, none of them very friendly.'

Everyone had heard of Fidel but, 'Che?' Pavana asked.

'You know, Dr Ernest Guevara?'

'Oh, yes,' Pavana said, but she really knew very little about it all.

'Very left wing and radical?'

'Ah,' Pavana said in a knowledgeable tone.

Well, bearded conspirators or no, Pavana needed to explain about her experience with the water heater, and to find out how the wretched thing worked. She certainly did not intend waiting until eleven p.m. – the time Gail had indicated she might get back from a dinner engagement – on a freezing cold night to have a bath. She could quite see, already, that London was a place where one had to exercise an enormous amount of personal initiative.

On the plus side, the room was fairly large, easily accommodating a roomy old-fashioned wardrobe set between the two beds. Overstuffed armchairs with dingy chintz slipcovers squatted to the left and right of a hissing gas fire, which consumed a quantity of coins morning and evening. If the chairs were not attractive, at least they were comfortable. At odd times, the thin, faded brown carpet, with a design of the most unlikely yellow roses, undulated with a disconcerting suddenness, startling Pavana until she discovered its movements were caused by draughts from the ill-fitting windows. What did you think it was caused by, she asked herself, annoyed by her susceptibility to 'fears and fancies', the Ghost of Christmas Past?

The sky continued to be overcast, and the day bitterly cold, 'one of the worst winters London had seen for a long time' the weather commentator had said, and Pavana had no difficulty in believing that the day would turn out to be as miserably cold as had been forecast. Her clothes were totally inadequate for a winter of any kind, let alone one of this intensity. It was a matter of urgency that morning to shop for a warmer coat, heavier sweaters, warm pants and boots. She checked her dwindling packet of pound notes, picked up a map, switched off the fire and left the depressing room with its peeling wallpaper and the couch with the sagging middle. One had to be careful always to remember to sit on the end cushions, or sink into a hole where the springs seemed to have gone beyond further repair.

As she descended the unlit, narrow staircase, she found herself increasingly fearful of facing the city, to which she had travelled with such excited anticipation and, no doubt, overly high expectations. She would probably wind up boarding a bus heading in the wrong direction, become disoriented and indecisive in the huge, crowded shops and discover that her funds were inadequate to purchase the items she needed. Or most likely she'd settle, like she did yesterday, for sitting in a café somewhere in the West End drinking cups of coffee, mesmerized by the fascinating variety of people in the London streets. The alternative was returning to the room upstairs, and that she couldn't, wouldn't do; there was an exciting world out there and she intended to try and become a part of it all.

Beneath her feet the stair carpet was red, with worn, straw-coloured patches in the middle of almost every step, the result of how many footsteps she didn't care to contemplate. The click of the bathroom door made her quicken her steps guiltily across the landing. The tub was undoubtedly still black with soot. One never knew who one would meet on the stairway – West Indians, Italians, Africans and a number of other nationalities – muttering apologies in diverse accents, avoiding one's eye, wary of contact, of involvement. Pavana understood their feelings only too well.

Just before she reached the final landing, where the pay telephone was located, she heard a man laugh and, peeping over the banisters, saw two people engaged in quiet conversation. Pavana giggled. The conspirators were early afoot and in front of the open basement door – surely a damaging clue? Still, neither of them looked particularly furtive, nor intimidating.

She recognized the woman as Helga König, a student who assisted the housekeeper in return for free lodging. Her blonde hair, parted in the centre, fell straight to her shoulders. She looked to be in her mid-twenties, very thin, and neatly dressed in a wine-coloured woollen sweater and dark grey trousers pushed into the tops of leather boots.

99

The man may have been about the same age, Pavana couldn't tell, but he did have a generous beard and curly hair and must have been just under six feet. Both heads were bent intently over a calendar open on the hall table, littered with a number of uncollected letters. Although they murmured quietly, the man's voice resonated in the hallway. Helga was saying, 'But why? Have the meeting in my flat. It's a lot easier and cheaper too.'

'You don't mind?' He tucked a wisp of hair behind her left ear.

'Why should I mind? I'll be in Düsseldorf by then, yes?' She wound the ends of his scarf around his neck. They both turned as Pavana reached the spot in the long hallway where they stood.

'Good morning,' he'd said, stretching out his hand. It felt warm, dry, reassuring. 'Helga told me you'd arrived. Don't you remember me? Abrams, Alex Abrams, from the Stann Creek Valley? I remembered your name the moment I heard it.

'But this is unbelievable!' Pavana exclaimed. 'It was at a christening, wasn't it? About ten years ago . . . your father was the godfather for my cousin's baby. I had no idea you were here. Gail never mentioned it. How are you doing?'

'Fine, absolutely fine, except for the weather, of course. God shouldn't send sinners to hell. He should send them to England!' Later on Pavana discovered he told this joke to every newcomer, but at the time she thought it the funniest thing she'd heard in a long while. The three of them stood there laughing like old friends.

'Is your room comfortable?' Helga asked, her voice gentle and concerned. 'We hardly ever see Gail, how is she?'

'Oh, Gail is fine, but she works day and night on her paintings. She gets invited out a lot, too.'

'And your room?' Alex asked.

'The room is all right,' Pavana said. 'But could you show me how the water heater in the bathroom works? It blew up on me this morning. I'm afraid the bathroom is in a mess. If it's necessary, I'm willing to pay . . .'

Again they laughed in genuine amusement. They seemed so kind. Pavana found herself joining in. Helga said, 'Everyone has problems with it sooner or later. I'll show you how to use it later this evening, if you wish?'

'Thanks,' Pavana said, taking a surreptitious peep down the basement stairs. All she saw was a neat kitchenette. Helga and Alex were still

100

looking at her with friendly amusement, and Pavana was suddenly conscious of how she must look to them. Gail's cast-off coat was too tight around the hips and bust, the sleeves were too short, and she'd shoved all her hair into one of Gail's peaked, woollen caps. 'Well, thanks again,' she said, suddenly anxious to be away from their scrutiny. 'Right now I'm off to conquer London Transport and Oxford Street, with its teeming hordes.'

'You're unlikely to win those battles alone, not in your first week anyway. Tell you what, I'm walking towards the Edgware Road myself, perhaps I can give you a few pointers along the way? The buses and underground are quite easy to use really.'

'Thanks,' Pavana said.

He kissed Helga on the forehead.

'Are you returning early tonight, Alex?' she asked, her manner bright and eager.

'I must go to a meeting at the union after lectures,' he replied, 'but I shouldn't be too late. We'll talk further then.'

'I'll leave some dinner in the oven for you.'

'Don't go to any trouble. You work hard enough here all day, and you have to be up early for your flight.'

'It's only a casserole. I have to eat myself, ja?'

Alex whispered something in her ear which made her laugh, and she smiled lovingly into his eyes.

'See you later then,' she said to him, and to Pavana, 'Ring my bell when you come in and I'll show you how the heater works. Ask Alex to recommend some shops.'

'Thanks,' Pavana said, 'I will, and . . .'

'Let's go,' Alex urged. 'There's a bus due in a few minutes.'

Outside, the cold air made Pavana gasp and shiver. She had walked only a short distance beside Alex when she skidded on the icy pavement covered by the snow. She made a grab for the iron railings which ran the length of the connecting houses, missed, and dropped on her bottom with a heavy thud. A milkman, bottles clanking in a wire carrier, picked up Pavana's bag, while Alex helped her to her feet, brushing the snow off her coat. She ached all over.

'Weather cold enough for you, sunshine?' the milkman asked. He, too, seemed amused. 'Not hurt, are you?'

'Not much,' Pavana replied, holding on to the railings and picking her way slowly and carefully along the sidewalk. God, this is embarrassing, she thought to herself, feeling as if all the people on the street were watching her. Of course, they weren't, but she felt stupid, nevertheless.

Alex looked at his watch. 'Don't you have a pair of boots?' he asked.

'She won't get far in them slippers, mate,' the milkman called. 'Not in this weather, she won't.' He grinned, looking at her red pumps.

I must look like a real back-of-the-bush immigrant, Pavana thought. Her calves felt frozen.

'I did try to buy some yesterday,' Pavana said, 'But . . .'
Did he think if she had some boots she'd be wearing these silly shoes? And after all she'd managed quite well yesterday. His presence made her nervous, and because she was nervous she became annoyed. What the hell, she hadn't asked for his help.

'Not enough money, eh?' His tone of voice was gentle, even understanding, but it also suggested that he had met her type before. What did the man think, that she was about to ask him for a handout?

'I was about to say that I took a bus going in the wrong direction from the stores. And I do have enough money for my needs, and I mean to earn some more before I enter the polytechnic in September.'

'A student, eh? And I thought you were here to conquer – that's your word, isn't it? – a blond, blue-eyed Englishman, who will whisk you off to a cozy, firelit cottage, far from the filth and confusion of Belizean streets.'

His voice was teasing, amused.

'Listen,' Pavana said, pausing by the railings. 'It was good of you to offer to help me, but I can manage quite well. I wouldn't want to make you late for your lectures. You go ahead. I really wouldn't mind.' And she really, at that moment, didn't.

'Here,' he said, extending his elbow. 'Hold on to my arm. We'll need to walk a bit faster if we're going to catch that bus.' Pavana tucked her hand into the crook of his elbow. He pressed it in a friendly manner to his side.

'I recognize that look in your eyes,' he said. 'Don't be so defensive. It's a Belizean disease.'

'Who's being defensive? Besides, Belize is not *all* filth and confusion. You should know that better than most. Or perhaps life in Düsseldorf is more your ideal? A well-regulated apartment in the right neighbourhood, and on Sundays a walk through the park to the nearest beer

102

parlour to lift a stein in hearty cheer? I really don't know how you'd manage with such a disciplined routine, however. We Caribbean types are notoriously easygoing, even a little irresponsible some might say.'

Alex laughed. 'I was only teasing.'

'I imagine you'd be quite safe there, far away from the orange pickers whining for more credit in your father's commissary.'

There, that should wipe the smile off his confident face, and it did. He looked annoyed, then thoughtful, as if considering something.

'I mean to return home, one of these days,' he said. 'I'll probably enter politics eventually. I'm reading law at one of the inns here. But it gets very discouraging at times. I don't have the background for a lot of the subjects, so I seem to be always cramming.'

No orange groves and whining citrus pickers for him, Pavana thought, that was quite clear.

'Oh, I understand exactly what you mean,' she said, her annoyance forgotten. 'I feel so relieved to be able to get some kind of higher education. Wasn't I lucky to get a place at the polytechnic? I feel like that cliché, the late bloomer.'

'Well, late or not, I was very glad to see a new face from home this morning. We aren't that commonplace in London. Perhaps now you're here, we'll see a little more of Gail as well. She's been a little elusive so far.'

Pavana could hardly wait to see Gail's face. What fun it would be to tell her that she'd met two of the leftist devils at the door, the very door, of their hellish den. What a coup, an absolute coup. And they hadn't been in the least bit unfriendly, but rather helpful and charming in fact.

'I'll show you where to get off the bus on Oxford Street, and give you the names of a few shops where you should be able to buy reasonably priced boots and a coat. At the corner, over there, is the laundromat we use, and up ahead is a café where we eat sometimes. It's cheap and the food is acceptable. And you'll want to meet some people, of course.'

Pavana looked around eagerly as he pointed out various places, the off-licence, the grocery store and a drugstore, which he called 'the chemist'.

'It's good of you to go to so much trouble.'

'Not really. The same was done for me. We'll start with my sister Moria, and a few of her friends. Moria is a trainee nurse at the Charing Cross Hospital, not a very good trainee, I suspect. I would never in my right mind trust myself to her ministrations. She'd probably let me die a slow, lingering death.'

It was Pavana's turn to laugh. 'What a thing to say about your own flesh and blood! Don't you two get along?'

He looked at her for a moment, a question in his eyes which Pavana was unable to interpret; then, as if satisfied about something, he turned his attention to the buses and traffic along the Edgware Road. 'Here's our bus,' he said, grabbing her hand. As he led the way to a rear seat at the top of the double decker, he asked, 'What will you study at the poly?'

'Journalism,' she said, sinking into a seat beside him, glad of the chance to rest her frozen, aching feet.

'Hmmm,' he said, quirking his bushy eyebrows in an interested way. 'Most of the women I know here go into nursing, except for Helga and Gail. I shouldn't think you'd have too many opportunities to use your training at home, to earn a living I mean.'

'I'll just have to use my own initiative, I guess,' Pavana said. 'But it's what I've always wanted to do.'

'That's an optimistic approach, in any case, even if there's no money in it,' he said, lapsing into a silence he occasionally broke by pointing out some building that he thought would be of interest to her.

Some weeks afterwards, she had learnt just how much he had put himself out of the way, that day, to accompany her to Oxford Street, and that he had been late in fact for an important lecture.

From that morning, and during the six months Helga remained in Düsseldorf assisting her mother with her father, who eventually died from a malignant tumour, Alex and Pavana drifted into a relationship of mutual dependency and friendship.

He taught her to move confidently through the bewildering maze of London streets, taking her to museums, to the theatre, to movies, and to Fleet Street and Blackfriars, showing her the *Times* and the *Daily Express* buildings. In return Pavana helped him to memorize his notes for his examinations, helped him write speeches which he gave at various meetings, cooked meals for Gail and himself and, after she obtained a typing job in the classified advertising department of a London newspaper off Fleet Street, lent him money when his remittances were late.

She also worked for the Friends of Belize Committee, organizing meetings and editing a monthly news sheet. A significant portion of her small salary occasionally went towards purchasing supplies for the committee, as the funds allocated by members for this purpose always seemed to be needed more urgently elsewhere.

She had been glad to have a role, to feel needed, to be near Alex, who constantly told her in front of his friends, 'What a wonder you are, Pavana. We couldn't do this without you.' She felt absolutely no pressure from him to be other than one of his very good friends. There were many other committees to which Alex belonged, such as some of those held occasionally in Helga's basement flat, but she had never been invited to attend any of those, which made Gail give her any number of 'I told you so' looks.

Without warning, the electric lights in the neighbourhood blazed on again, unnaturally bright after their long absence. Pavana's legs felt stiff and sore, as slowly she rose from the low veranda chair, blew out the candle and, in the bathroom, prepared dispiritedly for bed, reluctant now to let go of the memories she had allowed to resurface. In the bedroom, as she picked her skirt up off the floor, the wristwatch Alex had given her fell from a pocket. She examined the watch under the reading lamp by her bedside, as an archaeologist might scrutinize an artefact retrieved from the excavated garbage of the ancient dead.

Rummaging around at the bottom of her wardrobe, she unearthed a battered and seldom opened jewellery box. Unlocking it, she placed the watch inside, among other trinkets from her childhood and teenage years. She buried the box once again under old albums, old costumes and other oddments she was reluctant to relegate to the dustbin where they undoubtedly belonged. She never looked at them, had no more use for the things. Why had she worn the watch for so long as a reminder of an ancient belief and, she admitted it now, a symbol of hope for an eventual reconciliation between Alex and herself? Hadn't she always known that he had given it to her as a token of thanks and farewell?

Chapter 18

In spite of her resolutions at Stoner's party, Pavana had been forced to make another attempt to meet Alex. Ten days later she had gone uninvited to the West Indian Students' Union, which had once been an elegant house but was now an ill-maintained unprepossessing place. Alex, a dynamic speaker, was giving a talk on the long-standing dispute between Britain and Guatemala over the territory of Belize. Her unexpected presence in the audience had inhibited him somewhat, she felt, as two or three times during the hour he had faltered in his delivery, while the small audience of about fifteen students waited patiently for him to continue.

Afterwards he had accompanied her on the underground train to Chalk Farm, the station nearest the flat she shared with Gail. They walked past the flat on Fitzroy Road to Primrose Hill, circling a small park several times. She pulled her black overcoat closer around her body, turning the big collar up around her neck and ears.

He walked slowly beside her, one hand deep into the pocket of his brown overcoat, the other gesturing, fingers splayed, as he reiterated the points he had made, evaluating the response from the students, most of whom were younger than he was. Every audience was important to Alex. As he talked, she clung desperately to the thin hope that Alex still cared enough about her to reverse his decision.

Occasionally she would look sideways at his narrow, bearded profile, wondering how he could speak with such absorption in his subject, so much force, his chin jutting upwards as he recalled a particularly subtle question or, nervously smoothing his beard, remembered a crucial point he had not adequately developed. He spoke with such enthusiasm, such a sense of mission. It was as if the person who walked with him, who had once been so close to him, was not chilled to the bone – and by something other than the early December winds sweeping the brittle leaves across the park. She felt cast out from that stimulating world in which he had been her mentor.

She was back in her old world now, which was even more alarmingly cheerless and prosaic than she remembered. Would that her life did not sometimes seem like a hospital ward for the incurably diseased, but it did; and the knowledge that what she was about to do she considered to be the right thing, the practical thing, under the circumstances, offered her no cozy feeling of well-being.

That cold afternoon in the park, she began to understand that in Alex's day-to-day striving towards what he considered almost to be his territorial rights or political inheritance, an experience with one woman, or ten, no matter how genuinely felt at the time, was not necessarily encased in glass and made the object of frequent genuflections. He was not waiting all day, every day, for her to telephone; not vomiting in polytechnic lavatories; not beating his fist against his forehead in regret over stupid mistakes made and regrettable words uttered.

He was out and about struggling for recognition, involving himself in activities that would further his political career and enhance his self-esteem. Alex had many areas of vulnerability, but that vulnerability did not include marriage, which he would make in accordance with his own values. He considered her pregnancy a deliberate and cunning manoeuvre, and felt absolved from any responsibility other than the two offers he had made her.

'I've known Helga for a much longer time than I've known you, Pavana,' he'd said. 'But she's never put herself nor me in such a predicament.'

Even before her present crisis she had begun finding it extremely difficult to be as Alex wished. One of Alex's disappointments was that he had failed to transform her into a dedicated member of that regional group, the members of which, their formal education complete at least for the present, would soon be scattering in various directions, galloping to distant goals with such speed and skill that Pavana was unable to keep up with them. That he had done his best, and that she had tried, there was no doubt. She had learned to dress imaginatively on very little, a high value in that group although Pavana found them extravagant in other ways.

To the dinner parties she sometimes attended with Alex, she began wearing ethnic dresses from all over the developing world. Any embroidery could not be huge, gaudy flowers. To create the desired effect, geometric patterns were best, Alex said. Around her shoulders on cool summer evenings she would drape giant hand-made shawls, although she always had the silly feeling of being enveloped in a tablecloth.

But it was in the area of conversation at these dinner parties that Pavana sometimes had the greatest difficulty. She had too often, in a tone of voice not sufficiently dispassionate, disagreed with Alex and with his friends on certain premises which they at the time held sacred. Because she felt a sense of impermanence among them, and because she felt she wasn't taken seriously, it was often impossible for her to remain silent when confronted by ideas and assumptions at odds with her own.

Many times she argued her point of view vociferously even though, as happened quite frequently, at the end of the discussion she had learned a number of things which altered her own perception of certain issues. But putting her ignorance on display was not something Alex appreciated. Her questions and comments would not have been unacceptable, perhaps, if they had been backed by some well-known authority, or placed in the context of the ideologies on which they considered themselves advanced students, even experts.

Alex claimed, at the end of some of these evenings, that she spoke 'off the top of her head'. He was furious whenever, instead of quietly listening, she dismissed some of what she heard as 'so much more importation', and embarrassed him unintentionally when she made statements like, 'My aunt would never agree to that kind of life. She hates people telling her what to do', or 'My cousin, the one that lives in Crooked Tree? He was born stubborn. He would leave the country at once, walk to the United States, if he had to do so.' And, 'Maybe you wouldn't really be sorry if the present population of Belize all migrated to the United States? Would you then allow full-scale immigration from the surrounding countries to fill the gap? I suppose then you would have a proper *campesino* country, people appropriately ignorant and oppressed on which to practise these ideas? And who is to finance all this? Would the new immigrants accept you as leaders?'

She and Alex sometimes quarrelled after these evenings out together, and so she had found herself lagging farther and farther behind in the race for his attention, approval and company. And just when she had mustered the strength to accept the end of their relationship, she discovered that she was pregnant.

Since he had always been too busy to meet her, she had been forced to

108

tell him of her predicament on the telephone. It had thrown Alex into great consternation and distress, as it would have thrown most young men with his ambitions, she supposed. He had become extremely angry and his overriding concern, thoughout their long conversation, had been that Helga should not learn 'just yet' about Pavana's situation. Helga believed, at least she convincingly appeared to do so in spite of overwhelming evidence to the contrary, that Alex and Pavana were good friends 'from home', nothing more.

Alex had apparently told her that this was the case, and he was about to make that fiction the truth. Or maybe, from his point of view, it had been the truth all the while. The night after he left her surprise birthday party in the café near the polytechnic, he and Helga had become engaged to be married.

She had never for one moment considered informing Helga, and it angered her that Alex had implied that she was scheming and spiteful. What was even more galling was the knowledge that she did not measure up to the standards Alex required in a wife. He had never told her so, and there was no doubt how disgusted he would be if confronted with such an idea, but this was her perception and she would have to live with it.

'So, Pavana, how do you think the discussion went today?' She was startled by the friendliness, the ordinariness, of his voice. He was used to her thoughts straying whenever he talked at great length and he was smiling, amused perhaps that she was just as he knew she was.

'All right,' she said. 'Not your very best but still very good.'

'I wrote my talk by myself. I missed your help while I was writing it last night. And it was hard to concentrate with you sitting in the room . . . I kept thinking . . .'

'Did you, Alex?'

'I do think about you, whatever you might choose to believe. By the way, who told you about the meeting this afternoon?'

'Julian did. He knew that I'd been trying to see you.'

'Ah, yes, the Belizean Englishman. Did you receive the cheque for the surgeon's fees? I left it with Gail at the flat when I stopped there a few evenings ago. She said you'd gone out with Julian and Dora.'

'Why didn't you let me know you were going to drop by the flat?'

'It was a spur-of-the-moment decision. Is it adequate for your needs?'

'What?'

'The cheque.'

'Of yes, thank you very much. I know you are having a lot of other expenses at this time . . .'

'Don't apologise, Pavana. You've made a decision. The least I can do is to support it, although I still think you are making a mistake.'

'Then you haven't changed your mind, Alex?'

'I can't at this stage. Try to understand, please. That's one of the things I've always liked about you, your common sense, your ability to empathize with other people's situations.'

'I am trying to understand, Alex. That's mostly what I've been doing every day for two weeks. I remember how gentle and sweet you used to be towards me.'

'Don't, Pavana, don't start that, please,' he said, hugging her to his side. 'It's the one thing I am counting on you *not* to do.'

'Remember, Alex, remember, the cricket matches, the parties, the trips to the zoo over there, studying together, and you did say we would get married one day. You did, Alex, you did.'

'Situations change, Pavana, you know that very well. I can't break my word to Helga.'

'Why not? You broke your word to me!'

He took hold of her hand and held it tightly, using his handkerchief to wipe the tears spilling down her cheek.

'I hate to see you so hurt, Pavana. Quite honestly, I thought you were more able to take all this in your stride. On the phone you sounded so reasonable, which is another great thing about you, Pavana, your ability to cope with situations that would send other people under.'

'You don't know me very well, if you believe that, Alex . . . and I thought you did, I thought you did . . .' She hated herself for the tightness in her chest, her streaming eyes and nose, her inability to breathe properly.

'Pavana,' he said, pulling her head to his chest, and she of course so glad to be held close, to rest against his shoulders. 'Pavana, let's live together. I've told you, there's no need for you to face this alone. The house by the river at home is not very large, but it's more than adequate. We could be together sometimes. I care about you very much. You know that.'

'How do you think Helga would feel about that?'

'I think she'd make allowances. Helga is strong that way, sort of able

110

to create her own reality and live within it. So what do you say, Pavana? We could still work together as we planned, and you know how much I need you to help me write my speeches, help me rehearse and all that. What do you say?'

Pavana knew an opportunity when she saw one, so she looked at it carefully from every side. She could well see how Helga would be able to create her own reality for much of the time, living as she would be in a self-contained home on a hilltop overlooking acres of citrus orchards, surrounded by mutual friends and members of Alex's family, several miles from the nearest town. There, she would have every opportunity to paint the flowers and the wildlife of Belize for the guide book which she was planning to publish in Germany. Helga had spoken enthusiastically about wanting to do this on the very first day they'd met.

'Alex,' Pavana said, 'do you remember the joke about the baby called "Diploma"?'

'No,' Alex said, his face already preoccupied, perhaps with the arrangements and adjustments he would have to make.

'You must remember. It was a common joke at home. A grandmother is walking along a street in Belize pulling a baby girl behind her and saying, "Hurry up, Diploma. Come on, Diploma." A friend at a water pipe shouts to her, "Why are you calling that baby Diploma?" And the granny replies, "I sent my daughter to England to study, and this is what she sent back!" '

'That's awful, Pavana,' Alex said, letting her go.

'That's how I feel, Alex, awful.'

'Sad, too,' Alex said, his face bleak. 'I wish you'd been more careful. I wish I'd been more careful.'

'Belize is home for me too, Alex. I wouldn't be successful at that kind of intrigue. I wouldn't want to be.'

'You're exaggerating the difficulties, surely. Men with second homes are commonplace in Belize, in the region for that matter. Look at all the women we know who thrive in that system. Sometimes . . .'

'Well, I know very well I wouldn't. Besides I'm too cowardly to face this alone. Too proud, I suppose, to prove that I'm cut from the same cloth as most of the unmarried women at home.'

'And much too ambitious for that sort of life, eh? The new Caribbean woman, eh? I won't ever be able to forgive you, you know, nor Julian for helping you.'

'Forgive me? I am not asking for your absolution, Alex. Where were you when the decision was made? You left me to make it and I did.'

'Perhaps I should accept some of the blame for that. But quite honestly, I never thought for a minute you'd really go through with it. When I saw you at the meeting today, I thought you'd come to tell me that you *would* accept my offer and return to Belize as soon as you could. I felt really happy as we were walking earlier.'

'I am *not* blaming you, Alex, just myself. I don't seem to have very much political skill, do I? Caribbean women like myself, well, we seem to love with no strings attached, more so than other nationalities, take Helga for example.'

'Don't, Pavana . . .'

'I heard you say today that political naïvety leads to victimization. You said that one should always be careful to negotiate from a position of strength. Helga is so smart.'

'I am sorry to see you like this, Pavana, really sorry that we can't reach some kind of compromise.'

'I know you think I should settle, Alex, but I can't.'

They had reached the steps which led to the ground floor flat of the house in which Pavana lived. She couldn't look at his face for fear that she would weep for the loss of the tenderness and admiration he had once held for her, for the assumptions he had made about her, weep for the loss of her faith and trust in him, for the assumptions she had made about him, for being unable to accept his efforts at compensation, for being unable to love without condition.

'If you change your mind, Pavana, let me know.'

Pavana did not reply. She walked up the steps and put her key into the lock.

'Thanks for the money, and everything, Alex.'

'Listen, Pavana, since you've put it in those terms, I am quite aware that political debts accumulate and have to be repaid. I'll call to find out . . . the day and time, and all that. Take care.'

He walked quickly away from where she stood and she watched him until he turned the corner. He didn't look back and she didn't follow him, although she wanted to do so. They had both travelled too far from each other, and in different directions.

Chapter 19

The meeting with Stoner Bennett had also revived for Pavana unwelcome memories of another bleak winter day early the following year. She had stood with Julian and Dora on the station platform at Folkestone, waiting for Alex and Helga to complete the formalities prior to boarding the *QE2* sailing within a few hours for New York.

Helga was as magnanimous, cheerful and organized as she had always been. Five years older than Alex, she looked five years younger. Gone were the long purple skirts, the flower in her hair, the shawls and the beads. She looked extremely elegant in a dark coat and black shoes with very high heels. He blonde hair had been expertly and expensively cut and, as they approached, Pavana watched it shining and swinging from side to side with every movement of Helga's head.

'It's like a dream, you know, that we are leaving London after such long years,' she said, her blue eyes brilliant with excitement. She stroked the side of her nose as she always did when she felt nervous, lowering her hand to cover her capped teeth as she laughed.

The years of waiting for Alex to complete his studies were over, and her dreams of adventure in a tropical paradise were about to become a reality. Alex couldn't help smiling, with love and pride at her efforts. She would be the ideal wife for a man with a political future: a gracious, hardworking, creative hostess for the home far from the city, on a hill with a view of the sea, which he was planning to build some day.

'You will visit us when you return home, yes?' she said to Pavana, the accent, so appealing, so enchanting to Alex, very pronounced in the excitement of departure. Helga fingered the thin leather strap of the small handbag dangling from her shoulder, tilting her head expectantly towards Alex to see how well she was doing. He smiled enthusiastically, nodded and hugged Pavana briefly, relieved that all seemed to be well after all. His familiar scent filled her nostrils, and his beard grazed her cheek.

'But of course Pavana will visit us when she gets home, won't you, Pavana?' Alex said, but his eyes kept shifting from side to side, conscious of people looking curiously at Helga and himself.

'Oh, but why not?' Pavana said, when it was her turn in the ritual, her neck aching, proud that no tears shone in her eyes, glad that only her throat felt constricted and that her face must show an equal casualness, grateful for the bulk of the winter coat in which she had invested.

'Terribly sorry we can't wait until your ship sails, old boy,' Julian said, looking at his watch. 'I'm afraid you and Helga will have a rough time of it on the Atlantic at this time of the year. Good luck to both of you and keep in touch.'

'You must do the same,' Alex said, shaking hands first with Dora and then with Julian. 'We'll be very interested to hear how your job goes in East Africa.'

'The warmer weather will be very welcome, I assure you,' Dora said, 'whatever else happens.'

'Thanks again for coming,' Helga called. Pavana waved, then followed Julian and Dora walking quickly towards the train for London.

They entered a compartment which smelt unbearably musty. Pavana took a seat opposite Dora and Julian. As the train moved off, she strove to think of sensible questions to ask about their journey to Nairobi in June. Instead she kept remembering the reserve in Alex's eyes and the happiness in Helga's.

'You handled that extremely well I must say, Pavana,' Julian said, lighting his pipe, smiling at herself and Dora, obviously relieved that the whole tiresome business of saying goodbye was over.

'Yes, well done, Pavana,' Dora said. 'I couldn't, wouldn't have done it. I can't understand why you bothered in the first place. Masochistic, that's what you are.'

'Oh, I don't know about that,' Julian said. 'I think I might have done very much the same myself.'

'Well, good for you,' Dora replied. 'That was exhausting.'

Indeed, it was difficult for Pavana to recall clearly now, why in the end she had decided to go. Had it been another virtuoso performance to demonstrate how broadminded she had become? Was Alex convinced that, in spite of their former intimacy, she had grown so sophisticated, so civilized that she could laugh, joke and wish them well, all of which she had done, and not miss a heartbeat?

If Julian and Dora were to be believed, she had succeeded; her pride had been amply served, for all the good that had done. In retrospect, perhaps the main reason why she had gone was to make the break with Alex, in her own mind, absolutely final; gracefully final. She wanted him to believe that she was just fine; and that things were now as they had been before. Julian was the only one who knew the truth.

'You must be very excited about your trip to Kenya, Dora,' Pavana said at last. 'I know Julian says he can't wait to start his new job.'

'Julian is, yes,' Dora said, her drawl very English. 'I am not so sure I want to live abroad. Not at the moment anyway. There is so much in England I haven't seen and done. Kenya is supposed to be very special, though, isn't it?'

'So I've read,' Pavana replied.

'In any case, Pavana, what are your plans for the future?' Dora asked, stretching out her hand to Julian, who clasped it tightly. They seemed such a loving couple.

'Oh, nothing much beyond finding a job. I'll stay on in my flat and . . .'

'But why on earth don't you return home?' Dora asked. 'It sounds, from what Alex and Helga were saying, that you'd have far greater opportunities there than you ever will here.'

'That's probably true, but I feel a need to stay in London for the foreseeable future.'

'That's best for now, I'm sure it is,' Julian said.

Dora's lips tightened; she looked surprised and disapproving. Pavana was glad that Julian had kept her secret.

'Job, Dora,' Julian said, putting his two arms around her shoulders and looking into her eyes. 'We must think job.'

'Must we?' Dora asked, moving closer into the shelter of his arms.

'We must. What about your old agency? There might be something there, wouldn't you think?'

'I suppose there might be,' she said doubtfully. 'But I still think the very best thing . . .' She fell silent, and then said, 'It wouldn't hurt to ring up old David Hoyle, I suppose. I should say goodbye to him in any case.'

'Good idea,' Julian said. 'We'll do that first thing on Monday, shall we?'

Dora kept her promise and towards the end of the following week

115

Pavana had been interviewed by David Hoyle, the director of Project Child. A month later she had begun working with the agency on a temporary basis. Pavana had been glad to lose herself in her work, helping to write fundraising articles for a newsletter sent monthly to several thousand potential contributors to the Project Child fund. The agency supported health-related development programmes in a number of developing countries.

The fifteen staff members were on the whole congenial, and she soon made a number of friends among them. The routine of the working week was occasionally enlivened by visiting field staff who told fascinating stories about their life and work in Nigeria, Afghanistan or Bangladesh.

She became a permanent staff member shortly before the twins were born. Afterwards, the Brownes, a middle-aged couple who lived in the basement flat with a small garden to the rear, agreed to take care of Lisa and Eric for a small weekly sum, enabling Pavana to return to work shortly after they were born.

As the years went by, she received a number of pay rises, and it wasn't until the twins were nine years old that she began trying to find a better-paying job with other development agencies. But it was proving to be a more difficult task than she had anticipated. Jobs like hers seemed to be in great demand. Project Child was a relatively young agency, operating on a shoestring budget, and it had become obvious to her that prospects for any further advancement, at least in the near future, were very poor.

On a Friday evening in July, a week after the twins' eighth birthday, she had still been feeling bad that they had not after all been able to afford a trip to visit friends for a weekend in Cheltenham. The twins had been looking forward to seeing the farm again, and the renovated old cottage with the huge fireplace in which they could stand. But they had taken the change of plan very well, and seemed quite happy with their trip to the theatre instead. Nevertheless, the initial disappointment on the twins' faces had renewed Pavana's determination to find a better-paying job as soon as possible, even if it meant moving to another part of the country.

All during this time she had corresponded regularly with Julian and Dora, who had at first worked in Kenya, then Tanzania and were now in Somalia. There was little in their letters to her about the personal details of their lives, except for the lively accounts of their son's activities and long descriptions by either Dora or Julian about the United World

116

Agency, and the development projects in which they were both professionally involved.

However, she saw them each time they returned to England on leave or for short visits. They would either invite Pavana and the children out to lunch or would spend an evening with them in the flat. The children enjoyed these visits from Uncle Julian, Aunt Dora and Basil, two years younger than Eric and Lisa. On the living-room walls, and in the two bedrooms, were daily reminders of these visits: camel bells, a brass tray, embroidered hangings, a small handmade rug, a Masai warrior carved from wood, two African paintings, and other mementoes in which Pavana and the children took great delight.

That same evening she wrote a long letter to Julian and Dora explaining her situation, and asking their advice on people to contact in other development agencies, as they had several times said they would be willing to assist her in any way they could. But she had had no reply from them, and months later she was still being interviewed for jobs for which she was either over-qualified or not qualified enough.

On her return home from work one dreary February evening she spied a letter in Julian's handwriting among the bills and circulars lying on the doormat. Her hands were trembling as she slit open the bulky envelope.

6 January 1978

Dear Pavana,

I must apologize for not replying before. You will be surprised to learn that Dora and I have separated – temporarily, I hope. She has returned to live with her parents in Brighton until she can find a job and a house. Now that Basil's seven, he'll be going to boarding school, although he will be spending some of his holidays with me here. It is rather a long story and I won't bore you with the details at present, except to say that Dora has become involved with someone else.

I am now in the process of trying to decide whether or not to renew my contract with United World, or to return to England at the end of this one. My return to England will depend to a great extent on whether or not Dora and I are able to resolve our difficulties.

I note from your last letter that you are trying to find another

117

job with better prospects. I can well understand that as the twins get older you must be finding it hard to make ends meet on your present salary. Because of our own problems this past year, I have not kept in touch with friends based in London agencies as I used to do, so I cannot offer you much advice in that direction at this time. I am enclosing, however, one or two names that you might try contacting.

In your present situation, I suggest that you give some thought to taking a job overseas. There is a vacancy for an administrative assistant, to myself, here in our office. Although it would not be a professional advancement for you, the job does offer a salary three times what you are presently earning, much of which you should be able to save. In addition, you would be entitled to housing and educational allowances (there is quite a good international school here), two weeks' paid annual leave, aside from the home leave at the end of two and a half years if your contract is renewed. The job and your life here would not be without frustrations, but I think you would find it, on the whole, satisfying.

Of course, I need not tell you how much I would enjoy having you and the children here. I think Lisa and Eric would enjoy this part of the world. Basil loved it and was very sorry to leave.

Please let me know if you do intend to apply for this position, so that I can try to facilitate things for you from this end. The name and address of the person in New York to whom you must send the enclosed application is also attached. Write as soon as you can. Happy New Year.

All the best,
Julian

Chapter **20**

Pavana stared transfixed at two identical, emerald green parrots, their heads to one side, gazing quizzically at her from their perch in the papaya tree in the garden below the veranda outside the kitchen. Alex lay, arms outstretched, eyes blank, in a pool of blood on the floor. She stood barefooted in the middle of the kitchen, all escape barred by the mass of broken glass which littered the floor.

Outside she could hear the angry roar of the rioting crowds rushing up and down the neighbourhood streets, and smell the acrid smoke from the flaming torches they waved with purposeful menace above their heads. In mounting terror, she listened to the rattle of the garden gate and to the scrape, scrape, scrape of footsteps on the concrete steps to the kitchen. They were going to get her, this time. Suddenly Stoner, a terrifyingly sharp machete held in his upraised hand, loomed malevolently in the doorway. As he brought it down with all his strength Pavana screamed, 'I didn't do it, Stoner! I didn't!'

Someone was holding her close, someone was saying, 'Hush, Mom, hush, you're home now, you're safe.'

Whimpering in terror, Pavana opened her eyes to gaze into Eric's brimming with concern and love. In bewilderment, she gazed around the familiar bedroom. Sunshine fell in soothing waves on the painting of a Masai warrior leaning on his staff, a number of sheep grazing near his feet. On the opposite wall a herd of zebras galloped through the tall, golden grasses of an East African savannah towards distant mountains wreathed in clouds.

She glanced at her wrist to check the time, and the absence of the familiar band brought the events of the previous day back to her mind with shocking force.

'What time is it, Eric?'

'About a quarter to seven.'

'We'll be late,' Pavana said, disentangling the sheets around her legs.

'No we won't, Mom. We've had breakfast. If we start walking in about half an hour, we'll be on time.'

'We'd better not, Eric, walk, I mean. Maybe Jen can give us a ride, otherwise we'll have to call a taxi and hope one will turn up.'

From the kitchen came a soft clatter of cups and saucers. As she tried to rise, avoiding Eric's eyes, Lisa entered the room carrying a mug of coffee. Pavana accepted it gratefully.

'You have time to drink it before you dress, Mom. Don't rush. Was it a bad one?'

Pavana nodded, not trusting herself to speak. They had taken charge of the morning routine, were being brave and so must she be, brave and tough like they were trying to be, although the roar of the lawn mower next door made her head ache even more fiercely. Eric and Lisa sat one on either side of her bolstering her with their strength, their love and, she prayed, their forgiveness.

'We'll talk about it sometime, Mom,' Lisa said.

'Sure we will,' Eric said. 'Except we don't have time right now.'

'That's true,' Lisa said. 'It's getting late.'

But there was so much she wanted to tell them. She yearned to sing a paean of love to Lisa and Eric, to explain that she had meant to give them a magical childhood but, as was her usual way, had chosen to forget that magic includes goblins and ogres as well as good fairies with magic wands. During their childhood with, it had seemed then, the whole world for a neighbourhood, there had seldom been any shortage of fairies, of the right sort, with an infinitely varied collection of magic wands. In addition Pavana had always been there keeping their feet to sunlit paths, ensuring that their nightlights rarely if ever went out.

Still feeling more than slightly disoriented, Pavana sat on the bed between them, staring through the narrowing window of her motherhood, seeing emotional danger for them on the road to adulthood, wanting to set up signposts like those they had giggled at in East African gameparks: 'Detour!', 'Watch Out!', 'Elephants have right of way!' But those days were almost gone, and she must respect their new-found maturity and their ways of coping. Confessing 'her sins', Pavana realized, might provide her with a temporary psychological release but it would no doubt be an intolerable burden to them.

Now it seemed what they needed was the mother they knew back again; they wanted her strong, smiling, cheerful. In time, they would

120

want to know from her perspective how it was that they had come into being during those London days long ago, and why she had chosen to act as she had done. Until then, like Red Man across the street, she would simply have to sling her burdens once more across her back and carry on until her children were ready and able to help her.

'That was good,' she said, putting the mug down and hugging them close. 'I'll call Jen.'

'Are you sure you're all right now?' Lisa asked, as they left the bedroom.

'Positive,' Pavana said, going to the telephone. 'Did you turn on the water heater, Eric?' she called, raising her voice in a deliberate signal of her return to strength and vigour.

'Ages ago,' he replied. 'In fact, I'll turn it off now. The water must be boiling.'

'Lisa, maybe you can start closing the bedroom louvres?'

'Right,' she said as Pavana dialled.

She closed her eyes against the glare from the kitchen windows, listening to the telephone ringing in the apartment below.

'Jen,' she said, 'sorry to bother you so early. Are you driving Morris to town this morning?'

'Oh, hello, Pavana,' Jen said, surprised at her question. 'As usual, why?'

'Could we get a ride with you?'

'Sure. Does the Land Rover have a flat?'

'I think it's totally wrecked by now.'

'Wrecked! How come?'

'I parked it on Church Street yesterday during the demonstrations and . . .'

'You were downtown yesterday? What for?'

'I had an appointment, you know, about my new job? We never imagined things would reach such proportions.' Pavana cleared her throat. 'It was scary.'

'I know it was. And the situation is likely to get worse. Listen, why don't I ask Morris to arrange for a mechanic from the office to get the car to a garage for you?'

'Would you mind?'

'Cho, man, you know better than that. Oh, and while I have you on the telephone, how would you and the children like to go out to Pelican

121

Island with us for the weekend? We'll leave early Saturday morning and return Sunday night. Give us all a break.'

Pavana calculated swiftly. 'Just a minute, Jen, I'll ask Lisa and Eric.' She called to them. 'Would you like to go out to the caye on Saturday?' She was grateful for Jen's offer, which she hoped would help divert their thoughts from yesterday's events. As Lisa and Eric shouted their agreement, Pavana said, 'Thanks, Jen, we'd love to go, and thank Morris for his help.'

'You can thank him yourself, we're all driving downtown together, aren't we? Twenty minutes?'

'Oh, yes, that's right,' Pavana said. 'We'll be ready.'

In the bathroom Pavana turned the shower on full blast, giving herself up to the water pounding her face and body. She tried not to let it, but Alex's face, his bloody shirt and the memory of their early months together would not be so easily banished.

As she dressed she continued to recall the weeks subsequent to their first meeting, how her silly, romantic, lonely spirit had revived, turning sharply upwards in response to Alex's warm, friendly welcome, his guidance, his protection. She had found his conversation many-textured, informative, his experiences intriguing, but best of all, from the very outset, he had seemed to like her, to admire her, to find her attractive and interesting, a rare occurrence in her brief history. She had felt absolutely no inclination to look her gift horse in the mouth.

The depressing bedsitting room, which seemed at first to have few attractive attributes, was transformed under his advice. It became a warm, cheerful, happy place where hours of conversation vanished like minutes. On returning home from work or, later in the year, from the polytechnic, the thought that he would soon be in it banished exhaustion or depression, even on the most gloomy days.

She purchased cheap ornaments, which she knew now had been tacky, fresh flowers when she could afford them, and cheerful curtains for the windows, stuffing the cracks with newspapers to prevent draughts. She no longer noticed any smells in the bathroom nor in the hallway, nor did she actually 'see' most of the other tenants on the way in or out of the house.

In the evenings, record albums in his hand, he bounded up the stairs to help Gail and herself prepare moussaka or couscous, or fish salads and, sometimes, strangely spiced, stir-fried vegetables. He seemed always to be in the middle of some exciting activity and, as he talked, one could see onself reflected in his eyes, knowing that one was taken special notice of, and the smile, beneath his huge, hooked nose, was always a pleasure to watch, his lips well-shaped, his teeth even. He had been a beautiful man.

As they worked, Pavana's description of the people she met during the day, what they said and what she thought of them were all of interest to him. On one of those evenings she had said, 'So, today, this man, probably an old colonial type, phoned up and said he wanted to advertise for a sleeping partner. My God, I was shocked, and of course we'd been warned to watch out for prank callers. It's a most conservative newspaper, so I said, 'I'm sorry, sir, but we don't accept that kind of advertisement at this newspaper.'

'He became absolutely incensed, spluttered about foreign types like myself working on *his* newspaper, and informed me that he had been advertising for sleeping partners for more years than he cared to remember. He called the manager of the department and complained bitterly. It was embarrassing, especially when I had to call him back, apologize and copy his advertisement down. He kept asking, "Have you got *that* right?" The manager explained all about sleeping partners to me afterwards. I felt *so* ignorant.'

It hadn't been a joke to Pavana, but Alex laughed until his eyes watered, and even Gail, who was not sure she was all that enamoured of Alex, laughed heartily. They would stop laughing for a minute, then Alex's eyes would meet Gail's and the laughing would start all over again.

Pavana had watched them uncertainly at first. She had never considered herself in the least bit 'funny'. She reacted, over-reacted to stimuli. But here, obviously, must be an unsuspected talent. With certain people, she could be entertaining – what a joyful discovery. She had even been able that evening to laugh at herself. Triumph.

As they ate together, plates on their laps, he told them about the places where he had first tried different dishes, and how he had learned to cook the ones he liked. To unsophisticated palates like Gail's and Pavana's, these recipes were delightful surprises. On their own, even in restaurants, they would have hesitated to order them, much less assemble the ingredients to cook them.

Alex loved certain kinds of music, and shared with them those record albums that he thought they might enjoy. Rodrigo's *Concierto de Aranjuez* or Lalo Schiffren's *Tribute to the Marquis de Sade* seduced their emotions, making those evenings fiesta-like. In their imagination they trailed him eagerly up and down the streets of Athens, watched from a hillside the translucent blue of the Mediterranean, wandered in and out of old temples, sat on ancient, fallen columns looking out over the sea, visited the statue of Poseidon in a museum. And after dinner they scrutinized photographs of Alex and his friends seated on the grass below the Leaning Tower of Pisa, or of him standing on a bridge in Florence.

'That's why I'm nearly always broke,' he told Gail and Pavana, helping himself to the nuts and dates he had brought that evening. 'I travel whenever I can. You should try it, too. It's great fun. You musn't get into a rut – school, home, work, school. Make an effort.'

'Oh, we will! We won't!' they'd chorused, and had meant it, had even started to save.

Later, much later, when the romantic patina of their relationship had worn off and his enthusiasm for her company was on the wane, Pavana had felt unimaginably desolate, wondering what she had done to cause him to no longer care.

'You haven't *done* anything,' Gail said in great annoyance. 'Buck up, girl, the world is full of men, big, small, thin, fat, get your coat! Try thinking with your head next time, instead of your heart!'

'All right, all right!' Pavana had shouted, slamming the door of their room which had once more assumed its dingy, uninviting appearance.

Oh, but still, she thought, clumping down the stairs after Gail, it did not seem possible to have felt so close to a person for so long, to feel wanted, accepted, whole; it didn't seem in the realm of things that boredom, on his part, should soon set in, that close interest could dissipate into wariness, a studied politeness, an avoidance of contact. She felt as if she had metamorphosed from a graceful, colourful, tropical bird, flying freely through the days, into a loathsome vulture, trapped and skulking in the hallway at night, listening for his distinctive slam of the hall door, or to his voice laughing uproariously in Helga's flat.

She had struggled desperately to reverse this trend, to stave off jealousy, to hold his interest, even to the extent of sleeping with him, but she didn't like doing these things, being that way. She hadn't been able to carry it off. Later on, she realized that Helga kept herself inviolate, and he continued to treat her like a madonna. What does that then make

124

me? Pavana wondered another evening, as she waited in vain for him to arrive. His whore? And a cheap one at that, she said to herself, ruefully scraping the soggy salad, reeking of olive oil, into the dustbin. It was during this depressing period that she and Gail found a flat and moved out of the bedsitting house.

During the early headiness of it all she had made no demands on him for permanence of any kind, had asked for nothing, except for the joy of loving and of being loved for herself. Many years later, after long experience, she had reluctantly begun exploring the possibility that some people, like herself, perhaps like Stoner, are not lovable in the continuous sense. She did not contemplate this probable condition in any self-pitying way; it was an attempt at analysis, a query, a wonder, a small lament.

The qualities that brought her rewards in other areas – initiative, a little charm, a certain high-spirited zest for new experiences, satisfaction in the pursuit of goals which stretched her imagination and energy further than it was practical to attempt – those qualities did not seem to be tender in the affairs of the heart.

'Love', it seemed then, was a competitive business, demanding dedication, self-denial, discipline, continuous practice, cunning manoeuvres, guerrilla tactics: the same, she supposed, as in any other profession. It seemed to brook no diversions, would tolerate in her no other aspirations. It had been a lesson and she had been a diligent student, but life seemed so much duller for having learnt it.

Once it was really all over, she had no idea that somewhere in her being certain standards of 'love' had been irrevocably fixed; that it would be difficult to find again, or to sustain if found, what every human being needs through the stages and ages of being: the touch of a loved one, the miracle of union, of shared laughter and intimate secrets. She had not understood then that the exciting, satisfying image of herself she had seen first in Alex's eyes was not one she would easily recognize, even if seen in someone else's eyes.

After a while, through necessity and the fear of rejection, she had eschewed romantic love from her life, except for the usual, harmless flirtations and affairs of the mind in which everyone indulges from time to time. She had concentrated almost entirely on her children and on her small ambitions. But time is notorious for its talent in undermining the intensity of pain, for here it all was again, worse than ever.

By the time Eric pounded on the bathroom door, she had managed to form a few resolutions. After her class at Sacred Heart she would go to Belmopan, meet Mrs Elrington and begin familiarizing herself with the work ahead. At the end of the workday, she would try to visit Alex. There was only one hospital in town and one private clinic. Finding out where he had been taken would be the least of her problems.

'Mom! Ready?'

'Absolutely,' Pavana said, emerging from the bathroom.

Chapter 21

Pavana stood on a third-floor veranda overlooking the tennis court in the centre of the grounds, where about a hundred agitated students had gathered. At five minutes before eight the bell rang, silencing the earnest, clamorous, young voices, and Pavana walked into her sunny classroom to stand behind her desk. Tall palm trees poked their heads over the railings of another veranda to her left, and as she listened to the scraping of shoes on the stairs she wondered at the restlessness which had continued to grow within her during the past several weeks.

How could she seriously contemplate leaving these young people, to many of whom she had become attached? She enjoyed teaching, liked having to study hard so she could always feel prepared when she stood in front of her classes, liked discussing with them some of the experiences she had had abroad. It was a fairly secure position, one where she was not only needed but felt wanted.

However, the series of proposals announced recently had only served to stiffen her resolve to accept the position in the Ministry of Community Development. She too felt helpless in the face of the bafflement, anger and sadness with which most citizens viewed not only the proposed agenda but a vast array of other difficulties facing the country. Like most people, she also felt the need to make some small contribution which could possibly help to change the situation for the better.

As the teenagers filed in to take their places at their desks, it was immediately apparent that at some stage during the literature class the debate, started outside, would have to be continued. A few of them slapped their palms softly on her desk, breaking the rule of silence to whisper, 'Strike, Miss Leslie, let's strike.'

'Miss Leslie won't strike, eh, miss?' Julie, a tall, gangly girl with her uniform belt open and hanging to the sides, called from her desk near a door to the rear of the classroom.

'I don't think I like that smile, Miss Leslie.'

'Why not?' Pavana asked, watching Julie's clever, mischievous eyes sparkling as she winked at her classmates.

'It might seriously affect my grades.'

Pavana joined in the general laughter, too boisterous, too prolonged, and when the second bell rang she led them in the required prayer. Is that what they saw? she wondered, looking at the thirty-five faces as they made the required responses. A nice, nearly middle-aged teacher in black patent leather pumps, dark blue skirt and a white blouse? An easy-going teacher, on the whole, one who if not antagonized could be relied upon to give one a passing grade if one's marks were anywhere near seventy? A teacher who stayed clear of conflict, of controversy, and one who could always see too many sides to any issue? She could even hear herself: 'An excellent defence of your point of view, Julie, but there are other angles of vision, other perspectives on that issue. Shall we examine them before you make a final decision on where you stand?' Or, 'Shouldn't we strive, in the paper we are about to outline, for a more balanced viewpoint?'

Did they believe she didn't feel passionately about anything at all? Didn't she have any strong convictions? Of course she did, Pavana told herself, except she rarely displayed any passion in the classroom or anywhere else, anxious as always to avoid open confrontation with her students who were representative of the many races in the country and who came from all economic and social classes.

'Roger Mais's main character, Brother Man,' she began, not waiting for them to sit down and ignoring their cries of, 'Wait, miss, wait', 'was a man of peace. He wanted to help change the lives of the poor in his neighbourhood. He was involved in non-violent protest against the conditions under which large numbers of people were forced to live in Jamaica at that time, and still do. Partly because he was a Rastafarian, his motives were suspect, his good intentions were misinterpreted, and he was made to suffer out of all proportion to his actions.'

She paused, waiting for the transformation from literature class to political discussion which, she knew, was bound to happen. This was evident from the agitated glances among them, the scowls, the eyes fixed firmly on the floor or on the blackboard or gazing vacantly out of doors; the shuffling feet, the flipping of pages back and forth, the scraping of chairs, clearing of throats, the whispers.

It had been an unwritten rule for years that teachers should not discuss politics in the classroom. Today she would break it, for although she understood the reasons for the rule, she did not agree that it should be obeyed in all circumstances.

She made no attempt to impose order and tried no diversionary tactics to gain their attention. She prolonged the pause, disconcerting a few of the quieter, more studious pupils who looked at her with surprise and disapproval.

A plump student at the back of the room lumbered to her feet to pursue a sheet of paper blowing towards the veranda. Segura was ten pounds lighter than she had been at the beginning of the school year, when she had broken down in one of Pavana's classes weeping bitterly when one of the girls referred to her as 'La Buddha Segura'. Pavana had urged the class to support Segura in her efforts to follow the diet which the doctor had ordered for health reasons and the girls had done so, standing guard over Segura at recess to make sure she ate nothing she shouldn't. Their support had helped her greatly.

Segura felt indebted, and scowling at the class she said, 'I know Roger Mais was writing about Jamaica in the 1930s, miss, but our grocery store is in a neighbourhood similar to the one he describes. We all want to help make our neighbourhood better, you know, the drugs, the crime, the poverty. But we can't all be Brother Man, can we? Good intentions are not enough.

'People need jobs and so on. Don't you think this agreement would encourage more local people to invest in Belize? How about the politicians? Didn't *they* have good intentions when they signed the agreement? And look at the mess, miss.'

'It's not yet an agreement,' Pavana said, 'it's a list of topics for future discussions which could lead to an agreement. Good intentions were undoubtedly a part of their motivation. But we must also remember that it was, I understand, a condition for our independence that Guatemala,

Belize and Britain try once more to find a compromise acceptable to all parties.'

'Do you think that maybe Guatemala will invade after independence if the British troops leave?' another girl asked. 'My parents crossed into Belize some years ago to get away from the fighting in their region of Guatemala . . .'

'What kind of compromise?' another student interrupted. 'Guatemala believes this land, or part of this land, is theirs by rights inherited from Spain. If that agenda becomes an agreement, they may want to use the islands off-shore as military bases instead of for picnics, and use the country in various ways for economic gain. We'd be a colony again, is the way I see it.'

'Getting back to Brother Man,' another student said, 'and the work he was trying to do in his community, miss. It's difficult to do anything here. The same party has been in power since before I was born. People are afraid to speak their minds or to do any kind of community work because the politicians immediately interpret their involvement as politics, and unless the politicians are given the credit they do not support the projects. A lot of people are afraid to lose their jobs and their promotions.'

From the rear of the classroom, Julie called, 'A lot more could be done, but we are too easy-going, miss, the lot of us. We're glad to have other people do the work, make the waves and take the responsibility. We don't worry overmuch unless there is a crisis like these heads.'

The voices in the classroom were rising and tempers were beginning to flare. On the veranda, the teacher who would conduct the next class peered into the classroom as somebody was shouting, 'Don't talk to me about community service! You can't run around helping your neighbour when your own family is in need.'

A few minutes before the bell rang, Pavana said, 'For homework, I'd like you to write a short essay explaining how you would settle the border dispute between Guatemala, Britain and Belize. Your answers should reflect your grasp of the historical, cultural and political events leading to the present crisis.'

Groaning in protest, banging their books on their desks and scraping back their chairs, the students rose as was customary at the end of each class. As Pavana was about to leave, Julie spoke above the voices of a few teenagers still arguing back and forth.

'Excuse me, miss.'

'Yes, Julie?'

'Do you think these heads are a good compromise? Some people in here feel we should do what is asked for a secure independence. Others feel that if we do, we'll continue to pay a debt we don't owe until the country we know disappears entirely. What do you think, overall, I mean?'

The teacher at the door was signalling to Pavana, looking pointedly at the clock on the wall. The classroom was quiet for the first time since the students had entered. It was a challenge and there was no shirking it.

'No, as it stands, I do not believe the agenda for agreement is a good one. Undoubtedly we need a solution, which may include a compromise of some kind. However, it must be one which allows us to maintain the way of life we know, and the latitude to be able to improve on it. That way includes a humane democracy, law and order, the rights of the individual as well as those of citizens as a whole. We value human life, free speech, the freedom of a responsible press, the right to employment based primarily on merit; health care, education and so on.

'In the light of these and many other considerations, including those we talked about here this morning, I do not believe that the close association with Guatemala implied in the agenda for agreement is practical, nor would it ensure the preservation of our society as we value it, nor help it to continue its development along the lines we presently envision.'

'Thank you, miss,' Julie said, looking startled at the length and firmness of Pavana's reply. Pavana walked quickly towards the door, grateful that the pandemonium had subsided and that the maths teacher hovering anxiously outside the door would enter a relatively subdued classroom.

'You'd best be careful, Pavana, especially in these times,' the young teacher whispered urgently. 'The next thing you know they'll accuse you of discussing politics in the classroom!' She smiled to show she wasn't really afraid, but the fear was palpable in her eyes, and the tiny hand she placed on Pavana's was cold.

'Thanks for the warning, Ellen,' Pavana said, walking towards the stairs, hearing that her own voice was unsteady.

She was still glad that she had spoken her mind, whatever that was worth in a climate where most people were busily hiding theirs. She was grateful, too, to still be able to do so without fear of becoming a missing person, arrested in the middle of the night. She wouldn't face a firing squad at dawn. Neither would she be thrown into an unspeakable pit somewhere in the jungles of the hinterland. Nobody would pitch her mutilated body down a well, pull out her fingernails, deny her food and water or leave a tap dripping water on her head. It was possible that she could lose her job, of course, in some seemingly plausible way.

Victimization, in a vast array of guises, was the most effective mode of terror being practised, and since she was already feeling the flick of its thorny tail she had little more to fear nor to lose. What the events of the past week had done, however, was to change her from being a passive observer of what was becoming almost a benign form of dictatorship, with all its trappings, into a passionate opponent of its policy of rewarding friends and punishing its enemies. In addition, she had an awful suspicion that the opposition party would probably do very much the same.

Vicky was waiting for her at the bottom of the stairs. Her face was flushed an ugly purple.

'What's up, Victoria?' Pavana asked, remarking to herself that Vicky's eyes became almost hooded when she was disturbed or angry.

'Blue news, Pavana, the very bluest. Jackie Lee was over at the Peace Corps House last night. Guess who's in the lead for deputy at the Women's Unit?'

'Not Brenda Kirkwood!' Pavana said, immediately associating her name with Jackie Lee.

'I expect you'll hear the glad tidings, if Jackie is on target, from Mrs Elrington today . . .'

'I expect so,' Pavana said. 'Look, I've got to take a taxi to the bus station, if I'm to reach Belmopan by ten-thirty. I'll call you as soon as I can.'

'I'll expect a blow-by-blow account!'

'Those files will probably knock me out cold,' Pavana said. 'But I'll do my best.'

Chapter 22

Except for the deep rumble of the minister's voice from the conference room the ministry was relatively quiet, the typewriters silent, the corridors almost deserted, when Pavana hurried in that same morning after the one-hour bus journey. In the rooms on both sides of the corridor officers sat at their desks, heads bent over their files, their faces grim. A few, feeling more secure, lounged in the doorways, smirking openly at the escalating row in the conference room. Locating Mrs Elrington's room, Pavana sat on one of the chairs for visitors placed on either side of the doorway.

Minister Simon Galvez, intending to be heard, raised his voice.

'Mrs Elrington. I cannot allow you to put windows in the walls, nor to partition this room into cubicles. If I do not choose to hold conferences in it, the ministers who come after me may wish to do so. Besides, I am thinking of holding one . . . very soon.'

Still blustering indignantly, he charged into the corridor, his fleshy face looking peeved. The good looks which had helped him win the votes of at least a few hundred women had blurred, his eyes, nose and mouth much too small for their fatty surround.

'I hope you will reconsider the matter at a later date, Minister,' Mrs Elrington said, in a persuasive, reasonable voice, closing the door with an emphatic bang on the jumble of old filing cabinets, broken desks, chairs, tables and boxes, placed there over the years, and probably for the most part forgotten.

Mrs Elrington's twenty-five years in the ministry showed plainly on her face at that moment. She looked sick and tired of the whole business as she followed the minister and his permanent secretary, Mr Edward Kelly, down the corridor. Except for the colours, Mrs Elrington's clothing was more or less the same every day: a blouse with a floppy blow at the neckline, a tailored skirt reaching mid-calf and comfortable black shoes with thick rubber soles, such as nurses wear in hospitals.

Pavana noticed a black linen jacket draped over the back of the chair behind her desk. Perhaps she wore that to important meetings.

A few feet from the foyer, where Pavana had entered, the minister stopped in mid-stride, bumping into the permanent secretary who staggered a little, nearly injuring himself with the point of the extra-large black umbrella he carried, furled, in one hand.

'I've done everything I can to help you, Mrs Elrington, but it's not easy, you know, being a minister. I'd just as soon return to my farm, but I am here at the express wishes of my townsfolk. I have a lot of people to serve, Mrs Elrington, a lot of people.'

Conscious of the listening public officers, he sighed heavily. Then as if with a supreme effort he permitted a jocular note to return to his voice, suggesting that he was determined to humour Mrs Elrington, who had been used to serving colonial public servants from the United Kingdom and could not as yet, if ever, be expected to understand the ways of the new Belize.

'What more do women want, Mrs Elrington?' the minister asked, turning to the permanent secretary with an arch, youthful smile.

Mrs Elrington's eyes widened slightly, as if surprised at the question, but she smiled, answering seriously.

'Indeed, Minister, I am sure the entire country is impressed that a Women's Unit has been established in your ministry, particularly the women in your constituency.'

The minister looked around him, gratified, inclined to linger. He folded his hands behind his back, moving up and down on his heels and toes.

'However, Minister, we must now carry through . . . better health services, training, jobs, shelter, food, programmes to enhance women's self-esteem, and a greater awareness of their own potential.' Mrs Elrington voice was still reasonable, still persuasive. 'It means liaising with all the ministries, which means space here in the capital where we can work, hold meetings, conferences and so on.'

The minister looked annoyed, then knowing.

'Women's liberation. We don't need that here. Our women are free to rise as high as they please, if they wish to do so, which I don't believe they do, at least I haven't met many.'

Mrs Elrington's expression, a long look at the minister, managed to convey that she was quite sure his statement needed examination. But

133

she allowed this comment to go unchallenged, deciding to deal with the issue immediately at hand.

'Now, Minister, if we had space in the conference room, we could put the Women's Unit, Home Economics and Income Generating in one room, where they could learn to become colleagues, working together. Eventually,' she added on a note of triumph, 'they could become a department with their own head! Why, one day there may even be a Ministry of Women's Affairs.'

The minister looked horrified. 'A ministry, Mrs Elrington? Heh!' He looked puzzled, suspicious. He continued rocking back and forth, toe to heel, heel to toe, thinking. Finally he said, 'I didn't quite understand that the Women's Unit was to be such a grandiose affair, Mrs Elrington. As far as I can recall, I understood it was to train women to be better wives and mothers, an extension of the Home Economics Unit, so to speak. I had even mentioned to Mrs Carillo . . .'

Pavana casually picked up a magazine, pretending to be engrossed in it, but her heart was beating faster. No wonder Mrs Carillo had looked so disappointed and upset at Jackie Lee's meeting. She'd thought . . . Mrs Elrington was speaking again.

'I could arrange to brief you again, Minister. We've been planning and working for about two years, as you know. We missed you at the meeting last month . . .'

'So sorry about that,' the minister said, 'An urgent problem in my constituency. But yes, Mrs Elrington, perhaps I should be re-briefed.' He jingled the keys in his pocket. 'I can see where this new unit may be quite useful. But we must have the right people, of course. Cabinet is insisting upon it. Please make a note of that, P.S., a meeting with Mrs Elrington, soon, this afternoon?'

'Will do, Minister,' the permanent secretary said, looking pained that a senior member of his staff had insisted on placing his minister in such a publicly embarrassing situation.

It was amazing, Pavana thought to herself, but Edward Kelly's physical appearance had not changed all that much since she last saw him all those years ago at his wedding in St John's Cathedral. If anything, he seemed taller, slimmer, trimmer, still walking as though he was the leader of a military parade, head up, shoulders back, shoes brightly polished, trousers sharply creased, immaculate long-sleeved white shirts even in the most humid weather.

A stranger looking at the two men would immediately assume that P.S. Kelly was the minister. The grey at his temples added to his air of good breeding and distinction, of being in command, as he was. Like Mrs Elrington, like Mrs Carillo, the public service was his whole life. He had risen through the ranks, serving several ministers, to his present situation. Like other permanent secretaries, he was one of the country's real rulers.

'P.S. Kelly,' the minister was saying now, again pitching his voice to be heard in the silent rooms along the corridor, 'what is your advice on this matter of the conference room?' He looked helplessly at P.S. Kelly, who was swinging the umbrella by its handle back and forth on the forefinger of his right hand.

Pavana quickly discerned that P.S. Kelly was a cold, calculating man, perhaps even cruel. He had the most peculiar, watery, light brown eyes, and she could already see how the attentive yet blank expression in them, as he glanced up and down the corridor, could make a person feel insignificant, guilty, willing to do almost anything to gain his approbation. He also seemed to be a supremely confident man, and Pavana guessed that he tolerated no challenges to his authority, which she suspected he felt Mrs Elrington was attempting. The minister, demoted Pavana had been told in a recent cabinet reshuffle, was absolutely dependent on him.

'Minister,' P.S. Kelly said, 'it is my opinion that you made absolutely the right decision in the first place. The unit has brand-new offices and furnishings in Belize City. The Decade for Women, you will remember? Funds from the United Nations?'

'Of course, I remember now that you remind me,' the minister said, looking sternly at Mrs Elrington as though it had been proven that she had been trying to manipulate him.

'And, Minister, as you rightly pointed out, Miss Leslie – that's the newly appointed director, Minister – will only be coming to Belmopan once or twice a week for meetings and other work. She does have a desk here, with Paul and Tony, Minister. We can't allow special privileges, set unfortunate precedents, even if the unit is financially independent . . . for the time being anyway, two years, I believe.'

'Now I recall. Yes I See, P.S.'

'We could go on as we are, would be my suggestion, no need for an absolute decision of course, as you said.'

'Quite right, glad you agree with me, P.S. Kelly.' He turned to Mrs Elrington.

'Perhaps we can discuss this again, Mrs Elrington, at a later date, once the work of the unit is actually much further advanced?'

'As you wish, Minister,' Mrs Elrington said, following the men through the foyer to the offices they occupied at the other end of the building. As Pavana stood up, she remembered Miss Junie Silver and the baby she had stabbed, which led her to thinking about Alex, the blood on his shirt, about Stoner Bennett and about Lisa and Eric . . .

'Ah, Pavana, my dear,' Mrs Elrington was saying, 'let me introduce Minister Galvez. Minister,' she said, placing her hand on his arm and drawing Pavana forward, 'this is Pavana Leslie, the new director of the Women's Unit.'

'How do you do?' the minister said, his nose twitching as if he smelt rotting fish, steadfastly keeping his eyes somewhere between Pavana's neck and her chin. Pavana shook hands with P.S. Kelly, who smiled and welcomed her to the ministry. The minister said, 'I had to go against some of my colleagues in the cabinet, you know. I hope all will go well.' He managed a ghost of his jocular laugh. 'What was the name?'

'Leslie. Pavana Leslie.'

'Which Leslie is that? I have a few Leslie families in my constituency. Any relation to them?'

'Not that I know of,' Pavana said. 'My parents are originally from Toledo. They lived for a while here in Belize City and now they live north, in Corozal.'

'Ah, those Leslies. They've had quite a success with their bus service, haven't they? Do I know them, P.S.? Have they ever been into the ministry, for example?'

The P.S. shook his head doubtfully.

Pavana was about to say a little more about her parents, but the minister had lost interest and was about to continue walking towards his office when they heard the click-clacking of heels on the plastic tiles of the foyer. The minister bounded forward, emitting joyous exclamations of greeting.

'Brenda! Brenda Kirkwood!' the minister was saying, shaking her hand vigorously, reluctant it seemed to let go of it. His face wore a look of immense relief, as if his ministry had been under siege and loyal troops had now arrived to effect a long-prayed-for rescue.

'Miss Kirkwood is considering joining us, Minister, as deputy to Miss Leslie in the Women's Unit,' the permanent secretary said. 'She's meeting Mrs Elrington at eleven-thirty, I believe.'

'Wonderful,' the minister said. 'I've known your family for many years, haven't I, Brenda? Very bright family, great supporters of mine.'

Brenda Kirkwood's infectious and bubbly laugh gurgled along the corridor.

'Thought I'd join the ministry and give you a hand, Minister,' she said, her large, golden eyes fixed on the minister's face as if she had never seen a more charming sight. 'I hear you need help to get this place in shape.' She glanced around as if eager to begin a day's work, laughing all the while. Brenda was the very picture of a woman and development officer, in an elegant tan dress and brown leather pumps. She wore a ziricote wooden necklace with matching earrings. A narrow bandeau, embroidered with Mayan designs, held the mane of hair off her face. Brenda carried a leather briefcase and a furled umbrella. In the pause her wristwatch, large and blackfaced, gave a tiny reminding beep.

'You're early for your meeting, Brenda,' the minister said. 'Sorry I missed you on your previous visits to the ministry. But if you'll come to my office now I'll give you a briefing, if you don't mind, Mrs Elrington?'

'Not at all,' Mrs Elrington said, looking as if she minded very much.

'Hi, Pavana,' Brenda said, biting her lips and then bestowing her dazzling smile. 'Glad to see you're getting involved. I'm hoping we'll get a chance to work together.' She turned to Mrs Elrington. 'Eleven-thirty then, Cora? Here in your office?'

Mrs Elrington agreed, and as the minister led Brenda along the corridor, he asked, 'So what do you think of our new Women's Unit? I am relying on you to explain it all to me.'

The minister's great, booming laugh resonated throughout the ministry, signalling that all was well in his kingdom again. It was a calculatedly joyous laugh, deep, full-barrelled, reassuring, if for the moment one had nothing to fear; but if one had, and most people in the ministry did, it had the effect of an unexpected explosion, shockingly loud, heart-stopping.

Chapter 23

On her return from Belmopan, after spending most of the afternoon poring through the Women's Unit files, Pavana walked to the private clinic, converted from an old mansion, where Alex had been taken for medical attention. Growing in high, dusty banks on either side of the stairs were overgrown bushes of pink oleander. Pavana broke off a small cluster, shaking it vigorously to get rid of the worst of the dust clinging to the pointed leaves.

Then she climbed the stairs to the first-floor veranda and entered the cool reception hall, with its ceiling to floor windows wide open to the riotous colours in the garden. She crossed the pinewood floors to the mahogany desk, behind which a young nurse sat, studying a file from the stack on a table to her left.

'Are you a relative?' she asked, after Pavana had stated her name and requested permission to visit Alex. The nurse cast disapproving dark eyes on the flowers in Pavana's hand before looking her up and down, as though the purloined blossoms provided adequate reason, if not irrefutable evidence, for suspecting that Pavana was there with the sole intent of doing Alex further bodily harm.

'No,' she said staring steadily back at her. The tensions of the past two days had left Pavana in a contentious mood, and several facetious remarks occurred to her, but she banished them immediately. The nurse was only doing her job, as was the policeman rustling a newspaper in the opposite corner of the room.

'I'm not sure Mr Abrams can receive visitors.'

'I see,' Pavana said, continuing to stand before the desk.

Perhaps in the end the nurse was somewhat reassured by the school uniform Pavana still wore. With the air of someone going against her better judgement, she said grudgingly, 'But have a seat, I'll check.'

She locked her files in a drawer of the desk and, snapping the keys on to a ring on her belt, disappeared through a door to the rear of the hall.

She was gone for several minutes while Pavana, under the policeman's sober scrutiny, sat like a prisoner in the dock on the edge of a chair, waiting, in some apprehension, to know whether or not she would be able to see Alex that day. It had been difficult enough making up her mind to come here in the first place, and she didn't relish the thought of returning home to Lisa and Eric without getting a chance to speak with Alex.

On her return the nurse nodded curtly to Pavana, who followed her through the same door and down a long corridor. The nurse silently indicated a room with the door ajar. Pavana knocked diffidently and when Alex called, 'Come in,' she pushed the door wider and entered the room.

He was fully dressed and seated at a table near a window, his head bent over a mass of papers. As he turned, a look of complete surprise crossed his face.

'Pavana! The nurse said Miss Leslie, but I couldn't think it was you. Marvellous to see you.'

His left arm was in a sling, he extended the other and Pavana placed her hand in his familiar grasp. He accepted the flowers, which had leaked white sap drying to sticky black dirt on Pavana's fingers and palms. His words were welcoming, but his eyes grew wary, querying.

'And proferring poison,' he laughed, 'disguised as exquisite blossoms. Dusty, too,' he added, making a small *moue* of distaste as he examined the leaves with his fingertips.

'Are they really poisonous?' Pavana asked, then railed at herself for reverting so rapidly to the role of *naïf*. But this was Alex all over: throw the person offguard with some bit of extraneous or esoteric information, giving himself the chance to set the conversation on the course he preferred it to go.

'Indeed they are. However, since I don't intend to eat these I'll accept them as a gesture of goodwill. You, obviously, are ignorant of their deadly properties.'

'The sap will stain your shirt, I know that much,' Pavana said.

'An even greater gesture of magnanimity on my part then. I enjoy feeling virtuous occasionally. It's a terrible strain living up to my image as villain cum pariah in these chaotic days.'

There was more than a tinge of bitterness to his voice, that voice which had always been her undoing, those rich, vibrant tones which could hold, had held, thousands in thrall. He was different now. Even before he'd begun courting the ruling party, or perhaps it was the other way around, she'd been hopeful that he would stick to some of his earlier ideals. She wondered if it had all gone, the passionate commitment to championing the cause of the poor and the oppressed. Pavana, who had listened in recent months to some of his radio speeches and interviews, thought they lacked the intensity of his old convictions, but she couldn't be quite sure.

Alex did not ask her to sit down, nor did he sit himself but stood leaning against the table at which he had been working. The pouches under his eyes made them appear smaller, and there was a certain cynicism to his face, suggesting that he had listened to a hundred thousand voices all wanting something, and that he was now waiting to hear the one hundred thousand and one request. Pavana wondered what it was he saw in her own face.

'Were you very badly hurt?' she asked.

He touched the bandage on his shoulder as if he'd only just remembered it was there, shaking his head dismissively to make sure she understood that he was in no need of her interest nor her pity.

'To what do I owe the honour of this visit?' he asked, smiling his old sweet smile. 'Obviously, concern for my physical condition did not bring you rushing, and with flowers, mark you, to my bedside.'

'I've accepted the job as head of the new Women's Unit. I started work officially today.'

'Congratulations. I did my best on your behalf, and for Mrs Elrington. Sorry I wasn't able to do more. All debts squared away, I trust?'

'I didn't ask for any political favours.'

'You've got one anyway.'

'I wanted to thank you . . . for your efforts.'

'Consider it done, Pavana.'

Alex removed his horn-rimmed glasses, putting them with thoughtful slowness on to the table. He rubbed wearily at his bloodshot eyes before squinting down at her, a puzzled expression on his face, far more deeply lined, and haggard than she'd noticed the evening before in that fading light. His right arm gripped the chair tightly, as if needing further support.

She glanced at it, remembering those evenings long ago when even his arm, with its long, silken black hairs, the slender wrist, the elegant hand with its meticulously pared nails, could fill her with tenderness, believing she could have always the sweetness of loving a man such as this. Well, it was too late as well for all that. She'd had her chance, such as it was, and she'd blown it; although now, as an adult, she realized that events would probably have evolved the way they did whatever she'd done.

'Do you think I'll make an effective head of the unit?'

'We haven't spoken in years, how should I know?' He shrugged.

'I thought you would because you are . . . . you . . .'

'Is *turncoat* the word you're hesitating to use?'

'Well, you and Stoner were for years members of organizations opposed to the present political parties.'

'And we failed? But that was something quite different. The opposition party condemned one faction as racist, the other as communist. We were at each other's throats. Everyone wanted to become the maximum leader.'

'Maybe it was also because the ideologies of both factions were imported, alien to Belizean values, traditions and all that?'

'I'm quite familiar with that line of discussion, Pavana, and to be truthful I find it unproductive. Soon you'll ask me if it is true I wanted then to turn Belize into a socialist state, next you'll talk about Cuba and Grenada. Then will come a discourse on totalitarianism, victimization, nepotism and corruption. You'll tell me it's in my character, and there we'll both be, right back in Primrose Hill.'

'I was trying to discuss the reasons why black power and socialism could not sustain the early enthusiasm you and Stoner helped others to generate throughout the country. But what was great about it all was that those organizations did inject a new spirit into the country, a new awareness of political alternatives; so you accomplished a great deal.'

'What's that supposed to be, some sort of consolation prize?'

'I'm talking like this because the unit is another new idea, another importation and . . .'

'You don't want to make the same mistakes we did? Well, if the worst comes to the worst, as it probably will, you'll have the satisfaction, won't you, of having educated the masses, injected a new spirit into the country?'

'After yesterday . . . and now today in the ministry, I'm really not sure

I'm up to this. Perhaps I should have stayed in the classroom, at least there . . .'

'You're safe. No conflicts with aspiring, not to say *turncoat* politicians? You are a typical Creole, Pavana, in spite of that international veneer. You want life cushy, cozy, well-ordered, like an English storybook. Mrs Elrington sent me your *résumé*. I read it with great interest.

'Go back to the development set where you can sit in the evenings eating three-course meals in westernized houses, while you discuss the plight of developing countries and the low specimens of humanity who inhabit them. That's your *métier*, isn't it? Of course, it might sicken your soul the slightest bit to hear them talk in scornful, degrading terms about the begging-bowl mentality of Third World contries, but what the hell, it's a small price to pay for such civilized company, isn't it?'

'You read my *résumé*!' Pavana hated the scorn she heard in her voice. 'What do you know about the way I think, or the way I feel or the way I've lived? You also ran away from the true fight. You are helping to consolidate a power that is becoming absolute. If you really had the country at heart, you would continue to encourage healthy dissent, like you did in the old days, even if you lost every election. Why didn't you stand your ground? Who ran to safety and privileges of power?'

'I sincerely want to contribute to the development of Belize. The only road untried led to a role inside the ruling party where I do have some support for my ideas, and I've chosen to travel it.'

'Aren't you the one, Alex, who used to preach from every rostrum you could find that the saving remnant of a country is that group of people who vote, speak and act for the good of the country, instead of strictly along party lines?

'Look at what happens when they do. The ruling party stonewalls. There's absolute silence on the radio about the demonstrations, and there is no doubt about it, after this is all over, victimization will spread like a blight along the corridors of the ministries in Belmopan, and elsewhere in the country. Isn't that what happened to most members of the groups you and Stoner supported?

'Those people with the courage to speak out will continue to leave the country if they are victimized for exercising those rights. What will we have then, total power on one side or the other? Don't you care about these things any more, Alex?'

'Slave mentality is what drives that group away, no matter what excuses they use. They prefer third-class citizenship in America or wherever to being first class in their own. Nationals at the head of government are abhorrent to them unless they are the bosses, then they strut around like macaw parrots, treating the ordinary people with condescension, arrogance and disdain. Set up your soapbox among that lot, Pavana. They are the ones you should make your constituents. I've made a lot of mistakes but I never left Belize, and I never will. You've asked for my advice. I've given it, now for God's sake leave me alone.'

Chapter 24

A long, wooden pier stretched far out into the sea. Two boys, truants from school, sat at the very end of the pier, casting fishing lines into the emerald-green waves sparkling in the late afternoon sunshine. Alex stood against the window frame, leaning his head on his arm. Pavana wondered if he was in pain, wondered whether they could be friends again.

'You may or may not believe this, Alex, but I really was very sorry when the movements petered out.'

He didn't turn around, nor did he reply.

She wanted to add, but didn't, that in London, as she'd read the newspapers her parents sent her from home, she could sense the excitement in the country, hear the hopeful roar of the crowd. She could feel their enthusiasm and affection for a number of bright, attractive young leaders, Alex and Stoner among them, who with their energy, education and commitment would provide, perhaps, alternatives to the two dominant parties.

From afar, she and thousands of others had willed these two groups to combine forces, to overcome personal ambition and ideology, racial, class and economic barriers, which would enable them to formulate a practical plan of action acceptable to the electorate.

After some time, the two organizations did try to combine their strengths, but it had all turned out disastrously. In racially diverse Belize, the faction to which Stoner had passionately committed himself was forced to reduce its fiery black power rhetoric, which lost them a tremendous number of followers who were mostly city-bred, black and poor.

And neither blacks, *mestizos*, Maya Indians nor any other group showed much enthusiasm for socialism, espoused by the faction that Alex supported. Everybody assumed that socialism, whether democratic or scientific (nobody quite understood the difference), was a euphemism for the dreaded communism.

In addition to the battle for leadership in the newly formed organization it had, as was to be expected, alienated the established political parties, who viewed the activities of these young men as a potent threat to the status quo.

People tried in various ways to express their gratitude to these courageous young men, although they did not find it possible, then, to vote them into office, which was what they seemed to want more than anything in the world. And it really was with the greatest reluctance that the population turned once more to the seasoned politicians, many of whom had grown cynical, corrupt.

Alex exhaled deeply as he turned from the window.

'Thank you anyhow for the late expression of solidarity, and for the flowers.'

'Sorry they couldn't be primroses,' Pavana said, picking up her handbag from the floor.

He straightened up, removed the oleander from his shirt pocket and dropped the wilting blossoms into the wash basin. Gathering his papers together, he slipped them into his briefcase and snapped it shut. He poured a glass of water and tipped two capsules from an envelope on to the table. As she watched him, a quotation she had read, perhaps in one of Julian's books, stole into her mind, 'Revolution is not for moderates. In times of upheaval, hardness is power. From Alexander Kerenski to Arturo Cruz, nothing changes: the man of qualms, of balance, of ambivalence is lost.' Where had she read that, where? As she struggled to remember, Alex said, 'I hope you will excuse me, Pavana, but I'm being discharged this afternoon and I'd like to be prepared when Moria arrives.'

'Of course, Alex. I wouldn't have dreamed of visiting you at a time like this, only . . .'

'Only, what?' He glanced sideways at her as he placed the capsules on his tongue and drank the entire glass of water.

Pavana forced herself to go on.

'Only, last night, after you were . . . shot, Stoner approached me on Prince's Lane. He asked me to speak to you, to use my influence with you is the way he put it.'

'My, my, my,' Alex said, looking at her in an avuncular manner. 'A new recruit on the Action Committee? Times have changed, Pavana.'

'Oh no, it's because of . . . well, Stoner wants to know what advice you plan to give the cabinet, regarding a referendum on the heads of agreement.'

Alex removed a travelling bag from the closet and placed it on the bed.

'I don't know the answer to that question yet, and even if I did I wouldn't reveal it. Besides, opinion in the cabinet, the last I heard, has swung to the hardliners. They want to deal firmly with the situation and hope that the protests subside.'

'He wants you to try and use your influence with them, to speak out, get them to agree on a referendum. Go to the country, if necessary.'

'Stoner should know better than that. The cabinet is definitely not as enamoured of me as they once were. Last night was an effort to prove my loyalty, my gratitude to them for saving me from political oblivion, for taking me into the fold, to prove my devotion. The two ministers with whom I still have some credibility are in the same position as I am.'

'The Action Committee is planning to support the Public Service Union, he says, in a countrywide strike unless the cabinet agrees to a referendum.'

'Well, I'm very much afraid I cannot assist him with any advance information. He knows very well that a defeat on the referendum would force the government to resign and to call an election, which he wants of course.'

'He wants you to get in touch with him, Alex.'

'I'm sorry. I can't at this time. The minister and I have agreed to march with people all over the country, to meet with them during the next few days to explain to the public the details of the agenda which the party is fully supporting.'

'If you don't meet with him, or do something, Alex, he says he'll publish an anonymous article in all the newspapers on your reasons for having him expelled from the Independence for Belize Committee in London.'

'He was expelled for undermining my bid for re-election.'

'Stoner has a copy, he says, of some memo you destroyed. He says he has hesitated to use it until now but he will, if you force his hand.'

'Bennett is bluffing, Pavana. Just go home and forget about the whole thing. I will.'

'He's not bluffing, Alex, not altogether anyway.'

'What gives you that impression?' The question was almost a bark, harsh and frightening.

Pavana felt as if her knees would not hold her up any longer. She dragged the chair from beneath the table and sank down on it, feeling the sickness in her stomach rising again. She stared through the window at the two boys still fishing on the pier, before she said quietly, carefully, 'He told me about the money you borrowed from him in London.'

She heard his sharp intake of breath, but couldn't turn to look at him.

'He now knows why you borrowed it.''

Alex placed his hand on her shoulder.

'He couldn't know, not for sure anyway. But I must say Stoner understands you quite well, your terror of any kind of scandal or gossip. Besides, as I told you, he's bluffing. I wouldn't worry about it if I were you.'

'The twins do resemble you somewhat, if one is looking for a resemblance.'

His grip tightened, he was almost shaking her.

'Twins? What twins?' He crossed to the window, blocking out the view. There was no place to look but at him.

'My – our – children, Lisa and Eric. Stoner knows you're their father. I had to admit it to him last night. It's one of the reasons I came home, to talk to you about it, have you meet them.'

Alex's mouth twisted into an ugly sneer and he looked at her with an expression of absolute disgust. Pavana cringed before the ugliness of his gaze.

'Do you expect me to believe that? After all these years?'

'You can believe what you like. Stoner also plans to write about our relationship in that article, distort things in some way, use the children's names, God knows what else he plans to say. You would know that better than I would.'

Pavana watched Alex staggering, like someone old and frail, to the bed. He sat on it, his head propped against the pillows. He rubbed his hand across the area of his head where he was balding. She felt a momentary pang of tenderness, remembering the shock of curly hair he once had. The lines at the corners of his mouth were now deep indentations, enclosing his mouth like exaggerated parentheses. He closed his eyes, shutting from view the horror, fear, disgust Pavana had seen so clearly in them. Alex was exhausted.

She observed the grey in his beard, in the long tendrils of hair curling on to the edges of the bandage across his chest where his shirt buttons were open. He opened his eyes, and now they were puzzled and sad.

'But against my advice you insisted. We agreed.'

'I couldn't go through with it.'

'Why did you change your mind? Not from any high moral ground, surely?'

As she listened to his voice, indignant, incredulous and fearful in turn, railing against what she had done, Pavana continued to feel that overall she had made the right decision in excluding Alex from their early lives. It would have been humiliating, intolerable, watching the twins wait for his letters to arrive, for his visits, if he had felt inclined to make any, for invitations to visit him.

She would never have been able to request nor accept money from him for their support. False pride or not, it had been a value, without which she would have felt a continuing loss of self-respect, given the educational advantages in life she had had. Alex had not, after all, forced her to do anything she had not wanted to do.

She had given freely of herself, and the children were the result of that decision, her choice, and Pavana believed passionately that a woman should have the right to decide whether or not to have a child. She also believed that a woman should be prepared to face the consequences of that choice.

The arrival of unwanted children into a hostile environment was no picnic, neither for the mother nor the child. She had chosen to have her children because she had discovered she wanted them. If she had underestimated the difficulties of raising one child, to say nothing of two, without male support, she did not regret one moment of it all. It was not so much an intention 'to deceive' or an 'act of revenge', as Alex was now saying in harsh tones; it had been an act of self-protection, of survival, of trying to continue becoming the person she wanted to be. In those last months, Alex had become obsession. She had begun to feel diseased.

'Why?' Alex was demanding. 'Why?'

She answered him adult to adult. 'I wanted, needed to have them. Maybe it was completely selfish, hard to tell, but somehow my decision felt like the right one, still does.'

Pavana walked to the window and looked out. The young boys had gone, like the sunlight. She thought of Lisa and Eric at home by now, going through the routine of their day. She wondered what their thoughts had been during the past twenty-four hours.

Alex had been silent for a while, but as Pavana turned to go he placed his hand on her arm, rubbing it softly up and down, pressing his body close to hers. He bent his head and kissed her neck. She felt the thick bandage through the blouse of her uniform.

'If you had changed your mind,' he said persuasively, 'why was it necessary to hide it from me? They are my children, too, as you say. I find what you did cruel and unforgivable.'

Harsh words, harsher thoughts rushed through Pavana's mind but she stifled them, keeping the faces of Eric and Lisa firmly in her mind.

'Do you?' she asked mildly.

If he had forgotten, she hadn't – couldn't – forget that winter day in the private London clinic, when she'd sat on the edge of the bed in the room she had been assigned, burdened with the consequences of her decision. She thought of the doctor's face, young and sympathetic, as he had returned to her all the money she had paid in advance; how carefully she had counted it before stuffing it deep into her bag.

'It's not too late to change your mind back again, you know,' the doctor had said. 'I take it there's no possibility of marriage?'

Pavana shook her head.

'Shall I have the receptionist call a taxi for you, once you're dressed?'

'Oh, no thank you, Doctor. Alex, that's my friend, he's promised to come and get me.'

He patted her shoulder.

'It's a pity that . . . I mean you would have been able to return to your college, made something of your life. A tremendous amount of sacrifice brought you to this country, I believe?'

148

Pavana nodded.

'Well, think it over, let me know in the next week or so if you reverse your decision.'

'Thank you,' Pavana said.

Later she sat on a chair in the grocery store, the Christmas music sounding like a dirge to her ears, waiting for Alex to walk through the door. Everything would surely fall into place once he did. It had been well after noon when she'd telephoned the bedsitting house in Maida Vale again, but Alex was still out. Thinking he might have been delayed, she'd sat there for another two hours before picking up her overnight bag and leaving the busy store.

She'd stood in a cold drizzle on the crowded sidewalk watching the traffic hurtling by. In the end, feeling too ill and upset to face the long ride by bus or train, she'd hailed a taxi, sinking gratefully into the commodious back seat, closing her eyes against London, and upon the hopes and dreams she had hoped to make a reality there.

As much as she longed to remain where she was, she recognized the fantasy and gently disengaged Alex's arm from around her shoulder. She was sure he could see the conflicting emotions on her face.

'What was so terrible about the offer I made that day in the park? I wanted to offer some protection to you and the baby . . . babies. What was so shameful about that? So disgraceful? Why were you so outraged? You acted, over-reacted, I thought then, as if I were urging you to commit some criminal act instead of making a practical arrangement.'

'All my life, I'd struggled to break free of certain cultural patterns. I didn't want to end up being supported by you but only while you approved of my actions and decisions, having more children with you or, if you left, with somebody else, perhaps ending up with a patchwork quilt for a family. I wanted to be able to stand on my own feet.'

'What makes you think you're so different from most Caribbean women that I know? They accept their lives, it seems. Even like it, since as boys we are raised to become the men we are. How can you be so different?'

'I am not different, but I wanted to be. I wanted some control over what happened in my life, not have its outcome dictated by what I considered to be a youthful mistake.'

'And have you achieved that? Control, I mean. If you have, it seems

149

to me you cheated yourself, and the children, to get it. I feel cheated, too. Why the hell didn't you tell me?'

Pavana looked at Alex, whose face had become indignant and righteous all over again, thinking that whatever price she had paid had been worth it.

'I would have told you if you'd kept your promise to pick me up at the clinic, if you'd phoned or asked someone else to phone. But I sat there in limbo, not knowing what to think. I was furious that it all meant so little to you. I tried to see you, went to your room and well, you know what happened that night. I couldn't see what could be salvaged after that, what the point would be . . . in telling you.'

Chapter 25

That evening, after her arrival from the clinic, Pavana dropped her overnight bag on the divan in front of the boarded-up fireplace. She prowled feverishly back and forth across the small living-room of their newly acquired flat, hoping desperately that Alex would call to say he was on his way to see her. Gail was out, and although Pavana had plans to make and chores to do, she felt unable to lift nor lay; she could think of little else except her desperate need for the sound of Alex's voice. She rang the bedsitting house in Maida Vale over and over again, but no one picked up the pay telephone on the landing.

As the hours dragged on and on into night and as her hopes dwindled, she became obsessed with her desire to be with him, to feel the comforting warmth of his gentle hands moving slowly up and down her back. She wanted to sit on his lap with her arms around his neck, his beard against her cheek, to watch his expressive eyes tell her he wanted her lips on his own, to watch them tremble, become soft, vulnerable, reassuring, to feel that beloved face growing warmer beneath her fingertips, at least one more time; to hear him murmur over and over as he used to do, 'I love you so much, Pavana, so much.'

He did, he loved her; she didn't really need his words to know that. Why then had he let her go? Why wasn't she good enough? Was he, in some way, ashamed of her? Was it that her background was not prestigious enough for the life he planned for himself? She had tried in so many ways, in every way she could think of, to demonstrate how very much she loved him, and he knew too that she always would.

'Alex!' she cried aloud. 'Alex!'

What needs hadn't she filled? Was it because of their differing political views? Her character flaws were quite numerous, but hadn't she under his tutelage tried to overcome the worst of them and in many cases succeeded? And who was there in the world, dear God, who was there without flaw? Alex's weaknesses were almost legendary, but she hadn't rejected him because of them.

In the harsh glare of the bulb above the bathroom mirror, she peered critically at her face, trying to discover there the reasons for his withdrawal. Why, oh why, was she unacceptable? She had to hear the reason from his own lips; he should, would, could tell her. It might be a mark of nobility to learn to live with uncertainty and ambiguity, but she hadn't yet fully developed those resources, didn't know if she ever could, or would. She needed to hear from Alex that their relationship was really ended, and the reasons why.

At about nine o'clock, when she could no longer endure the empty flat and the silent telephone, the tension overcame her battle for self-control. She pulled on her woollen cap, her boots, coat and gloves and left. At the Chalk Farm station she bought a ticket and sat huddled on a seat in a crowded compartment of the rumbling train, travelling through the underground tunnels to Maida Vale. She still had a key to the bedsitting house, and she let herself into the quiet, dimly lit hallway.

Alex's room, number twelve, was right at the top of the house and she ran the entire way up, arriving almost breathless outside his door. She knocked and knocked but he was not there. Running all the way down again, she stood outside the door of Helga's basement flat, angry, jealous, frightened, absolutely beside herself. She knocked, and when Helga opened the door the second movement of Roderigo's *Concierto de Aranjuez* came flooding into the hallway.

'Is Alex here?' she asked Helga, who was wearing a warm, dark blue robe. Her hair smelled newly washed. She looked extremely surprised to see Pavana, who had never knocked on her door this late before even while she lived in the bedsitting house, and she had moved away, hadn't she? Instinctively, both of them had stayed clear of each other.

151

'Not just now, but I expect him soon. Shall I give him a message?' Helga was quite accustomed to giving Alex messages of all kinds from all kinds of people.

'No,' Pavana said.

'Are you all right?' She had come right out into the hallway, and Pavana could see her painted toenails, a pearly pink, peeping through her fluffy, pale blue slippers.

'Yes,' Pavana said, but it was obvious she wasn't. She couldn't even meet Helga's eyes, so overwhelming was her terrible jealousy. Not even the *Concierto* had been special to the relationship between Alex and herself, which, it seemed, had been peripheral, easily sloughed off.

'Come in and wait, at least for a few minutes. You look frozen. It's terrible weather, yes?'

Pavana followed her down the basement steps through the tiny kitchen and into the comfortable living-room of her flat, which was now filled with Alex's possessions. Had he moved in with Helga? Pavana sat in an armchair and picked up a book off the coffee table, piled high with Alex's books and record albums. The book was called *The Little Prince*, and since it seemed to be a children's book, she flipped the pages idly, wondering why it was there.

The music was filling Pavana's soul with an unbearable melancholy. It's not her fault, she said to herself over and over. Be angry with yourself, with Alex, but not with Helga.

'Alex taught me to pronounce English words properly first of all from that little book,' Helga said. 'Would you like some tea or coffee? I'm making some for myself.'

Pavana shook her head and Helga, switching off the record player, came to sit on the arm of the chair, patting her shoulder briefly, kindly.

'You look very ill,' she said. 'And you have lost a lot of weight, yes? What's the matter?'

On Helga's left hand, a beautiful ring with a bright diamond winked in the light of the lamp. Pavana couldn't tear her eyes from the ring.

Helga said shyly, holding her hand proudly before Pavana's gaze, 'Alex chose it for me. It's very lovely, isn't it?'

'It is . . .' Pavana said, thinking of her birthday party in the café near the polytechnic. It must have been an expensive and extremely busy day for Alex, Pavana reflected with bitterness. He had given her a costly wristwatch, and Helga an exquisite diamond ring.

Afterwards, for many years, she had tried and failed to understand – and still couldn't understand – what madness took possession of her in that moment. Nor could she forgive herself. She'd wrenched the book in half, tearing the pages to shreds and, standing up, deliberately flung the pieces all over the carpeted floor. Through a blur of jealous rage, she saw Helga's face flame with horror and distress, her face crumple and the tears flowing down her cheeks as she bent to pick up the scattered fragments of her precious *Little Prince*.

Pavana grabbed the lapel of her robe so hard that it tore open, tugging hard at the pale blue nightgown until it ripped open from shoulder to waist. As Helga raised her arms in self-defence, Pavana grasped her cruelly by the hair and gave her a stinging slap across the face. She didn't even notice the door opening until she heard Alex's shout.

'Get out of here at once, Pavana, get out!'

To her dying day she would never forget the tenderness in his voice as he gathered Helga into his arms that evening.

'*Liebling, liebling*,' he had said again and again, following her around the room, helping her to pick up the torn pages of the book.

'*The Little Prince*, Alex!' she cried out. 'Why, ah, but why, did she do that? You *will* tell me, Alex!'

He had walked to the door and slammed it on Pavana skulking on the dark staircase.

That night, on leaving the bedsitting house for the last time, she had walked many miles before she reached her flat. Somewhere along the way she threw the key into a hedge. Overcome with grief, she had not felt the cold nor had she been afraid of the dark streets. Appalled by what she had done, Pavana felt she now deserved, perhaps always had done, whatever fate chose to mete out to her. She'd have to take it on the chin and survive somehow.

Once inside the flat, Gail was still not home, and Pavana pounded on the walls, howling in anguish, calling Alex's name over and over again. But of course he never phoned, never came.

She had been so young then, young in a way that had little to do with age. What had she known about the strategies for survival, long-term planning, using one's head as well as one's heart and, in some cases, forgetting about the heart altogether?

Alex had been, still was, an attractive, charming man, whose dynamic personality and commitment to a cause drew people to him in droves. He was self-centred, used to the adoration and submission of women of all ages and all kinds, and skilful in manipulating them to serve his needs and interests of the moment. A hug here, a caress there, a kiss on the cheek, an intimate smile across a dinner table – there were few tricks Alex didn't know.

Every woman, starved for affection, was susceptible in ways that he himself seemed to find at times distasteful, despicable. His saving grace was that he did not find these qualities altogether admirable in himself, and only in Helga had he found good sense, stability, an intelligent, clear-eyed vision, an absence of the flattery he found debilitating.

Now in this other clinic, as Pavana lifted her eyes to his face, she witnessed his anguish as he recalled Helga on that terrible evening. He was missing her dreadfully, his guide, his mentor, the one upon whom he had always relied for sound advice in times of trouble, and he had probably never been in greater trouble than he was now.

But even with Helga, he had never been completely honest. Pavana wondered whether it was even possible, in any relationship between human beings, to be completely honest. Like so much else, she supposed, it was all relative. As she watched the tears in his eyes, she wondered if he had ever been completely honest with himself. Is that possible for any human being? She didn't know. Perhaps the well-known truism about truth being elusive also applied to knowledge of one's self and honesty about one's motivations.

Alex lived several lives simultaneously, always had done. And if by unhappy chance any two, or more, of his lives crossed, he made a choice, absenting himself from those he found the least necessary for his interests at any given time.

'That afternoon,' Alex was saying, 'I was unavoidably delayed at a meeting. I couldn't get away. You know how those meetings used to be. When I arrived at the clinic, you were already gone. I meant to call you as soon as I could that night after I returned, but then . . . In any case, what happened has happened. There is little point in looking back. I rarely do, or I couldn't go forward.'

Pavana heard his words, but she wasn't sure whether or not she believed them. It was quite likely that he had entirely forgotten his promise. It just hadn't been a priority. In any case, it didn't matter so much now and as he had said, there was little to be gained in looking back for too long on that particular evening.

'I was sorry to hear about . . . the accident, Alex, about Helga's death. I read about it while we were in Somalia.'

His face jerked, as if she'd slapped him.

'What you've just told me, about us having children, I mean, would certainly have killed whatever was left of our relationship, if Helga was alive. She and I, we never had any children. It was the source of a great deal of unhappiness between us, not for me so much but for Helga.

'That night we were driving on the Western Highway to Belize City. We planned to stay in an hotel, away from everybody. Helga was planning to catch her flight early the following morning. We were quarrelling violently. I didn't want her to return to Germany, didn't want her to leave me, but, well . . . Moria was becoming more and more of a problem for her, and there were other things in my personal relationships outside the home that she couldn't accept.

'She refused to believe that I could change, would ever be any different. She was weeping, telling me she had to go to her family, needed their support, that it wasn't the kind of life I'd promised her we would have together. That I'd broken our contract, that kind of thing. I was frantically trying to dissuade her, not concentrating on my driving as I should have been. I'd also had too many drinks before dinner.

'At about mile thirty-nine on the highway, I drove into the rear end of a truck, parked without lights at the side of the road. I swerved but the top of the car, on Helga's side, was ripped off in the impact. Helga was decapitated. I myself was in a hospital in Mérida for several weeks. Those are the memories I live with every day.'

'How absolutely horrible, Alex. Helga was so much for us, for the developing world, wanting to help, to be a part, and above all she believed so much in you. Do you know, Alex, after that night, after what happened in her flat, I felt that to handle it on my own was the least I could do to make up for what I'd done. I felt very ashamed. I still do.

'It changed me completely. I never wanted to lose possession of the self I was trying to become, ever again. That's probably the most important reason why I never told you about the twins. If Helga had lived, in spite of my promise to the children, I don't know whether I'd ever have told you.'

155

Chapter 26

Alex held out his hand and Pavana put her hand in his. He squeezed it hard.

'That's something else we share at any rate, our guilty feelings about Helga, those painful feelings of regret.' He resumed his packing.

'The question now I suppose is where do we go from here?'

Pavana looked out the window. She couldn't ask.

'I suppose you'd like me to see the . . .' he couldn't bring himself to utter the words.

'Lisa and Eric? Not if as you say you're so busy . . .'

'I won't ever be not busy, at least not for the foreseeable future. But I feel I should do something, at least talk with them, particularly if Bennett is serious about publishing that article.'

'You needn't,' Pavana said.

He closed the drawers carefully, one by one.

'I think we should explain to them . . . what we can.'

'You said you didn't believe . . .'

'Oh I believe all right,' Alex said, his face grim. 'I think I know something about you, whatever you may think about me, and God knows I'm sure it's plenty, although I wouldn't like to hear any more about it I quite assure you.'

'You met them once, last year during Children's Week. They were so impressed, felt so privileged that you talked with them. They are at Sacred Heart Elementary. Do you remember?'

Pavana pulled a wallet out of her bag and passed a photograph to him. He took the picture, a particularly good one of the twins. He peered at it, recognition for a moment replacing the distress on his face.

'Them?' he asked. 'I remembered thinking how much they reminded me of you. My eyes kept following them whenever they were on the stage.'

'Last night after you were shot I was forced to tell them about you. I'd hoped to do it differently. I thought maybe somehow we could talk with them together. They say they don't want to meet you now. They'd be too embarrassed, that's what they told me. I think they are trying to pretend I never said what I did.'

'I am not in the least bit surprised,' Alex said. 'We'll have to contrive something soon, in any case, unless you're dead set against it. After all, you know them.'

'No. No. I'm not against it . . . it would be a relief, a great help to me, to us . . . if . . .'

'Well, that's something at any rate,' Alex said. 'False pride does have its limits, I'm glad to know.'

They were both silent as Alex continued looking at the photograph.

Pavana asked, 'What was in that memo, Alex?'

He passed the photograph back to her and, placing his bag near the door, went to sit on the edge of the bed, his legs stretched out on the floor. He cupped his injured arm with his right hand and stared at the blank wall opposite, as if he saw a lost world peopled by supporters who had long since vanished.

'You understand, Pavana, how things can become distorted when taken out of context. I became attached to a number of left-wing students and other young radicals, so we thought ourselves, who were committed to social justice, democratic liberties and so on. I am sure you remember? It *was* the thing to do, but I was sincerely committed to trying to change things for the better in Belize. As you know, we formed a small group of our own which met occasionally, sometimes in Helga's flat. I didn't ask you to join because, well, our views were different, to say the very least.'

'I was in agreement about social justice and all that, Alex, but I couldn't see *how* you were going to bring it all about, and who was going to pay for it. I was afraid that it would all end badly, become a repressive instead of libertarian programme.'

Alex swallowed hard.

'Helga believed, though, so did Stoner in the beginning, and a number of our friends, not Julian Carlisle, of course, but many others. The numbers were surprising.

'The memo suggested that we draft a socialist constitution for Belize. It contained a number of other ideas which I realize now were idealistic, impractical, like nationalization measures, the collection of money from

157

sympathizers and the eventual, if necessary, establishment of economic as well as diplomatic relations with Moscow.

'At the time they were all around us, these ideas, it was like the air we breathed, heady stuff. The memo also included suggestions for the drafting of a manifesto for a socialist party in Belize. I can't remember clearly all that it contained, but I am fairly sure those were some of the main points; not necessarily in that order. But it was never circulated. Helga advised me to destroy it, to wait; and later on, realizing she was right, I did destroy it.

'That's what started the rift between Bennett and myself. Against Helga's advice I showed it to Stoner, a Belizean like myself, to get his reactions. He was horrified. Like you, he felt that I would gradually abandon the libertarian political programme. He accused me of wanting to become another Castro. He felt that I had swallowed whole the Marxist–Leninist line. Stoner and I, we were close. It never occurred to me that Stoner would copy it, which was easy enough to do. He had it for a couple of days, at least.'

'But all that happened a long time ago. Who cares about that now, surely . . .'

'He knows I am hoping to run in the next election. He could, for example, suggest that unknown communists have been financing my political career from the start, guilt by association, that kind of thing.'

'Have outside agencies been financing you?'

'Of course not, Pavana. I feel this has been one of my biggest failures. I somehow have not been able to get across to people the fact that many countries have, and have had, socialist governments at one time or another without the sky falling in. A left-wing orientation is necessary in the national political spectrum, to balance the excesses of the right. Socialism does not need to be evil, undemocratic. But people think in terms of Cuba and Grenada, and well, you know how much people fear that that sort of thing may happen here.'

'So what are you going to do?'

'I don't know if there is anything I can do. This government seems in danger of collapsing in any case, if not during this present crisis then the next. But there again, against Helga's advice, I threw in my lot with them and somehow I'll have to see it through.''

Pavana was silent in the face of an overwhelming sadness and despair that the brilliant vision, which Alex had once symbolized for so many, had diminished, disintegrated into what seemed to her merely a hungry quest for power at any cost. She had no difficulty imagining how disillusioned Helga must have become with Alex, how disappointed at his abandonment of their once mutual political vision. She remembered that Stoner, too, had expressed that same sense of betrayal.

The silence between them grew longer and, misinterpreting the expression on Pavana's face, Alex asked, 'Do you think you will be able to handle the scandal if Stoner publishes that article, linking us together? It'll be brutal, make no mistake about that. Your credibility at the Women's Unit will be severely compromised. The women's arm of the party feels they should have been consulted before your appointment. They feel overlooked, threatened. They've lobbied certain cabinet ministers. Something like this could chain you to your desk, serving time for the remainder of the year, you do understand that.'

Pavana nodded.

'I must handle it. But the children, I worry about the effect all that would have on them.'

'We've been over that. We'll talk with them. They'll have to learn to live with a burdensome paternal inheritance, I'm afraid. Stoner can't possibly get anything on the streets before Monday at the earliest.'

'What about the meetings? He might say something from the rostrum, mightn't he?'

'I doubt if he will, not until after we talk in any case.'

'What would prevent him?'

'He's nothing to gain from speaking out too soon. Besides that, he still feels some sense of loyalty towards me, I believe. We grew up together in the valley, as you probably know.'

'I'm sure I must have known, but I'd forgotten.'

'Oh, yes. His mother moved here to Belize City when he was about twelve or thirteen.'

Pavana began moving wearily towards the door. 'I see,' she said, her hand on the handle. 'Well, we are going to Pelican Island this weekend with friends. We live in their upstairs apartment. I can't disappoint Lisa and Eric. They are looking forward to the trip. I wouldn't know how to explain. It couldn't be contrived.'

'I could try to get out there sometime over the weekend.'

'Do you think you'll be able to do that?' Pavana asked, looking at his bandaged arm.

'Oh, sure,' Alex said, 'somebody can fly me out as soon as I can get away. Besides, Simon Galvez and one or two other ministers will be out there. I need to talk with them in any case, and one or two other people who have promised to help us during this crisis.'

'We'll be at Holiday House, near the Turtle Grass Hotel. I'll look out for you.'

'Do that. I'll get on to Stoner as soon as I can, but if he contacts you before then, tell him I'll be in touch.'

'All right, Alex, see you then,' Pavana said, listening to the click of the door as Alex closed it. She stood for a moment in the deserted corridor before hurrying out of the clinic.

On the street Pavana paused for a moment near the open gates. The sky had clouded over and the sea was growing choppy. Across the street, to her left and a few yards down, she saw Moria locking the door of her car. For a moment, Pavana considered saying hello, but then she changed her mind. She wished she'd thought to bring a light jacket. The wind had turned quite chilly, and she had gooseflesh all up and down her arms.

Chapter 27

The day after she'd spoken with Alex. Pavana sat at her desk concluding preparations begun by Mrs Elrington and Mrs Carillo for the one-day workshop to be held in Boom the following weekend. On the floor below, a home economics class was in progress, and she could hear Mrs Carillo's voice as she instructed the women who had registered. Pavana had had little time to reflect on the conversation with Alex, nor about the trip to Pelican Island. But as it neared four o'clock she found that she was very glad it was Friday. It had been an exhausting week.

She was looking forward to a more relaxed evening with Lisa and Eric, to a hot bath and an early night. She had much to think about.

Brenda Kirkwood, already on the job with the title of training officer, was on the telephone calling the panellists, reminding them of the workshop date and arranging pickup times where necessary. As she replaced the receiver, the telephone immediately rang. Brenda answered.

'Women's Unit. Yes, Cora, I'll tell her, certainly."

She replaced the receiver.

'That was Cora. She said that she's just returned from Belmopan and that she'll be here in a few minutes. I wonder what she wants so late on a Friday afternoon?'

'To see how we are getting on, probably,' Pavana said. 'Here, look at this programme and tell me what you think of it now.'

Active in community affairs, Brenda was a storehouse of political intelligence and Pavana was soon beginning to rely on her for advice, for it was obvious that she understood the depth of political paranoia in the country far better than Pavana did. Brenda's knowledge of linkages between politicians and community members was astonishing, and during their first working day together she constantly jogged Pavana's elbow, steering her away from landmines and pitfalls as they tried to maintain a balance in the selection of committee members, panellists and other volunteers who would, they hoped, work with the unit on a continuous basis.

As Brenda pored over the programme, Pavana picked up the list of workshop participants and noticed a surprising thing. There was no representative listed for the Belize Women's Democratic Organization, the women's arm of the ruling party. She distinctly remembered typing it in on the draft. Recalling what Alex had said, Pavana wondered how Brenda could have overlooked such a glaring omission, particularly as there was a tick opposite the women's group of the opposition party.

'BWDO isn't on the list, Brenda,' she said. 'Shouldn't we call to check whether they are planning to send a representative?'

'No?' Brenda asked, not sounding as surprised as she should have done. 'I'll do that right away,' she said, beginning to dial. Pavana observed her closely, noticing a slight discomfiture in her expression. It was hard to decide whether she was upset at having overlooked something so important, or because Pavana, whom she considered politically naïve, had noticed the omission.

'They must be closed for the day,' Brenda said, replacing the receiver. 'I'll call them first thing on Monday morning.'

Pavana decided that she too would follow up on that telephone call.

She made a note on the growing list of things she hoped to accomplish during the week before the workshop.

'Pavana?' Brenda suddenly said, looking up from a number of papers on her desk. 'You should *do* something about our situation, and very quickly.'

There was an edge to her voice, and Pavana realized she was referring to their first conversation that morning after Pavana had returned from her literature class at Sacred Heart. Pavana felt certain now that she was annoyed because Pavana had noticed BWDO's omission from the list. On her arrival at the unit at about ten o'clock, Pavana had found her engrossed in a number of women and development conference reports sent to the ministry from various parts of the world.

'Otherwise, it is highly possible that we won't be allowed to attend a single overseas conference, including the Mid-Decade Conference in Copenhagen. But the minister will go to Copenhagen, you may be sure, or he'll send someone acceptable to the cabinet.'

'It's a bit early to be thinking about that, isn't it? But I agree. We should sit down with Mrs Elrington and think through a number of strategies. Do you have any suggestions?'

'Mmmm,'' Brenda said, biting her lips and then smiling, her golden-yellow eyes sparkling again. 'Not at this very moment, but I'm sure to think of something.'

'I'll be glad to discuss them with you,' Pavana said.

There was silence for a while as they worked, until they heard the door of a vehicle slam downstairs. Brenda glanced out a window overlooking the street.

'It's Cora,' she said. Leaning forward on her desk, she added placatingly, 'You know, Pavana, we all want what is best for the unit. So perhaps I should tell you something I heard in the ministry.'

'What's that?' Pavana asked.

'Cora is thinking of retiring, so you shouldn't rely too heavily on her. Bertie Slighson, the Assistant Social Development Officer, is likely to succeed her if she does retire.'

Pavana stared at her.

'Who told you that, Brenda?'

'A reliable source, I can quite assure you.'

Pavana thought about Bertie Slighson, a tall muscular man nearing middle-age. Quite good looking, with a dimple in each cheek, silvery hair and a suntanned skin, Slighson was considered an action man. The Ministry of Community Development was a place where things were nearly always threatening to fall apart, and sometimes did, with the most terrifying political reverberations. Bertie had made himself useful to everyone, from the minister, whose constituents' needs were numerous and varied, to the harassed office messenger in the Belmopan Registry, unable to locate important letters he had been instructed to post the previous day.

'Ask Bertie,' was the cry in the ministry. 'Bertie knows. Bertie can do it. He'll get it done.'

In the brief conversation Pavana had had with him at the ministry the previous day he'd said, 'My approach to the unit coincides with PS Kelly's. It's just another government unit. There's nothing special about it, as far as I can see. I don't understand the need for one myself, to tell you the truth.'

Mrs Elrington came into the room breathing heavily, 'Those stairs will be the death of me,' she announced, seating herself at a table piled high with workshop materials. 'But the view from up here is worth it, isn't it?' she said, looking out through the numerous windows of the office.

As they discussed the workshop, Mrs Elrington said, 'Oh, by the way, Minister Galvez will not be able to open the workshop, as he had hoped. But I think the permanent secretary will represent him.'

'That's a pity,' Brenda said, her voice low, regretful, managing to convey the idea that she fully understood why the minister was not going to attend. 'Do you suppose the women will feel that the unit does not have the backing of the government?'

'Nonsense,' Mrs Elrington said. 'It happens all the time. He's promised to attend the next one.'

'We'll see,' Brenda said, rising from the table. 'My goodness, is that the time? Did you want to see me for anything in particular, Cora?'

'No, I thought I'd come along and let Pavana know about the minister's change of plans, and talk with her about a few other matters.'

'Then I do hope you'll excuse me. I'm going out to the caye for the weekend, so I've got to fly.'

'Certainly,' Mrs Elrington said. 'I'll see you next week, I expect.'

After she and Pavana had discussed a number of matters to do with the running of the unit, Mrs Elrington said, 'Oh, by the way, Pavana, I almost forgot the real purpose of my visit. I hesitate to ask you this. It is a favour and you really don't have to agree, although I hope you will.'

'You know that I'll try my best to do whatever you ask, Mrs Elrington,' Pavana said absently, her mind preoccupied with Brenda's remarks about Coral Elrington's plans to retire.

'You do remember Jackie Lee Baines? The UN consultant who helped us to obtain funds for establishing the unit?'

'Yes, of course I remember Ms Baines,' Pavana said, suddenly wary.

'What a dynamic woman! Such a worker. She knows exactly how to get things done around here, understands strategies, is absolutely committed, knows how to manoeuvre. I do so admire her. A powerhouse of ideas too, you know, my dear.'

'Oh, I know,' Pavana said, shuddering involuntarily.

'Well, she's back in town,' Cora Elrington said, a sparkle of hope in her eyes, her face animated. 'Such a stroke of luck for you and me, especially with our plans for the unit. She's agreed to help us develop plans for some of our other units as well, and she needs a base somewhere in the ministry to do her writing.'

Mrs Elrington frowned. 'As you know, space is extremely limited in Belmopan, so I agreed she could have a desk in your office, as you don't yet have your full staff appointed.'

'You did what?' Pavana asked, flabbergasted. Jackie Lee Baines would not *only* occupy a desk, no matter how much she tried. She was an extremely aggressive personality, experienced, ambitious, wily, a hard-driving consultant, competitive, effective, all the qualities Pavana didn't have and some she didn't care to have.

Pavana suspected that she was underhanded, a wheeler-dealer. She was not the kind of person by whom one could be guided or helped and retain any self-respect. She would take over; one would have to submit or she would fight one, with great subtlety, to the death. Apart from all this, her expertise was quite genuine and bureaucrats in many ministries depended on her access to UN funding.

Brenda, with her appetite for experience, power and travel, would naturally join forces with her. From what Vicky had said, and from Pavana's own observations, they were already friends. Together they would be an unbeatable combination. Pavana would rapidly become a figurehead before she could get herself established.

Pavana forced herself to be reasonable, knowing that the paranoia raging like a disease in the country had probably finally invaded her soul, inch by wretched inch, and was beginning to win the battle she had waged with it for so long.

It was burning within her now like malaria. She struggled against the wild beating at her temples, in her throat. She strived for the balance on which she prided herself, for a view of the thing from detached heights, but the knowledge that Jackie Lee Baines from the very start had considered her a poor choice, inexperienced and insufficiently militant, and had no respect for her whatsoever, made her so fearful that she said, 'I'm sorry, Mrs Elrington, but it just wouldn't work.'

'Why ever not?' Mrs Elrington said, her eyes hardening. 'You could learn a lot from Jackie Lee about women and development issues, particularly as you aren't allowed to represent government overseas at conferences, seminars and workshops. She could help you to network, absolutely essential in this kind of work. Besides, I've already given her my word! I was so sure you would agree. Honestly, Pavana, your attitude is quite a surprise to me.'

Pavana understood that Mrs Elrington herself was already beginning to feel the loss of power and influence, particularly if rumours of her imminent retirement were travelling through the corridors of the ministries. But though Pavana liked, admired and respected her, it was proving difficult for Pavana to change her mind, as much as she wanted to do so.

Jackie Lee Baines would have little to gain from assisting Pavana. The woman gathered and hoarded information in a most disturbing way. Information and its judicious use was the lifeblood of her career. She exchanged it, bit by grudging bit, for a price, and Pavana already knew that because of her own attitudes and values she would be unable to pay it. She could not barter her self-respect to become a successful puppet, even if it meant giving up the directorship of the unit which she was beginning to value highly.

'I'm sorry you didn't consult me before you made that decision,' she said, watching Mrs Elrington gripping the arm of the chair tightly. She was angry, her eyes wide, her nostrils flaring as she took deep breaths, her voice erratically rising and falling.

'It seems that I've been mistaken about you, Pavana. I thought you'd be cooperative about this. Jackie Lee will be shocked and hurt. It was her hard work that helped me to get funds for the unit. In a sense you owe your present position to her.' She inhaled deeply.

'When I first told her about you she was surprised, but most accommodating, although she did have Brenda Kirkwood in mind for the directorship.' Mrs Elrington glanced slyly at Pavana, who was swiftly re-evaluating the woman seated before her.

'I understand your point of view, Mrs Elrington,' Pavana replied, 'but I cannot agree. I wish there was some compromise I could make, but in this case there isn't.'

Evening had crept in silently and swiftly. Pavana rose and switched on the electric lights, feeling extremely tired and dispirited, knowing that she was probably in the process of losing a valuable ally, perhaps her only one. She worked so much better in cooperation rather than in competition, in harmony rather than in conflict. But this apparently was the real world, and here she stood.

'Well,' Mrs Elrington said, 'I can see you are not about to change your mind. I think you may regret your decision. As you know I supervise twelve other units and my time now is severely limited. I had hoped Jackie Lee could assist me if she had workspace here.'

'I know your intentions are good, Mrs Elrington.'

'Good luck with the workshop, in any case. We can discuss any final details when you visit Belmopan next week.'

'Thank you,' Pavana replied. From a window, she watched Mrs Elrington's striding angrily towards the ministry bus, obtained through the United Nations courtesy of Jackie Lee Baines.

Chapter 28

As Morris parked the car on a grassy verge near the lighthouse, opposite the empty playground at Fort George, Pavana could have sworn she spied Stoner in the subdued crowds waiting on the seawall. It was already nearly ten o'clock on Saturday morning. After the chaos in the centre of the city, the distant sailing boats and, closer to shore, the motor boats, yachts and doreys lent to the area that air of festival associated with the city's annual regatta, which had taken place on the ninth of March, thirteen days before.

As Lisa and Eric jumped with alacrity on to the deck of the *Sin Verano Final*, Pavana anxiously scanned the faces onshore, seeking Stoner's scarred, determined face, the narrow eyes flicking restlessly, seeking an advantage. But as the boat began easing away from the concrete seawall, she decided she'd been mistaken and gave herself up to the tranquillizing motion of the waves and the sweet, fresh smell of the wind tugging playfully at the ends of her headscarf.

Their little party found a place in the stern of the boat, and Pavana stood with the twins at the railing gazing backwards at the red-roofed houses, casurinas and coconut trees rimming the curving shoreline. The morning had not got off to an encouraging start. The tense and exhausting drive through the centre of town to pick up the Johnsons, business colleagues and friends of Jennifer and Morris, underscored all their fears of what would happen during the days ahead.

Another gigantic rally and demonstration had taken place the previous evening, and the streets were littered with debris. Teenagers and adults wandered the streets purposefully, carrying sticks, rocks and broken bottles, waiting for another chance to show their disapproval of the agenda for agreement. At street corners policemen, soldiers and members of the riot squad waited too, knowing it was only a matter of time. By nightfall there would be scores more arrests, more injuries, more fires. Who could tell what would happen next, where it would all end?

Jennifer and Morris, usually at their most pleasant and amusing at the prospect of a party, especially one on Pelican Island, had squabbled with each other from the moment they left Sapodilla Street and all the way through the town. Morris was forced to drive with agonizing slowness, bumping in and out of potholes, starting and stopping along the narrow, crowded streets. As he turned into Albert Street from Orange Lane, Jennifer said nervously, 'Take your hands off the horn, Morris.'

'How do you expect me to get through this crowd without blowing the horn?' He sucked his teeth belligerently, bringing the car to a stop on Albert Street, where crowds of picketers were converging on the radio station.

'If somebody throws a molotov cocktail at this car it'll be your fault, Morris. We can't just sit here, we'll be arrested. Reverse!'

'What do you think I'm trying to do? Don't start assigning blame, woman. It wasn't my idea to drive downtown in this madness.' He reversed slowly, turning down the nameless lane bordering Independence Park. At the stop sign, he cursed the flow of traffic, slamming his foot on the brake.

'Oh, look!' Eric cried. 'The soldiers are pushing people away from the door of the radio station. What a stinky smell!'

'It must be tear gas,' Lisa said. 'It looks like a war. How will we ever get out of this crowd?'

'You'll get us all killed,' Jennifer was saying. 'Look, Morris, that policeman is signalling to us. I don't like the look in his eyes.'

'I want to see him come over here,' Morris muttered, quite unlike his usual uxurious self. 'See if I don't let him have a piece of my mind.'

'What, Morris?' Jen was saying. 'You're mumbling. What is it you want me to do?'

'Do you want to drive, Jennifer? I have no problem with that.'

'In this?'

'Then shut up.'

'Don't shut me up. If you'd hired the guard from the agency like I suggested before all this started, you wouldn't be fussing and fuming like you are now.'

'I couldn't get a guard for love nor money, m'son. And you know it. Don't confuse the issue. I need to concentrate.'

'Do you think they'll burn our house, Mom?' Eric asked, as Lisa and himself fidgeted in their seats, trying to see everything at once.

'Don't be so silly,' Pavana replied, but she didn't say it with very much conviction. Everyone had reason to worry.

'I hope the boat doesn't leave without us,' Lisa said, raising her voice to be heard above the squabbling in the front seat.

'Oh, it won't,' Pavana replied automatically, but she was far from being sure about very much.

Very late the previous evening, after her return from the Women's Unit, the slamming of car doors and the raised voices in the usually quiet street had brought the twins rushing on to the veranda to watch with Pavana flames and smoke rising above distant rooftops. The

168

Income Tax Department on Queen Street and a number of surrounding buildings and homes had been reduced to ashes. A second fire broke out at St Mary's Rectory on North Front Street, not far from Pavana's office, then a third near the William Harvey School in Dolphin Street.

Fire-fighting efforts were sabotaged by the surreptitious cutting of the rotting water hoses, while panic accelerated throughout the centre of the city where most dwellings and business houses were constructed from wood. In the end the British forces, stationed near the airport nine miles away, were asked to send in fire tenders which helped the local fire fighters to bring the situation under some control.

Pavana had received no further communication from Stoner, but she expected to hear from him sooner or later. That, coupled with apprehension about Alex's possible visit to Pelican Island and the unfolding events at the Women's Unit, had made her jittery. On Thursday and Friday nights she had several times wandered around the apartment checking doors and windows she had already secured, peering cautiously through the louvres overlooking Sapodilla Street, half expecting to see the flaming torches of her horrible, recurring nightmares. But each time she saw only the ugly, long-legged carpenter birds stalking crabs along the street, and heard only the casurinas whispering their secrets to the night.

In the other five districts, demonstrations were also taking place, and Pavana had begun to seriously worry about her parents, retired and living on the outskirts of Corozal Town. Although they had known for years that Alex and herself were once friends, Raul and Carrie Leslie had never met him, and Pavana had never actually admitted to them that Alex was their father. Naturally they greatly loved Lisa and Eric, but a barrier had risen between Pavana and her parents.

'Jesus Christ, Morris, you've got to get us out of this,' Jen said, peering through the windows at another group of pickets advancing on the radio station.

'Whose idea was it anyway to pick up Peter and Viv? I told you to let them find their own transportation. But no, you were determined to get the hostess of the year award!'

'There they are!' Jen said, almost shouting with relief. 'Waiting for us on the steps of the Treasury Building.'

'That shows some sense anyway,' Morris grumbled. 'We'd never have made it to their house.'

'Thanks a lot,' Pete Johnson said, squeezing into the front seat beside Jen. 'We were just about to give up and go home.'

The twins moved nearer to Pavana to make room for Viv, who, even as she made her apologies, continued to stare through the windows repeating, 'Unbelievable, really incredible.'

'A shocking state of affairs,' Pete was saying as Morris continued to make his way towards the Swing Bridge. He gave a loud sigh of relief as he drove across without incident and turned right, speeding towards Fort George and the *Sin Verano Final*.

In the stern of the boat Pavana watched as Morris helped the twins to bait their hooks with sprats, showing them the correct cast of the lines into the voluptuously curving waves. As soon as possible she would tell them about Alex's possible visit, although now she was hoping fervently that he wouldn't be able to make it. What had seemed so absolutely right at the clinic on Thursday afternoon now seemed totally wrong.

Pavana wiped the sea spray from her face with a towel, and retrieved her handbag from among the variety of beach paraphernalia. She accepted a drink gratefully from Jen, whose smile was still strained, and then retrieved from the bottom of her bag a letter from Julian, which she had received the evening before. She wanted to read it again, before talking with Lisa and Eric. Julian had written from his flat in Ovingdean, Sussex, on the first of March. It was hard for Pavana to believe that so much had happened since that time,

Dear Pavana,

Thank you for your last letter, which I received several weeks ago. You cannot imagine how delighted I was to get it. Again, I must apologize for not replying immediately, but since my return home on leave (nearly three weeks ago), all my time and energies have been focused on dealing with lawyers, etc. Dora and I have agreed to divorce. She plans to marry again, once the divorce is finalized. I expect she will be given custody of Basil, although she seems quite amenable to the idea that he should continue to spend his long holidays with me. So much for the smaller mercies.

I am not yet certain about any future assignment with United World as, my recent memories being what they are, I am not particularly eager to return just yet to East Africa. At the moment United World is the process of expansion, and from what I

170

gathered from Hawkins, dour as ever, there is talk of possibly opening an office in Belize. I've strongly hinted to Hawkins that if negotiations there are successfully concluded, I would very much prefer being assigned there as United World representative. Hawkins, by the way, sends you his regards.

I noted that your new job with the Ministry of Community Development starts very soon. I am tempted to offer you tremendous quantities of advice, but shall restrain myself until my long-overdue visit to Belize later this year, which I expect will now have to be some time in July or August. I am hoping that Basil will be able to accompany me. The thought of our possible holiday in Belize is helping to take his mind off our present difficulties. Next week I am travelling to New York headquarters for further discussions with Hawkins, who, I'm afraid, seems set on re-posting me to East Africa. If anything positive results from my visit, I'll telephone immediately, as our holiday dates may be affected. Basil and I send our best love to you, Eric and Lisa. We hope to see you quite soon.

All the best,
Julian.

P.S. It was most interesting, if not totally surprising, to read about old Alex Abrams' role as *éminence grise*. I can well empathize with your feelings of ambivalence towards him. My feelings about Dora are very much the same. However, if on your rounds along the labyrinthian-sounding corridors of your bureaucracy you do happen to see Abrams, you might mention my plans (albeit tentative) to him, if you deem it wise, that is. See you soon. Fight fiercely.

Love, Julian.

In her hand, the thin pages crackled in the wind. She felt immensely cheered by the thought of Julian's possible visit. As the boat ploughed its way through the sparkling waves she held her face up to the sun, feeling her neck muscles relax. Julian, even through his letters, had always had a bracing effect on her spine.

Chapter 29

A squeal of excitement from Lisa and Eric made her open her eyes. Eric had caught a fish and she watched as with Peter's help he carefully reeled in a medium-sized red-tailed snapper which was soon flapping on the floor of the boat. As he knelt to examine his catch, he noticed the letter in Pavana's hand.

'Who's it from, Mom?' Pavana watched his strong hands as he hooked another sprat on to his fishing hook.

'Your Uncle Julian.'

'Uncle Julian!' Lisa said, turning sideways on the seat beside Pavana, holding her fishing rod carefully with two hands.

The twins both wore T-shirts, shorts and sneakers, and Pavana noticed their changing bodies and the inches they had both grown during the past year. They would soon be taller than she was.

Eric cast his line back into the water. His voice was casual.

'What did he say?'

'He's hoping to visit us in July or August, with Basil.'

'Oh good,'' Lisa said, not at all surprised. ''He said he would.'

'I'll teach Basil how to fish,' Eric said.

'You're not an expert yet, Eric. Mr Johnson helped you. Don't think I wasn't watching.'

'But I will be by then,' Eric said, frowning in concentration.

'You wish,' Lisa laughed.

The twins turned back to the sea determined to catch more snappers before Pelican Island was sighted.

In spite of their verbal gaiety and banter with the twins, there were strained silences between Morris, Jen, Peter and Viv, obviously fearful that they would return to the city to find their businesses looted, or their homes gutted by fire.

Peter and Viv lived on Regent Street above their small hardware store in the centre of town. They had recently partitioned the ground floor, renting the second half to Morris and Jen who, with one large bus, had

172

opened an agency called 'Explore Belize'. It was Morris's second attempt at a business venture, and Peter's first.

Pavana joined Lisa and Eric, staring fixedly at the rolling waves, alert for any tug on their lines. On the roof of the boat, a few passengers shouted encouraging instructions. She said as calmly as she could, although her heart was beating rapidly, 'Guess who I saw on Thursday afternoon, you know, when I was late getting home?'

'Who?' they asked simultaneously.

'Alex Abrams. I went to visit him at the clinic. He's much better.'

'Oh, him,' Lisa said dismissively, not taking her eyes off her line. 'Come on,' she said to the frothing waves. 'Come on, fish.'

Eric swallowed, narrowing his eyes against the sun.

'So?'

'You mustn't be surprised if we see him on Pelican Island today or tomorrow. He's going there to help the representative do some campaigning, and he might stop by to say hello.'

'Shh, will you, Mom?' Eric said. 'I really have to pay attention here.'

There was a shout from Morris to Lisa.

'Easy now, easy,' he instructed, passing his rod to Pavana, going to stand behind Lisa, helping her to reel in another snapper.

'It's a tie,' Lisa laughed joyously, swinging her fish into the boat. 'It's a tie, Eric, and there's Pelican Island!'

Morris pulled a knife from the pocket of his shorts and began scaling the fishes, slitting them expertly, gutting and rinsing the snappers in the sea.

'Awesome,' Eric said. 'Where'd you learn to do that?'

'I was a scout,' Morris said virtuously. 'Earned nearly every badge there was.'

'I've just had the best idea, Mom,' Lisa called. 'When Uncle Julian and Basil arrive, we can bring them to Pelican Island with Uncle Morris, Aunt Jen, and Mr and Mrs Johnson.'

'We'll teach them to catch fish and clean them,' Eric said. 'I can't wait until they get here.'

'Me, neither,' Lisa said.

Morris opened his eyes very wide, and drew himself up, pulling in his paunch.

'Are you telling me you have another uncle? I'm jealous. And I'm not giving any more fishing lessons. That's the end of those.' Deliberately, and with great hauteur, he examined the fishing rods with a view to putting them away.

'Oh, please,' Lisa said, giggling. 'Just one more?'

'Not if you like him more than me,' Morris said slyly, looking from Lisa to Eric, who stood with bait in their hands, eager for another try.

'Well?' Morris persisted, as Viv, Jean and Pavana joined in the laughter.

'We do like him better,' Lisa said, a little shamefacedly, as Morris covered his eyes in despair.

'That's because we've known him nearly always, Uncle Morris,' Eric said. 'He's like our dad.'

'Why didn't you say so before?' Morris asked, removing his hands from his face. 'All is explained. A dad is a dad after all. I had one myself. Look, I'm not an unreasonable man. I'll give you another lesson now and more later, provided you don't forget all about me once he arrives.'

'He's bringing Basil, that's his son,' Eric said.

'Another son? Lucky man,' Morris said, and for a moment there was an expression of genuine envy on his face. 'When they arrive then, the three of us can give them lessons, how about that?'

'You are wonderful, Uncle Morris,' Lisa said.

'Oh, I know it,' Morris said, keeping a serious look on his face.

'Let's start, we're nearly there,' Eric said, beginning to cut up a number of sprats.

'But in return you'll have to tell me about this other uncle, my rival,' Morris said, continuing to bargain.

'We will, we will, but let's hurry,' Lisa said, putting a piece of sprat on to her hook.

Pavana sat between Vivian and Jen, ostensibly listening to their comments about the ongoing crisis in the country but really straining her ears to hear what the twins were telling Morris about Julian and Basil. She felt grateful to Julian all over again. The thought of his visit overshadowed everything else for the twins. The meeting with Alex, if it occurred, had been reduced to an unpleasant duty which they'd get through somehow. It would be something else that would be interesting to relate to Julian, who, undoubtedly, would put the whole thing in its proper perspective.

Chapter **30**

That first night on Pelican Island Pavana woke suddenly in the long, narrow room of the box-like, two-storeyed structure which Jen called Holiday House. At the far end of the room, Lisa and Eric slept soundly beneath an open window which let in a view of the gibbous moon, coconut trees and the lighthouse. She sat up against the pillows listening to the wild roar of the waves crashing across the barrier reef, and to the high winds rustling the fronds of a thousand coconut trees. But those were sounds she loved, almost as much as she did the drumming of raindrops on zinc rooftops and the cool feel of wet sand between her toes.

A faint, fishy smell emanated from the bathroom where Lisa and Eric had stored two conch shells in the shower stall. The luminous hands of the clock on the bedside table indicated that it was nearly midnight. She hadn't been asleep for long.

Making a quick survey of the room, she noted the jumble of clothing in the old-fashioned mahogany wardrobe, swimsuits and towels draped across the bedrails, and the collection of shells on the floor in the corner opposite her bed. Overhead, where Jen, Morris, Viv and Peter slept in similar rooms, all was quiet. The ceiling fan gave a small rattle as a strong gust of wind blew through the room.

Satisfied, Pavana closed her eyes, snuggling further beneath the fresh-smelling sheet. She pulled the pillows more comfortably under her head, ready to abandon herself once again to the delicious stupor induced by the roaring waves, the wildly blowing wind and the swishing of the palm fronds. Almost immediately she heard it again. This time she identified the sound, the clicking of domino pieces on the table outdoors. 'It's probably a cat,' she thought, hoping the animal would not follow its nose to the bag of garbage left near the steps. Well, she'd worry about cleaning up any mess tomorrow. It was lovely to feel so drowsy.

Waiting for sleep, she reflected on the day which, except for one disturbing incident, had turned out all right after all. Once the business of arrival and settling in had been thankfully concluded she sat on the

175

sand at the base of a coconut tree, enjoying the activity on the beach and at the nearby Turtle Grass, a sprawling hotel with numerous patios and verandas.

It felt faintly luxurious sitting there listening to the slap of dominoes on the makeshift table, Morris's jokes, the laughter of Peter, Viv and Jen, the excited squeals of the twins dashing in and out of the water among a group of newly found playmates. Finally, she watched the sun's splendid exit. For a few minutes it seemed to pause in exaggerated uncertainty, changing from orange to red, before disappearing suddenly behind the mangrove swamps, lagoons and creeks to the west of the island.

However, since their arrival, even as she'd followed the flight of magnificent frigate birds, or observed on the trunk of another coconut tree a Jesus Christ lizard, wondering if it really could skitter upright on its hind legs over the surface of the water, she had been waiting for Alex to appear.

Each time a light plane flew towards the landing strip her heart beat faster. But after sunset, when there would be no more flights from the mainland, and an hour or so had passed, Pavana relaxed, feeling reprieved. She enjoyed her dinner of fish and lobster, contributing her small stock of corny jokes to the general hilarity of the evening. Each time she told a joke, the twins groaned, 'Not that one again, Mom!'

Afterwards they'd all taken a long walk along the beach towards the village, drifting idly through the boutiques of several hotels. They bought ice-cream for the children before going to sit for a while on one of the long piers jutting out into the sea, from where they could get a better view of the boats belonging to the islanders who caught fish, shrimp, conch and lobster for a living.

As they started their return journey to the house, Lisa and Eric lagged behind the adults, staring speculatively at a couple walking hand in hand along the beach. On the bench in the park, a young man plucked at the strings of a guitar, his only audience a lone policeman sitting on the veranda of the tiny station house overlooking the park.

On their arrival, Morris announced, 'I don't know about you people, but I'm still hungry, m'son.'

'Why don't we go to Turtle Grass?' Viv asked, 'They make good pizza.'

176

Reluctant to let go of the evening, everyone agreed with that idea. So they continued on to the hotel to sit at outdoor tables with large thatch umbrellas. A marimba band played for a reception on the patio and people wandered in and out of the hotel, laughing and talking as they made their way to the other bars and restaurants on the island.

Infected by the atmosphere of fiesta, Pavana allowed Lisa and Eric to persuade her into the hotel, where they were keen to get a closer look at the seashells displayed on the walls of the lobby and in showcases along the walls. An obliging salesman selected the shells Lisa and Eric indicated, while Pavana wandered over to the display window of the gift shop, from where it was possible to see as well as hear the marimba band; and watch, through an arched doorway, the gaily dressed people laughing and talking as they milled around the patio.

Entering the shop, Pavana lingered for several minutes, examining hand-painted blouses, strawbags, and jewellery made from shells and black coral. As she bent down to have a closer look at a painting leaning against one wall she heard Minister Galvez's voice, which couldn't be mistaken for anyone else's. In public, he always spoke at the top of his voice, when he wasn't laughing at his own or somebody else's joke.

Looking through the window, she saw him emerging, none too steadily, from the patio through the arched doorway. A number of people were with him, including, to Pavana's astonishment, Brenda Kirkwood, looking like the essence of tropical womanhood.

The halter neck of her floral print dress showed off her smooth, brown back. She was tossing her long brown hair all around, smiling and chatting with Minister Galvez, his matronly wife on his arm; he looked as if he had never seen a more welcome sight. The party crossed the lobby and disappeared through the doorway.

Much to the surprise of the woman carefully hanging a number of ironed cotton dresses on to a hanger, Pavana said, 'Way to go, Brenda. Way to go.'

'*Sí?*' the woman asked.

'*Nada, gracias,*' Pavana said, and quickly left the shop. She went to find Lisa and Eric who still stood by the showcase of shells. Eric said, 'Uncle Morris came to tell us the pizzas are outside.'

'Let's go get some,' Pavana said, but really she'd completely lost her appetite for pizza.

In the room, as she was once more drifting into sleep, the domino pieces clattered on to the table and Pavana sprang out of bed impatiently, determined to shoo the intruder away. Switching on the outside light, she opened the door. For a moment, she could hardly believe her eyes. Stoner sat on one of the canvas chairs, picking up the pieces scattered before him. His appearence shocked her. His hair was matted, his face unshaven, his clothing dirty and dishevelled.

Chapter 31

'Where's Alex, Pavana?' he asked, making no attempt to speak quietly. 'He told us he was scheduled to make an appearance at a reception at the Turtle Grass, but he didn't show up.'

'Us?' Pavana asked, keeping her voice low, hoping hc would take a hint.

He gestured towards the beach. Two men leaned against an upturned boat, their cigarettes glowing in the dark. Stoner was looking at her suspiciously. What did he think, that she had Alex secreted in the room behind her?

'I don't know where Alex is. Maybe he couldn't make it, gone back to the clinic or something. I have to go, Stoner.' She closed the door softly, glancing towards the twins' beds, but they hadn't stirred. She'd done what he'd asked and she wasn't about to do anything more.

A sharp rap sounded on the door. Furious, Pavana opened it just a crack.

'I have children sleeping in here,' she hissed at Stoner, who stood at the top of the three steps, his face inches from her own.

'We mustn't wake Alex's children, must we?' he asked.

'No, we mustn't,' Pavana said, pretending she hadn't heard the note of derision in his voice. 'Have some consideration, Stoner, it's late.'

'Too late for me?' She smelled stale liquor on his breath, and a sweetish smell she didn't recognize. Was it marijuana? Whatever it was, it had certainly altered his personality.

'I'm not your typical Caribbean male, you know, hung up on the double standard.'

'Good God, Stoner, what *is* this? I did what I could, didn't I?'

'Don't worry, Anna Banana, don't worry. I'm not going to rape you or anything. Do you have anything to eat in there?'

'Only some biscuits, I'll get them.'

'Any tea or coffee?'

The outrage was plain on Pavana's face.

'We've just been released,' he said, pitching his voice to a fake whine, deliberately obsequious.

'Released?'

'As in released from gaol?' He grinned wickedly at what he doubtless considered her newly acquired bourgeois sensibilities. 'There is a war on, remember? Easy for you to forget, I suppose, out here in your dolly house.' He gestured disparagingly at the table still littered with broken coral, dominoes and seashells. She followed his glance to the barbecue, the two-burner kerosene stove and the bag of garbage.

'We're broke,' he added. 'Are you going to provide us with sustenance to strengthen our manly limbs for the righteous war or what?'

'I'll get the biscuits,' Pavana said. 'But I'm not going to make you any tea, Stoner Bennett.'

She closed the door and rummaged around in a box of groceries until she found a packet of sweet biscuits. That ought to hold starvation at bay. Opening the door again, she shoved them out to him. But Stoner wasn't on the steps, he was back at the table stacking dominoes.

'It's a damn shame the way you're treating your children's relative,' he said, not looking towards the doorway.

'What are you talking about?' Pavana stepped outside.

'I came here to discuss it with you, but since you're skulking in there play-acting the endangered female, and a hard-hearted, inhospitable one at that, I won't.'

'Don't then,' Pavana said, stepping inside.

'It's your funeral,' he called.

As she tiptoed back to bed, Eric raised his head from the pillow.

'Who's making all that noise?'

'Stoner Bennett. Playing drunk. Not to worry.'

'What's he want?'

'Tea and biscuits, at this time of night, can you imagine?'

179

'He must be crazy, Mom. Go to bed.'

She lay on her back, dispirited, unable to dismiss Stoner's words from her mind. Was he really drunk? He was still outside, clicking the domino pieces. She had never known Stoner to lie; exaggerate, yes, for the sake of a good joke, mostly at his own expense. She slipped on her rubber thongs and pulled one of Eric's giant T-shirts over her pyjamas, fuming as she did so.

What did Stoner think? That this was still, or at least a continuation of, the old London days, when on numerous occasions they'd sat together in Alex's flat, drinking tea, waiting for him to return from classes, from another interminable meeting, or mysterious assignations of one kind or another? Stoner probably saw little difference, only now he had finally found the major commitment of his life, the overthrow of these heads of agreement, and a chance simultaneously to even the score with Alex. His past failures would now be forgotten; he would come at last into his own.

She picked up the biscuits again, careful in case the crackle of cellophane disturbed Eric; the three mugs clinked alarmingly as she moved them off the table; the tea, sugar; she wouldn't bother about milk. To save time, she placed everything in her straw bag, grabbed the kettle and went outdoors, determined to have a showdown with Stoner once and for all.

But what was this? The legendary hero-to-be, the man among men: his head was down on the planks placed together across two stumps to form a makeshift table. His shoulders shook. He didn't even notice that she was outside. Was he crying? Maudlin from drink?

'You're not crying are you, Stone?' Pavana asked. She sometimes used to call him Stone in the old days. He didn't look up immediately, surprised perhaps that she had come outdoors after all. Pavana looked around for his friends or colleagues whatever they were, and saw them walking up and down the far end of the pier extending from the beach opposite the Turtle Grass Hotel. Were they angry with him or what, she wondered, for bringing them on what had turned out to be a wild-goose chase?

'You need some tea in truth, Stone,' she said. 'Devil drink, and whatever it is you've been smoking, has weakened what is known as your moral fibre.'

Funny, but she couldn't ever remember seeing Stoner drunk. And

180

marijuana? Not like him, at all. His idea of fun was eating shark steaks, fried locusts and every kind of exotic concoction. He'd gone out with many girls, in the old days but, like Moria, he'd always shied away from any kind of permanent relationship with anyone, as far as she knew.

She rattled the matches, walking towards the stove near the halved drum which Morris had made into a barbecue.

'Let me do that, Anna Banana,' Stoner said, getting up and taking the matches out of her hand. 'Almost like the old days, isn't it?'

'Almost, Stone,' Pavana said, carrying the kettle to the vat, raised on concrete slabs off the ground. The rustling fronds of the coconut trees no longer seemed soothing. Turning on the faucet, she watched the two figures pacing up and down the pier. Overhead, the branches swished ominously, creating within her all over again a terrible unease. On her return, Stoner was staring intently at the flames he had lit.

'So what were you guys in prison for?'

'Burning flags, marching in illegal processions, possession of firearms, things like that.'

'How long were you in gaol?'

'About eighteen hours. I've lost track. Some of the brothers and sisters are still there, for allegedly setting fire to buildings, and so on and so forth.'

'Hmmm.' Pavana said. She knew that ever since the protests against the agenda had started, dozens of known activists were regularly stopped, searched, taken out of their homes in the middle of the night, held without bail and generally harassed. Stoner, staring into space, didn't seem interested in discussing his ordeal, and it must have been an ordeal. This seemed to Pavana downright strange, and uncharacteristic.

'Oh, and Stoner, what is this relative business you were talking about? Are we related in some way?' This would not have surprised Pavana in the least for, like most people in Belize, she had relations she didn't even know about. As a young girl she'd heard several stories of brothers and sisters marrying, not knowing they shared a father or a mother. A lot of women, for various reasons, sometimes refused to reveal the fathers' names, or often the fathers refused to acknowledge paternity.

In the old days nearly all their friends used to speak incessantly, often boastfully, sometimes untruthfully, about their families 'back home'. But she had never heard Stoner mention a single member of his family.

181

Even so, Pavana half-expected Stoner to begin some complicated story going back at least seventy-five years to prove they were far cousins or something like that. But no, Stoner was walking away from her to the vat, leaning against it, his back to her, his shoulders shaking again.

She watched him through the fronds of the coconut trees. Should she say something? Better not, she thought. When the water boiled, she poured it on the tea bags in the mugs and put the biscuits on a plate.

'The tea is ready, Stone,' she said. 'Do you want to call your friends?'

'They won't want to come over here,' he said. 'I'll take it to them.' He washed his face at the faucet and dried it with his handkerchief. 'I guess you're going back to bed now, right?'

It was tempting, but she shook her head,

'I'll wait.'

On his return, he sat beside her in a canvas chair, sipping his tea and eating the biscuits. She remembered that Stoner had never been one for desserts, nor any kind of sweet foods.

'A side effect of my miserable and impoverished childhood,' he used to say at Julian's dinner parties.

'Do you know who's coming to Belize soon, Stoner? Julian Carlisle, for a visit.'

'Really? It'll be nice to see the old fruit,' which is how Julian used to refer to him.

'Jolly nice of you to come, old fruit', Julian would say to Stoner at the door of his flat. Stoner used always to make a funny face behind Julian's back.

'My mother visited me me at the gaol,' Stoner said. He'd turned his chair so he could stare out at the sea. He lit a cigarette. The wind had dropped and the sandflies had come out. Pavana scratched her ankles, then her arms, then her face.

'Once I remember,' Stoner said, 'sitting with Alex in the Edgewater Café, the little restaurant near the bedsitting house where you lived before . . .'

Pavana nodded, not trusting herself to speak. Stoner was extremely agitated, getting out of the chair, walking a little distance beyond the shadow of the thatch, never directly looking at her, returning to the chair. He began stacking the dominoes again, idly with one hand, the expression on his face shifting with his thoughts. It now seemed reflective, tender unto tears.

'I was begging Alex to let me share his flat with him. I placed my hand over his, pleading with him. He punched me in the jaw. All I ever wanted to do was to serve Alex, ironic really.'

Pavana decided to sit on the sand in the shadow of the table. She couldn't bear the glare from the naked electric lightbulb a second longer. Her eyes were burning, her back ached, and she felt incredibly tired. Stoner seemed not to have noticed.

'I've always cared about Alex very deeply. We grew up together as children, and I literally worshipped not only him, but his entire family, for what I took at the time to be their kindness to my mother and me.'

Stoner paused, as if he expected her to comment, so Pavana said, 'I can well understand that, Stone.' She leaned her head against one of the massive tree stumps supporting the planks and closed her eyes. The dominoes crashed to the table.

'There were times, during those days, when we had very little food, no kerosene for the lamps, none certainly for the stove, and we groped around in the darkness, my mother and I carrying candle stubs from one corner of the room to another. That's all there was, one room, attached to rooms occupied by other workers, in a long row on the edge of the citrus orchards, near Abrams Creek. We used to swim there a lot, Alex and I.'

The sandflies had become really vicious. Pavana stood up and walked slowly to the steps. She sat on the top one, as though she was a nightwatchman for the room where the twins slept.

'On those nights, when we had no more credit at Abrams Commissary, I would peer constantly through the window, which got on my mother's nerves, at the path through the orange groves, hoping that someone from the bungalow on the hilltop would remember us below. Alex would sometimes visit us, Moria too.

'And quite often Mr Abrams himself, who seemed quite an old man to me then, with his white hair and stooped shoulders, would visit us. Perhaps my mother had sent him a message, I don't know, and she would go outside to talk with him. On her return, she'd have money and food, and the next day she'd buy fresh candles, gallons of kerosene, meat and vegetables, and we'd be all right for a while, managing on her wages.

'So my childhood passed. I never questioned why we moved to Belize City, nor where the money came from to send me to high school.

Perhaps subconsciously I knew, and instinctively refrained from questioning my mother, who as far as I remember had laboured unceasingly for the Abrams, picking fruit, housekeeping occasionally.

'When we left, I was glad. I thought I never wanted to see those hills again, nor smell oranges rotting on the roadside, nor to lug boxes and crocus sacks to the highway, where the fruit was piled into trucks. I never wanted to eat fish seray, nor plaintain *fu fu*, nor hear the beat of drums in any ceremony for the dead. I wanted to get away from all that for ever.

'After high school, I worked for a few years in the Civil Service and helped my mother to start the little grocery store she has now.'

'Then you went to London?' Pavana asked.

'Followed Alex to London, is more the truth,' Stoner said, his expression bitter. 'Alex was always my role model. I wanted to do everything he did, be as much like him as possible. At the time I fooled myself that I was going because, like Alex, I was going to get a law degree.'

'Ah,' Pavana said, as if that explained everything, only it didn't, and she waited.

'I flew to Jamaica,' Stoner said, 'worked there for a while, and wrote Alex week after week although he didn't reply that regularly. Finally he sent a letter, encouraging me to join him in London. It was hard to save the money, but I did.'

On the pier, the two men were still walking back and forth, waiting for morning, perhaps, and the first boat back to Belize City. Neither she nor Stoner wore a watch, and she wondered what the time could possibly be. Two o'clock?

'My mother came to see me in gaol,' Stoner was saying, beginning to stack the dominoes again. 'You know, she and I, well, we're close – at least we used to be close before I joined the Action Committee. I'm an only child, so she's always given me a lot of her time. She was very upset, and has been ever since the committee started its activities. I tried to explain it all to her again last night before we were released, I said to her, "Mama, I feel the agenda is not right for Belize. That's why I joined the action committee. It's wrong to remain silent."

'"But Stoner," she said, and she was crying and carrying on, "I need your help in the shop. It's hard for me to do everything."

'"This won't last for ever," I told her. "It's something I need to do for Belize, and for myself."

'"For Belize!" She was shouting at me. "Then why are you hounding Alex Abrams? His father came to see me at the shop to ask you to stop! How do you think I felt with all the customers standing around?"'

Stoner swallowed.

'I said to her, "Mama, love, Alex Abrams and other officials and ministers have been sent out to sell the heads of agreement to the country. They have to be stopped."

'"But why must *you* be the one to do it? He's got a right, same as you, to his beliefs, as his father said!" My mother was almost beside herself.

'Then, I said, he has to be persuaded otherwise. He still has a lot of influence on people in this country. His whole family does.

'My mother cried, "He was shot! You and Alex used to be friends. His father and I were both glad about that, at least."

'I gave up at that point, Pavana,' Stoner said. He came and sat beside her on the step. 'I could see that I wasn't going to get anywhere. Besides, I understood her loyalty to the Abrams family. For most of my life I'd felt the same. So I didn't say any more. I sat there watching her cry. Then she said a horrible thing, the thing I suppose I'd always suspected and feared. She said, "He's your own flesh and blood, Stoner, your half-brother!"

'You know, Pavana,' Stoner said, lighting another cigarette, 'At the time I felt no softening within me, just a greater rage, a greater hatred for Alex, who I see as betraying me time and time again, and now in my view is about to betray the country, wrapping himself in the flag, pretending he believes this is right for Belize, all for the sake of power. He and I are not flesh and blood. It was merely an accident of birth.'

Stoner sounded tired, his head resting against the wall of the house. Pavana sat there staring at the moonlight glimmering on the waves. She was glad now that she had told Lisa and Eric about Alex and that Alex knew about them. Unpleasant to do as it had been, late as it had been, with consequences to come as she had no doubt there would be, still she had done it.

'I'm sure Alex will get in touch with you, Stoner. He's just delayed . . . or something.'

'Naw,' Stoner said, curling his lips. 'He's sending me another

185

message. Alex has done this to me before, even when we were friends, so called.'

'He's going to contact you, Stoner, really.'

'Well, I can't hang about like his flunky waiting, neither will those guys.' He gestured to the pier.

'What will you do?'

'It's more like what I'll *have* to do. Time has run out on me. From here on, I have to follow orders from the Committee, or get out. And, as I've told you, Pavana, they intend to overthrow the agenda by any means necessary.'

Chapter 32

At breakfast the following morning, Morris, looking relaxed and well rested, whispered in Pavana's ear, 'I do believe you have a secret lover, Pavana. Did I hear sweet murmurings in the night?'

Pavana smiled faintly, feeling her lips tremble, conscious that the twins were observing her surreptitiously. She had a splitting headache, the pain intensifying with every insistent bite of the machete into the young coconuts Peter was husking on a tree stump near the rainwater vat. There was no sign of Stoner, nor of his friends.

After he'd left, stumbling across the sand towards the men on the pier, she had crept indoors feeling completely defeated, to lie wide-eyed staring into darkness until the sky lightened. She had showered, the fishy smell of the conch shells increasing her feeling of nausea, before going outdoors to walk up and down the beach, hoping that the breeze from the sea would clear her head. It hadn't worked; the air was still, the sea motionless.

Later, when Jen and Morris came downstairs, she'd helped to fry snappers and to make johnny cakes, baking them in a huge iron pot set over the barbecue fire. Across from her the twins ate without much appetite, drinking sweet, hot tea from enormous mugs, their faces subdued, as they stared steadfastly out to sea.

They'd had a swim before breakfast; on their return, Lisa wrapped a towel around her swimsuit, pulling her hair into a neat, uncompromising plait at the back of her head. Now and then she cast a curious eye along the beach in the direction of the Turtle Grass Hotel.

Eric had undoubtedly told her about Stoner's request for tea in the middle of the night, the clicking of the dominoes and Pavana's long talk with him outdoors, for he hadn't been asleep when she finally went in. Feeling her eyes on him, Eric tried to smile reassuringly, but in his dark eyes, fringed with long lashes, she saw not only empathy but also reappraisal. He had kept close to Lisa all morning and was unusually solicitous, pouring her orange juice, urging her to eat. Childhood, it seemed, had gone.

Peter's machete was stuck in the tough green husk of a young coconut. He pounded it repeatedly on the stump, his long, thin face set in a determined grimace. As the coconut finally split open, Pavana heard him give a long, low whistle. Everyone looked in the direction of the Turtle Grass Hotel. He called over his shoulder, 'Isn't that Alex Abrams? What the hell is he doing playing on the beach at a time like this?' He brought the coconut to the table and set the halves before the twins, who stared at the soft, quivery meat of the young coconut as if the very thought of eating it made them feel horribly ill.

'It's himself,' Morris replied, sipping his coffee appreciatively and squinting down the beach. 'Is that his sister?' He whistled. 'Look at that figure.'

Moria, in a silver and black bikini, her long hair piled on the top of her head, had her arm loosely linked through Alex's.

'One arm is in a sling,' Jen observed, removing her sunglasses to watch Alex, in dark blue swimming trunks, his unbuttoned shirt blowing like a sail in the wind. The waves surged on to the beach. Seagulls flew squawking above the dark heads. 'I do believe they're headed this way.'

Pavana felt exposed, like a hermit crab which had lost its shell. She casually pulled Eric's T-shirt over her navy blue swimsuit, her heart beating in a mixture of excitement and dread.

'Alex did say he might look us up if he came out to the caye today,' she said, pouring herself a cup of coffee.

'Are you a friend of theirs?' Jen asked in betrayed tones. Her look of incredulity made Pavana feel like a collaborator of the most devious kind. *Was* she a friend of theirs? Lisa and Eric were staring at her, their faces pinched and bleak.

'We were very good friends, once, in London,' she replied.

Morris gave a low whistle.

'Is that how the land lies, Pavana? he asked, quirking one bushy eyebrow as though to ask, 'Was it him out here last night?' She ignored his unspoken question.

'Body Guards too.' Viv said, painting her lips the colour of her coral pink swimsuit. She ran a comb through her short, crinkly hair, looking expectantly down the beach.

'I hear, my love,' Viv called, her voice rivalling the seagulls, 'that he lives with a Salvadorean refugee who turned up on his doorstep. Two children and another on the way.'

'Oh,' Pavana said, dreading what she would say next, wanting to throw sand into Viv's sympathetic eyes.

'Collected a pile of insurance when his wife died in that car accident,' Peter grumbled, pouring himself a glass of orange juice. 'At least that's what I heard,' he conceded.

'Never takes the Salvador lady anywhere with him, though,' Viv was saying, 'always his sister. Well, what can a poor refugee woman do, except be grateful for the luxurious life in that big white house on the hillside?'

'Easy for that kind to be liberal,' Morris said, easing his bulk into a chair near to the twins. 'Money from way back, plus his salary as adviser. But who knows, maybe he's flat broke; I hear he's campaigning and that's never cheap.'

He cleared a space on the table. 'How about a game of dominoes? Lisa? Eric?' The twins shook their heads and he stared at them, obviously perplexed.

Alex and Moria had paused by an ancient anchor mounted on cement, a few yards from the pier on which Stoner and his friends had walked up and down the night before. Alex was vigorously shaking hands with two young fishermen standing near a boat drawn up on the sand. The fishermen raised their hats as Alex and Moria walked confidently towards the group at the makeshift table under thatch.

At their approach Morris, Viv and Jen scrambled to their feet to shake hands. Peter, settling his lanky frame more comfortably in his chair, merely waved his glass of juice as Pavana introduced everyone.

'Enjoying the lovely weather?' Alex asked, removing his black sunglasses, dangling them in one hand. He smiled winningly at the twins. Pavana could think of little else but the sound of his voice reverberating in the air.

Jen, determinedly loyal, said, 'We made a great escape from Belize City. I suppose you had the same idea? How is your . . . wound?'

'This sling makes it look a lot worse than it really is,' Alex said, his hand on Pavana's chair. 'A flesh wound, nothing to worry about.'

'We were very sorry to hear about the incident,' Morris said, rearranging the chairs around the table. 'Pavana mentioned you were friends in London?'

'Oh, yes,' Moria said, hesitating slightly before sitting in the chair Morris offered, 'We're very old friends.'

Alex carried a canvas chair and placed it near to Lisa and Eric. They had uttered no word of greeting but, as Alex chatted to them quietly, they seemed to relax. Lisa proffered her half of coconut and a spoon, remembered his wounded arm, scooped the flesh of the coconut on to a plate and passed him a fork. Whatever it was he said, it caused Eric to smile. He, too, scooped the flesh of his coconut on to Alex's plate, and the twins watched fascinated as he ate the whole lot.

'Have they arrested anyone?' Jen asked.

Alex looked across the table at Jen, who was smiling brightly at him. For a moment it seemed as if he couldn't imagine what she was talking about.

'Oh,' he said, his gaze returning to Lisa and Eric. 'The police have a few suspects. Others have told me that Red Man's gun probably went off accidentally . . .'

'Red Man!' Peter snorted sceptically. 'I believe it was politically motivated myself.'

Viv glanced warningly at Peter and said to Alex, 'Would you care for some juice? Or johnny cakes? The fish is all gone, I'm afraid. How about you, Moria?'

Moria, too, was staring at the twins who were smiling a little now as Alex examined a brain coral the size of a skull, which the twins were planning to take home. The three smiles were almost identical.

'That's very kind of you,' Moria said, 'but we've only just had breakfast. Actually, we've booked Captain Trejito's boat for a ride to

189

view the reef. We wondered if Pavana would like to join us for an hour or two.' She looked at Pavana, who looked at the twins.

'Eric and Lisa are invited, too, of course,' Alex said. 'Have you ever been out in a glass-bottomed boat?'

The twins shook their heads, looking at Pavana, who smiled encouragingly.

'Would you like to go with us?' Alex asked Lisa and Eric. Alex's expression was so anxious and uncertain that it would have been difficult for Lisa and Eric, who loved to dive in any case, to refuse his invitation. They nodded, running off to collect their diving gear.

'Would anyone else like to join us?' Alex asked politely, looking around the table. The others murmured excuses.

As they were preparing to leave, Alex said, 'It's quite a delight to watch the underwater life. I always find it a very relaxing thing to do. Have you ever been out on one of the boats, Pavana?'

'To be truthful, I hadn't realized there were glass-bottomed boats on Pelican Island now. Such is progress.'

The expression in Alex's eyes was shielded by the huge sunglasses in which Pavana saw only herself. He took the straw hat from her hand and plopped it on her head.

'You're getting cynical in your old age, Miss Pavana,' he said. 'Come on, Eric, Lisa, let's go, it's quite a walk, and old Trejito will be in a disgusting temper if we're late.'

The twins called goodbye to the group under the thatch, giggling at the lugubrious expression on Morris's face as he told them to enjoy themselves.

Pavana walked between Moria and Alex, as she had done so many times before up and down the streets of London. Perhaps her happiness showed for Alex laughed, putting his arm around her shoulder as they watched the twins racing each other along the beach. There were disturbing things she wanted to discuss with Alex, but for these few minutes perhaps they both needed to pretend. Moria dropped back to talk with the men in Alex's entourage, an unpleasant reminder that it was an unnatural time.

Chapter 33

'Ready, *Capitán?*' Alex asked, waving goodbye to a sullen bodyguard leaning disconsolately against the shaded wall of the thatched-roofed *cabaña* at the end of the slatted wooden pier. The burly guard did not respond to Alex's cheerful wave. His dark brown face was swollen like a puffer fish, sensing danger in the immediate vicinity. He waited until Alex, Morris, Pavana, Lisa and Eric settled themselves around the wooden railings rimming the giant window of glass, set in the bottom of the boat. Then he shrugged, stalking off quickly to join his companions huddled together at the shore-end of the pier.

'*Sí, Señor,*' the captain replied, as the outboard motor finally kicked into life. Edwardo, his assistant, a thin, muscular teenager, threw the rope on to the deck and jumped after it. He positioned himself on the raised deck, his feet dangling in front of a large padlocked cupboard where passengers stored diving and other gear for daylong trips beyond the fringing reefs.

Captain Trejito turned out to be a frail-looking, wizened seaman, around seventy years old, with white, curly hair cropped unevenly close to his head; his face was a mass of wrinkles, his eyes light grey and clear, sparkling in the sunlight. He sat aft, steering the *La Reina Belizeña* over the relatively shallow water in which, eventually, patches of massive brain coral appeared, hulking like convoluted boulders beneath the glass. Further out, a stream of fishes, an intense deep blue, darted through a bed of stagshorn coral growing like a miniature and fantastical forest, in which grew clumps of sea feathers and sea fans undulating in the waves.

Held in thrall, oddly shy and awkward with each other, the adults and young people peered underwater at the wealth of marine life, living in symbiotic but often destructive relationships, life feeding upon life on the crowded barrier reef. The window of glass made the sea seem tame, like a giant aquarium, through which one could walk fully dressed, feeling absolutely safe from the watery abyss.

191

It wasn't until Edwardo dived overboard, harpoon in hand, his red trunks flashing in the sunlight, that the silence was broken by the twins' excited exclamations as the young man appeared beneath the boat. He swum with supreme grace as if the sea were his natural habitat, moving swiftly through schools of parrot fish, groupers and other vividly coloured fish, some silvery, others purple and blue or green and yellow. He pointed with the harpoon to a moray eel backing under a coral ledge and to a stingray burrowing into the sand. As they followed his progress, Edwardo spiked a crayfish, surfacing with a splash to throw it triumphantly over the side.

In the cool shadows of the boat, Pavana watched Alex's animated face as, together with the twins, he moved to the stern, waiting for Edwardo to surface with another crayfish for the burlap sack resting near the captain's bare feet.

Moria also watched. At first she was silent, plaiting her straight brown hair into two long braids, tying them in a coronet around her head. Thoughtfully, slowly, she rubbed suntan lotion into her smooth pale skin, over her arms, body and legs. Looking up, she caught Pavana's eye.

'So, how is it going at the Women's Unit?' she asked. It occurred to Pavana that for the past few minutes Moria had not smiled or said very much. She seemed distracted, her expression guarded. But now she seemed to have reached some resolution.

'Not too promising at the moment,' Pavana replied, 'but I expect things will improve.'

Pavana looked from Moria to Alex, and then back to Moria again. It was proving difficult to tell Alex, who seemed determined to have a good time, what she had learnt from Stoner. But she watched for an opportunity.

'That's what Alex has been telling me; too bad about your contract and all that.'

These days it took only a kind word, a friendly smile, or a sympathetic look to start up the ache in Pavana's throat, and she was determined today of all days not to give way to emotion. So she conjured up in her mind the fantasy in which she had several ministers pinioned to their benches in the House of Representatives, while they listened to an endless list of grievances from an irate women's group.

It always worked. Before long, as she related her difficulties during the past few weeks, she had Moria sitting next to her shrieking with laughter, wiping the tears of amusement from her eyes.

'What's the joke? Let us in on it,' Alex called, laughing in delight, pleased that they were getting along so well together.

'Never you mind,' Moria called back. 'Your job is to relax and entertain your guests.' For the first time she smiled in a genuinely friendly way at the twins, one on either side of Alex.

'You are funny, Pavana,' Moria said, patting her hand. 'You get yourself in such a state, and these people are really so easy to deal with, once you understand that they too are insecure and in need of reassurance. We are not all ogres, you know. I'll have to teach you a thing or two, bring you into the fold.'

'That's not been my experience so far, Moria. I've met with such a lot of pettiness and vindictiveness, when people are not timid and evasive. Perhaps my job should be a political appointment in truth, although that was certainly not my understanding of it from Mrs Elrington. The minister will not be attending our workshop in Boom, and because of a foul-up at the office BWDO may have a valid excuse for not attending either. It's very worrying, what with one thing and another.'

'Perhaps that's where I can help,' Moria said, a bright smile on her face. 'I've long been a loyal foot soldier in BWDO, and you'll be delighted to know that last month I was elected deputy head of that doughty organization. I'll be sure to attend the workshop, and bring as many members as I can with me.'

'You'd do that?' Pavana asked doubtfully.

'Oh, yes,' Moria's eyes sparkled. 'I'm already involved in a battle royal over there with Beulah Stephenson,' she replied gleefully. 'I mean to liven things up more than a bit, I can tell you. And I think our first task is to get behind the unit and support it.'

'It's certainly worth a try,' Pavana said, looking at Moria's determined face. She didn't have to think very hard to realize Beulah's leadership was being challenged by Moria. Perhaps she too was heading for the House of Representatives. Pavana did not fool herself that Moria's offer of help was in any way altruistic. She couldn't have changed that much. Moria kept her gaze fixed on Pavana's face, as if trying to gauge her reaction.

'Maybe you can tell me,' Pavana said. 'I've tried a few times to make an appointment to speak with Beulah Stephenson at the House of Women, but she's always too busy to meet with me.'

'Well, Beulah has always supported the old guard, as you know, and she knows Alex supported your appointment, and we're not too popular with her. Besides, she's getting all the information she thinks she needs at the moment from a number of women in the ministry, including your deputy, Brenda.'

'Brenda! She's on the island, did you know that?'

'Oh, I know that. Alex and I met her in the hotel dining-room having breakfast with Simon Galvez and his wife. We all had a cozy little chat. Brenda was telling the minister how excited she was to be able to be of assistance to BWDO, through the Women's Unit.'

'I'm amazed, truly,' said Pavana, thinking that it hadn't taken Brenda very long to begin the process of undermining her authority through informal contacts with officials and politicians.

'Of course, as you know, she would have been made director long ago if it wasn't for Mrs Elrington's opposition. Cora has had quite a few sticky moments with Miss Kirkwood during the past few months.'

'So I gathered, except I don't understand the reason why.'

'It's just regular old politics, Pavana. Mrs Elrington is pro the opposition party as you know, and she doesn't want the unit to be used, through Brenda, for political purposes by the ruling party. Ergo, you.'

'Well, I'm afraid my philosophy is pretty much the same as Mrs Elrington's. I am trying to work with all women regardless of their political, religious or any other kinds of belief, and . . .'

'That's exactly your problem, if you don't already know it, which I know you do. With no strong constituency in either political camp, you're vulnerable. It'll continue to be rough going, and the unit will only be able to move so far.'

'I understand all that,' Pavana said, 'But given . . .'

'Now here's my idea, Pavana. We should be natural allies, you and I. Why don't we work together?'

'You feel I should pick a political side?'

'Under our present system it's the only way, otherwise you'll only continue to be ignored. Alex and I would like it very much if we three could work together again like we used to do, Pavana.'

Pavana didn't reply immediately. For a moment or two the years

194

slipped away, and she was back in Stoner's Bayswater flat watching Alex and Moria dance.

'Let me think about it for a day or so, will you, Moria?'

'Oh, sure,' Moria said, but Pavana could see disappointment, even annoyance, on her face. 'You'll need to prove your loyalty, though, if you intend to survive beyond your present contract.'

Pavana could not meet Moria's gaze, for she already knew she could not promise to support BWDO exclusively, nor its equivalent in the opposition party. Pavana was sure her feelings on the subject were plain on her face. She had to resist being persuaded or pressured into serving certain women's groups and not others, certain villages, certain towns, for the benefit of one political party or another.

Surely the unit was established to upgrade the miserable situation of most women, not to use its funding primarily to bolster a single political party. The unit should be able to work with the government of the day, like other units and departments. However, the politicians had long regarded women as their traditional territory, to serve their needs and aspirations. It must be quite disorienting for them to absorb the fact that women were now beginning to work for the upgrading of their own status. She'd better tell Moria now, and not wait.

Moria was back on the deck smoking a cigarette. Pavana hoisted herself up to sit beside her.

'You won't do it, eh, Pavana? I told Alex I didn't think you would, but I did do my best.' She smiled. 'I'll still attend the workshop by the way.'

'That's something at any rate,' Pavana smiled in return, continuing to sit beside her, watching Alex, Lisa and Eric as they assisted Captain Trejito who was dropping anchor near a number of other boats, crowded with diving enthusiasts. Lisa and Eric slipped on flippers and masks, jumping overboard to join Edwardo, who seemed eager to show them the wonders of the reef.

Chapter 34

'They swim very well,' Alex said wistfully as the twins, one on either side of Edwardo, swam easily through the waves, faces down, peering at the reef below. Pavana didn't reply, but the unkind thought 'No thanks to you' did arise unbidden in her mind; she didn't ever want to be mean-spirited, but especially not today. The day meant so much to her, and to Lisa and Eric. As she removed Eric's T-shirt, Alex took it from her.

'You don't look much older, Pavana. You look great, as a matter of fact.' The slight surprise in his voice, and the memory of Mr Grant's comment on the plane, made Pavana laugh out loud, simply because she suddenly felt good.

'Thanks, Alex, you don't look too bad yourself,' she replied, and meant it.

Moria was still smoking in the bow of the boat, apparently observing closely the activities of the divers in the water but probably only waiting for Pavana to swim away before relating their conversation to Alex.

'Does Moria know about Lisa and Eric? And about Stoner?'

'I've told her just about everything.' Was there already a slight edge to his voice?

Pavana pressed on.

'Stoner came to Jen's house in the middle of the night looking for you. He said you'd promised to meet him earlier at the Turtle Grass.'

'I couldn't get there until early this morning. I was at an emergency meeting which lasted half the night.' He was definitely impatient, probably in some physical discomfort too, although he continued to deny it. 'Besides, we wanted to spend some time with you and . . . Lisa and Eric. I'll catch up with Stoner later today.'

'He's very upset, Alex, about . . . he told me that . . .'

'I'm sick to death of the whole business, Pavana,' Alex interrupted. 'I'll handle it from here on, OK?'

'OK,' Pavana said, climbing down the ladder. When her eyes were on a level with Alex's hairy legs and bare feet, she said, 'The water feels wonderful. Sorry you can't swim today.'

He hugged his injured arm.

'You're not sorrier than I am,' Alex replied. 'We'll have to talk later today, you and I.' Looking up, Pavana thought she saw in his eyes much of what used to be there before. Amazing, Pavana thought, simply amazing. Does he just switch on and then switch off? Or was she just older, more experienced, more able to recognize these things for what they were? Or was it simply her imagination treading a familiar groove? She'd heard of far stranger things.

Floating on her back, she looked again at the golden chain gleaming in the mass of hair on his chest. I can't take the chance in any case, Pavana thought, whatever it is.

As she was about to swim away, the captain's voice, raised in a mixture of fright and outrage, startled Pavana. Clambering quickly back into the boat, her heart beating wildly, she was just in time to see Stoner crawling out of the stowage space from among fishing nets, lines and greasy tools, his clothing oily, perspiration rolling down his face.

The captain stood barring his way, an enamel lunch carrier in one hand, the padlock in the other.

'A stowaway?' Moria said, laughing, giving Stoner an insolent, dismissive look. She sat cross-legged on the deck, above the stowage cupboard, still smoking, an air of resignation in her posture. Her eyes were locked with Stoner's. She seemed prepared for anything, and beyond caring.

'You have an absolute bloody nerve,' Alex said. 'Get off, Stoner, before I have you thrown off.'

'You and which army?' Stoner laughed. 'Strong language, Alex Abrams, considering I've been hanging about this island for over twenty-four hours waiting for you to show up. It's caused me considerable embarrassment as a matter of fact. Still, the wait's been worth it. You know how drawn I am to you, Moria, and old Anna Banana over there, from the old days.'

The captain was incensed.

'I don't want trouble on my boat. You get off. I don't get myself involved in politics.'

'Oh, but peace and love, Captain Trejito,' Stoner said, keeping his eyes on the captain. He splashed water on to his face, smiling at the group as he removed his shirt. 'I'm along for the ride at the invitation of Mr Abrams, soon to be the Honourable Alex Abrams, if his party wins another election. Who knows? Maybe Prime Minister Abrams, one of these days.'

'Do you know this man?' the captain asked Alex.

'I know him, but I had no idea he would hide like a thief on your boat,' said Alex, walking past the huge pane of glass in the bottom of the boat towards Stoner, who continued to smile. 'I am very sorry he scared you like that.'

'Stoner is very good at surprises, aren't you?' Moria asked as, muttering angrily under his breath, the captain made his way aft. He opened his lunch box noisily, his expression grim and unappeased.

'The only way to survive,' Stoner said, 'in my present line of work. But most especially when I consort with my enemies.'

'Are we your enemies now, Stoner?' Moria asked. 'Well, well, well. Tell me about man's ingratitude.'

'Don't try sarcasm with me, Moria,' Stoner said, sitting down and lighting a cigarette. 'Alex agreed to meet me out here, and I came, at great trouble and personal expense. Nobody gave me a complimentary airplane ride out here. But then, I don't have any contracts or concessions to influence.'

'You poor, poor man,' Moira said.

'Yes,' Stoner said, 'I'm a poor man.'

'What's this I hear then, Stoner?' Alex said, his voice harsh, 'You've hired yourself out as a messenger *bwoy* for the opposition?' He stretched his legs out luxuriously, until his bare feet touched the rim of the window of glass. 'In addition to accosting unsuspecting matrons on the public thoroughfare? Shame, shame.'

Stoner lounged on the long wooden seat on the right-hand side of the boat, opposite Alex.

'You're not in the House, yet, Abrams. So don't practise your rhetoric on me.'

Although Pavana was listening keenly, she glanced occasionally out to sea where, a five-minute swim away, Eric, Lisa and Edwardo were exploring the reefs with seemingly inexhaustible energy, cavorting like porpoises in the relatively shallow, surging water. Beside her in the stern of the boat the captain gnawed at the remains of a fried grouper, the skeleton of the fish curving delicately in his two gnarled hands.

It was nearly noon, and the captain would soon be pulling up anchor; their two-hour ride was nearly at an end. Pavana felt relieved. The day was in ruins anyway. She thought about Alex's bodyguards waiting patiently on the pier.

'People link us to the opposition party, but our aim is really to get a referendum on the agenda. After that, we'll disband.'

'Such public spirit, Stoner, inciting young people to violence, burning, looting, smashing up the city, although it doesn't take much, I'll agree.'

'And I'm afraid it will continue, unless you can persuade your cabinet colleagues to hold a referendum.' Stoner was trying to speak reasonably but his voice was edged with anger, and a much deeper emotion which Pavana recognized.

'I don't have that kind of influence, Stoner. I keep telling you that. Besides its only an agenda for discussion.'

'The public service will go on strike if the people's wishes aren't respected, and the Action Committee will support them.'

'When the House of Representatives meets next Friday, the issue will be debated, and the decision of the ministers made public. Until then . . .'

Stoner stood up, walking around the railings to where Alex sat.

'Feelings are running pretty high in the country. I know your minister isn't unsympathetic to the people's feelings.'

'Yes, but how many other ministers would support him in any call for a referendum? Not enough, I'm afraid.'

'So,' Stoner said. 'Are you telling me that you can't, or won't, do anything to try and change the course of events?'

'I don't really see what I can do. The few ministers who would take my advice are in the minority, out of favour as a matter of fact, for allowing all this free expression to go so far.'

'You could resign.'

'Oh come on, Stoner. Why would I want to resign? This whole thing is being blown out of proportion by people like you. An agenda is not a treaty.'

'As a show of solidarity with the people,' Stoner continued. 'Besides, it would save your face all round. I am giving you a chance to save your political career.'

'You are, are you? Generous all of a sudden. Why?'

'Ask Moria. She knows a lot about the kind of agricultural projects under way up north.'

'Explain to me, Moria, what is he talking about?'

'God knows,' Moria replied, turning her back to them and gazing towards the shore.

'And me,' Stoner replied. 'I've heard that whenever you return from one of your shopping trips to Miami, your handbag is stuffed with US currency for certain public officials, in payment for facilitating the exportation of a certain weed, ditto for other illegal substances, who knows?'

'That's a dirty, lowdown lie, Stoner Bennett. Prove it, you bastard!' Moria's face became suffused with ugly red blotches, her eyes were shiny, glazed with anger and fear.

'I may be a bastard,' Stoner said, jabbing the air with a forefinger. 'But I don't need proof of your activities to damage your . . .' he hesitated, his lips curling in disgust. 'Your so-called brother. A rumour will do.'

'You're bluffing, Stoner,' Alex said.

'Am I?' Stoner laughed until tears streamed down his face.

The captain, still sitting beside Pavana, was becoming extremely agitated. He gripped Pavana's arm, his long nails grazing her skin.

'Is he drunk?' he asked. 'Or crazy?'

Pavana shook her head, closely observing Stoner's tightly closed eyes, his shoulders heaving in uncontrollable mirth.

'Let's go back now, please?' she said to the captain who, needing no persuasion, scanned the sea. He whistled shrilly. Catching Edwardo's attention, he beckoned frantically, pointing to his watch. Edwardo waved his arms in return and almost immediately, together with Lisa and Eric, began swimming towards the boat.

'I think you should get off now, Stoner,' Alex said. 'There's no point discussing this any further.' He glanced towards several passenger boats within shouting distance of *La Reina Belizeña*. 'You shouldn't have any difficulty getting a ride.'

'That's right, Stoner,' Moria said, her voice conciliatory. 'It's too upsetting. Perhaps we can all have a drink later, discuss the whole thing . . .'

'I don't give a damn if you're upset,' Stoner said. He turned to Alex. 'Look, I'm trying to make this easy for you . . .'

'Don't do me any favours, Bennett.'

Stoner's voice rose sharply.

'Unlike the way you treated me that night in London, when you had me voted off the Committee for Belizean Independence. You distorted the truth, when you weren't telling outright lies, using your prestige and rhetoric to swing the votes. I was a fool then. I should have distributed copies of that memo.'

'If you had it, why didn't you?'

'You know why I didn't. You had me over a barrel, because of my mother, because of my gratitude to your father, and because . . .' Stoner stopped as his voice began to falter.

In her mind, Pavana completed his sentence, 'And because you loved him, like I did.'

'In any case,' Stoner said, 'I do intend to publish it now unless you resign. Your resignation would strengthen the union's negotiating position, and could influence the vote in the House next Friday. If the cabinet reaches consensus in favour of a referendum, we would stop our activities immediately.'

'It could bring the government down,' Alex said.

'So? Have you heard of any government which lasts for ever? Although I must say these past twenty-five years have seemed like for ever.'

'I personally would like to continue helping to guide the country towards independence later this year. We're in the middle of the process.'

'We've waited this long,' Stoner said. 'Surely we can wait another year? Come on, Alex, you couldn't be that power-hungry.'

Moria jumped off the deck and stood close to Alex.

'Don't let Stoner push you around, Alex.'

'Shut up!' Stoner shouted.

Pavana waited in anxiety for Alex's reply. Which way would he go?

Swinging his legs off the railing, Alex stood for a while looking underwater through the glass. Then his expression hardened into the now familiar lines of arrogance and the certainty of power – or perhaps he had simply run out of choices.

'I don't believe you're thinking rationally, Stoner. I'm not resigning. Do what you like, publish what you like.'

Pavana's hopes, never high, plummeted. He couldn't, wouldn't, return to them. There would be no joining of forces, no fighting for a cause bigger than himself, no sacrifice, no resurrection. Alex didn't have the courage to risk being out of power again.

Moria placed her arm around Alex's waist. She gazed up at him abjectly, as if grateful for deliverance, but Alex removed her arm slowly and carefully, not meeting her eyes, and Moria's colour flared up again.

'He's lying, Alex!'

'I'm neither a judge nor a jury, Moria. I don't want to discuss it.' He turned to Stoner, whose disappointment was almost palpable.

'Are you going to leave?'

'You feel like a god, don't you, Alex Abrams? You and your party will live for ever, right? *Que viva*, and all that.'

'I feel all right,' Alex said wearily, his face ashen, his whole posture indicating defeat.

'Who wouldn't feel all right,' Stoner said savagely, 'with your two women beside you, and one at home? You want me gone, do you? I'm a low form of life now, am I? But I remember that night in my flat in London how you pleaded with me for a loan . . . to engage in well . . . violence of a particularly nasty sort, I now realize. The churchmen won't be too happy to read about that in the papers, will they? It might spoil your entire campaign, put you out of politics for good . . .'

Alex sprang forward, shoving Stoner to one side of the boat. His unexpected ferocity caught Stoner off guard and he fell, striking his face on the edge of the open cupboard door. Blood trickled from a small cut above his eyebrow. He rose slowly to his feet, a smile on his face, his eyes narrowed to slits.

'I respect a violent man,' Stoner said. 'Here, my brother, let's shake hands and discuss the issues like civilized people.'

Alex glanced at him warily, suspiciously, his injured arm held protectively against his chest. Blood had soaked through the bandage and stained the sling in which it was cradled.

'There's no need to get personal, Stoner.'

'Hard to avoid in a small society like ours,' Stoner said, advancing nearer, his hand outstretched. 'But the point is well taken, and when all's said and done, you are my brother.'

'And cut out that brother crap. It's sickening.'

'Oh,' Stoner said, 'but you are my brother – half-brother, but still flesh of my flesh, blood of my blood, and all that good stuff, ask our daddy.'

It was Alex's turn to be taken off guard. His hand was already outstretched and Stoner, grasping it fiercely, pushed Alex over the railing and on to the window of glass. Springing on top of Alex, Stoner banged his head against the glass. He lifted him up and then pushed him down again, hard.

'Beg, Abrams, beg,' Stoner chanted. 'Beg.'

Alex did not cry out, nor try to defend himself. He seemed almost to welcome the pain, surrendering himself to it. His eyes, full of hatred and disgust, challenged Stoner to do his worst.

Moria, cowering in a corner near the storage cupboard, screamed continuously at Stoner, 'Stop for God's sake, you'll kill him!'

But Stoner, beyond hearing or caring, continued to beat Alex's head against the glass. Blood now trickled from the bald spot on Alex's head and, overcoming her shock and terror, Pavana looked out to sea. In another minute, Lisa, Eric and Edwardo would be on board. Her one thought was to stop Stoner before the children reached the boat.

Cautiously, she crouched down on the floor of the boat and reached for Edwardo's harpoon. The captain uttered a soft moan as her fingers curled around the handle.

Moria's screaming stopped abruptly and she watched Pavana with petrified eyes. Slowly she crept forward. Stoner raised Alex up again and, in the instant before he pushed Alex down, Pavana pushed the harpoon hard against Stoner's back. He screamed in agony and Pavana watched the blood streaming down his brown skin. He cursed her viciously.

'Stop, Stone,' she said. 'Stop, he's not worth it, and you'll hang.'

Stoner sprang over the railing, grabbed the harpoon and swung it, striking her face and shoulder. The pain was excruciating, boring into her, making her cringe.

'My children, Stoner, my children!' Pavana shouted, staggering backwards, raising her hand to stave off Stoner's rage. She closed her eyes, waiting for the next blow from the harpoon.

'Poor bastards,' Stoner said. 'The poor little bastards.'

Pavana opened her eyes, stifling the urge to whimper. Stoner, the harpoon upraised, was looking with hatred at Alex, slipping and sliding as he attempted to rise off the glass smeared with his blood and Stoner's, mingling indistinguishably, reddening Alex's hands and clothing. Stoner hawked and spat on Alex, the huge, frothy glob of spittle landing on Alex's mouth. Alex gagged, vomit sliding down his chin on to the hairs on his chest. Stoner grunted in disgust, flung the harpoon on to Alex's body, hunched over in agony, and dived overboard, the cut on his back still trickling blood.

The wind was up, the waves surging. Pavana staggered to the stern of the boat. She wouldn't faint, never had, never would. These were the consequences, she had to take them – could, would, take them, not give in, survive. She kept her eyes away from the captain and Moria, frantically throwing water over Alex's inert head and body, slapping his face, calling his name. They were forcing the captain's rum down Alex's throat and he was gasping, moaning. Oh, Alex. Her own shoulder and cheek felt like a giant mass of pure pain, but it was as nothing compared to her mental anguish. It mustn't show, wouldn't show.

As the children reached the bottom of the ladder she called reassuringly, 'Alex has been hurt. He's been fighting with Stoner, but don't worry. They'll both be all right. We're going back to the island now. Let's get your things together.'

It was a hard ride back to Pelican Island. Pavana, sitting between the twins, trembled as if she had a fever, her shoulder aching even more now, and she refrained with difficulty from touching the bruise on her cheek which felt as if someone had thrown boiling water into her face. Lisa and Eric stared moodily out to sea, towels clutched around their bodies as if they were terribly cold.

Moria sat in the bow of the boat, cradling Alex's head on her lap. His eyes were closed and he made no sound. Edwardo knelt on the floor, holding Alex's body firmly against the seat, keeping him from falling as the boat bounced and leapt through the roughening waves.

Chapter 35

It was simply exhaustion, she was sure. Shuttling back and forth between her classes at Sacred Heart, the Women's Unit in Belize City and the ministry in Belmopan, she found herself away from home for as much as twelve or thirteen hours on really busy days. In addition, the horror of that afternoon on the glass-bottomed boat had stayed with her and she had been unable to sleep properly, plagued by nightmares. Many nights, jerking awake, she would sit up in bed reading until dawn, afraid to fall asleep again.

And most evenings, as soon as homework was finished, the music of the pan flutes stole out from Eric's or Lisa's room, and she had no one with whom to share the unbidden memories which the music always evoked. Memories of Eric and Lisa, on brown horses, tearing across the fields at their old school in East Africa, horses and riders silhouetted against the sky.

Memories of Julian, who had watched with her, that late afternoon from the shadows of a thorn tree, both of them riding too, with all the intensity of their beings, until night closed in; and then they'd gone, she and he, to an hotel, where they sat at a table in the open air.

She remembered the tangy taste of prawns on lettuce leaves, the ice-cold cider and the freshly baked loaves of bread. It was cool there in that neglected garden, with its flagged paths winding in and out among the trees. In the weeds and grasses to the rear of the garden, four tiny brown dik-diks stood silent and alert, merging with the browns, greys and smoky blues of the evening, and Julian, finally trusting, had spoken.

'Dora always claimed that life overseas turned her into an alcoholic. Who can tell about these things? In any case, she blamed me for it, and she blamed my work. In the beginning she enjoyed it thoroughly, particularly when we lived in Kenya. She lost weight there, and grew her hair again, as long as it would go. Perhaps I should have complimented her more, not only on her appearance but on her very real achievements at United World.

'Don't ask me why I didn't, Pavana. I don't know why, except I'm not very good at that sort of thing, at being . . . romantic. I always feel it's a bit of a put-down for women, especially when I admire their intellect as I did do Dora's. I couldn't understand why she needed that sort of constant flattery in our relationship. I didn't expect her to flatter me, not in the least.

'She often went out on her own to parties and things, which she resented. At the same time she had a tremendous need for the never-ending round of social occasions which, at first, must have seemed glamorous and exciting to her.

'But out here, things took a different turn. Sometimes I'd return home in the evenings, late from the office, to find her out cold on the floor, once completely naked on the bathroom floor. I wonder to this day whether or not Basil saw her that particular night.

'I can't remember the exact day she stopped working at United World, which accelerated the problem. She just did, claiming she was totally fed-up with what she called "the mealy-mouthed development set". One evening I arrived home to find her nearly drunk, laughing uproariously, a copy of the *Washington Monthly* in her hand. She said, "Look, Ju Ju, I found this at the club. There's a marvellous poem in it, ever so funny, you must hear."

'I asked her where Basil was.

'"In bed," she replied, waving the magazine at me. "What do you think I'd done now? Abandoned him in a mosque? Take that look off your face, Julian, you're so bloody stuffy, and serious all the time. You can't carry the burden of the black race on your back *all* the time, you know; besides, I thought it was only white men who did that. In any case, have a drink and listen. It's *so* funny."

'I sat beside her, with a whisky and soda, and she read the entire thing, about twelve or so verses. She was delighted to find confirmation of her ideas in print, so she said. But I felt devastated. I re-read it several times one day, when she was out. The first verse went, and I may not be quoting correctly:

> Excuse me, friends, I must catch my jet –
> I'm off to join the development set;
> My bags are packed, and I've had all my shots,
> I have traveller's cheques and pills for the trots.
> The development set is bright and noble,
> Our thoughts are deep and our vision global;
> Although we move with the better classes,
> Our thoughts are always with the masses . . .

'You're giggling, Pavana . . . it *is* funny, all right, I admit it. No, Pavana, at the time, I didn't laugh! Maybe I was, am, stuffy, but I didn't find it funny then, or now. And I was hurt, and furious.

'Later that night, during and after dinner, Dora continued her harangue, on and on – it was a way she had, which I absolutely hated –

about the shortcomings of my profession, my life's work, everything I live for. Finally it got too much, and I threw my plate violently into the air, the food – I forget what it was – splattering against the wall, the table, Dora's hair, everywhere. And I shouted, my God, how I shouted. She was alarmed. As you know, I'm not given to violence of any sort.

'"Tut, tut, Ju," she said, "If I didn't know your sterling qualities, I'd say you'd had much too much to drink. Best be careful, old boy, alcoholism is endemic to your profession, isn't it?"

'Other times, she'd spend entire days at the club, playing tennis with her friends, swimming, and drinking of course. On the nights we entertained, she'd plunge herself into an orgy of housekeeping, working herself up to fever pitch, raging at the servants, driving them on to ever more perfect dinner party productions, making them shine the brass trays and the copper until they glittered, that sort of thing.

'One evening, it was one of her better days, I urged her to go to Nairobi, or to the Masai Mara, or to any of the places in Kenya that she loved, to try and pull herself together. She did go, spent about three months there, that's where she met Ken, the fellow she hopes to marry, totally English of course, lives in England, travels back and forth frequently. I don't know for sure what he does, never asked.

'She was a lot better after her return. Our quarrels became more infrequent, but they never entirely stopped. One night we had a huge quarrel. Basil must have overheard. We were very noisy. Dora, that same night, began drinking again, for the first time in several weeks. I felt it was because she was so idle, bored, had been for months, and I said so. Well, yes, I had said it several times, Pavana.

'I remember her saying, among other things, that she didn't know the language, couldn't learn yet another one even more difficult than the last, and wasn't living the life she wanted to live. She wanted us to pack it all in and return to England. I tried to explain why I couldn't, my commitment to my work, but she said it was all a "load of codswallop", and that she had decided to leave, and would take Basil with her.

'I was livid. I took her by the shoulders and begged her to reconsider, for Basil's sake if not for mine. I went to close the double doors so Basil wouldn't come in, and when I turned around she was pointing a gun at me, wanting me to leave at once, that very night. I suppose Ken must have given her the gun. She was convinced that I intended to harm her. Strange how people you care about deeply can become your enemies,

207

eh, Pavana? I was fighting mostly to keep Basil, although I did love her very much.

'But my kind of love, well, I suppose I am a little, maybe, quite dull. She never understood how hard and long I'd struggled simply to reach where I am now. Anyway, I lost the battle of course; moved into another house until they finally left. I still miss Basil, especially on school occasions like tonight. I don't know if Dora has stopped drinking and I worry very much, even miss her too, sometimes.

'She could be very good company when she wanted to be. She claims to be able to offer Basil a more stable home life, regular schooling and so on, than I can. To be fair, Basil did want to go with his mother. They were good friends, so far as I could see. So there you are.'

And afterwards, in silence, hand in hand, they'd walked back to the school, entering the auditorium filled with the haunting trilling of the pan flutes. They had sat in the numbered chairs, still holding hands, waiting for the curtain to rise on that term's theatrical production, the cool sweet night air stealing through the open doors.

Julian had kept his eyes averted from hers for a while, his head turned towards the outdoors, gazing at the stars, at the splendour of the African night. There had been many such bitter-sweet hours, and times, and days, and evenings with Julian for the three of them, and she supposed that the twins, although they rarely spoke of them, must be plagued with these memories, too.

Chapter 36

In the air-conditioned studio of Radio Belize, about mid-morning the following Monday, Pavana was preparing to broadcast an interview she had taped with one of the women attending the workshop in Burrell Boom the previous day. She was seated at a table beside Elsie Rodriquez, a programme organizer, who smiled reassuringly as the red light flashed and a technician signalled through the huge pane of glass. A medley of folksongs indicated the start of the programme.

'Good morning, everyone. This is Pavana Leslie presenting your

Weekly Forum, a programme in which we discuss the contribution women make, and can make, to the development of our country, region and world.

'Last week, you will remember, we interviewed a successful shop-keeper in Corozal, who explained to us the way in which she started her now thriving grocery store, and how she conducts her growing business. Today we have a recorded interview with Sarita Williams, who attended the Women's Unit workshop held in Boom yesterday.'

Elsie and Pavana sat quietly as the tape began.

'Good afternoon, Mrs Williams, it's good to be having lunch with you in the lovely riverside village of Boom. I am happy you felt able to attend our workshop today.'

'Good morning. I am glad to be here, too. It makes a nice change for me and for the other women. We don't get out much. The truck picked us up right on time.'

'What is your life like in Hicatee Landing, Mrs Williams?'

'My life? What can I say? We live as we live. There is no road to our small settlement so our life is quiet. We have no complaints.'

'Tell us a little about your family, Mrs Williams.'

'My family? Well, God has been good to me and my family. Of course we work hard, but we are mostly healthy. My husband and I have ten children, and we are grateful for them.' She laughed. 'Sometimes I give them a little trouble you know. My mouth is a little fast. So my husband has to punish me sometimes, but I deserve it. He punishes me because he loves me. He's not like some who beat their wives for little or nothing, especially when they are drunk. My husband says I talk too much. He likes a quiet woman. I keep trying to improve my ways.'

'How do you manage with so many children, Mrs Williams? I suppose the older ones help you a lot?'

'Oh yes, especially with the water-carrying you know, gathering firewood for cooking, all those kinds of things. The river is a ways from our house. We have no vat as yet, only drums to catch the rain, and when those run out, the children go back and forth. They also help my husband with the little planting and so on. And of course I do a little bit myself.'

'How many daughters and sons do you have, how are they divided, I mean?'

Mrs Williams's laughter rang out again. 'We have five daughters and five sons. God sent all our daughters first, which made my husband very unhappy with me. He and I, well we'd both hoped for a boy or two first. Everybody wants that, don't they? But finally God answered our prayers and hard work. We had the five boys in a row, too. It's quite a joke on the Landing. As I said, we are very happy.'

'How did you manage with schooling for your children?'

'Oh, sometimes, when we could spare them, they came here to Boom for school. They walked. It's only a few miles. Sometimes, if we had money, they used the bus or the truck. The mobile clinic used to visit us, but that's broken down now. No spare parts as yet, but it'll soon be fixed.'

'You seem quite contented with your life, Mrs Williams. But is there anything you would have done differently, if you could start all over again?'

'Oh, no. I am quite content. God is good, the government is good, people are good. I have no complaints, as I have said.'

'Did you dream of doing anything else when you were a younger woman? Do you dream of anything now?'

'Dream? I don't dream too much any more now. When I was younger and my first children were babies, I used to dream like everyone else. I used to dream of piped water outside the door of our house so I could get a little time to sew. Of course, the children are bigger now, but I suffer from stomach pains some days, and my eyes aren't too good any more. I used to dream of a kerosene stove, that I do remember. We have a fire hearth, which is good enough. I realize that now.'

'Well, it's been a privilege to talk with you, Mrs Williams, and I am really glad you came to our workshop. What made you decide to attend?'

'Well, as I said, it's a nice break, a chance to see some of the other women and talk with them. My eldest daughter is the one who encouraged me to come here with her. She didn't want to come alone. She is still a young mother, you know, and she still dreams of things like electricity, running water, a flush toilet and a telephone. She hopes the workshop will help us.'

'Thank you very much for talking with us today, Mrs Williams. I hope your daughter's dreams come true and that you feel better really soon.'

'I enjoyed the workshop, especially the lunch, that was very good.'

The technician signalled, and Pavana concluded the programme.

'Next week, we will be talking with Elvira Jones, a mother and teacher in Boom. Until then, think about your own needs and aspirations and those of your families. Discuss them with each other. Write to us about them, and we'll try to read as many letters as possible. I hope the rest of your day goes as you hope it will. Until next week, this is Pavana Leslie saying goodbye.'

As the folksong melody was repeated at the end of the programme, Pavana followed Elsie from the studio. In the corridor, Elsie asked, 'Do you have a few minutes?'

'Yes, sure,' she replied, following Elsie to her office.

Elsie offered Pavana a seat and then sat behind her desk, situated between two windows overlooking a busy intersection of Regent Street near the Court House, Independence Park and other government buildings. Tape recordings, scripts, files and papers covered her desk, bookcase and a nearby table. Pavana sat on the edge of her chair, anxious to return to the Women's Unit where she had meetings scheduled for most of the day.

'We are getting a tremendous response to the programme,' Elsie said, handing Pavana a packet of letters. 'It's educational, and I like your interviews with the rural women. Today's was one of the best yet.'

'Thanks,' Pavana said, examining the envelopes.

'I hope they allow us to continue it,' Elsie said, getting up to stand by the window. 'Good Christ,' she said softly, peering down at the soldiers positioned at intervals all around the station. 'This place is getting more and more like a concentration camp with every day that passes. Soldiers on the roof, at the bottom of the stairs, at the entrance. I don't know how much more of this I can take.'

She turned around, jerking her head in the direction of the Chief Programme Organizer's office.

'Belmopan phoned just before you arrived today.'

'What's up?' Pavana asked.

'Nothing yet, but someone, probably some foot-licking permanent secretary, phoned to say that from now on all my programmes should be more upbeat, positive, more in line with the new and progressive revolution, whatever that means.'

'I try to present balanced programmes,' Pavana said cautiously.

211

'Oh, I know you do. But they want something that praises the good works of the ministry. They're not interested in the needs and aspirations of women, which they interpret as criticism, or complaints at the very least.

'In any case, I told them I wouldn't change the format of the programme. If the Information Office wants to broadcast propaganda hour after hour, they can do that themselves.'

'What do we do now?' Pavana asked, thinking of the other tapes she'd made.

'We'll keep going for as long as we can.'

'That's brave of you.'

'It's not brave. I just don't care any more. I started out in this job as enthusiastic and full of ideas as you are right now. And look at me, my hands are shaking and I practically jump out of my skin every time the telephone rings. There must be a less stressful way to earn a living. The demonstrations have only made the paranoia around here that much worse.'

'I am sorry the programme is adding to your difficulties.'

'Don't be sorry. It's my last act of defiance, you might say.'

'Last?'

'I'm getting out of here before I lose my personality altogether.'

As Elsie walked with her to the top of the stairs, Pavana had a fluttery feeling in the pit of her stomach. Elsie was an ardent supporter of the ruling party, and something more than she had let on must have occurred, because Pavana had always found Elsie to be exactly what she'd said was wanted – positive, upbeat, and all for the new and progressive revolution.

'Good luck, Elsie.'

'The same to you,' Elsie called, returning swiftly down the corridor.

A soldier, face impassive, gun slung across his shoulder, unlocked the door leading to the street. Pavana eased herself through the narrow opening. Outside the door about two or three hundred people milled up and down, carrying protest signs, keeping vigil at the radio station, which still had not reported any news about the ongoing protests against the heads of agreement.

As she continued her way down the narrow lane, someone in the crowd muttered, 'Traitor.' Keeping her face neutral, Pavana turned into Regent Street and began walking towards the north side of town where

212

the unit's office was located. But the single word uttered by an anonymous voice in the crowd had found its mark, reminding Pavana of an unpleasant exchange between Brenda Kirkwood and herself at the end of the workshop the previous day.

Chapter 37

Burrell Boom is a picturesque village on the Belize River, famous for its plentiful cashew trees, nuts and wine. During the days of its prosperity, many years before, Boom was one of the sites in the country used as a trapping point for logs floating downstream. At the Community Centre, shortly before eight o'clock that Sunday morning, Pavana, Brenda, Vicky, Mrs Carillo and other ministry personnel worked with community members to get the centre prepared for the workshop, scheduled to begin a mid-morning.

Pots of fern decorated the front of the hall, and women helped to stick posters on the wall and to arrange tables, benches and chairs. As they completed their task, truckloads of people began arriving from the outlying towns and villages. The panellists, experts on health, education, employment and the law, spoke with the villagers about the situation of Belizean women.

The daylong workshop turned out to be a very lively one. As the afternoon discussion was drawing to a close Pavana, tape recorder in hand, sat with Brenda and a group of women near the front of the hall, listening to a participant from Bermudian Landing.

'Radio Belize says we are to unite to build a nation.' The villagers, in a holiday mood, laughed loudly again. The whole day had gone much better than Pavana had dared hope. 'But tell me something, Nurse, are we supposed to have more and more children? We have been doing that for years but the population hardly grows at all. The young people go to America, or wherever, as soon as they can, because there are no jobs for them.'

'I am from Double Head Cabbage,' another woman rose to say. 'Every so often we get government workers out here, no offence meant, you understand, asking us these same questions, having meetings and what not, but we don't see that much improvement in our lives. We need the training that's been promised us for so long to use what we have better, and to learn new ways of making money for our needs.'

A member of the Crooked Tree Women's Group added, 'Don't think we are ungrateful. We think government is doing a great job allowing us to have these workshops and things to express our ideas. Miss Leslie said earlier that the Women's Unit is our voice. Well, we are going to try and use it, if it is still going when we get ready to say something.' The villagers laughed again, knowingly.

'However, one meeting like this is not enough. We need regular meetings. You have heard our views about family planning, health problems, the school, electricity, water and so on. What we want to know is what does this new Women's Unit plan to do to make a change in our situation?'

In her response, at the formal close of the workshop, Pavana thanked all those who had participated and then continued, 'Our job here today is to record the needs and aspirations which you have expressed, and to incorporate them into a five-year plan which we hope to present to the ministries for the necessary action. The research officer, when appointed, will begin the work necessary to document the situation of Belizean women from the viewpoint of Belizeans. The training officer, using the small amount of money at our disposal, will continue to organize more workshops, based on the needs and aspirations expressed by women all over the country.

'This does not seem like very much, I agree, when basic needs for the most part have not been met. It is not enough, as you have said, to present reports. The Women's Unit will need your participation in the design and implementation of programmes and projects not only for women, but for the country as a whole. Women need to become an integral part of the decision-making process, to make sure that money spent by government is used to upgrade not only the situation of women but of their families as well. As you know, this has not always been the case.

'But this is still not enough. You must know your real needs and your aspirations for the future. Your voices must demand change, and you must be willing to take an active role in the challenges ahead of us.

'This may mean that women's groups with common interests and goals will need to come together, to lobby your political representatives or to travel to Belmopan to make your views known. It is said that the development of a country comes from within a people, not from without. Change in our lives, if change is what we need and want, must be done by ourselves.

'Our desire to improve our situation must be so strong that we are willing to take great risks to help devise ways and means to improve the way we live for ourselves, our families, the country, the region, even the world. However, I believe that we can do it, if we continue to strive together. We can't be afraid. Tell the politicians you meet, at every opportunity, about our workshop here today, and about your expectations for the future.

'On behalf of the Women's Unit, I can only pledge our determination, during the years ahead, to assist the women of Belize in overcoming the obstacles in the path of our development. This we shall try to do for all women, regardless of race, colour, creed or political persuasion.

'In the final analysis, however, as officers in the unit will come and go, it is the women of Belize as a whole who must devise strategies to ensure that the unit continues to do the work for which it was designed. I thank you.'

As the afternoon wore on, the hall seemed to become more crowded. A 'boom and shine' band struck up a familiar tune. People began singing and Pavana, Brenda, Vicky, ministry personnel and the panellists joined the circle of men and women dancing around the room singing at the top of their voices.

'We are women, we can do it if we try, we are women, we must strive, but never cry.' As the musicians packed away their instruments, Vicky, hair streaming out behind her and her face flushed with triumph, came rushing over.

'Wasn't that just the way, Pavana! Aren't you glad now that you took the job?' Pavana nodded, and Vicky continued, 'Boy, I'm so thrilled to be in on the start of something like this. Listen, I've been offered a ride back with a few women, ministry women, to Belize City. Do you mind if I go ahead?'

'No, onward and upwards,' Pavana laughed. 'See you next week.'

'Right,' Vicky called excitedly, and she was away.

It had been a most exhilarating and rewarding day. It was hard for Pavana to believe that in Belize City and in other parts of the country the agitation against the heads of agreement was still continuing, but it was and everyone knew it.

Since the weekend at Pelican Island, she had had no word from Alex, Stoner nor Moria, who was not present at the workshop but Pavana had not expected her to be. Pavana felt as if a great burden had been removed from her shoulders. She could begin now to build a new life for the twins and herself. And the workshop that afternoon had shown her the direction she should take in the immediate future.

For about an hour Pavana and the others helped the villagers to clear the hall. As they worked, she began thinking about setting up smaller meetings with women leaders to address the issues which had come up at this workshop, and the ones held before by Mrs Elrington and Mrs Carillo.

As they walked across the grass towards the bus belonging to the Women's Unit, Brenda, laughter in her voice, called loud enough to be heard by Mrs Carillo and Ferdie Williams, the male head of the Income Generating Unit.

'That was quite a performance, Pavana! And here was I thinking you'd be shy onstage in front of two hundred women. Talk about hidden talents!'

Although it was supposedly said in humour, and Brenda's smile was very much in evidence, neither the look in her eyes nor the mocking lilt to her voice was altogether complimentary.

'Yes, very nicely done,' Mrs Carillo said, panting and wheezing as she hurried fretfully towards the bus. 'Oh, I do hope I won't be too late to catch my bus to Belmopan. I don't want to sleep in Belize City tonight. My family . . .'

'You were as good as the minister, Pavana,' Brenda interrupted as they took their seats in the bus, Pavana beside the driver and the others to the rear. Pavana could hear the rattle of Brenda's necklace of shells as she settled herself between Mrs Carillo and Ferdie.

'Oh, better, certainly better,' Ferdie added, blowing the smoke from his cigar through the window. He was the type of person who seemed always to have three or four times the salary he actually did. Pavana often wondered how he did it.

He was overweight, flashily dressed, his fingers weighted down with rings. Looked at from a certain angle, though, he could be considered good looking. His smooth dark skin was unblemished as a baby's, his thick black hair barbered in the latest fashion. Ferdie was very obviously taken with Brenda's style, but Pavana had experienced the greatest difficulty in getting him to discuss in any depth the income-generating projects for women groups which he supervised.

'All the projects are doing very well, extremely well. You must come visit one of them with me some day.'

Pavana had been unable as yet to pin him down to a specific date for visiting any of his projects. But she had heard Mrs Carillo muttering about a chicken project in the Cayo District which was not doing at all well.

Brenda's voice could be heard, Pavana was sure, right to the back seat of the bus.

'I mean the poor women must have been stunned, absolutely stunned, Pavana – all that extremely stimulating talk at the beginning of the workshop about drafting a proposal for the establishment of a women's communication network, training in non-traditional fields of endeavour, and what not.'

As the bus stopped briefly to let out a few villagers who had been attending the workshop, Ferdie said, 'The Information Department won't be too happy to hear about the competition from this new network you are planning, Pavana.' He laughed. 'They're bound to think you're trying to set up an alternative government. It won't be popular with them, I promise you.'

Brenda chuckled at the very thought.

'I wonder what the minister will say when he hears about all this excitement?' she asked. 'I almost had the feeling that I was at a BWDO rally during election time.'

As the bus moved off again, Pavana turned around to face the three people in the seat behind her. Mrs Carillo was dozing, her head bobbing up and down on her chest with every jolt of the bus on the rutted road.

The windows were open, and Brenda had one hand on her hair in an effort to keep it from blowing forward. She and Ferdie were smiling at each other, the perfume from his cigar filling the bus. Although Pavana was growing quite angry, she managed to keep her voice mild as she said, 'Well, Brenda, I hope you'll let us know the minister's reaction to the workshop as soon as you talk with him. It would be useful to have that information as we review our plan of action later this week. By the way, did you enjoy the reception at Pelican Island?'

217

Brenda did not immediately reply, but Ferdie asked, 'Pelican Island? How did you get invited to that shinding, Brenda? I thought it was held by the Tourism Association for ministers, permanent secretaries and that ilk?'

Ferdie, who jealously guarded any privileges associated with the Income Generating Unit, looked at Brenda, waiting for her reply.

She shrugged her shoulders.

'Oh well, Ferdie, you know how it is. I just happened to be out there that weekend, and met the minister and his wife in the hotel restaurant, quite by accident really. They invited me to join them. I didn't see you out there, Pavana.'

'Oh, we move in different circles, I'm sure,' Pavana said, forcing a laugh into her voice. 'Oh, and did you notice, Brenda, that both women's groups from the political parties were represented at the workshop?'

'Oh my God,' Brenda was saying, clapping her hand against her forehead. 'I am so glad BWDO turned up, after all! Do you know, I'd forgotten to telephone again. I blame you, Pavana, too much to do, too much excitement.'

'At that rate, Beulah Stephenson will soon chuck you out of the Belize Women's Democratic Organization,' Pavana said, raising her voice. 'I understand she runs an efficient shop.' Mrs Carillo raised her head and said sleepily, 'Didn't know public officers could belong, Brenda?'

'I'm not exactly a member,' Brenda said. 'I just go along there occasionally to help them organize their groups, and what not. Besides, except for you, Rosa, we're not exactly public officers yet, are we?'

'Well, well,' Ferdie said, throwing his cigar through the window. He fell silent. Mrs Carillo leaned her head against the back of the seat and closed her eyes. There was no amusement in Brenda's face as she stared steadily at Pavana, who said, 'Your talk today was excellent, Brenda. And everything was so well organized in your group.'

'Thanks,' she said, shifting her gaze to the road. She was silent for the remainder of the drive, but it didn't take much imagination to speculate that she was probably already planning her strategies for the days ahead.

Pavana did not delude herself into thinking that she was any match for Brenda. She could even imagine a scenario where one day Brenda would become the Unit's director. As the bus rolled along the winding

218

roads, she discovered something new and exhilarating about herself. Although she greatly valued her position as director, the thought of losing it did not scare her, nor did it unduly dismay her in any way.

She would not try to compete with Brenda; she would not try to emulate her strategies, which Pavana was sure she couldn't do successfully in any case. And it did not matter whether Brenda or anyone else thought her values were the values of a simpleton. She would simply, or not so simply, continue trying to do her best for as long as she could.

Chapter 38

From her desk the view through the louvred windows of her office in Belmopan, beyond the low bank of red hibiscus, was of the House of Representatives, overlooking a broad plaza, other ministries and a variety of administrative buildings. Gathering up her notes, Pavana walked along the corridor to the permanent secretary's office for the meeting which he had requested. In the sunny room, P.S. Kelly continued leafing through his files while Pavana sat in a comfortable chair, well below the level of his desk, observing the blue hills in the distance.

A young, pretty junior officer, who worked in the long-established Home Economics Unit, entered the room breezily, ignoring Pavana. With a great flourish she set before him a plate of hot *panades*, made of raw corn tortillas stuffed with beans or fish, folded and then fried. Dressed in a tight blue dress, she sat on the arm of his chair, brushing invisible specks from the collar of his spotless white shirt.

As she watched Marion's weekly ritual of ministering to the P.S., Pavana reflected that if she had been able to advocate for the advancement of the Women's Unit with the occasional home-made cake, tamales or potato pound, particular favourites of the permanent secretary, her early weeks at the unit might have evolved differently.

P.S. Edward Kelly munched appreciatively, dipping a half-moon stuffed with fish into the small dish of burning hot red peppers and diced onions floating in brown vinegar. He offered the plate to Pavana who, looking at the hypocritical smile and the cold, watery brown eyes, and at Marion's measured gaze, shook her head.

'Good, P.S.?' Marion asked.

'Mmmmm, hot, just as I like it,' he replied, wiping his fingers on an immaculate handkerchief.

'I got up before light to make them. I wanted to surprise you.'

'Thank you, Marion. I always remember how you take care of me. Do you make *panades*, Miss Leslie?' Pavana shook her head.

'You should ask Home Economics to teach you. They invite me to complete dinners in their kitchens every so often. I always enjoy myself at these demonstrations of their skill.'

Leaning forward to look into his face, Marion said, 'I was thinking, P.S.'

'Yes, Marion,' he said, continuing to flip the pages of the Women's Unit file.

'We need a vehicle to attend a cake-decorating workshop in Benque Viejo.'

'What's happened to the Home Ec. bus?'

'Not working, P.S. We are waiting for spare parts.'

'Again? That bus is always in the workshop.'

'You know how the roads are, P.S. They break up the vehicle, and we travel back and forth such a lot.'

'You'll have to wait until the Home Ec. bus is fixed, then, Marion.'

'Oh, but P.S., we told them we were coming today. Couldn't we borrow Miss Leslie's vehicle? The Unit isn't doing anything today, and we'll be back by four.'

The P.S. looked a bit sheepish as he patted the soft hand on his shoulder.

'You are a good messenger, Marion. I hate to refuse you anything. I may really have to recommend to the minister that we promote you to that vacant Home Economics Officer position in Toledo.'

Marion did not look particularly thrilled at the prospect of a permanent assignment in Toledo, the southernmost district, often inaccessible by road during the rainy season.

'That sounds good, P.S.,' she said, doubtfully, 'but the bus, we need a vehicle today. The officer in Benque needs the equipment we borrowed.'

Pavana listened to the exchange intently, shifting her eyes to the distant hills. Part of her job was to facilitate training for the Home Economics Officers so that eventually they would become Women and Development Officers. But already she could see that Mrs Elrington's plan would not be so easily effected. It would take a number of years, and may even have been ill-conceived.

Most of the women enjoyed their work as Home Economics Officers, pensionable positions firmly fixed within the bureaucracy, with the possibility of promotion to other positions like that of Welfare Officer, to which many of them aspired.

The title of Women and Development Officer was not yet a pensionable post, and who knew if it was ever likely to become one? Although they had been assured that they would not lose their pensions, many of the Home Economics Officers were not so sure they wouldn't, and Pavana could well understand their fears. Besides, as far as people like Marion could see, it was a lot more study and work for exactly the same pay.

The Permanent Secretary tapped his fingernails reflectively on the side of the empty plate which he pushed away. He looked through the window at the office block across the Plaza, where the Premier's office was located. It would soon be time for his weekly briefing and he was becoming restive. He glanced towards Pavana, but she continued to stare through the window.

'Miss Leslie obviously needs the vehicle today, Marion, to attend a number of meetings here and in Belize City.'

'Oh, P.S., you are letting me down,' Marion said, pushing out her lips in mock reproach.

The P.S. rose from his desk, placing his arm around her neck.

'For my sake, Marion, try to get the Home Ec. bus on the road. I'll see now whether I can borrow a vehicle you can use today.'

'I knew you wouldn't let us down, P.S.!' Marion said triumphantly. 'I'll bring you a nice pound cake today from Benque.'

'Do you make pound cake, Miss Leslie?' the P.S. asked, giving Marion a gentle push through the door. His eyes as he spoke were deliberately wide, friendly, but not sufficiently so that Pavana did not catch in them definite displeasure.

He sat down again, idly turning the pages of the file.

'Miss Leslie,' he said, his voice pained, reluctant. 'About the radio programme . . . I've been glancing through the scripts in this file, and I can't see a single reference to the Ministry nor to the Minister, who is displeased about that omission.'

'I'll try to remedy that in the future, P.S.'

'It's not only those omissions to which the minister objects, although he'll be delighted to hear that the omission of his name and his Ministry was an oversight.' He made his eyes surprised and innocent. 'Though how you could forget the Minister's name and his ministry I can hardly imagine, Miss Leslie.'

'I did consider the matter carefully, P.S., and decided that the radio programme would receive a more positive response if it was presented as an educational programme rather than . . .'

'You should have consulted me, Miss Leslie. Are you suggesting that our Minister's name, our Ministry, one that serves the public with so much sacrifice, so much dedication, might harm your radio programme in some way?'

Pavana watched the P.S. warily. He was extremely cunning and she didn't trust him in the least. She asked, 'Did you say the Minister has other objections to the radio programme, P.S.? Women all over the country are responding enthusiastically. They so badly need to be recognized for their contribution to the development of Belize. They are particularly concerned about its economic development, in which they need to participate more fully . . .'

'Please, Miss Leslie,' the P.S. said raising a hand for silence. 'Please, I wish you would try a little harder to understand that you are working for government. Expectations are being raised which the Minister feels cannot be fulfilled.'

He paused, listening to raised voices in the Minister's office. He glanced at the doorway and then, satisfied that the Minister did not need his assistance in his meeting with Mrs Elrington, lowered his voice confidentially, persuasively.

'Let's start all over again. The Minister gets no credit and he is understandably a little upset.'

'The response we've had is exactly because we've made no explicit reference to the Ministry.'

'Please, Miss Leslie,' the P.S. said wincing. 'There are no stars in a government bureaucracy. We work behind and through the political figures. That's a difficult lesson to learn, I know, for people like yourself entering Government Service at your age and at this level. I have made

222

a number of allowances for that, and given you a great deal of latitude. Try to be a little less of a one-man – pardon me, one-woman – band. We work in concert, so to speak.'

He chuckled and Pavana tried to smile, but it was too difficult.

'P.S., are you implying that the minister feels that I am using the radio programme as a medium for my personal advancement?'

'Oh no, not deliberately of course. We wouldn't dream of accusing you of that. Nevertheless, that is what the minister is beginning to feel. He is such a thoughtful man, too, quite understanding of your position, your inexperience, your commitment. Do you know what he said to me last evening while we were together at a function in his constituency? The minister is a great one for working long and late hours, as you know.'

'I know, P.S.'

'He said, "P.S., we must assist Miss Leslie, guide her, bring her into the fold, into the Ministry family. She is a committed and hard worker. Help her to see our point of view. Maybe we could start with the radio scripts, P.S.?" That's what the minister said, always a generous, forgiving man.'

A look of scepticism must have crossed Pavana's face for the Permanent Secretary said, his voice slow, casual, 'One of your own officers, Miss Kirkwood, was present during our conversation.'

Pavana swallowed.

'Does he want the programme censored?'

'Miss Leslie,' the P.S. said, growing exasperated. 'Why must you choose these unfortunate words? All I am suggesting is that in future I read the scripts, suggest a few changes here and there, if they are needed, and indicate a number of progressive women who could be interviewed, nothing drastic, you understand?'

'I think what you are saying is absolutely disgraceful.'

'I've spent a lifetime in the service of the government, and I've seen programmes come and go, people, too. People, newcomers especially, seem to always insist on re-inventing the wheel. You'll get used to it, in time.'

'I don't think I'll ever be able to do so.'

'I've seen that also,' the permanent secretary agreed. 'But you're upset at the moment. Try not to say anything you'll regret later. For the next programme, my suggestion is that you get Mrs Carillo to help you include some recipes, and interviews with women in her programme, also in Mr Ferdie Williams's. They'll suggest the right people.

'Mention that it's a six-month series. At some point you can interview the Minister, at another time Mrs Elrington – who is definitely retiring around the time the series will end – some of the people in the ministry, and so on. I'd be quite willing myself to be interviewed, if you get stuck for a programme one week.'

'At this rate, the unit will subside into mediocrity, into another government programme that does little innovative to inspire . . .'

'Who instructed you to create innovative programmes?' When Pavana didn't reply, he added, 'You are presuming too much. Don't try to rush change, that's my advice. You're creating enemies, playing into the hands of people who want you out of this job, numerous in this Ministry, I might add.'

The Permanent Secretary rose to his feet, setting the files into his out basket. As Pavana walked towards the doorway, he said, 'After this crisis is over, I'll arrange for you to have a discussion with the Minister. He's indicated he wants to speak with you, Mrs Elrington and, I believe, Miss Kirkwood.'

'Do you suppose he wants the workshops stopped, too, P.S.?'

'I have no idea, Miss Leslie. Good afternoon.'

Chapter 39

Sacred Heart was one of those schools which did not voluntarily close on Tuesday 31 March, the day of the countrywide strike, the scale and intensity of which took many people by surprise. Belizeans are prone to talking a lot, often harshly, but frequent and violent public demonstrations are not among their shortcomings.

Shortly before nine o'clock that morning, another brilliantly sunny day, Pavana and her students watched in mounting tension as the crowd of picketers on Orchid Street gradually grew larger, noiser. Six young men, neatly dressed in white shirts and dark blue trousers, leaned their bicycles against the rotting fence of the vacant house opposite, which

Pavana only a few weeks before had hoped to purchase in partnership with Gail and Robert. That dream had all but vanished, like the beautiful red helium balloon she had once bought with great delight at a church bazaar, shortly before one Christmas when she was about eleven years old.

On that long-ago afternoon, as she made her way across the dry and flattened grass, jostled by the crowds around the stalls, enticed by the tinkling bell of an ice-cream cart, the lovely balloon was suddenly whipped out of her fingers by an unusually strong gust of wind from the sea. She stood helplessly in the throng, gazing in consternation as the balloon rose skyward, higher and higher above her head, its string wriggling like a slender river snake. Pavana watched as it drifted away, feeling a sense of inestimable loss, and a sensation that she still held the string in her hand even while admitting to herself that the balloon had never seemed so desirable.

Shading her eyes from the rays of the sun, leaning her head back as far as it would go, she followed the progress of the balloon until it vanished, or burst, she wasn't sure which, far away from view. Afterwards, she wandered disconsolately up and down the aisles of the bazaar, her white socks sliding down into her shoes, the ground already littered with crumpled paper cups, drinking straws, bottles, scraps of sandwiches and cake.

The old-fashioned waltzes and military music blaring from scratchy gramophone records grated on her nerves, contributing to her feeling of disorientation. Even the two clowns in the children's tent, bumbling around in oversized army boots and repeatedly colliding with each other, shaking their pink woollen wigs in bewilderment, had lost their power to amuse.

Night falls swiftly in December, and shortly before leaving the bazaar she paused to buy one last chance at a fake fish pond, feeling oddly diminished and melancholy. She'd had to remind herself several times that it was only a silly old balloon, and that with three whole dollars remaining in the navy blue plastic purse, slung for security over her head and across her chest, she could still buy another one – two, if she wished; only she hadn't bothered that afternoon, nor at any of the other numerous fairs and bazaars of her childhood.

On her return home shortly before it was completely dark, she'd found her mother ironing clothes in the tiny washroom to the rear of the heated kitchen, redolent with the scent of black fruit cakes baking in the oven. Pavana had spent the entire morning shelling pecans, cutting them into tiny bits, and beating batter with a wooden spoon in a huge white enamel pan until her wrists ached. As a reward, she'd been allowed to go on her own, a rare treat, to the bazaar.

Without meaning to, Pavana found herself telling her mother about the loss of the lovely red helium balloon. Her mother, very thin then, with curly, greying, shoulder-length hair, did not say very much, but seemed to understand very well about the loss of helium balloons for she smiled ruefully and after a moment or so, said:

> 'What can a tired heart say?
> Which the wise world have made dumb?
> Save to the lonely dreams of a child,
> Return again, come?'

'Did you make that up?' Pavana asked, rinsing her hands under the tap. Her mother could make up lots of things and she did write sad poems sometimes. Pavana's fingers and palms were sticky from cut-o-brute, coconut tableta and the other sweets she had eaten compulsively, and in excessive quantities.

'No. We had to memorize that poem in school when I was about your age. I think a man called de la Mare wrote it.'

'Oh ho,' Pavana said, feeling strangely comforted. Lots of people, it seemed, understood how terribly sad it felt to lose a helium balloon, and hers had been an especially nice one, rosy-red, blown to just the right size. She'd never forgotten the poet's name either because it reminded her of a horse.

'Why didn't you buy another one?' her father asked, when he came home not too long afterwards. He sat on a dining-room chair, his back to the window overlooking Miss Erline's garden, twirling his straw hat around and around between his slender fingers, his forehead creased with the stress of another day's driving up and down the countryside.

'It wouldn't have been the same, would it?' Pavana asked.

'I suppose that's true,' he said, biting his underlip thoughtfully. 'Dreams come in different sizes, shapes, colours and feelings, not less valuable but different, don't they?'

Pavana nodded. It seemed her father, as great a reader as his wife, also understood about the loss of helium balloons.

Her parents had married young and it could only have been for love, since at the time neither had many pennies to spare. They seemed to have remained 'in love', and if one loved the other more, as is often the case in marriages, it was not discernible to the naked eye, at least not to Pavana's.

They had always regarded Pavana's survival as an absolute miracle, one which, with every birthday successfully reached, grew to mythological proportions. For of Carrie's several pregnancies and births – the precise number a closely guarded secret – Pavana alone remained.

For this deliverance from her 'wasteland of pregnancies', Carrie conducted perpetual thankful novenas to Our Lady of the Immaculate Conception, whose statue, three feet tall, occupied a specially constructed niche in the dining-room. Under her benign gaze, Pavana had eaten most of her meals during her last two years at home, as one would do with an aunt or a female cousin who had nowhere else to go, and who showed little inclination of wanting to go anywhere, or do anything else, except to stand on a marble pedestal, veiled and vestal, looking serene and sweet.

Pavana had taken to telling Lisa and Eric, whenever they were visiting Pavana's parents, that the statue was put into their lives as a test of their characters, of their patience, their tolerance, and that they should show themselves equal to its presence. And their endurance and tolerance should extend to the flowers, the candles and the incense, which did not, absolutely could not, affect the taste of their food, which they were to eat, all of it. And the candles and incense did not burn all day, every day, that was wilful exaggeration on their part.

'They do so nearly,' Lisa had giggled, hugging her carryall on her lap, as they'd driven north last December to spend the Christmas holidays with Pavana's parents.

'Except when Gramma and Grampa go out,' Eric said, laughing aloud as he looked eagerly down the road, cheering as Corozal Bay, sparkling in the mid-morning sunshine came at last into view.

Pavana laughed too, glad that the twins could not see her eyes in which some trace of sadness must surely show. She suspected that the candles and incense no longer burned in thanksgiving for her birth alone, but also for Lisa and Eric, referred to by Carrie and Raul (although never in the twins' hearing) as those 'fatherless children', who they considered to have been conceived, born and bred in circumstances far more mysterious to them than the Virgin Birth. However, they accepted Pavana's limited explanations 'in faith and trust', confident that the will of the Father would in time manifest itself.

Still, Pavana's seeming lack of faith and trust in her parents had set up a barrier between them, making many everyday conversations fizzle out, leaving a silence that was sometimes impossible to break. The strain was not quite so obvious when Pavana was with both her parents, but on the occasions when she was alone with either of them it soon became almost unbearable, for each parent hoped to be the one in whom Pavana would at last confide.

When Raul was nearly forty years old, twenty years before, he had left (or been fired from, Pavana was never entirely certain which) his job as manager in the sales department of a large agency which specialized in the importation of heavy equipment. This had come about because, Raul said, and this was all he ever said, 'of political differences between the owner and myself'. As time went on, he forgot 'the details'.

Raul had not been entirely sorry to leave, for he and Carrie had long been dreaming about starting a bus service. They bought a second-hand bus which travelled daily to Corozal Town, returning to Belize City late in the evening. At first Raul drove the bus while Carrie, very efficient with money, managed the makeshift office from their home on Kiskadee Avenue. The bus service prospered, and within six years they were the owners of six second-hand buses which travelled daily to each district in the country.

The continuing success of the bus service surprised even Raul and Carrie, but it enabled them to realize another dream, that of building a home of their own in the curve of Corozal Bay which they named El Paraiso. The house of their dreams was certainly a long way from Kiskadee Avenue in Belize City, and an even longer way from the sleepy village in the Toledo District, near the Guatemalan border, where Carrie and Raul had been born, attended elementary school and been married. They had travelled, a gruelling journey in the back of a truck, to Belize City for their honeymoon, and once there decided to stay.

Raul's and Carrie's parents had died many years before, while Pavana was still a young girl, and so she had no clear memory of them. Raul and Carrie didn't talk very much about their village, absorbed as they were in creating their new lives and rigorously training themselves at night school to become the people they wanted to be.

They had taken Pavana to their village just once, and she had only the vaguest memories now of friendly faces in cool, thatched houses offering her hot tortillas, stewed beans and bits of deliciously spiced meat; of dusty roads; and of swimming in a river in which women and girls swam naked while others washed their clothes, beating them vigorously on the rocks.

However, nowadays Raul sometimes told Eric and Lisa about an uncle whose eyeballs had been kicked out by a horse, or about a cousin of Carrie's who had been quite mad and would throw coins and dollar bills, family savings, into the street from an upstairs window of a ramshackle house. But although Lisa and Eric pestered him, Raul seldom seemed to know the stories in detail and would say, in pathetic tones, that it was such a long time ago, he was sure he had forgotten almost everything.

The loss of her dream house, its windows overlooking Orchid Street where picketers marched militantly up and down, and the memories of the helium balloon had led Pavana to thinking about Julian, who in many ways reminded her of her father. They had the same slender stature, the same sense of responsibility, the same tenacity, the same capacity for hard, grinding work. Julian, too, had offered her a dream, but because it was different from her dream of Alex – the latter an adolescent's dream, really – when all was said and done, she'd carelessly allowed the wind from the Indian Ocean, there at Mosque Bay, to whip it out of her hands. She had not had the wit to hold on to it tightly, not only for herself but for Eric and Lisa, whose dream it had been, too.

Standing there in her sunlit classroom, with the waving shadows of the palm trees on the concrete floor, and the tense faces of thirty-five jittery young women looking to her for guidance in this time of terrible trouble, it was extremely difficult for Pavana to understand that aspect of her character which had led her into making a fetish of Alex, or her idea of Alex, which now seemed to have very little basis in reality, and then swearing fealty to it. But perhaps such is the way of the human heart, or at least some human hearts; and in that moment she regretted afresh that she had not told her parents about Alex. In retrospect, they most certainly would have understood.

229

Chapter **40**

A stone crashing through glass shattered the absolute silence in Pavana's classroom and all over the school. She rushed with her students to the veranda overlooking the grounds, three floors below, just as the crowd, mostly adults muttering angrily, entered the open gates of the compound. The siege had begun.

For the past nine days, following their return from Pelican Island (from which time she'd still had no word from Alex nor from Stoner), there had been continuing violent clashes. Riot squads were unable or unwilling to control the frenzied protesters, driven to uncharacteristic displays of ferocity. People feared they were being unfairly asked to pay a bill they did not owe, and that they were in danger of losing all, or a portion of, their beloved Belize.

Of course, not everyone felt this way. The school administrators didn't. Pavana and a number of other teachers had wanted to close the school. They had in fact not wanted it to open at all on that dreadful morning, which started with a special service at the Wesley Church on Albert Street for those who intended to march in protest against the heads of agreement. By seven o'clock demonstrators were already picketing public buildings. Many schools in the city closed, and hundreds of young people marched through the streets, fully aware that for this action it was quite possible that they could be expelled from school.

When it became obvious that the strike was going to be overwhelmingly successful, those teachers at Sacred Heart who wanted to close the school were faced with the unpalatable choice of going home and possibly losing their jobs, or remaining with their students – which was no choice at all.

In the middle of the compound, a woman with a megaphone was reading a statement.

'We are asking the administration of this school to send the students home in protest against the heads of agreement. We are supporting the strike called by the Public Service Union. If the school is not closed in ten minutes, the Young People's Movement will arrive and forcibly close it.'

Then abruptly the protesting crowd departed, and an ominous silence once again enveloped the school. Across the street young men, small mounds of stones at their feet, stood in readiness.

As Alex had accurately foretold, during that dreadful afternoon on the glass-bottomed boat, the House of Representatives in Belmopan had met the previous Friday afternoon and passed a resolution to hold a referendum on any final treaty. No referendum, however, was to be held on the heads of agreement.

As the seconds ticked by, it became increasingly clear to Pavana that she would probably have the awesome responsibility for the safety of the students in the room, when all she wanted to do was to rush across the grounds to the elementary school and take Lisa and Eric home.

Although her students sat quietly, faces sombre, books on their desks, waiting for the signal that they could leave, the mood in the classroom was rising swiftly to one in which anger, fear and hysteria were mixed. Even the schools, it seemed, were divided along political lines: those that supported the government and those that did not. Tension was evident on the faces turned towards the street where the young men, working industriously, had expanded the range of their arsenal. To the collection of stones they had added clumps of hardened earth, rusty tin cans and empty bottles.

Stepping on to the rear veranda, Pavana looked anxiously towards the elementary school, built in the previous century. There all doors and windows had been closed and barred. Only several axes and a battering ram could break through those doors, but in her classroom the six huge doors, three on either side, made of thick, opaque glass, could be easily breached by any determined force.

Five minutes went by, then six, then ten, and there was still no word from the main office. The earlier decision, to keep the school open, was to stand. Should she defy the authorities and allow the students to leave? It was difficult for her to believe that the school wouldn't be closed in the face of the immediate danger. As she began trying to sort through the implications of letting the students go, Julie, from her vantage point at the back of the room, sprang to her feet.

231

'They're coming now, miss!'

As her classmates rushed to close the doors, Pavana caught a swift glimpse of militant young men, most wearing dark trousers, white shirts and peaked caps, pouring into Orchid Street, marching in determined, orderly lines towards the Sacred Heart compound. The classroom was in an uproar as students dragged desks across the room, erecting barricades at the doors.

'Leave one door clear so we can leave quickly if necessary,' Pavana called above the tumult, trying to speak calmly, although this unprecedented situation was threatening to bring her to the edge of panic, not so much for herself as for the safety of her students and Eric and Lisa. Violence, even the thought of violence, revived the sickening memory of the harpoon in her hand, the wound she had inflicted on Stoner, the blood trickling down his back.

Although she had probably prevented Stoner from fatally injuring Alex, the look on Stoner's face before he dived overboard left her in no doubt that he considered that she had sided with Alex and Moria. This was not entirely the case, but then the events of that afternoon had not been conducive to rational thought. It worried her that Stoner had placed her in the camp of people he now believed were his bitter opponents in what he considered to be the battle of his life, a struggle greater than his own welfare; a battle in which to him good and evil were clearly defined.

All over the school they could hear the terrible uproar, like the one in her classroom, as frightened students bolted and barred windows and doors, erecting ineffectual barricades with desks, tables and chairs. It was something to do, some attempt at self-defence.

In Pavana's classroom the frenzied activity had ceased and students stood around the walls, sat on the floor or at the remaining desks. The heat had become stifling as soon as the March wind had been shut out. A few students attempted nonchalance, even bravado, fanning themselves with exercise books, but a number were openly fearful, crying, giggling nervously or clasping their books tightly to their chests, prepared to leave at the first opportunity.

Once it became apparent that the authorities were not going to close the school, a mighty roar of male voices, angry and determined, preceded the sounds of breaking glass, shouts, screams and the incessant ringing of dozens of bicycle bells. Scores of rioting young men

232

poured into the school grounds and from inside the room they could hear the terrified screams of students as the rioters pounded up and down the verandas, banging on the closed doors, the chanting voices rising to a thunderous chorus.

'Close Sacred Heart! Close! Close Sacred Heart! Close!'

The sound reverberated through the room. Pavana was willing the authorities to negotiate, but it was evident from the escalating chaos outdoors that this was not to be the case.

'Now,' she said to the class, 'offer no resistance, whatever the provocation, which will be mostly verbal I am sure. I hope. Is that understood? Your main objective is to get off the grounds as quickly as you can.'

Most of her students answered, 'Yes, miss,' but not all.

There were a number of students in the class who supported the ruling party, but she couldn't tell for sure how many they were, or who they were, and how they would react if the classroom was invaded.

Footsteps were now pounding up the stairs to the third floor, dozens of footsteps, and in a minute shadows loomed at every door, the rioters battering methodically on the glass. Suddenly the door nearest Pavana's desk gave way, and bands of high school boys were falling into the room, sending the barricade crashing to the cement floor. They ran up and down the room, overturning other desks and chairs, dashing books to the ground, flinging papers into the air, emptying wastepaper baskets, pushing the girls off the chairs, urging them through the doorways.

'Home,' they chanted. 'Home, go home.'

Pavana quickly surveyed the room. Most of her students were rushing through the rear door, but two young women were still sitting at their desks, and two more were on the floor, refusing to leave, keeping their eyes down, as the boy rioters rampaged around the room, banging on desks, on chairs, on blackboards, stamping their feet, uttering wild noises, chanting all the while.

One young man, nearly six feet tall, his cap turned around so that the peak was at the back of his head, placed his hands on Deborah Stevens's chair.

Deborah had a terrible temper and it was now thoroughly aroused. Fiery with indignation, she swivelled around in her seat, peering up at him from behind thick-lensed glasses. She removed his hands from her chair. He immediately replaced them.

'Why don't you go home?' he asked. 'It's all over. The school is closed. No classes today.'

'No shopping today,' the other boys laughed. 'No working today, no banking today, everywhere will be closed. Home!' they chanted. 'Home!'

'No,' Deborah said, removing her glasses and slipping them into a pocket. She gripped the sides of her desk, her face set in defiance. Several other young men surrounded her, chanting, 'Get up, go, get up, go.'

She did not reply, but placed the whole of her upper body across the desk, face down, her arms hugging the desk.

'Go!' the fellow behind her chair said gently, beginning to rock her chair back and forth, while the others circled the room again, echoing his words.

Deborah, her black hair spread out all over the desk, shook her head slightly, keeping her tall, well-built body rigidly in place. Her voice was muffled, but without a tremor.

'You can't make me. It's my right to be in this school. I'll go when, and if I feel like it.'

Sucking his teeth in impatience and exasperation, the young man rocked her chair, harder, faster, backwards, forwards, until her grip loosened and she fell to the floor, hitting her head on the metal surround of an open doorway. Her glasses flew across the room, one lens leaping from its frame to break in half.

Pavana and the other students rushed to her aid, but Deborah was already on her feet. She grabbed a nearby chair and flung it with maniacal force at the boy rioter. He sidestepped nimbly while the chair sailed through the air, crashing against the concrete wall and causing an enormous framed map of the world to come tumbling down. Her feet crunching on the shattered glass, Pavana took advantage of the stunned silence, positioning herself between Deborah and the rioters. Forcing herself to speak very quietly, she said, 'It's obvious that we can't have classes today. Why don't you leave?'

Several young men, looking slightly ashamed of their actions, began half-heartedly to jeer and chant. One fellow picked up Deborah's glasses and held them out to her. She knocked them furiously out of his hand.

The young man in the peaked cap, obviously the leader of the rapidly dwindling band in her classroom, said, 'I'm sorry about this. It was an

234

accident. We are not supposed to injure anyone. We were to frighten you into leaving.'

'Well, you did hurt someone,' Pavana said, glancing at Deborah, slumped but standing against the wall, her chest heaving, one hand to her head, but still determined not to leave. The other three students were apparently of the same mind.

'I'll obviously have to report this incident to the police', Pavana continued. 'Your names, please.' She picked up a broken piece of chalk from the floor and approached the blackboard.

'Well?' she said when they did not reply.

'If you give us your word, miss, that these students will go home right away, then we'll leave, but not before,' the leader said, turning his cap around so that the peak faced the front.

'You have my word,' Pavana said, dropping the chalk on the ledge, clapping her hands briskly. 'Regina, Abbie, the rest of you, let's clean up this mess. It's time for us to go home.'

For a long minute the rioters stared at Deborah, who stared back at them without blinking. Then, as Pavana began closing the doors, the rioters – feeling perhaps that their faces had been saved – shuffled out of the classroom, down the stairs and out of the grounds, already almost deserted.

Pavana escorted a relieved but jubilant Deborah to the library where the first-aid kit was kept. The bump on Deborah's forehead had grown quite large but she didn't seem at all fazed, whereas Pavana felt exhausted and, for some reason, ravenously hungry.

Chapter 41

'I did it, miss,' Deborah was saying as they neared the doorway of the library, 'I didn't let them frighten me into leaving.'

'So you did,' Pavana said. 'You were very brave.'

'This morning before I left home, my parents told me that I have the right to go to school, the same as the right to go to church, or anywhere.

235

Nobody is going push me around. The anthem says it, *land of the free* is what it says, doesn't it?'

'It does, Deborah.'

'I have the freedom to choose, miss, and I chose!'

Pavana looked into Deborah's dark eyes, shiny with defiance and a passionate commitment. She looked as if she would have died rather than give in. Like everyone else, Pavana could almost hear the crackle of energy in the air, feel the intensity of the convulsions shaking the country, and she shuddered, wondering into what further quagmires the national psyche would have to descend before the awesome silence from the government in Belmopan would end.

The astonishing sequence of events during the past few weeks seemed to signal some sort of watershed in the country's history, indicating a distinct change in the mores of the Belize she thought she knew.

She couldn't help but feel reprieved by the countrywide strike called by the Public Service Union, which prevented her from travelling to the ministry in Belmopan or to the offices of the Women's Unit. Undoubtedly there would be some public service officers who would defy the union, but Pavana was not one of them, although she was not a member.

'Let's see what we can do about that bump on your forehead, Deborah,' Pavana said, looking around the library.

Several teachers including Vicky were attending to the minor cuts and bruises students had received in the general scuffle. Other students on work-scholarships were sweeping broken glass from the floor or replacing books on the shelves.

'Now buck up there,' Vicky was saying in a loud, cheerful voice to a weeping first-former. 'Goodness me, it's only a slight cut, pull up your socks, my girl, and give us a smile.' Slapping the plaster firmly on to the student's cheek, Vicky winked conspiratorially at Pavana, passing her a cloth full of icecubes for Deborah to press against the bump on her forehead.

As Pavana began writing down the telephone number of Deborah's father, Vicky said, 'I'll be through in a few minutes, Pavana. So much to tell you.'

'I know, same here,' Pavana said. 'But I'd better take Lisa and Eric home as soon as I'm done here. I'll ring you later. We'll arrange something.'

'Sounds good,' Vicky said.

Once she had successfully completed the telephone call to Deborah's father, Pavana sighed with relief. Before daybreak that morning she'd made a pot of conch soup, which the twins loved. She was also beginning to feel quite drowsy. Perhaps after lunch she would be able to take a nap. She needed time to think, too, about her sticky situation in the ministry. Stifling a yawn, she walked quickly across the grassy playing field towards the twins' classroom.

To her knowledge, the rioters had not even approached the elementary school. However, Miss Reyes, a short, motherly woman, looked distinctly distressed and harassed. It could not have been easy keeping twenty-five young people cooped up in the classroom for more than two hours.

'Oh, my God,' she said distractedly. 'Were they supposed to wait for you? I've never seen such an almighty confusion!'

'Yes, . . .'

'Parents in and out, children screaming, running about. There should be a law! I have a good mind to go straight to the Minister's office . . .'

'Have you seen them?' Pavana asked.

'Well, yes,' she said. 'I sat right here and saw them leave. They had their bags.'

'That's odd,' Pavana said. 'They usually wait for me here or near the Land Rover, or they come to my classroom.'

'They're somewhere about, I'm sure,' Miss Reyes said, the indignant expression on her plump, pretty face changing to one of concern. 'Why don't you check upstairs? They might be chatting with Steven Paine, he's a friend of theirs, isn't he?'

'That could be,' Pavana said doubtfully. Steven couldn't hang about after school, not even for games. His mother always picked him up promptly, and today of all days she would have been extremely anxious about his safety.

'Have a look in any case,' she said, pressing her fingers to her temples. 'I have a terrible headache, it's been too much, too much.'

Pavana climbed the long flight of stairs to Steven's classroom on the third floor but, as she had expected, it was locked and barred. Puzzled, she leaned against the veranda railing, scanning the extensive compound, searching for Eric's curly head. He'd been so delighted when; after considerable debate, she'd finally agreed he could grow his hair into 'a bush'.

237

If they were anywhere about, she could hardly miss his gangling frame, in khaki trousers and white shirt, ambling along beside Lisa, a coronet of plaits around her head, wearing the detested white pullover uniform. Pavana had had to let down the hem of it the evening before, steam pressing it carefully so that the first crease wouldn't show.

The Land Rover was in its usual place, parked in the shadows to the rear of the high school building, but the twins were not in it nor near it. They were not sitting on the seawall, which they sometimes did at recess. And, of course, there was nobody playing any kind of game. Two young girls about 8 years old, obviously under strict instructions not to move, sat on a bench outside the principal's office, swinging their legs back and forth.

'Hmm,' she said, to herself. 'They wouldn't leave without telling me, surely. In any case, where would they go on a day like this?'

Of course in the panic and confusion they might have decided to accept a lift with Steven's mother; highly unlikely, as Steven's mother would have certainly enquired whether they had informed Pavana. Still, it was just possible.

For some reason she ran down the stairs, all seventy-two of them, arriving breathless in the principal's office. She called home, staring at the wall behind the principal's desk, decorated with the students' drawings and paintings. She dialled and re-dialled, letting the phone in their apartment ring and ring. There was no reply. Of course they could be outside, playing basketball. It was not part of their routine in the middle of the day, when the sun turned the concrete driveway into a bed of live coals and they nearly always played barefooted; but then, it was not a routine kind of day.

As for Jen and Morris, it was quite likely they were still out west, in El Cayo, clambering up and down Xunantunich, with the group of university lecturers touring the Mayan ruins in Belize. They might be back. But they weren't.

She decided to call Steven, who was home.

'No, Miss Leslie,' Steven said. 'They didn't come home with my mother and me. Should they have?'

'Did you see them at all today, Steven?' Pavana asked, raising her voice.

'Let's see. Ah, no, Miss Leslie. We didn't have recess, you see, because

238

of the terrible riots. Miss Eloisa allowed us to peep through the cracks in the door and we saw . . .'

'Yes, Steven, I know,' Pavana interrupted. 'Thanks. Bye.' She hung up quickly, muttering to herself, 'This is getting ridiculous. Where can they be?'

She circled the grounds, questioning the caretaker and one or two teachers she met, then returned to her classroom, pulling the doors shut on that scene of devastation, lingering on the veranda, expecting the two beloved faces to appear at any moment with a perfectly reasonable explanation. She tried to think of what it could be. She wished they would hurry up. The feeling of nausea had returned and she was sweating profusely though her fingers were icy cold.

How could they have left the school grounds without telling her, or leaving a message? In the grip now of guilt and paranoia, Pavana wondered whether this was not one more portentous result of their trip to Pelican Island and that catastrophic afternoon on the glass-bottomed boat, of the longer hours she was now forced to spend away from home – a warning of their increasing independence, the distance between herself and them which seemed to be widening daily.

There was no help for it, she would have to telephone Julian later tonight, if she could track him down, once the twins were asleep. She needed to talk with him desperately, needed his advice about so many things, or at least his support. She'd call Vicky, too, postponing their talk for another day. Tomorrow she would have a long talk with Lisa and Eric, even if she had to force things out into the open. They couldn't go on like this.

With this new plan she felt somewhat better; it gave her the illusion of an attempt to pull back from the edge – of what, though, she wasn't quite sure. Hoisting her bag of books and papers to correct on to her shoulders, she walked slowly down the stairs and around the building, half expecting to see Lisa and Eric.

A young boy, perhaps eleven, bright of eye and very handsome, sat hunched on the fenders of the Land Rover, his hands on his knees. He wore a ragged pullover and grubby shorts held up with a belt, and he was barefooted. His expression was one of complete boredom, as if he had been sitting there, waiting, for a very long time.

Chapter 42

At her approach the young boy leapt off the fender and ambled across the grass, the end of his oversized belt swinging from one side of his slim hips to the other. He padded along, cracking his knuckles, head up, eyes alert, his whole bearing reminiscent of an athlete ready to make a dash at the sound of a gun. He looked like a boy accustomed to foraging along the riverways, bathing in the Haulover Creek, or like one of those boys Pavana sometimes observed as she drove around, who slipped easily, mysteriously, in and out of the mangrove swamps bordering the sea.

She was sure that he didn't attend school very much, if at all. He flashed her a bright smile, displaying sound, white teeth, and although there was definitely something furtive about those mischievous eyes it really seemed unnecessary for her heart to be beating as rapidly as it continued to do.

'This Land Rover belong to you?' he asked straightaway, looking a trifle sceptical as if anyone who owned a Land Rover was not a part of his everyday experience.

Pavana nodded. Then, imitating his caution, knowing the answer beforehand, asked in her turn, 'Do you go to school here? I don't remember your face.'

His hair was tangled and matted, as if some time earlier that day he had been swimming and had then allowed it to dry without bothering to comb it. Hair, matted or combed, was undoubtedly the least of his problems.

'I mostly ketch and kill, and I sell fish, other things, crabs in season.' He was studying her face very closely, if surreptitiously, adding offhandedly as if to reassure her, 'I'm in Standard Six, at Lake I.'

'You look very young for Standard Six,' Pavana said, walking towards the Land Rover. 'You must be very bright.'

'I do O.K. I only look young. I'll be thirteen in November.'

He hitched up his shorts and spat on the grass, not because he had a

240

cold or a cough or anything; it was his habit, simply one of the privileges of manhood.

'That's a coincidence,' Pavana said. 'I'm November born, too.'

'Not a bad month, is it?' he asked conversationally in a tone of voice which suggested he had considered the matter and had decided to speak to her on equal terms. 'Christmas time, of course. I sell a lot in November. But that's far away yet. Business bad right now.'

'What's your name?' she asked.

'Who? Me? Denzil Nathaniel Jones. But everybody call be Cobbo. Just ask for Cobbo, if you want fish, or crab . . . or anything.'

He folded his arms across his chest, looking at her as if he stood outside her gate selling fish; as if he had all the time in the world and he intended to spend it, all of it, right there on that patch of grass, as near to the door of the Land Rover as possible.

Pavana had hung around the school grounds, waiting for Lisa and Eric, for as long as she could, and was getting quite desperate. It was well after noon now, the school and grounds completely deserted, only the jagged holes in the windows and doors of the classrooms indicating that anything untoward had happened there that morning.

'I'm going home now, Cobbo,' Pavana said, keeping her voice steady, keeping it casual. 'My children are waiting for me to eat lunch. Would you like a lift?'

The last thing in the world she wanted to do was to give Cobbo a lift. Lake Independence – and if that was really where he went to school, he probably lived in that area as well – was quite some distance away and not along her regular route.

There was a shift in Cobbo's expression. His face became downcast, as if he was losing ground in an important transaction. Then it brightened as if he had decided to give it one more try. In spite of her anxiety, Pavana had to smile. It was obvious that there wasn't anything little or mean about Cobbo's character. However, it was also obvious that he considered himself a man of business, and as such he was going to do what he had to do by his reckoning.

'What's your name, miss?'

'Pavana Leslie.'

'And this Land Rover belong to you?'

'Yes,' Pavana said, impatiently, feeling as if she were in court

241

answering a misdemeanour charge. It crossed her mind that Cobbo may have stood before the magistrates' bench any number of times. She decided to force his hand.

'Please move out of my way, Cobbo,' she said, a slight, dismissive edge to her voice, reverting naturally to her combative girlhood days in the schoolyard, where she had learnt to give no quarter and to expect none. 'You may have all day to talk about horse dead and cow fat but not me, I'm a busy woman.' Arms akimbo, she glared at him. 'Move! You're holding me up!'

Cobbo remained cool. After all, his attitude seemed to say, he was quite accustomed to dealing with irate, nervous, old women like Pavana. It went with his line of business. But he did back away from the door, watching as she opened it and dumped the heavy bag on to the rear passenger seat.

'You don't have to act so vex up,' he said, as if slightly offended, 'when I come out of my way to tell you something.'

Pavana's heart skipped a beat.

'You have two children, right? Doubles, right?' He was hopping up and down, scissoring two fingers of one hand in front of her face.

'So what?' Pavana said, getting into the driver's seat.

'Well, they're not at home waiting to eat no lunch, I'll tell you that, Miss Leslie.'

He leaned against the hood of the Land Rover, looking like a man who had come on a mission of goodwill and, instead of the welcome which he had every right to expect, had been met with a rebuff, and not only that, unwarranted abuse.

Pavana wasn't fooled by that posture. She knew what was up, only she was uncertain just how to proceed. Until now, bribery had usually been outside her ethical code, and she still considered it to be so, but right at that moment she felt she would do anything simply to know where her children were. In this situation, a new set of ethics had to apply. Besides, as a businessman Cobbo must have his own code of ethics, she supposed, and he couldn't be expected to give away his goods and services. He couldn't afford such expensive gestures. She retrieved her purse from the bag, holding it carelessly against the wheel.

'Do you know them, Cobbo?'

'Not to speak to, but I saw them.'

'Where?' Pavana asked, extending a five-dollar bill.

Cobbo shook his head.

She added another one, and another. Fifteen dollars, and Cobbo still didn't seem interested. It was all the money she had with her. He said, still in that slightly offended tone of voice, 'If you really want to give me something, I'll take that basketball.'

'Basketball?' Pavana asked, trying to hide the tears streaming down her cheeks.

'You don't have to bawl. It's not a burying. A man's got to live.'

'For sure, Cobbo,' Pavana said, returning the money to her purse.

Moving swiftly, she went to the rear of the Land Rover and took out Eric's basketball, hugging it to her chest, hating to part with it. She told herself that was pure sentimentality in the face of the disaster which she now felt certain, had descended on them all.

'Where did you see them, Cobbo?' Her voice was strident, carrying on the air. Calm, she cautioned herself. This is an emergency, and you cannot allow yourself to be flattened by the first stiff wind that blows.

'The last I saw, they were standing in the Never Full Grocery on Pen Road with some men.'

'Which men, Cobbo, come on, which men?'

He shrugged.

'Will you take me there, show me where the grocery is?'

'Who? Me? My granny sent me out since early morning to buy bun and cheese. She frighten to go out in the riots. I have to go home.'

'I'll give you a ride home. We'll explain to your granny and then . . .'

'Well, I'm not exactly going straight home. But just go to Pen Road, and ask for Never Full. Everybody know where it is.'

'How did you find me?' Pavana asked, passing him the basketball. He took it, looking slightly shamefaced.

'They told me to come here and tell you to go to Never Full.'

'Well, I'd better get over there right away,' Pavana said, climbing into the Land Rover and switching on the ignition.

'I wouldn't say no to a lift to the Belcan.'

'Get in then,' Pavana said, her mind no longer on Cobbo but focused on the plight of her children, who could be anywhere by now.

She sped recklessly out of the school grounds, crashing in and out of potholes, driving instinctively, hearing only the echo of Stoner's words that evening outside Jen's holiday house on Pelican Island: 'They intend to overthrow that agenda by any means necessary.'

243

At the Belcan Bridge spanning the Haulover Creek she braked, allowing Cobbo to jump out.

'I remember now,' he said, 'who gave me the message to give you?'

'You do, do you? Who?'

'Mr Stoner,' Cobbo said quickly. 'He gave me a little flip to bring the message. Don't tell him about the basketball.'

'I'd really like you to come with me, Cobbo."

But Cobbo was off, shaking his head as he went, wending his way through the crowds gathered outside the market at the foot of the bridge, the orange basketball tucked securely in the crook of his arm. Driving across the bridge, Pavana caught one last glimpse of Cobbo, scuttling quickly along the footpath between the market stalls and the wide creek, moving sluggishly towards the sea.

She shuddered, remembering the story she'd heard about a twelve-year-old boy who had allegedly murdered another by throwing him over the railing of the Belcan Bridge, and of other unspeakable crimes which had occurred in the vicinity. And she thought of Eric and Lisa, their open faces and relatively trusting ways, and what seemed now a terrible vulnerability.

Chapter 43

Stoner had told her that night on Prince's Lane that he lived in 'a neighbourhood of criminals and drug addicts', but he probably exaggerated. To Pavana, Pen Road appeared to be a perfectly ordinary Belizean street with its requisite number of potholes, blocked drains, fruit and vegetable stands, grocery stores and bars.

As Cobbo had said, the Never Full Grocery and Saloon (Not Licensed To Sell Alcoholic Beverages) was not difficult to find. While still ten yards away, she could see the large signboard with bold, black lettering jutting out from the side of the house. To the left of the doorway, an old gentleman sat on a three-legged stool before a cart of oranges, peeling them one by one, getting ready for the evening trade. At his feet was a rusty two-gallon tin can half full of salt and crushed *habanero* pepper.

Pavana entered the shop quickly, expectantly, the relieved cry of joyful greeting dying abruptly on her lips. Lisa and Eric were not there, nor was Stoner. The shopkeeper was helping an old lady fill a plastic shopping bag with bread, rice, beans and pigtail. Disappointment had coupled itself with a blinding rage, and Pavana leaned against the doorway, lightheaded and beside herself.

Pulling herself together with a supreme effort, she approached the counter.

'Good afternoon. My name is Pavana Leslie. I think my children were here some time today. With a man called Stoner Bennett? A boy and a girl? They go to Sacred Heart School.'

The woman behind the counter, in her mid-forties, with an erect bustline, small waist and shapely figure, did not immediately reply. She reminded Pavana of someone. Her low, rounded Afro was streaked with grey, and as she spoke to the old lady, bent with arthritis, whose crippled fingers were hardly able to grasp the handles of the shopping bag, Pavana noticed wide spaces between the teeth of the woman behind the counter.

'Excuse me,' Pavana said again, unable to wait. 'Did you see them? The boy was wearing a white shirt and khaki trousers, and the girl had on a white pleated jumper over a white blouse with a pale blue tie. They both have backpacks, Eric's is red and Lisa's is blue.'

The woman behind the counter did not look at Pavana. Her face was made up like a squall. She opened the old lady's hand, laying on her palm a dollar bill and seventy-five cents in change, counting it out loud, taking her own sweet time as she did so.

'That's it then, Miss Sissy,' the woman said to the old lady. 'Think you can make it?'

'Sure, I can make it,' the old lady said. 'Don't I always make it?' She hobbled slowly to the doorway, carefully negotiating the step into the street.

'Excuse me, but did you see them?' Pavana asked, as the woman, giving her a baleful look, busied herself, straightening sweet jars, covering the barrel of pigtail, closing the sack of rice and slamming shut the doors of a glass box filled with bread.

'Please, did you see them?'

The woman grabbed a fly swatter and pointed it at Pavana.

'Don't you come in here shouting at me! I'm sick to death of it. This

245

shop belong to me after all. Eh.' Then reluctantly, as if Pavana was forcing the words out of her mouth, she said, 'I'm Stoner Bennett's mother.'

'Oh, that's a relief,' Pavana said. 'I was supposed to meet Stoner here, to collect Lisa and Eric. But I got the message only a short time ago, which is why I'm late.'

'Well, you can see they're not here,' Stoner's mother said.

'But did you see them?' Pavana asked, pressing on, desperate.

'I think I saw them, but I was busy at the time and didn't notice them particularly. They left before the police came, I think.'

'Police?'

'Turned the place upside-down. I only just finished putting everything to rights.'

'Do you know where Stoner took the children?'

'I don't know if Stoner took them anywhere. The police said they were looking for bombs, guns, ammunition. All kinds of children were in here.'

'Where did Stoner go? Is he coming back? Didn't he leave a message for me? I'm really worried about my children.'

'How should I know where Stoner is? Nowadays he comes here when he is hungry, leaves when he is full and takes my hard-earned cash from the till.'

'Where does he live?'

'He doesn't live in one set place. I couldn't say where he is now. He flies in here when he likes, as I said, pitching on my life like blue conkas, spoiling what he touch.'

'Do you mind if I wait for a few minutes?'

'Suit yourself.'

Dejected, wondering what her next move should be, Pavena sat on a chair at a table near the doorway, and tried to collect her thoughts. If Stoner's mother was going to be uncooperative, she had no alternative but to go to the police station on Queen Street. On a day like today, how much time would the police have to help her find Lisa and Eric? But she had to do it. She needed expert help. She'd drive over there and camp at the station, all night if necessary. That's what she'd do.

As Pavana was about leave, Stoner's mother placed a soft drink on the table in front of Pavana. She didn't want it, and as she tried to pay Stoner's mother made a dismissive gesture.

246

'It's not the first drink I've had to give away today. Drink it. You look like you see a ghost. Children are a trial, eh?'

'Are they?' Pavana asked, simply to be saying something, forcing herself to swallow the ice-cold liquid which burned her parched throat. She'd had no idea she was so thirsty. She drank quickly, anxious now to get to the police station. On the other hand, should she wait? They did say they'd meet her here.

'A bloody trial.'

'It was ever thus,' Pavana said, taking the bottle to the counter. 'Look, Mrs Bennett, if you know where Stoner lives, would you please tell me? I have to find him. Somehow or other he forced my children to leave the school grounds and brought them here. If you don't tell me where he lives, I'll have to go to the police.'

'Are you one of his women?'

'No, I'm not,' Pavana said, 'but I've known Stoner for a long time. We were students together in London.'

'Ha. London, eh? That's another laugh. The scrimping and saving I did to send him a little money while he was there. I believed by now he would have been some help to me, but I'm still feeding him, at least of late.'

'So sorry to hear that,' Pavana said, thinking about what Stoner had said to her that night on Pelican Island. 'I'd like to leave a note for my children,' she said, 'in case they turn up while I'm gone. Would you give it to them for me?'

Stoner's mother nodded, watching as Pavana scribbled in her notebook, tore out the leaf and handed it to her.

'Going to the station now, I suppose?'

Pavana nodded.

'Can't say as I blame you. Children are a trial. Stoner entered this world in violence, and looks like he's going out the same way. Turned really reckless. I don't like to say things like that about my own flesh and blood, but it's nothing but the truth, no secret now.'

'Well, thanks, Mrs Bennett,' Pavan said. 'Do you have a telephone here, in case I need . . .'

'I can't afford a telephone, and you don't have to keep on calling me Mrs Bennett. I'm not married yet. My name is Lynnette.'

'I'm not married either,' Pavana said.

'Oh no? That makes two of us,' Lynette said, 'although I'll bet you

247

weren't raped. Oh, you don't have to try and fix your face. If you're shocked, you're shocked, and there's an end to that.

'At first I tried to keep it quiet like you know, after we came up from the valley. Nobody around here knew, not a soul. But since Stoner join that gang breaking up the city, making bombs, setting fire to people's stores and the government's good buildings, going to gaol and worse things, well, the whole story is out, all over the city, what happened and what didn't. And I haven't even told you the half.'

'So sorry,' Pavana said.

'Oh, you don't have to be sorry,' Lynnette said, waving her hand towards her well-stocked shelves. 'I've made old man Abrams pay through his big, lumpy nose, believe me.'

'I see,' Pavana said, understanding better the reason for Stoner's murderous urge that afternoon on the glass-bottomed boat.

'It's the disgrace of it, you know? After all these years of hiding it, trying to live a respectable life. One of my enemies up the road, a woman who doesn't usually buy from me, she waltz in here this morning as soon as I open the door. "Lynnette, one pound of rice. I hear at market say old man Abrams whap you good under his orange tree. I bet you entice the old man."

'I pitched a cup full of rice right into the old fowl's face. If you look on the floor, you can see the grains. I've had quite a day, I can tell you. It's enough to make me puke, if I was the puking kind, which I'm not.'

Pavana blurted out, 'His son, Alex, Alex Abrams? He's my children's father.'

'To Christ?' Lynnette asked.

Pavana nodded.

'We're the same kind, you and me. Messed up by the same bloody family.'

'Well,' Pavana said, the tears coursing down her cheeks, 'I wasn't raped.' Lynnette came around the counter and taking Pavana into her arms hugged her like an old friend.

'Never mind, pet,' she said, 'we're in this together. We'll find Stoner if it takes us all night. And stop casting eyewater all over the place. In this town, you have to stand up and fight. Help me lock up the shop. Hurry.'

Pavana helped Lynnette to close and bolt the shutters. Outside, she let down the iron bar across the door, fastening it with a massive padlock.

'Closed till later, Tomas. Anybody ask, I'm out on business.'

'Gaol again, Señora?' Tomas asked, shaking his head sympathetically.

'No, personal.'

'Ah . . . *sí*,' Tomas said, pounding his salt and *habanero* pepper with a rounded stick.

Lynnette marched down the street, swinging her arms militantly as if the entire Belize Defence Force was at her back.

'You must forgive me, you know,' she said, 'for treating you so bad when you first come in looking for Stoner. Criminal or not, he's still my son.'

'That's OK,' Pavana said.

'But you look so high-minded, speak so nice, big school teacher and all, I could see from your uniform, that for no reason I get jealous. I think maybe you think you better than me.'

'That's only my looks,' Pavana said, remembering Cobbo and wishing he was with her.

'I know that now,' Lynnette said, hooking her arm into Pavana's. 'You and me, we cut out of the same cloth, and blood is always thicker than water, eh?'

Pavana nodded.

'We'll find your children if I have to beat the truth out of that simpleton Stoner sometimes sleep at. I'll introduce you to Vangie as Stoner's near relative. That'll shake her up a bit. How about that, eh?'

'That's OK,' Pavana said. There was a blister on her left heel, and the pain was striking her straight to her heart.

Chapter 44

It was nearly five o'clock when Stoner's mother slammed the gate shut, mindful of the chickens and hens scattering in alarm at their approach. 'Vangie! You have a visitor! Vangie!'

Stoner had indeed exaggerated, Pavana thought, looking around. If this was his base, he had been careful to choose one of the pleasantest spots on Pen Road. The house, painted white with green blinds, was very small, but it was not a shack. Situated well back from the street, it was surrounded by coconut, mango, papaya and other fruit trees. A fishing net had been flung across a fence to dry, and to the rear was an unbroken, magnificent view of the sea.

As Lynnette opened her mouth to shout again, a soft voice said from the doorway, 'There's no need to holler like that in my yard, Miss Bennett, don't you see me standing right here?'

Vangie stood, picking her teeth, one foot crossed over the other, resting her bulk against one side of the doorway. She seemed quite composed, as if she didn't have a care in the world and didn't want to be bothered by those that did.

'Bigger than ever,' Lynnette said, climbing the six steps to the veranda. 'That I can see.'

Vangie was a woman of gargantuan dimensions, over two hundred pounds, Pavana guessed, wearing a loose-fitting pale blue garment which reached almost to her feet shoved into rubber slippers with matching blue straps. Her hair, rolled in a quantity of yellow and pink curlers, was neatly tied with a blue scarf, the ends dangling on to her shoulders.

'But eh? Why you wearing that nightgown in broad daylight? You sick again?' Lynette straightened her black skirt, tucking her red blouse tidily into the loose waistband, aware, and showing she was aware, of the contrast between herself and Vangie, at least twenty-five years younger.

'This is a *muu muu*,' Vangie said, her lips curling slightly. She stared at the toothpick reflectively. 'Stoner likes me to look nice when I go ... when we have visitors.'

There were any number of three-legged stools on the veranda, enough for a small meeting, and Pavana imagined that Stoner had probably held a number of them there, but Vangie didn't ask them to sit down.

'You have visitors, then?' Lynnette asked, trying to peer through the doorway.

'You're here,' Vangie said, glancing curiously at Pavana who stared dumbly back at her, feeling as if a lump of ice had lodged in her throat. There was not a single sound from inside the house.

'Although,' Vangie continued, shifting her eyes, beady and black, to Lynnette, 'you don't exactly qualify. Last time you were here you

250

accused me of aiding and abetting Stoner and the brethren in criminal activities. You said you wouldn't come back.

'Now that you are back, I want to tell you that neither me nor Stoner are criminals, we're not getting anything by it, except abuse by the likes of you. Stoner is trying to save his country, that includes you and your *poco tiempo* shop down the road, not that you can appreciate it. Stoner told me how you insulted him this morning when he went there to get two cold drinks for the brethren, how you sucked up to the police. So now what do you want?'

Vangie hadn't raised her voice, but her eyes glinted dangerously.

Lynnette inhaled deeply, as if she intended to put Vangie in her place once and for all. Pavana gripped her arm fiercely.

'Please, Miss Bennett.'

'This lady,' Lynnette said, her voice vexed but controlled, 'is Miss Pavana Leslie. She's looking . . .'

'Evangeline Brooks, at your service,' Vangie interrupted, 'from Orange Walk.' To Pavana, Vangie didn't look as if she was about to be at anybody's service.

'Miss Leslie is looking for her two children, Vangie. If you don't tell us where they are, she's going to the police.' She added, her voice sarcastic, 'I hope that this so-called people's revolt doesn't include kidnapping people's children, Stoner's flesh and blood besides. Where is he?'

Lynnette went to the doorway and shouted down the corridor, 'Stoner? You in there, Stoner? Miss Leslie is here wanting her two children!'

Vangie moved away from the door and went to sit on the top step, gathering the folds of her *muu muu* between her knees.

'You can shout and holler all you like, Miss Bennett. Stoner is not here.'

'Well, where is he?'

'I told you,' Vangie said. 'Out helping to kill those heads. But you're welcome to search the place if you like, satisfy yourself, if you think I'm a liar.'

'I hope you don't mind if . . .' Pavana said.

'Mind? Why should I mind? The police have been in and out of here at least ten times this week.'

Pavana followed Stoner's mother down the corridor of the small house to a room to the rear. Miss Bennett rapped on the door then pushed it open. Pavana stared about her, stunned. The room was almost an exact replica, except for the window with its view of the sea, of Stoner's old room in the Bayswater flat in London, even to the poster of the revolutionary in the cane chair, beret on his head, gun in his hand. She recognized some of the books on the shelves, and although it surely couldn't be the same one, Stoner still slept on a camp bed, an army blanket thrown over one end, a single pillow at the other.

'Well, you can see nobody is here,' Miss Bennett said. 'Your children are probably at home by now. Bad as Stoner is, he's not the kind to kidnap children.'

'Unless somebody forced him to do it,' Pavana said, her eyes trying to take in every detail of the room. There was something familiar about the way in which Stoner's pillow was scrunched up against the wall. She glanced at it, then glanced at it again, the memory of Eric's pillows on his own bed, in his own room, in their apartment, making her want to weep. On an impulse she lifted the pillow.

'It's Eric's book!' she shouted to Miss Bennett, standing impatiently at the door. 'They were here!' Frantically she peered under the camp bed and scrutinized the floors, shelves and table, searching for evidence that the twins had been there – a clip from Lisa's hair, anything – but there was nothing more that she could see. Conscious that the minutes were ticking away, she clutched the book to her chest and rushed down the corridor to the veranda.

Vangie was still sitting on the top step with the folds of the *muu muu* gathered between her knees.

Pavana held the book out to her.

'This is my son's book,' she said. 'I found it in Stoner's room.'

'Stoner has lots of books,' Vangie replied, with a show of indifference. 'I can't keep track of them. He's a great reader.'

'They were here, in this house, and I want to know where they are now.'

'Sit down,' Vangie said to Pavana, gesturing to the space beside her on the step. 'You look as if you're about to faint.'

Pavana sat, her head swinging as if she had vertigo, repulsed by the fanatical gleam in Vangie's eyes. She had resumed the reflective picking of her teeth, ignoring Lynnette, then she said abruptly, apropos of nothing, 'That your real hair?' She gestured with the toothpick towards Pavana's plait.

252

She nodded.

'Nice. Thought it was a switch. Hairdresser down the road sell plenty. Expensive though.' She glanced at the book Pavana cradled like a baby against her chest. She frowned worriedly, then began breaking the toothpick into tiny pieces.

'It's my real hair,' Pavana said, feeling strength surging back through her veins. Vangie knew something about Lisa and Eric, wanted to tell her, but didn't know how to begin.

Lynnette, looking anxiously around the yard, must have felt that way too, for suddenly she abandoned her confrontational stance and sat down on the bottom step, surveying the yard appreciatively.

'I never said this before, Vangie, but you and Stoner not doing bad with those fowls. I bet you are turning a real profit.'

'Not too bad,' Vangie replied, a faint touch of pride in her voice.

'I wouldn't mind buying a couple, if I could meet your price.'

For a woman of such enormous bulk, Vangie was light on her feet. She was inside the house and back in seconds, a milk tin of cooked rice in one hand and a covered straw basket in the other.

'I wouldn't sell you,' she said to Lynnette, who was staring at the basket in open-mouthed surprise. 'You can have any two of my hens you like.' There were dozens of hens wandering about the yard and Vangie gestured carelessly towards them as if she had plenty more where those came from.

Lynnette wasn't slow either.

'Well, if you're sure,' she said, taking the basket reluctantly. 'I mean I can afford to pay.'

'Cho man,' Vangie said. 'I wouldn't charge you, you're almost my mother-in-law after all. I'd catch the hens for you but this *muu muu* would get in my way.'

'I have my eye on those two pullets over in the corner,' Lynnette said. She pointed to where two fowls squatted in the dirt, near the chicken coop, almost hidden by the fishing net draped across the fence.

'Go right ahead, catch them. And excuse my *desgracias*,' she said, gesturing to a clothesline at the very back of the yard near the sea, on which gigantic undergarments were drying, puffed out by the wind.

'Is that what they are?' Lynnette asked, her face tortured into fake surprise. 'You know I sat here thinking they were pillowcases? I must surely need an eye test.' She wandered off into the yard, scattering the

253

rice grains, calling, 'Come chicky chick, here chicky chick, pretty chicky chick.'

'You have one like her around your house?' Vangie asked.

Pavana shook her head.

'Well you're lucky. That woman doesn't like the best bone in my body, nor in Stoner's no matter what she tell you. Can't figure out why. If I had a son, I'd love him. But she hates Stoner, only he act like he don't know. You love your children, don't you?'

Pavana nodded.

'Where's Stoner now?' she asked Vangie, who was staring malevolently at Lynnette crouching low trying to grab one of the two hens.

'Stoner had to leave town. I was just putting on my clothes to go find your house when you came with her. Stoner telephoned your house he said but nobody answer. I was going to take a taxi.'

'Where are they?'

'You don't have to worry, those are Stoner's exact words. Your children are all right, except that they have to stay with the brethren until Alex Abrams cancels his plan to speak at that rally government is planning for tomorrow night.'

Pavana leapt off the step.

'Tomorrow night? They think they can keep Lisa and Eric away from home until tomorrow night?'

'They're long gone on the bus by now. Why don't you call Mr Abrams, then? I'm sure everything will be all right. Stoner told me you are all family together. In my family we all stick together.'

'Stoner and Alex are no family to me,' Pavana said. 'They're my enemies, and Stoner has my children, and I'm going to the police station right now. You tell Stoner I'm taking him to court!'

Putting Eric's book into her bag, she removed her shoes and raced towards the gate, leaving it to swing wide open. Several of Vangie's fowls scurried, clucking, into the street. She heard the women shouting her name, but she didn't pause; she kept right on running until she reached the Land Rover. As she switched on the ignition, the sun dropped beyond the horizon. It was nearly night.

Chapter 45

The nervous young police officer, laboriously writing down Pavana's statement, was sympathetic but noncommital. He was interrupted several times by the telephone, or by two other officers as harassed and overworked as himself, who were heroicially attempting to deal with the uproar in the station house and the compound on Queen Street, one of the town's main commercial streets. He apologized.

'Excuse me, but each officer is doing several jobs. Most of the men are on the street. Now where were we? Ah yes, description of children. Now.'

It took a long time for Pavana to make the full report to the officer, a conscientious, intelligent man, tall, skinny, with a high forehead and bony face. Every now and then he pressed his fingers against his eyeballs, and when he removed them they were watery and red, the result of his long hours of duty. Finally, the report seemed reasonably complete to them both.

'I'll need to take advice on this,' he said. 'It's not a regular case, not a regular case at all. The name of the children's father you say is Alex Abrams, so that makes for some complications.'

He hesitated, rubbing his hand over the stubble on his chin, and took a sip of the tepid coffee on his desk blotter. 'Even political. I'll have to take advice.' He looked at her questioningly.

'Well, take it then,' Pavana said, then added, 'please,' not wishing to antagonize the young officer, who was obviously scared to death of the statement he held in his hand.

'It's not so easy. We may have to call in CID. The commissioner is in conference. The rioting has spread countrywide, and of course we must still deal with routine cases.' He'd already repeated the same thing several times.

'Yes, yes, of course.'

'But, we must be resourceful, yes, very resourceful. I suggest that you try telephoning Mr Abrams again, and your home. I'll use the outer office to try locate the commissioner. Yes, yes, much the best course. But I must warn you, I doubt whether we will be able to produce an immediate result. It may be several hours. With Mr Stoner Bennett involved as well, ahem, to be truthful, the case is not within my competence.'

'Please do your best,' Pavana said.

'It may mean that the commissioner may even be forced to consult the permanent secretary in the Ministry of Home Affairs – that's our ministry, you understand me?'

'Yes, yes.'

The officer looked appalled at the very thought.

'Not within my competence at all,' he repeated, stacking the sheets of paper on the blotter before pounding a stapler into the pages. He stood up and placed his peaked police cap on his head, looking like a man about to rush into a screaming mob of rioting citizens, expecting to be trampled to death underfoot.

'Even the very highest authority,' he said, his voice choked with awe.

'Please, do anything you have to do,' Pavana said, feeling she understood what it must be like to pronounce on someone a sentence of death.

'Just hurry, please.'

He sat down again.

'Try Mr Abrams again. He might be able to help. We don't want to be precipitate.'

Pavana dialled, her fingers fumbling, knowing that there would be no answer from Alex's home in the Stann Creek Valley. The operator had told her earlier that the telephone was off the hook.

'Still off the hook.'

The officer cleared his throat, trying to choose his words carefully.

'And the number of his Belize City residence is unlisted and you don't know the number?' The officer was obviously puzzled.

'That's right,' Pavana said.

'Hie!' he said. 'There's no way around it. Keep trying your home in the meantime.'

Pavana nodded, anxious to oblige, beginning to dial again as he finally left the room which resembled a prison cell with its barred, dingy windows, bare, unscrubbed floors, naked lightbulb, and the scent of stale urine mingled with disinfectant emanating from the unspeakably dirty bathroom. There was, of course, no answer from the apartment.

When after fifteen minutes the officer still had not returned, Pavana walked into the outer office to find him. There were three officers on duty, which seemed to be the evening's quota, but P.C. Ronald Smith was not among them.

'P.C. Smith?' the new officer asked. He was a shorter man, thick set, with broad shoulders and a small waist. He was light complexioned with a stiff, bristly moustache and a very pink tongue,

'Off duty, miss, for a few hours. All we're allowed for the time being.'

'Off duty?' Pavana asked, horrified. 'But what about my statement? My children have been abducted. I don't know where they are – P.C. Smith said . . .'

The officer interrupted her smoothly.

'All in order, miss. Your statement's in the pipeline. P.C. Smith has reported the matter. We've been in contact with the commissioner. We are waiting for instructions. The word is out. These things take a little longer in times like these.'

'Pipeline?' Pavana asked, 'Can't we do something in the meantime?'

'Do?' The officer smoothed his moustache then mopped his forehead with his handkerchief. 'You can wait in the office if you like, or sit out here. Perhaps the best thing would be for you to go home and we'll contact you there as soon as we have any news. We're working on the case, only we're shortstaffed. Excuse me.' He turned back to a gentleman at the counter who wished to report a burglary of his home in St Martin de Porres.

Pavana went to the front door of the station house and looked out upon the night, at the ceaseless activity on the stairs leading from the street to the main office, at the people moving back and forth on the street. She listened to the screeching of police cars going in and out of the compound, watched handcuffed, desperate men and women being led to the rear of the station house, and she wondered about the length of the pipeline in which her statement had been placed.

Almost without knowing it, she had walked down the stairs and into the street, standing beneath a lamp post near the corner of Queen Street and New Road, the barred, broken shop windows, and the unusual number of policemen and soldiers walking up and down, making the whole street eerie and unfamiliar.

She could go home and wait as the officer had suggested, or she could try to find Alex; somebody must know where he was, and the most likely person was Moria. A policeman was strolling purposefully towards her, swinging his nightstick, a speculative look in his eye. That decided her; she couldn't hang around the streets and the police station all night.

After circling the streets indecisively for a few minutes, she drove to the filling station on Freetown Road and then headed for the Northern Highway, driving towards Alex's house on the river, the one which he had offered her as a home all those years ago, in the park that cold afternoon in Primrose Hill.

Chapter 46

Alex's house on the river, like many of those along the Northern Highway, was fairly large, solidly built from concrete, surrounded by giant old trees. She knew the exact location of the house, and drove into the garden, parked on the driveway, walked up to the massive front door and pressed the bell. For a few minutes, dogs barked ferociously inside the house before Pavana heard someone murmuring soothingly to them.

The savage barking descended into a whine as a face appeared at the window and a light above Pavana's head was switched on. The door opened and a Mestizo woman, in her late fifties, obviously a maid, stood wiping her hands on an apron and smiling in a friendly way. But she didn't unlatch the chain on the door.

'*Buenas noches, Señora,*' she said.

'*Buenas noches,*' Pavana said. 'Is Mr Abrams or Miss Abrams at home?'

'No, *Señora,*' the maid sounded breathless as if she'd hurried from a long way to answer the doorbell. Behind her, two fierce-looking dogs of indeterminate breed kept up a continuous growling.

Over the maid's shoulders, Pavana saw an elegant, luxurious room, with oriental rugs on the parquet floor, wall hangings from Mexico, bookshelves, comfortable chairs, coffee tables, paintings of birds, which Helga had probably done, and numerous framed photographs on the walls. To her tired heart, mind and body, the room looked inviting, safe.

But even as she looked longingly inside she knew that this was only an illusion.

'Do you know when they will return?'

'No, *Señora*,' the maid replied. From somewhere in the depths of the room a parrot screeched, 'No, *Señora*! No, *Señora*!'

'*Quite tu boca!*' the maid yelled, and the parrot echoed, '*Tu boca, tu boca!*'

'*Sí, Señora?*' the maid asked, obviously anxious to do her duty.

'May I have the telephone number so I can call later?'

The maid looked extremely anxious, as if she had a cake baking in the oven and was in a hurry to get back to it before it burned.

'I would like, *Señora*, but it is not allowed.'

'Do you know how I can reach Miss Abrams?'

The maid looked puzzled.

'Find her,' Pavana explained, using all the persuasiveness she could muster in her voice and in her gestures. 'I must speak with her.'

'You will telephone to London, *Señora*?'

'London?' Pavana asked. 'Miss Abrams is in London?'

'But *sí, Señora*.' She waved a hand as if to indicate that Moria had left a long time before.

'When do you expect Mr Abrams back?'

'The maid looked nonplussed.

'Any time, *Señora*. I am always here. You have a message, *Señora*?'

She removed a pencil and notepad from her apron pocket.

'Yes, yes, of course.'

Pavana wrote down her telephone number, name and address, the reason for her call, and asked Alex to get in touch with her as soon as possible.

'Thank you, *Señora*. Good night, *Señora*.'

As she was about to close the door, Pavana asked. 'Would you mind if I waited for Mr Abrams?'

The maid's round, plump face looked distressed and regretful at the same time.

'It is not allowed, *Señora*.'

'Of course not,' Pavana said. 'Good night.'

'Good night, *Señora*.'

The heavy mahogany door closed with a thud and a click of the lock. The light was switched off. Pavana walked back to the Land Rover and sat in it for a while, looking at the gleam of the river through the mangrove trees and the shrubbery, at the speedboat on a trailer in one of three garages, at Moria's car, at the lovely house, lamplight shining through the windows.

Switching on the ignition, she said out loud, 'I will have a shower and have something to eat. I will call my parents. I will call the police. I will try to find Alex.'

She sped towards the city, trying to plan, slowing down only for the sleeping policemen placed at danger points along the road. It was urgent that she return to the apartment and to the telephone, but it was the last place she wanted to go.

Chapter 47

Jen and Morris had still not returned and the house was in complete darkness. Inside the apartment, she switched on all the lights, outside and in. Without Lisa and Eric, the entire atmosphere of the apartment had changed. It had turned sullen, unwelcoming, closing in on itself, revealing its nastiest side. Everything in it, the unmade beds, dishes in the sink, the rumpled cushions on the chairs, unwatered plants, books on the floor and the table – all the paraphernalia of their everyday lives – adopted an accusatory stance.

It was eight p.m., nearly twelve hours since Lisa and Eric had rushed across the school grounds to their classroom, the last she had seen of them. Had they been forced into a car at gunpoint? Lisa and Eric would never have willingly got into a strange car with people they did not know. If, after the rioters had closed the school, she had not lingered with Deborah for so long in the library, perhaps Lisa and Eric would be with her at this minute. 'If! If! If!' she cried aloud.

Perhaps they would be home at any minute, tired and hungry, and the place was an absolute mess. She crawled on her hands and knees across the beige carpet, picking up the pink and red rose petals fallen from the brass bowl on the top shelf of the bookcase. She'd just retrieved the last petal from underneath the dining table when the telephone rang.

'Hello,' she said cautiously, praying, Let it be Lisa and Eric, let it be.

There was a crackle on the line.

Overseas? she thought to herself, surprised and more than a little confused. Overseas?

'Pavana?'

'Yes.'

'This is Julian, can you hear me?'

'Julian! Yes, I can hear you!' Pavana said, her joy in receiving a call from Julian tempered by her anxiety not to linger too long on the telephone. Supposing the children were trying to call.

'You sound very strange,' Julian was saying. 'Are you crying?'

'Lisa and Eric have disappeared. They've been taken by a group fighting against the heads, they're trying to force Alex to speak out against the heads of agreement. We're having terrible riots and they've closed the schools...'

'I've just heard about it on the news here in the hotel. That's why I'm calling. What about Lisa and Eric? What did you say?'

'They've been taken.'

'Who took them away? Who?'

'I'm not sure, but Stoner, remember Stoner Bennett, he works with this group. No, no, he's not the leader, but a member, very influential member. Right now they're trying to prevent Alex ... yes, Alex Abrams, from holding a counter rally and demonstration at a meeting tomorrow night. I'm very frightened, Julian. I'm nearly at the end of my rope.'

'So you should be, it sounds awful. Have you been to the police?'

'Yes, they're doing what they can, but what with fires and bomb threats, it's hard...'

'Have you talked with Abrams?'

'I can't get hold of him. I've tried and...'

'You absolutely must get hold of Abrams, no matter what you have to do. Listen, I'm in New York, visiting headquarters, but I'm taking the first plane to Miami and will get to Belize as soon as I can – some time tomorrow, or the day after.'

'You're coming to Belize tomorrow?'

'Yes, of course. Don't you want me to?'

'Oh I do, Julian, I really do, we do need your help so badly, but...'

'Then that's settled. I'll take a taxi from the airport.'

'Julian?'

'Yes?'

261

'It was a mistake to bring them home for such a long time, I mean ...
it's all turning out badly and I feel guilty, wretched.'

'No, it wasn't. You did what you needed to do. You're frightened at
the moment, who wouldn't be? But don't buckle. Find Abrams
immediately, are you hearing me?'

'Yes,' Pavana said, wishing he was already there in the apartment
with her. It was proving to be a lonely, terrifying business.

'And keep on top of the police.'

'I will, I will.'

'I love you, Pavana.'

'And I love you, Julian.'

'Fight fiercely.'

'I will. See you soon.'

'Very soon,' Julian said.

Pavana replaced the receiver and impatiently wiped away the tears
spilling down her cheeks. Julian loved her. He was travelling all those
miles to help them, because he cared about them. And Alex and she
were in the same city, and she couldn't find him, he hadn't contacted
her, not once since that afternoon on Pelican Island.

She washed her face under the kitchen tap and drank a glass of water,
taking care to avoid the eyes of the African mask. And all of a sudden
things didn't seem so hopeless; she did have some resources. There was
no need to imagine that the worst had happened until she had proof that
it had. Besides, wasn't that one of her better qualities? At least her
parents always said so, and Julian, during those days when they worked
together in East Africa, hadn't he often said to her, 'Follow through on
this one, Pavana. Get to the bottom of it, no matter what it takes, or how
long.'

As she began organizing herself for the hours ahead, the memory of
the love in Julian's voice kept surprising her as she worked. But the
greatest surprise was the discovery that she loved Julian, had understood that the moment she heard his voice. It had been like hearing the
voice of a husband who has been away from home for a long time.

Chapter 48

All that night she sat by the telephone. She called her parents and told them what had happened, kept calling the police who reported that they were working on the case but had no definite news as yet. At dawn she drove to Alex's home but the maid, already awake and fully dressed, told her that he had not yet returned home, nor had he called.

Back in the apartment, she telephoned Alex's home in the Stann Creek Valley, but the telephone was still off the hook. At eight a.m. she called the headquarters of the ruling party. A man's voice, polite but distracted said, 'I'm sorry, but...'

'It's urgent,' Pavana pleaded. 'I must speak with Mr Abrams. Is he there?'

'One moment.'

A minute later he was back on the line.

'Sorry, Mr Abrams is in a conference and can't be contacted at the moment. Except in an emergency.'

'This is an emergency. His two children have been abducted. Tell him to call me at once, please.'

The man sounded doubtful, as if he didn't quite believe her story. 'I'll give him the message as soon as he returns.'

'Isn't he there? I thought you said he was in a conference!'

'Well, he is, but the conference moves from place to place, organizing for our rally tonight. I myself don't really know where Mr Abrams is at this exact moment.'

'What time is the meeting tonight?'

'The one at Cinderella Plaza?'

'Is there another one?'

'All over the country, ma'am.'

'Where is Mr Abrams going to speak?'

'At Cinderella Plaza, that starts about seven-thirty or eight. But if I were you, I'd go to the police.'

'Thanks,' Pavana said, hanging up.

Pavana spent that day, as she had spent the night, calling the police, the ruling party headquarters, Alex's home in the Stann Creek Valley. Her parents called several times, but she still had no news about the whereabouts of Lisa and Eric.

'They'll be back soon,' she repeated to herself, as she began alternating her telephone calls with household chores. At about five, just as she was putting on her shoes to go back to Alex's home on the river, and to Stoner's on Pen Road, the telephone rang.

'Pavana Leslie,' she said, breathing hard. She'd been disappointed so often that day. There was a pause at the other end of the line, then, 'Afternoon, Miss Leslie, this is one of the brethren calling on behalf of Mr Bennett and the Action Committee. Did you reach Mr Abrams? We haven't been able to do so, and according to our information the rally is still going ahead, and he's to be the keynote speaker.' The voice on the other end of the line sounded so everyday, so pleasant, his Creole drawl so unthreatening.

'I've been trying and trying ... sir,' Pavana said quickly. 'Excuse me, but do you have my children with you?'

'Oh yes, ma'am. Would you like to speak with them?'

'Yes, yes, please,' Pavana said, the moments seeming to drag endlessly before Lisa's voice, tremulous but in control said, 'Hi, Mom. We are all right, sort of. Did you speak with Mr Abrams yet? He'll help you, I know he will.'

'I'm still trying to find him, love, but no luck so far. I won't stop until I speak with him, don't worry. Where are you, Lisa? Try to tell me, please.'

'We're fine, really, Mom. I love you,' Lisa said.

'I love you very much, Lisa. Are you sure you're all right?'

'We're pretty good, but so tired. We have to climb ...'

Someone took the receiver from her hand, then Eric came on the line. 'Heigh ho, Mom.'

'All well, Eric? I found your book. It helped.'

'Very high up,' Eric said, his voice steady. 'Listen, Mom, I'm to tell you to find Mr Abrams, tell him what's happened. They want him to resign.'

'Tell them I'm working very hard to try and contact Alex.'

'Do you think you'll be able to?'

'I'll do it, Eric, somehow. I love you.'

'Love you, too, Mom, bye.'

'Hello, Eric? hello ...' she said into the telephone receiver, but they were gone.

Chapter 49

There was little else she could do now, except to go to the rally at Cinderella Plaza. Before leaving the apartment, she called the police station and told P.C. Ronald Smith, once more on duty, where she would be, and about the telephone call she'd received from Stoner's 'brethren' earlier that afternoon. She also reported her brief conversation with Eric and Lisa.

'We expect something to break soon, Miss Leslie,' he said sympathetically. 'Commissioner has put some excellent men on the case.' He coughed apologetically. 'I'm still involved, of course.'

As she drove to Cinderella Plaza, Pavana switched on the radio and fiddled with the dial. Radio Belize was still off the air. The previous day, protesting crowds had gained entry to the radio station, forcing most bureaucrats to vacate the premises.

In a nearby government compound, a public servant had been injured by a tear gas canister on his way home from work, and in previous days Pavana had heard numerous other stories of injuries suffered by adults, students and children; and about 'peaceful' picketers, many of them women, who had been arrested and herded into the police station compound and to gaol.

Now as she looked around the crowded streets, it was obvious that feelings in the country had escalated to new heights. The ruling party was at last about to break its ominous silence and its supporters, many of whom were thirsting for retaliation, for war, were converging on Cinderella Plaza.

The residents of Belize City are not overly fond of investing funds, public or private, to erecting monolithic statues to leaders, heroes or heroines, whether living or dead, so the plaza itself was little more than a modest-sized, depressing area of ground between Freetown Road and Kelly Street, surrounded by weathered wooden houses, warehouses, shops and stores.

During regular times, the plaza was also used as a taxi stand and as a base for a number of the city's unemployed men, who amused themselves by observing, with seeming insouciance, the flow of traffic through the plaza. But who could tell what their thoughts might have been?

Pavana drove to the Barracks, a relatively broad road going to rubble, bordering the sea. She parked the Land Rover there on the green, opposite the stadium, where as a young woman she had first seen Alex become a national football hero. She hurried across the street, crushing underfoot the blood-red blossoms fallen from an African tulip tree, its branches overhanging the stadium wall.

During the hours she had spent by the telephone in the apartment, she had made a giant placard, nailing it on to a board ripped from an empty packing crate. Using one of Eric's broad-tipped markers, she had written in huge letters:

URGENT, MUST SEE YOU.
LISA, ERIC IN DANGER.
PLEASE HELP.

Hugging the placard against her body, Pavana moved easily through the crowd, and as she listened to the angry voices flying backwards and forwards around her she began to seriously fear a violent clash between supporters of the ruling party and those groups opposed to the heads of agreement.

She was thankful that in spite of her general disorientation and anxiety for her children's safety, she had had the good sense to wear blue jeans, tennis shoes and a lavender long-sleeved shirt, which reached almost to her knees – colours which no one could consider inflammatory.

The plaza was ablaze with lights, and an MC occasionally stepped up to the microphone on the platform, several feet off the ground, to shout above the blaring music, 'Come one, come all to this gigantic rally at

266

Cinderella Plaza. Show your support for your government, and for your ruling party.'

Huge banners and yellow and green flags nailed to the lamp posts and surrounding buildings fluttered in the breeze, and party marshalls wended their way through the crowds exhorting, cajoling, bringing people to fever pitch. But underneath the obligatory gusting of the party line, Pavana thought she detected uneasiness; a lot of the old fervour seemed to be missing, and here and there she discerned an undertone of disenchantment from party supporters, who worried aloud about the implications of the heads of agreement.

She shoved and pushed her way through the crowd, the placard held like a shield against her chest, until she was in the front row, two yards from the platform, rapidly filling with politicians, filing onstage one by one or in twos or threes. The children's voices and Julian's sang in her ears, their words of love buoying her up, reviving her inner strength which had dwindled alarmingly during the past twenty-four hours.

She knew Alex well enough now to understand that nothing, short of a bomb, would prevent him from speaking tonight. But she wanted to make certain he knew that Eric and Lisa were in danger, and that she needed his help to get them released. But where was he, that genius of persuasive rhetoric? She kept her eyes on the platform, and her elbows out. A big, burly man, with a protruding stomach and bulging eyeballs, was pushed forward by the crowd into her line of vision.

'I was here first,' she shouted into his ear. 'Get out of my way!'

The man, sporting baggy yellow trousers and a bright green shirt, wearing several massive gold chains around his neck and a heavy gold ring on every finger, glanced at her placard, the words hidden from view, and making his own assumptions, said, 'That's the way, Mis'lady, give 'em hell,' and, squeezing into the crowd next to her, shouted party slogans which raised a deafening cheer.

By the time the meeting began, the plaza was jammed. The speakers passed before her in a blur. She heard little of what they said, only knew that it was said ineffectually and that the noise of the crowd was just so much more seawater pounding against her eardrums, until all the politicians except Alex had spoken.

Just like him, Pavana thought, knowing it was all theatre, to make a dramatic entrance. And so he did, dressed in dazzling white except for a narrow black belt around his slender waist. He came bounding up the few steps to the platform, looking vigorous, fresh, as if he'd only just emerged from the shower – which he probably had, his hair curling in wet tendrils about his ears.

Pavana had to admit that under the bright lights he made a splendid figure, tall, handsome, winning; the bald spot in the centre of his head was the only indication of his age. Every gesture he made, every step he took, seemed filled with a new recklessness and resolve, his vigour diminishing the other politicians on the platform, on whose faces fear, uncertainty and a loss of self-confidence were plainly written.

Pavana's heart did not skip a single beat. It was as if she stared at a stranger, or an adversary, across enemy lines. As he stepped up to the microphone he stretched his arms wide, acknowledging the roar of the crowd, smiling, waving, keeping the cheers loud and long. It was as if he meant to force the political leaders on the platform to acknowledge that the people in the plaza were roaring for a warrior, for a lion, for him, Alex Abrams; and from this day forth he was not about to kow-tow to anyone, but they were now forced to take him into account in any future election.

With a sudden movement Pavana jerked the placard high in the air, waving it above her head as she shouted. 'Alex! Alex Abrams!'

He looked down, saw the placard in her hand. She knew he read it, but with the adrenalin of power flowing through his veins, intoxicating him like nothing could, and with his extraordinary facility for concentrating fully on one thing at a time, he never looked below him during his speech but continuously swept the crowd with his eyes, glowing with a violent resolution to which everything else was subjugated.

'My beloved Belizean people,' he began, his voice low, soft, as if moved almost to tears, bringing one hand slowly upwards, an elegant gesture, his golden watchband glinting in the hot, white lights, pausing as if reluctant to interrupt this outpouring of love and affection.

'My beloved Belizean people,' his voice grew deeper, resonating over the plaza, into the streets, alleyways and the surrounding neighbourhood. So, Pavana reflected in the pause, that was what he had been doing all day, writing his speech, memorizing and practising it; for Alex was ready, his moment had arrived, the gods had given him one more chance, probably his last chance, and nobody understood that better than he did.

'There has been a breakdown in law and order in the land. There have been acts of violence, directed against government buildings in support of the opposition's campaign against the heads of agreement. Our young people are constructing molotov cocktails, schools have been forcibly closed, our flag has been burnt. The residences of your duly elected representatives have been stoned and their lives, and the lives of their families, threatened, endangered. Business houses have been damaged and looted, resulting in the loss of untold numbers of dollars. Buildings have been burnt, bonfires lit on bridges bringing traffic to a standstill, and still it goes on, beloved Belizeans.

'This threat to our internal security seems set to continue for the foreseeable future, and it is escalating into violence which is rapidly spreading to every corner of the country. We have been patient. We have been silent; but we can no longer stand idly by watching the hard work and progress of the past twenty-five years wiped out by an opposition who has vowed to use any means necessary to overthrow your democratically elected government. They have written on placards, on T-shirts, on the walls of buildings, and on fences in cities, towns and villagers, the terrible slogan: "Kill the Man and Save the Land".

'Are we conch, with no blood flowing through our veins, to put up with this? Don't we love our country, our government, our party? Which man, or men, my fellow Belizeans, are they plotting to kill?'

'My friends, the opposition claims that these outbreaks of violence and criminal behaviour are in protest against the heads of agreement. They claim we are handing over our sovereignty to Guatemala, and that this is why they are destroying the city and are planning to take human lives as well. They are destroying it, they say, because they love it, and us.

'I say this is nonsense, my fellow Belizeans. They want power. They want this government overthrown by any means necessary. Because we have served the people loyally and well, because we love the people and the people love us, they are afraid, my fellow Belizeans, afraid that unless they violently wrest power from our hands they will never achieve it through the democratic process.

'And in this they are right! For they have shown themselves to be élitist, disorganized, envious of each other, greedy, power-hungry and lacking in imagination. They can produce no plan for the development

269

of the country. They are too proud to go to the people, except of course at election time. They are not willing to put in the long hours necessary to develop a viable plan for a nation's progress. They are not willing to study the business of administration, to sacrifice as we have done, selflessly, seeking as our only reward the welfare and love of the people.

'But they are willing – more, eager – to destroy what others have so carefully built up. We are the architects of Belizean independence, and they are jealous of that. But independence, whether they like it or not, is close at hand. We cannot allow them to sabotage this dream, simply because they are afraid of our hard-earned independence, afraid that we cannot govern ourselves, are not ready to govern ourselves but must rely on the British governor and on the United Kingdom for guidance and handouts for the rest of our lives.

'And what after all, my fellow Belizeans, are these heads of agreements that they are using as an excuse for spreading near anarchy throughout the land? They are merely, beloved Belizeans, an agenda, which sets out a number of points or headings or subjects for future discussions with the United Kingdom and with Guatemala. We have reached no agreement on any of these topics. Later this year, further talks will be held to discuss these headings. And as we have repeated time and time again, any agreement we reach will then be put to the people to express their opinion in a referendum. Have no fear. There is no need for a referendum on the present agenda, because there have been no decisions made.

'So what are we to do tonight at this juncture in our history? How are we to deal with these saboteurs of the peaceful, progressive Belizean revolution? We must show, in the streets as we have always shown at the ballot boxes, that we support our government. Tonight is the beginning of that demonstration of our political will and of our determination to support our government in its decisions. Tomorrow, let us march from all corners of the country, from every village, caye and town, let us fly the green and yellow in support of law and order, and in support of our duly elected government, the government of our beloved Belize. Long may it live!'

Alex's voice was drowned by the roar of the crowd. On the platform, he was hoisted on to the shoulders of a group of men, once more their hero, and carried through the cheering crowd to his vehicle, already surrounded by men and women in full war cry. He never looked back.

Determined not to let him get away, Pavana kept close to the group of men carrying Alex, waving and bowing to supporters screaming his name, although the vast majority of spectators lining the streets watched silently, knowing his speech had been less than honest, that his talk had been directed at the already converted and to his party's hardliners. If a hero's function is to inspire people to be better, to do better, what had Alex become in their eyes? Pavana searched their faces trying to guess their thoughts, but of course she failed.

Pavana scrambled into the rear, assisted by the willing hands of Alex's foot soldiers, and as the truck sped along Freetown Road it soon became apparent to her that the driver was headed for Alex's house on the river.

The truck bounced along the rutted road leading to the Northern Highway, reminding Pavana forcibly of the night three weeks before when Aex had stood in the rear of a truck similar to this one, moving slowly through the crowd on Prince's Lane. Ripping the placard to tiny pieces and dropping them on to the floor of the truck, she uttered a brief moan, a small elegy for something iridescent which had been lost a long, long time ago.

Chapter **50**

As the driver brought the truck screeching to a halt on the driveway, Pavana jumped out, following three men who were accompanying Alex to the door. The truck, packed with supporters shouting, '*Que viva!*', roared off into the night. A stream of light from the open double doors flooded the tiled entrance. The men walked swiftly up the steps, their excited voices carrying on the air. They waved their arms in extravagant gestures, slapping Alex on the back, laughing together in a deep rumble of satisfaction. When she was about three feet away from the porch, Pavana called, 'Alex! I must talk with you about Lisa and Eric. I need your help.'

He swung round as if he'd been unexpectedly stung by a battle ass, a fly with a ferocious bite – one with which he was well acquainted having grown up in a home surrounded by hills and miles of uncleared land. From the comparative darkness of the driveway she watched him standing in the light, his bushy eyebrows knotted in a ferocious scowl. Conscious that his companions had paused to stare curiously at Pavana, he waved them into the house before returning to the driveway.

'I got your message and meant to call later. What is all this about?'

Pavana told him, her breath coming out in painful gasps. He listened without interrupting, his arms now folded against his chest, his eyes shielded by his long lashes, the wind from the river ruffling his hair so that curly tendrils blew across the bald spot on his head.

Towards the end of her story, his face grew ashen. He turned away abruptly, staring into the darkness, unwilling perhaps for her to witness the terrible struggle raging within him – to see in his eyes the hunger for power, beginning to grow into overwhelming proportions, to know that he was still on that dangerous high which only the roar of the crowd could produce in him.

'I am one of your beloved Belizeans, remember?' Pavana said. 'The ones you spoke about in the plaza? And I need your help!'

'You'd better come indoors,' he said reluctantly.

Although he did not refer to the placard it had obviously disturbed him greatly, and not least because he had ignored it, for every now and then he glanced at her hands as if he expected her to produce it suddenly and thrust it into his face.

'Drinks, anyone?' he asked, attempting to smile at the men lounging around the living-room, calling to him excitedly about their plans for the following day's demonstration.

'Help yourselves, please,' Alex said, indicating the tray of drinks on the buffet, looking relieved when the maid appeared carrying a tray with glasses and paper napkins.

Glancing around, obviously regretting that she was there at what for him was an inopportune time, he said, 'You'd better come this way, Pavana,' leading the way into his study overlooking the garden.

'Sit down, Pavana, for heaven's sake, sit down.'

He poured her a cup of coffee from the thermos on his desk, then poured another for himself.

'Now, let's see what can be done,' he said, picking up the telephone directory. He called the police station and asked for the Commissioner of Police.

'This is Abrams here, Commissioner. Look, I understand that a report was made about two missing young people. Lisa and Eric Leslie. You have it? Good.' He listened for a while, drumming his finger on the curving mahogany desk.

'Yes. Oh, yes,' he said. 'They are my daughter and my son. Leslie is the mother's name.' His eyes avoided Pavana's. She stared at the tiled floor with the small rugs set before the three comfortable armchairs, while the cup of coffee cooled on the table to her left. The walls of the room were lined with bookcases and filing cabinets. Her fingers were icy cold as she listened to Alex, hugging her bag tightly against her chest.

'You're working on it? Excellent. Well, just as soon as you have something, anything, please let me know. I have the mother waiting here.' He consulted his watch. 'I should be here for another few hours at least. We've a meeting scheduled for tonight. Yes. Yes. Thank you, Commissioner.'

'Well?' Pavana asked.

Alex stood up but before he could reply the telephone rang. He picked it up.

'Abrams,' he said, sitting down, his expression changing from exasperation to absolute fury as he listened. Putting his hand over the receiver, he asked, 'Would you mind waiting outside for a minute?'

Pavana nodded, re-entering the noisy living-room where the men sat huddled together, their heads bent over a number of papers on a circular coffee table, talking, telephoning, planning, with sandwiches, drinks and ashtrays at their elbows. Unnoticed, she walked to the window overlooking the mangrove trees and the wooden pier jutting out into the river. She looked around the extensive living-room; the parrot was nowhere to be seen, but occasionally the dogs barked from the rear of the house.

After about fifteen minutes, Alex appeared in the doorway, hesitating a little as if trying to get his bearings. He glanced at Pavana, who returned his look questioningly, then at the men who immediately began congratulating him all over again on his triumph in the plaza.

'No stopping you now, Alex, are you ready? We've already contacted a number of the organizers of the march for tomorrow night.' The man who had spoken was the tallest of the three, a handsome, middle-aged man, greying at the temples, trim and physically fit as though he was careful about his diet and led an active life. Alex didn't reply so the man added, 'Seems like we won't get finished here until some time after midnight, if you don't mind. We'll do all this while you get your speech for tomorrow ready. There are a few points we think you should include...'

Alex walked away, slowly, towards the buffet. He poured himself a stiff drink, the whisky sloshing over the rim of the glass and on to the floor. He plunked three icecubes into the glass, one by one, each gesture emphatic, angry.

'Here's to nothing,' he said, a bitter twist to his lips, swirling the ice around in the glass and drinking the contents almost at once.

'Another drink, Jim?'

'No thanks,' the man addressed as Jim replied, his smile shrivelling to a frown of disapproval as he watched Alex pouring himself another drink.

'It's off,' Alex said. 'The demonstration tomorrow is to be cancelled.'

'Cancelled?' the three men asked simultaneously. Disbelief wiped the smiles and enthusiasm from their faces.

'Cancelled,' Alex repeated. 'The governor, so my sources inform me, is planning to declare a state of emergency tomorrow. A curfew is to be imposed.'

'But he can't do that!' another man exclaimed, flinging his pen on to the table. He heaved himself off the sofa and walked heavily over to Alex, waving a paper in his face. 'This is our country. We are in charge, running it!'

'That was exactly our minister's view, Fonzo,' Alex said, 'which he expressed forcibly to his colleagues, but it turned out to be a minority position.'

'And?' Jim asked.

'Well, to cut the dreary details short,' Alex said, 'the governor, so I was informed, wanted to know what gave our minister the impression that Belize is *our* country. As far as the governor's information went, Belize is still a British colony.'

'I vote we march in defiance of the governor. What the hell,' the third man said, his pale face erupting in red blotches. 'Who does he think he is, ordering our people about?' He walked to the tray of drinks on the buffet, a short, portly figure, wearing two-inch heels which clicked alarmingly on the floor.

'I understand how you feel, Sanch,' Alex said, pacing back and forth between the front door and the door of his study. 'Nevertheless, he is the governor, with authority over the British troops stationed at the airport camp. It is a deterrent to Guatemala. The Belize Defence Force numbers what, six, seven hundred? Perhaps we *should* show some sense of responsibility in a situation like this. Everyone is fearing an armed clash between the two sides...'

'It's all bloody well for you to talk about responsibility,' Sanch said, waving his hand around the room. 'And it's a bloody fine time to be bringing it up as well, but some of us have a lot more, a lot *more* at stake here besides those goddamned heads of agreement.' He jabbed his finger in Alex's face. 'Which you have been selling up and down the country! Our businesses, our way of life, are going to go down the drain if we don't do something!'

Alex gave him a sour look. 'You've got plenty,' he said. 'How much more do you need?'

'If we march in defiance of the governor's order,' Jim said quietly, 'the British troops will leave, is that the implication?'

'There was absolutely no mention of troops going anywhere,' Alex replied.

'Then how come you're so responsible all of a sudden? You were all fired up, got us all fired up, and now poof!' Sanch was shouting, waving his drink around. 'If I ever saw a conch, Alex Abrams, it's you, no bloody blood. Toughness is what is needed now.'

'We can put that to the test if you like, Sanch,' Alex said wearily, finishing his drink but showing no inclination towards belligerence.

Jim joined Sanch, who was raging around the room.

'Belizeans are usually a law-abiding set of people, Sanch,' Jim said, 'I don't think we could get many of them into the streets if a state of emergency is declared. You must admit that even though we had a very good crowd at the meeting tonight we weren't at full strength, not by a long shot.'

'All the more reason to stick to our plan,' Fonzo said, hitching up his trousers over his paunch. 'If we allow the opposition to kill the heads, the result will be much the same as if we had a referendum. It's admitting defeat.'

'So which is it to be?' Sanch asked, jutting out his chin pugnaciously. 'Is the Belize City march on or off, Abrams?'

'Off. You can't be more sorry about that than I am.'

'Let's get to hell out of here, Fonzo,' Sanch said, and without saying goodbye to Alex they marched furiously through the door, slamming it violently behind them.

'I vote we call it a night, Alex,' Jim said, glancing at Pavana who still stood gazing through the window.

'You can take my car,' Alex said, handing Jim the keys. 'Perhaps you can give Sanch and Fonzo a ride back to town?'

'Of course,' Jim said, looking deeply disappointed. 'The three of us are willing to stand by you, go all the way...'

Alex shook his head.

'It wouldn't work, *compadre*, not now.'

'You could have done it, swung the tide, I mean.'

'I like to think that,' Alex replied, following Jim to the door and closing it softly behind him. He leaned his head against one of the carved panels while the maid crept quietly about the room, clearing away the plates and glasses, breaking the silence with muted chinks and tinkles.

A clock chimed the hour. Pavana counted the strokes: eleven p.m. and the police had not called back. Out there, somewhere in the middle of the chaos convulsing the country, Lisa and Eric were depending on her to get them safely home.

'I'm *not* a conch,' he said suddenly, lifting his head, running his fingers through his hair.

'Of course not,' Pavana said, wondering just how much help Alex, with the best will in the world, would be able to give when he himself was in the middle of a grave personal and political crisis.

Chapter 51

'Is that all, *Señor*?' the maid asked Alex, but glancing at Pavana, who still stood stiffly at the window, clutching her bag.

'That is all, Dominga. Good night,' he said, stumbling dazedly towards the buffet.

Pavana experienced a moment of panic. What shall I do if he asks me to leave? she thought wildly. He mustn't.

'Unless you want something, Pavana? Sandwiches? A drink? You look as if you could use one.'

'Nothing, at the moment,' Pavana said. Alex poured himself another drink and stood, glass in hand, staring across the room at his reflection in the window overlooking the garden, mangrove trees, pier and river.

What mirage did he see? Pavana wondered. His dreams of political glory going downriver, power slipping from his grasp, the end of his political career? He had apparently thrown everything into organizing the aborted demonstration. But Pavana could hardly believe, and it was entirely possible that the same thoughts were crossing Alex's mind, that those dreams had been crushed only by the British governor, who must surely have had some consultations with the ministers Alex served in his capacity as adviser.

He was not an elected representative. Perhaps he had been sent a message from the politicians, too. Was it a reply to his rhetoric on the platform earlier that evening? If so, Alex must be finding it particularly galling that he had not been invited to participate, if participation there had been, in the decision to declare a state of emergency the following day. Did his exclusion signal to Alex that he would not, in spite of his demonstration of public support, be asked to run in the next elections?

Lisa and Eric were now probably the people furthest from his thoughts. After all, Pavana conceded, trying to see things from his point of view, who were they? Two young people who had dropped suddenly into his life a few weeks before, claiming him as their father, children whose mother had not contacted him for nearly twelve years.

I may have hung my memories, like religious icons, along the walls of my mind, Pavana reflected, every day drifting from one to the other, genuflecting, lighting candles, dusting and polishing the images every day, but Alex hadn't. And she'd always known he hadn't; it wasn't his way. Therefore she was more than a little startled when he said. 'So, Pavana, how do you think it went, the speech, I mean?'

"All right,' Pavana replied, as she had done that cold winter afternoon in the park near Primrose Hill, all those years ago. She shrugged. 'Not the best you can do. But maybe that's still in the future.'

'A little less than honest, eh?' He stared at her over the rim of his glass, his dark eyes apparently quite sober.

'As you say,' she replied, shrugging again. She leaned against the wall feeling the coolness of the concrete through her blouse, watching Alex as he leaned against the buffet, his legs crossed, one hand in his pocket, unconsciously elegant and attractive even in crisis.

'Alex,' she ventured, trying to speak carefully, 'I know how terrible you must be feeling. I am sure you must be absolutely shattered by ... everything.' She paused, and when he didn't reply, continued, 'But would you mind telephoning the police again? It's been nearly an hour...'

'It's been a day of shatterings, all right,' Alex said, glancing at his watch. 'But please,' his tone held a trace of sarcasm, 'don't think I've lost sight of your problem. It's been forty-five minutes precisely since I spoke with the commissioner. I'll call again at 11.15, if we've no word from them by then.'

Pavana turned to look through the window, to hide the impatience on her face, the fear, the desperation.

'It does take a little time to contact all the police stations in the country. Why don't you sit down, Pavana, make yourself at home?' Was it her imagination, or did he emphasise the last word, so that it hung in the air between them: 'home, home'.

Maybe not, she thought to herself as she made her way to one of the chairs, gaily upholstered in tropical greens and blues. They reminded her of chintz, stirring up memories of her old London bedsitter, which in turn caused her head to swing from exhaustion and fear.

She eased herself into the depths of the chair, at eye level with a number of enlarged, framed colour photographs on the table holding the lamp, startled to find herself gazing into the laughing, beautiful faces of Helga and Moria, in strapless swimsuits, standing together beneath several coconut trees, on some island beach, in a perpetually happy pose. Her hands trembling, Pavana picked up the photograph, staring at it for a moment, before returning the heavy, gold-plated frame very carefully to its central position on the table.

'I took that at Half-Moon Caye, shortly after we arrived back home,' Alex said, his voice, for the first time, slurring a little. 'Those were good days,' Alex said, 'hopeful, bright, sparkling days.'

'I see,' Pavana said, closing her eyes against the months of days in London, after Alex and Helga had left, which she couldn't have described as sparkling.

'Well,' Alex said, a philosophical note entering the sadness in his voice, 'we can't all be Gandhis or Kings.'

'I suppose not,' Pavana said, listening for the quarter-hour chimes of the clock.

'Remember those years in London when we believed we were destined to pioneer a new breed of men and women in the Caribbean?'

'Mmm,' Pavana said, the drunken slurring of his words grating on her nerves. She hoped to God he wouldn't pass out before at least telephoning the commissioner again.

'Well, in spite of what you may think, I've done quite a few things I'm proud of, to move things along.'

'I know that,' Pavana said, listening to his footsteps pacing the floor between the door and the window. 'You have done some very great things, in fact.' His footsteps stopped abruptly. Turning her head, she found that he was standing behind her chair. He lifted her plait, weighing it in his hands.

'Please, Alex,' she said, gazing at him in desperation, 'let's call the police. I can't expect you to be as ... concerned about their welfare as I am, but ...'

'Oh, but that's where you are wrong,' Alex said. 'I am concerned, very much so. I've had a lot of experience with the police, in one way or another, and I know the commissioner very well. He will get word to us the minute something breaks. You'll have – we'll have – to wait.'

He didn't let go of her plait but continued to unravel it, exactly as he used to do in the bedsitting house all those years ago.

'I'd prefer if you didn't do that, Alex. Do not loosen my plait!'

But he didn't stop, his fingers moving swiftly, and soon her hair was bushing around her face and shoulders.

'There, that's better,' Alex said. 'Much better. It reminds me of you when you were you. Don't you feel a lot more relaxed?'

'I do not! And for Christ's sake, please stop that drinking!'

Alex had approached the buffet again. She softened her voice.

'We're in trouble, Alex. If you continue drinking like that, you won't be able to help yourself, or us.'

He fixed a gin and tonic and brought it to the table, placing it in front of her. She didn't touch the drink but kept her eyes on him, pacing back and forth.

'You certainly weren't thinking of helping me, were you, Pavana, when you waved that placard about at the meeting? It put me off, did you know that? I left two paragraphs out of my speech.'

279

'I was trying to warn you that Lisa and Eric were in danger. You didn't care about that, though, did you? I had to follow you here!'

'Yes, you did, didn't you?' Alex said, approaching her chair, sliding his hand beneath her hair, massaging her neck and pulling her head back so that she was looking into his face.

'Kiss me, Pavana,' he said. 'Hold me like you used to hold me, please. Let's make up.'

'I'm not angry with you, Alex. There's nothing on my part to make up.'

'You're not rejecting me, are you, Pavana?'

'I don't want to kiss you, if that's what you mean,' Pavana said. Then she added, cautiously, 'I've got a lot on my mind, even you should be able to understand that.'

Alex put his head back and began laughing uproariously. With the drink still in his hand, he staggered unsteadily around the room, his arms outstretched, as he said, 'You're rejecting me, Pavana, don't deny it, you're rejecting old Alex Abrams, the regular cock o' the walk, that man among men, a legend in my time, any time, a leader, a regular hero, isn't that what you predicted I would become . . .?'

'You're distorting what I said, if I said any of that,' Pavana shouted. 'And you're drunk!'

'Ah, I may be drunk, Pavana, but I do remember that I have achieved the ultimate in machismo! No door is closed to me, no bedroom door for sure, not even that of my . . .' He stopped, and Pavana watched with shock the tears rolling down his face, the ugly sneer on his lips. The anger in his voice was absolutely terrifying.

She tried to rise casually out of the chair but he was upon her, holding her firmly by the shoulders, covering her lips, face, hair with kisses, sobbing with desperation, his breath reeking of whisky. Any woman, she supposed, would have done at a time like this, but she happened to be the one closest to hand. She felt sickened, but there was a stirring of pity in her heart too.

Removing his hands from her breasts, she jerked her body out of the chair. He fell with a crash, knocking over the lamp, the table, the drink and the photographs. Alex's whisky spilled on to the rug and on to the slickly polished floor, and she watched him sliding dangerously through the liquid. He grasped her arms, pulling her close to him so that his lashes were on her cheeks, moving his mouth up and down her face.

Pavana stood completely still, allowing him to kiss her, allowing him to force her mouth open with his tongue which tasted faintly of stale onions, mingling with the nauseating smell of whisky and the familiar scent of his cologne, which she had always liked. It was funny, she thought, how certain things remained the same, but in another context, another environment, could assume an altogether different significance.

As he was beginning to undo the buttons of her shirt, she whispered calmly, deliberately into his ear, 'Are you going to rape me, Alexander Joseph Abrams, like your father raped Stoner Bennett's mother all those years ago?'

Alex's body went completely rigid, then slack, as if his breath had been punched out of him. His head drooped on to her shoulder, and feeling so sorry, so very sorry and sad, she rocked him, like she used to rock Lisa and Eric when they were in trouble or hurt, rocked him back and forth, staggering with him around the room, Alex refusing to let go of her arms, or to lift his head from her shoulder.

'Is that true, Pavana, what you said? You wouldn't . . .' He mumbled the words, slowly raising his head to look into her eyes, a deep furrow like a knife wound on his forehead.

'I don't know if it is true, Alex, but that is what she told me.'

'Papa!' Alex groaned. 'Papa!' his head drooping once more on to her shoulder.

He was perspiring profusely, and as Pavana smoothed his hair away from his face her glance fell over his shoulder on a photograph of his parents, lying among others which had fallen to the floor. Taken in middle-age, they were a plump, smiling, well-dressed, kindly-looking couple, the picture of wedded bliss.

Chapter 52

'Did you believe her, Pavana?' He stared into her eyes, willing her to retract everything she had just told him.

'At the time I did ... believe her, I mean. She seemed to be telling the truth. According to Lynnette, that's her name, because of Stoner's activities the whole town now knows.'

'Good Christ,' Alex said, moving away from her. He slumped on to the sofa, leaning his head against the back and closing his eyes. Beside him, Pavana sat upright, listening to the chiming of the clock, wondering if Alex was in a state of shock, as he had every reason to be. If so, she was going to telephone the commissioner, P.C. Smith, somebody, immediately. She tried to extricate her fingers from his grasp, but he gripped them harder.

'Alex, I'm extremely sorry I had to tell you like that, especially after the terrible night you've had, we're having, but I was afraid ...'

'That I was going to rape you?' He smiled, his lips still twisted in a bitter grimace.

'Of course not!'

'I was going to ask you to marry me.' He sat up. 'Will you?'

'Marry you?'

'Wouldn't that be the best solution all round? I'd made up my mind to ask you, *was* going to ask you that afternoon on the glass-bottomed boat. Moria knew.'

'You're the absolute limit, Alex, do you know that?'

'Well, what do you say?' Alex asked wearily, as if more than a little anxious to get the business settled.

'That's not possible now, Alex, you know that.'

'No, I don't know that,' he said. 'This is surely a better offer than the one I made you in London.'

'It is, and I'm grateful, but it's too late.'

'For goodness sake, be your age, Pavana. We're the ones with the two children between us. I want them ... and you, with me here.'

282

'Maybe that afternoon on the glass-bottomed boat it would still have been possible for me to think in those terms, but so much has changed since then. You never contacted me afterwards.' It would have been unkind to add that she now felt that she'd had a narrow escape.

'I was busy, had a lot to think about, to sort through, to do. You could have called, too, you know. Brought me flowers ... or something?' He tried to smile.

Pavana didn't reply.

'Or aren't you willing to saddle yourself with a washed-out would-be politician? You've always been very ambitious.'

'Don't be so childish, Alex. We're both older – I wish I could believe we're wiser, but I can't. In any case, my values have changed, and I'm going to marry Julian Carlisle, if he asks me.'

'Julian Carlisle?' For a moment Alex looked as if he couldn't recall who that was. 'The Belizean Englishman?'

'The very same.'

'Oh really?' Alex asked. 'You must be out of your mind. The man's married with a family. Do you think he'll give them up for you?'

'He's not giving them up for us. He's divorced.'

'But he hasn't asked you to marry him yet, has he? It seems to be the story of your life.' There was a sly perhaps even mean note to Alex's voice. Was he sneering at her? 'Is he willing to take on two more children? If not, you might consider giving them to me.'

'You must be drunker than I thought,' Pavana said, bundling her hair roughly on the nape of her neck and securing it with the clasp, which she retrieved from the floor. 'Perhaps you don't realize it, but I've always worked to support Lisa and Eric, and expect to continue doing so.'

Please God, keep them safe, she added to herself, as Alex poured coffee for them both and then lit a cigarette.

She thought briefly of her job in the ministry. Only a few days ago, after the meeting with the permanent secretary, she had momentarily considered resigning immediately. But she was glad she hadn't done that.

As she talked with Alex, she was forcibly reminded of the importance of the job to be done there, not only on behalf of women but on behalf of men. Her resolve stiffened. She would follow through, in spite of the obstacles that were inherent in the position, and a lot that weren't, at

283

least until the end of her contract. She was sure Lisa, Eric and Julian would support her decision. Lisa and Eric! Oh, God, where *were* they?

Alex was saying, almost conversationally, 'I can't imagine, Pavana, how you can contemplate with any equanimity marrying a man like that. He's not your type, never was, as far as I can remember. You even said that to me once when I asked you why you spent so much time talking with him at parties and things. No *frisson* is what you said, as I recall.'

'People's needs change, Alex, or hadn't you noticed?' She wanted to shout into his face, 'At least he's been a good friend to me, he's responsible, and won't leave me in the lurch when I need help, and I won't lie awake nights wondering where he is, and he won't do things to make me jealous, hinder my personal development, or make me feel feeble-minded.' But there was no point, no point whatsoever.

'In any case,' Pavana said, 'he's arriving tomorrow. He called me as soon as he heard about the rioting. He's very concerned about Lisa and Eric, and about me.'

'He is, is he? Well, Pavana Leslie, I have news for you. I'm not giving up my two children to Julian Carlisle without a fight, I can tell you. I've always hated that smug bastard, a real Mr Know-It-All. I intend to . . .'

The doorbell pealed its ridiculous melody through the house. Pavana jumped to her feet. Alex shouted, his voice unnaturally high, 'It must be them, the police.' He marched to the door, his movements exaggeratedly brisk, determined. Removing the chain, he jerked open the door.

'Oh, good evening, Mr Abrams,' the police officer said, peering into the room. It was P.C. Ronald Smith. He bowed to Pavana, who felt as though she was riveted to the floor. 'We've located the whereabouts of Stoner Bennett. He was last seen an hour ago in Corozal Town.' he cleared his throat respectfully. 'I'm on my way there now, sir, to assist in the investigation. The commissioner said you and Miss Leslie might care to accompany me.'

'Wonderful work, officer. Step inside. Just one moment.' He disappeared to the rear of the house, appearing after a few minutes with the maid, in her dressing-gown, yawning but seemingly not at all surprised, as if it was all in her day's work. 'Please take any messages, Dominga,' Alex said. P.C. Smith wrote down the telephone number of the police station and gave it to her.

Pavana felt as though she had received an unexpected blow on the back of her head. Corozal, where her parents lived, was about ninety-six miles north of Belize City. Had Lisa and Eric really been taken to Corozal? She tried to speak, to ask questions, but couldn't.

On the driveway, Alex opened the front door of the police car and after she entered got in beside her. P.C. Smith drove out of the grounds and on to the Northern Highway, practically empty at this hour of the night.

Chapter 53

Soon they were driving through Ladyville, a small town near the airport where only a few weeks before she had seen Alex advancing, his arms outstretched, to greet the delegation returning from London. As soon as this is all over, Pavana promised herself, Lisa, Eric and I will visit Mr Grant and Miss Erline. She was sure they would be able to advise her on her situation in the ministry.

P.C. Smith and Alex exchanged perfunctory remarks about the weather, the condition of the road, and 'the situation' which, in P.C. Smith's opinion, was now almost beyond the competence of the police, the Belize Defence Force and the British forces combined. Their hearts weren't in it, P.C. Smith said, and neither was his, if the truth had to be told. Every few minutes, the P.C. spoke on the car radio with the officers at the Corozal station but there was no further information about Stoner, nor about the twins.

As P.C. Smith talked with Alex, Pavana thought of Julian's kind, dependable face. What a tremendous solace it would be for Lisa, Eric and herself if he was really waiting for them at the apartment when they finally arrived home. She tried very hard to focus on this bright, positive image, rather than on the more morbid scenarios her mood seemed inclined to conjure up from the gloom and darkness of the car and from the silent, deserted countryside.

After a while Alex grew morose and silent too, his face becoming more sombre as they entered the Orange Walk District which together with the Corozal District comprised the country's sugar-producing regions.

The night breezes rattled the cane stalks, and as they drove deeper into the area, tall, thick metal poles appeared at intervals on both sides of the road, some bent into grotesque shapes, erected by the authorities to prevent light aircraft from using the highway as a landing strip.

However, marijuana producers from the surrounding towns and villages, or so P.C. Smith intimated, routinely twisted the poles back from the highway and the light planes continued their nocturnal landings to collect their cargo of marijuana for sale principally in North America. The sugar cane fields, the dense bush and the bent poles were beginning to unsettle Alex even further, for occasionally he groaned as if in agony, slapping his palm against his forehead, causing P.C. Smith to glance enquiringly over his shoulder at Pavana, who smiled faintly.

If Stoner's story was true, then Moria's income – spent lavishly, as Alex's home on the river seemed to testify – came directly from her involvement with the marijuana trade. Was she really a bag lady? Had she also used some of that money to help finance Alex's political career? If so, had Alex known about it? The chances were poor that Pavana would ever learn the answers to those questions, unless Moria was brought to trial. That was not likely, given her deep political cover and family connections, which would probably protect her from public exposure.

With a sudden insight into Alex's feelings, Pavan said, 'You must be missing Moria a lot, especially at this time, Alex. I only heard last night that she is in London.'

He glanced quickly, warningly, towards P.C. Smith. A spasm of pain crossed his face, the muscles of his jaw contracted, then relaxed.

'I plan to call her soon. She'll be anxious to know what's happening. Before I do, however, somehow I'll have to face my parents, talk with my father. I don't even want to think about it until I have to do so.'

Pavana framed her next question carefully.

'Is she returning home soon?'

'Oh, I think so. She's only having a break from all this.' He waved one hand towards the countryside then lit a cigarette. 'We've nearly always lived together, in the same house I mean. If things continue the way they've been going, I may join her in London, at least for a while.'

'That would be too bad, after all the work you've done since you returned home, and all the plans you have for the future.'

'Ah well. It's been a difficult, and long, re-entry in one way or

286

another. Funny, how I still consider it a re-entry, after what, fifteen years or so now. Not at all like I imagined it would be. But then Belize is changing rapidly. Perhaps we grow old, eh?' He grinned at her, but his expression faded swiftly to sadness.

'That could be,' Pavana said.

'And my personal life is quite untidy and neglected.'

'I remember,' Pavana said, 'you and Moria were always extremely close. In London I used to be quite envious, not having a brother myself, or a sister.'

Flicking his cigarette butt through the window, he clasped his right knee, resting it against the dashboard.

'Ah, Pavana,' he said, like one confiding a secret, 'if only we could go back, eh? Helga, after that first great year, began insisting that Moria move into her own place. The quarrelling between them became quite alarming, particularly when Helga discovered that Moria sometimes took a nap beside me in the afternoons. Well, she's always done that, ever since we were children.'

'I understand,' Pavana said, staring straight ahead at the empty, dark, winding road.

'Anyway my parents and I could see her point of view, so we encouraged Moria to renovate the house on the river, although it made us very sad to think she'd be living so far away from us. Moria is great fun. She makes us laugh, always full of vim and vigour, you know. She makes us forget calamities and responsibilities, which we needed to do at times. We are her world. She doesn't want any other. To live without her was difficult. She's very clever, too, about getting us out of unpleasantness. In any case, she used to be.'

'I remember that very well,' Pavana said.

'In the end, it was all a waste of time, effort and money, as Moria always said it would be. Helga complained that I spent too much time with Moria in the house by the river. But it couldn't be helped. I work in Belmopan most of the time, but I have any number of meetings and things in Belize City, cocktail parties and what not. Moria helped me to organize area meetings and parties, supported me in every way. I do miss her, as you said, but I miss Helga, too, in a different way. Helga was very sensible.'

He stretched his hands out before him, gazing at them as though he was staring at a map, as if they could give him a new sense of direction.

The elation of the earlier part of the evening, the terrible letdown of the cancelled demonstration and, later, drinking to excess, seemed to have left him chastened. He twisted and squirmed beside her as if he felt trapped, as if the enormous implications of Pavana's revelations, true or untrue, about his father, his subsequent proposal to her and his declaration to fight for Lisa and Eric, must have begun to trouble him in earnest.

He slapped his forehead again, muttering, 'Oh God, oh God,' then fell silent, the swishing of the car tyres sounding loud in the car.

'Moria,' he said, swallowing as if with difficulty, 'was extremely disturbed when I explained about Lisa and Eric, and that I planned to ask you to marry me. She didn't think you'd want . . . be able to live with us.'

He grinned reluctantly, sheepishly, and Pavana smiled in return, knowing it was a test, that he was willing her to repeat her earlier refusal.

Alex had not said one word about caring about her, or about Lisa and Eric. How could he, when Moria was perhaps his first love, his only love, although at a certain stage in his life he had cared very deeply about Helga too. Still, Alex must have felt some responsibility for the twins' welfare, at least he had been concerned enough to once again offer them some security. She'd always remember that as the supreme sacrifice on his part, on their behalf. Although her refusal of his offer would be most likely as great a relief to Lisa and Eric as it was to Alex. She placed her hand on Alex's, patting it gently.

'The problem won't arise, will it, Alex? It would be wonderful, though, really a big help if you continued to take an interest in the twins' welfare.'

'Of course. I wasn't myself, talking like that. Once this is all sorted out, I'll arrange for them to meet my parents. That's the first step.'

'That's that, then,' Pavana said, looking into his eyes, which remained the most familiar reminder of the Alex she had once known and loved, although now even his eyes, haunted and confused, were swiftly becoming those of a stranger. Perhaps it was the ageing process, as he had said.

'I suppose that does have to be that,' Alex replied. 'Wouldn't it be great if it didn't?'

'It would,' Pavana agreed. For the remainder of the drive he was

288

silent, dozing, his head drooping on to his chest, and finally he slept, his head resting awkwardly on her shoulder. Even in sleep his hands twitched nervously, and he groaned softly several times, causing Pavana to speculate on the terrible internal battles he must still be waging there.

Chapter 54

On the outskirts of Corozal Town she directed P.C. Smith to El Paraiso, and as he drove through the open garage gates Alex sat up dazed, still half-asleep, looking in befuddlement at the house ablaze with lights.

'This is my parents' home,' she explained. 'I must let them know we are in town and what . . . the situation is.' Her shoulder, instead of being grateful for its release, felt exposed, vulnerable, as if some integral component had been permanently removed – not surprising, perhaps, since apart from her children few others had rested so often or so easily there.

'All right . . . yes, yes, of course,' he said, fumbling with the handle of the door. He stood on the driveway looking curiously around as he lit a cigarette. 'Nothing new from the station, I suppose?'

Pavana shook her head.

'I won't be very long, P.C. Smith,' she said, hurrying up the concrete path lined with hibiscus bushes, their blossoms tightly closed for the night, and up the several curving steps to the double doors at the front of the house where Carrie and Raul, their faces anxious, peered into the night.

'It's Pavana, Raul!' Carrie cried. 'We've been so worried!'

'I can see, I can see,' Raul said. 'We've been calling your house all night, Pavana!'

She embraced them tightly; their arms around her had never felt so good. She wiped the hot tears coursing down her mother's lined cheeks shaking her head at the terrible question in their loving eyes.

As they drew her into the hallway Pavana wondered how she must look to them, her baggy jeans sagging over the tops of dirty tennis shoes, the crumpled lavender shirt reaching almost to her knees, her tangled hair, bundled roughly on to the nape of her neck, her eyes reflecting the terror in their own. Even though they rarely complained, she knew they were not all that robust. They had always wanted the children and herself to live at El Paraiso with them, had remained in it with that dream in mind, and had never understood why Pavana found this impossible to do.

'Those poor children,' Raul said, his voice hoarse, a downward tilt to his massive nose. He tied and retied the cord of his dressing gown, once a dark blue, but faded now from many washings. 'I still don't understand how something like this could happen.'

'She'll tell us, Raul, give her time,' Carrie said, patting his chest soothingly, although she sounded uncertain as though she was not altogether sure now that Pavana would ever tell them anything of substance about her life.

About to close the doors, Raul said in surprise, 'And who is that? A policeman? Special Branch, I suppose.'

Alex stood on the path for a moment, before climbing the stairs hesitantly. Pavana, breathless from a series of severe cramps in her abdomen, introduced him to her parents, watching their eyes widen at the mention of his name before their faces settled into polite expressions of welcome. There was a brief pause, in which Pavana could hear the reassuring crackle of the car radio. They would know the instant any news was received.

'Please come in, Mr Abrams,' Carrie said. 'Are you helping Pavana to find the children?'

Alex nodded, his eyes guarded but gentle and compassionate, thinking perhaps of his own parents.

'It's good of you,' Raul said, a puzzled frown on his forehead, 'to take time off from your other interests.'

Carrie had not yet changed for bed, and over her black dress she wore a heavy black sweater although the night was warm. Her rosary beads were wrapped around her knuckles and her eyes, usually bright and lively, were dull, the lids puffy from weeping.

As they followed Carrie and Raul through the dining-room, Pavana noticed that on either side of the Virgin were photographs of Lisa and Eric taken last Christmas at El Paraiso. The candlelight flickered across their open, laughing faces. Alex paused for a minute to glance thoughtfully at them, and Pavana reflected that Eric and Lisa were right, incense did taste peculiar. It could make a person feel nauseous; wanting to 'upchuck' was the way they described the whole miserable feeling of sweating hot, then cold, saliva accumulating in one's mouth.

In the living-room, overcrowded with old mahogany furniture, books, pictures and ornaments, Carrie removed her sewing from her chair near a window, offering the seat to Alex, who when he sat down seemed to Pavana so much a part of everything. If only things could have been different, she mused to herself, listening to the husky timbre of his voice as he spoke with her parents.

'It's strange, you know, in a way, to have you here helping us,' Raul said. 'I once worked for an agency – of course that was many years ago – connected in some way to your family. Marchand was the owner's name, Micomedes Marchand.'

'My mother's brother,' Alex said briefly, looking directly at Raul as if expecting a further disaster of some kind. But Raul didn't say any more. Pavana glanced at Alex to find him observing her, hating the fact that he knew all her defences were down. Getting out of Carrie's chair, he went to sit next to her on a couch near the door leading to the veranda.

'I'll help you to tell them,' he whispered, an ancient intimacy in his voice, one to which in the past she had always responded. Oh God, she thought to herself, why couldn't Alex be like this all the time? Why was he always at his best with her only when she seemed vulnerable or helpless? She could accept only now that in great part this was the nature of their relationship, always had been.

'Mama, Dad ... Alex ...' She stopped, wondering how best to proceed.

'I'm not sure how to say this Mr and Mrs Leslie,' Alex said. 'Lisa and Eric ... well ...' He hesitated, and Pavana finished in a rush.

'Alex is the twins' father. I didn't tell you before because I didn't want Alex to know about them, to feel any obligation towards us.'

'I see,' Raul said, gripping his desk, cluttered with papers.

'I have told you some of my reasons before, Mama? Dad?'

'Yes, you did, Pavana. We remember,' Carrie replied. 'You said that if we knew the name of the twins' father we might be tempted to contact him, or his family, and you didn't want that ...'

'Of course, we felt very unhappy about it all but we tried to respect your wishes.' Raul stopped, clearing his throat.

'Pavana told me about the children only recently,' Alex said. 'I was

291

married some months before the children were born, you see. My wife, Helga, died in an accident,' he added, dropping his eyes. 'Two years ago.'

'Very sorry to hear about your wife,' Raul said.

Pavana didn't believe she had ever seen her parents so distressed or embarrassed. She had tried very hard to keep her troubles as far away from their door as possible, knowing very well the misery and hardships of their earlier lives, remembering how they had tried to shield her from the worst of these.

'Are you two planning to get married now?' Carrie asked, her smile tremulous, looking at Alex and Pavana sitting next to each other on the couch. 'Is that why you are together?'

Raul opened the door to the broad veranda overlooking the beach and the sea. The wind rushed in, rattling the lamp shades and window blinds. Pavana wished with all her heart that she could have answered yes, to say she had waited all these years hoping that Alex would contact her, even a postcard, but had not received a single word from him. During these past years, it was as if their relationship had never been.

Raul was looking at Alex, who said, 'Pavana tells me she has made other plans for herself and for the twins. We've discussed it and well, after so much time, I ... well ... I am sure she has made the right decision.' He kept his eyes averted, looking at a distant corner of the room.

'I see,' Raul said, linking his fingers with Carrie's. 'Is the disappearance of the children connected with you, Mr Abrams, politically motivated in some way?'

'I'm afraid the entire thing has been politically motivated,' Alex said. 'To force me into resigning from office in protest against the heads of agreement, and then to have me speak out against them.'

'Which of course,' Carrie said, 'as a supporter of the government you couldn't do.' Her voice was low but she couldn't hide her anger, disappointment and shock.

'I wasn't altogether aware, Mrs Leslie, I mean I had no idea that my political convictions would lead to such extremes. There is no precedent for this. I came to say, really, how very much I regret that this has happened.' He stood up, as though an unpleasant but important interview had come to an end.

'Very good of you to even think of it,' Raul said, an edge to his voice,

292

the bleakness and despair in his eyes saying quite clearly that he didn't see anything good in anything at all, at the moment. 'Well, Pavana, what do you suggest we do now?'

'I'll stay as long as necessary at the police station. Alex is in contact with the commissioner and a few other people who can help. P.C. Smith, that's the officer who drove us here, feels that Stoner Bennett will soon be brought in for questioning.'

'Who's he?' Carrie asked, her voice still low, without much vigour.

'One of the leaders of the Action Committee opposing the heads of agreement. We believe he knows where ... where Lisa and Eric are,' Pavana said.

'Or at least he'll be able to give us some information on their whereabouts,' Alex said.

The four people moved awkwardly towards the door. Alex shook hands briefly with both her parents.

'Pavana used to talk a lot about you while we lived ... were students together in London. I am very glad to meet you at last.'

'Ah, yes, London,' Raul said, tilting his nose downwards, as if the city was spread out on the floor before him.

'London,' Carrie echoed, opening the door.

'I'll call later, or anyway as soon as I can,' Pavana said, hugging them close, remembering how sorry they had been to see her leave home all those years ago, but at the same time glad that their hard work had provided her with an opportunity they never had.

How blithely she had left, confident of her ability to wrestle with demons, certain of a triumphant return at some unspecified date. Only she discovered, after years of trial and error, that most of the 'demons', labelled nurture, values and attitudes, were within herself, and refused to be permanently banished by one giant blow. They reared up at unexpected moments, demanding exhausting mental encounters which she usually lost.

'Parents seem able to forgive their offspring most things,' Alex said, as they hurried down the stairs. 'Don't they?'

'I suppose that's true.'

'Why do you suppose the reverse isn't true?'

He was undoubtedly thinking about his father so she tried to think of something comforting to say, but couldn't.

'I don't know why that is, Alex.'

293

As they neared the car, P.C. Smith called above the crackle of the radio, 'Stoner Bennett and a few others were seen in a restaurant, Miss Leslie, Mr Abrams.'

'At least we know now he really is in town,' Alex said, getting into the car beside Pavana, who felt her spirits rise slightly. If Stoner was in town, it was likely that Lisa and Eric were nearby. She wondered if things would ever be the same between the children and herself, if they would ever forgive her.

Chapter 55

The sun was already shining brightly through the windows of the Corozal police station when Alex placed before her a cup of coffee and a fragrant, vanilla-flavoured bun, bought from a vendor. Pavana tried to smile her thanks, calculating that it was now getting on for eight a.m. on Thursday, 2 April, nearly forty-eight hours since she had last seen Eric and Lisa.

She and Alex had hardly exchanged more than a few words during the preceding hours. In a fleeting moment of regret, Pavana recalled that Alex used to be one of the few people she knew who shared her enthusiasm for rising early in the morning. But she wouldn't remember those long-ago mornings when they'd laughed and talked over several mugs of coffee, making plans. In any case, maybe they never happened. Maybe they were fragments of dreams remembered. Was something real if only one person remembered it?

Alex turned up the volume of the transister radio on the desk near where he sat a few feet away. He closed his eyes and leaned his head against the wall, listening to a recording of the governor's voice declaring a state of emergency and a curfew, under the extraordinary powers granted to him by the constitution.

Like herself, Alex seemed sunk beneath an almost unbearable despondency. She felt a surge of gratitude towards him that he had remained at the station, when it was evident from the muscles twitching in his jaw and from his fingers silently drumming the desk that he had a

294

number of important things to do. He was surely anxious to be released from what must seem to him something very much like imprisonment.

Even while she felt sorry for Alex and empathized with the conflict obviously raging within him, the declaration of the state of emergency gave her further reason to hope that she would soon be with Lisa and Eric again. This slight relief was soon chased by anxiety. Shouldn't she then be getting home? Supposing Lisa and Eric, exhausted and hungry, were simply dropped off in the street or on the highway? Even if they did manage to reach Sapodilla Street, they had no key to the apartment. How would they know where to find her?

It was after eight o'clock when she picked up the telephone and dialled, hoping that Jen and Morris had returned. They hadn't. Next she called her parents, who had spent the entire night as she had. waiting.

It was while she was speaking with her parents, who were assuring her that they could easily find someone to drive them to Belize City so they could wait at the apartment for Lisa and Eric, that Alex received a telephone call. He then walked swiftly through the door into the street.

After two hours he still had not returned, and as the day advanced Pavana began to sense a heightening of tension among the officers, the barking of orders into telephones, the quickening of civilian and official footsteps, the slamming of doors as the station house swiftly emptied. Eventually only one officer remained at his desk, answering the telephone which rang incessantly.

Some time afterwards P.C. Ronald Smith, sweating profusely, walked wearily into the station waiting-room. He had joined the search for the children as soon as they'd arrived from El Paraiso long before daylight that morning. As Pavana questioned him, he removed his peaked hat and mopped his forehead.

'Oh, Bennett is definitely in town, Miss Leslie, but we still have not been able to pinpoint his exact whereabouts. But as you can see, we are in the middle of another crisis. Members of the ruling party here in Corozal are definitely going ahead with their planned demonstration.'

'How about the state of emergency, P.C. Smith?'

'They're not worried about that. In any case, to enforce it will be a problem. Picketers are already in the streets, and the engines can hardly keep up with the fire alarms. We have a problem on our hands, I can tell you.'

'But what about my children, Lisa and Eric?' Her throat ached. She forced herself to speak calmly. 'Does this mean . . .'

'Oh, no, Miss Leslie, it's all part and parcel. Special Branch is still on the case, and they're competent. It's only a question of time. We are hopeful, very hopeful.'

'That's good,' Pavana said, refraining from asking just who was hopeful and why. P.C. Smith obviously considered it part of his duty to maintain a positive outlook, and she would try to do the same although it was hard to keep her eyes away from his face.

'We're doing all that can be done.' He looked sympathetic but tense, distracted. 'I'll have to telephone Belize City now for further instructions. The situation here has certainly complicated matters.'

As P.C. Smith dialled, Pavana heard raised voices in the street. With a sudden premonition she went to look through the door. Alex was at the corner of a sideroad, not too far from the police station, talking with Jim, Fonzo and Sanch, the same three men who had been at his home the evening before, as well as with several others who seemed to be vehemently urging some sort of action on him.

She hurried into the street, fearful for Alex. As she neared the spot where the group stood, she heard him reasoning with them about the importance of observing the law.

'Oh to hell with the goddamned state of emergency,' a man shouted. He raised a wickedly sharp machete above his head. 'We will bloody well march in support of the government, with or without you.'

Most of the men were armed and one of them, holding what Pavana supposed was a shotgun, spat on the dusty road and asked, 'Well, which is it to be? We haven't got all day.'

Alex stood with his hands in his pockets, his slender frame in sharp contrast with the bulky, pot-bellied men grouped around him. Jim, Sanch and Fonzo stood a little apart, their faces grim as they whispered to each other. Now and then they glanced derisively towards the men around Alex, sucking their teeth loudly, as if they considered the entire exercise a complete waste of precious time. If Alex had refused to lead the demonstration in Belize City, where he had a large group of supporters, why should he join them here?

Alex's white shirt and trousers were dishevelled and muddy, the black stubble of beard on his chin was mixed with grey. His face was haggard, his voice unconvincing, and there were black shadows beneath his eyes as he turned to speak to Jim, Sanch and Fonzo.

'Isn't that so, Jim? Sanch? Fonzo? The march in Belize City was supposed to be in support of law and order. Is it true that you've hired armed aliens to march in the demonstration?'

'I don't know who your informants are,' Jim replied. 'It's the first I'm hearing about it.'

Alex then turned to Sanch and Fonzo, who listened but wouldn't look him in the face, wouldn't support whatever else he was saying. They even seem embarrassed for him.

Pavana already knew what Alex's decision would be before he voiced it, but even so she experienced a terrible anguish, heard a terrible silence within herself which always signalled disaster. It was as if she had waged and lost a bloody battle and had been abandoned. She was certain that Alex must feel this way to an even more heightened degree, and he had decided to try and regain his lost prestige.

'What the hell,' Alex said, with the air of a man with no more to lose. 'I'll march.' Thrusting his fist into the air, he shouted, '*Que viva!*' the rallying cry of the inner circle of the ruling party, but the cry was weak, lacking conviction.

'*Que viva!*' the men responded, slapping him encouragingly on the shoulder, but there was little gusto to their shouts. Their enthusiasm seemed perfunctory. They remained huddled together, speaking in lowered voices, near vendors hawking garishly coloured plastic flowers, second-hand shoes and an assortment of old clothing jumbled together on their makeshift stalls.

As soon as the men left, hurrying across the street towards their vehicles, Pavana began walking to Alex, who stood, hands in his pockets, staring reflectively after them. But then she thought better of it and quickly retraced her steps. She doubted if he would hear a word she said.

As she entered the station P.C. Smith rose from his desk, retrieving his cap from the top of the filing cabinet.

'Miss Leslie,' he said, 'I'd planned that we would do this a little later, but why don't we go now? It's possible that we may catch a glimpse of Mr Bennett somewhere in the crowd.'

'Yes,' Pavana said, following P.C. Smith, thinking of Alex standing in the roadway.

297

Chapter 56

P.C. Smith and Pavana walked quickly in single file along the increasingly crowded and chaotic central streets. Up ahead, Pavana caught a glimpse of Alex jumping into a waiting car parked opposite the town hall. Large numbers of people, their faces grim, carried sticks, rocks, bottles and a variety of other missiles. Pickets paraded up and down, oversized placards in front of their faces or held high in the air. Above the babble of voices, the screeching of tyres and prolonged blowing of horns, the wailing sirens of the fire engines were seldom absent for long. At certain intersections, it was possible to believe that the entire town was on fire. Smoke billowed above distant rooftops, smudging the sky with an unnatural haze.

Although Pavana was quite familiar with certain areas of Corozal Town, a feeling of disorientation set in, and it was disconcerting to find herself being swept along by the feverish excitement of the mushrooming crowd. Her eyes raked the sweaty faces around her, searching for Stoner. Concentrating on her task, she soon became separated from P.C. Smith. She glanced backwards to see him helping another police constable trying to separate two young women waging a brutal battle, locked in each other's embrace, rolling over and over in the dusty road.

Pavana's skin felt bruised, inflamed, while the noise, which had reached maniacal proportions, matched the level of her internal anxiety – her desperation to find Stoner Bennett and to wring out of him the whereabouts of her children. The police had so far failed, as had Alex. It was all too apparent that it was up to her. She had no idea what she would do if she caught up with Stoner, but her determination to do so blocked everything else out. She stumbled over a broken fence paling and, picking it up, carried it militantly as she continued to scan the faces in the crowd.

She was amazed at the strength which buoyed her along, and she shoved her way to an intersection where the noise was greatest. As she had anticipated, Stoner was sitting in the middle of the street together with dozens of others, obviously determined to block the passage of the march. She rushed towards him, oblivious of danger, shouting his name over and over again, waving the broken paling to attract his attention. But the noise of the surging, intervening press of people was too great.

From the sidelines the crowd, gone wild, continued to pelt the oncoming marchers with rocks, dirt, sticks, stones, bottles and whatever came to hand, hurling obscenities too. A clod of earth came flying through the air, hitting Pavana's face with the sharpness of stone. Angrily, she brushed the dirt from her face and rubbed her eyes, trying to remove the grit grazing her eyeballs that was temporarily blinding her. Tears streamed down her face and into the corners of her mouth and she spat out the dirt, almost gagging at the thought of the filth it must contain.

From behind her came the sudden screeching of brakes, as the first truck in the march stopped about a foot from where she stood and one of the passengers in the cabin opened fire into the crowd. The agonized screams of the injured mingled with cries of fury and horror as violence threatened to become unconfined.

Pavana stared transfixed, disbelief mingling with terrible fear at the body of a man lying dead in the road, blood trickling from his chest, caking the dusty road. Pavana realized the frightening moans must be coming from her own throat, for beside her a man was shouting into her face, his own contorted by rage, as if he too could feel a murderous urge consuming his soul.

His body jerked back and forth, spittle appearing at the corners of his lips. Her anxiety was so overwhelming that Pavana could hardly distinguish one word from another. Giving up on her trembling mouth and wildly staring eyes, the man turned to continue his tirade to the more voluble, responsive group near where he stood. Averting her eyes from the dead man, Pavana flung the fence paling into a drain, looking about her, searching again for Stoner, but she'd lost him.

Forcing herself to join the throng of people moving slowly past the dead man, she feared that the crowd had grown to such a size that even if she saw Stoner, she would be unable to push her way through to him. The frantic energy that had propelled her along earlier vanished. Her plait felt like it was weighted with iron, dragging her down. She shuffled along, her two fists up, pressing against the people ahead of her, feeling others pressing against her back.

Just as she was about to extricate herself, to stand back a little to regain her sense of direction, a commotion up ahead caused the crowd in front of her to surge forward. Tear gas poisoned the air and people began pounding away down the side streets. There was general pandemonium and, pushed from behind, Pavana began running, making for the shelter of a store front. Ahead of her the scattered crowd parted, and Pavana saw Stoner darting back into the middle of the street, followed by a number of men, obviously still determined to set up a human blockade against the much reduced number of marchers. In one hand he held a rock with sharp points which he flung in the direction of Alex, now walking at the front of the marchers. His head held down to avoid flying missiles, Alex waved his hand to the left and to the right, while the jeering crowd taunted him with obscenities and references to the dead man lying in his blood.

Bottles smashed on the pavements, stones crashed against buildings, dirt and sticks seemed to be coming from everywhere, and the remaining marchers quickly scattered, trying to get away, melting into the general crowd. But Alex and about fifteen others held their ground, continuing to advance down the street, hands outstretched to ward off the raining missiles. A rock, thrown from quite close in, hit Alex on his forehead. Blood spurted and he staggered back, holding up one hand as if to ward off the next strike. Sensing that victory was at hand, Stoner uttered a wild yell and stopped to pick up another rock. As he did so, Sanch stepped in front of Alex, who was holding his head as if in agony. Lifting his rifle, Sanch aimed it directly at Stoner.

'No! No!' Pavana screamed with all her might, another futile voice in the roar of the crowd. Her mouth was opened in a continuous scream as she watched Alex, blood streaming from the cut on his forehead, stagger towards Sanch, obviously intending to wrench the rifle from his hand, but it was too late. The gun went off and Alex fell at his feet, shot through the forehead. Trapped in the middle of the pressing crowd, Pavana covered her ears to shut out the voices in the crowd calling to each other, 'Dead. Abrams is dead. Through his forehead. Dead.'

Somewhere within her, Pavana experienced a terrible sense of vacancy, as though the rifle shot had bored through her soul and a howling gale was pouring through the jagged hole, with no shutters to close against it. It was the kind of gale that she understood would howl there as long as she lived. Tear gas was again poisoning the air and she staggered to the side of the street, leaning against the shattered glass of a shop window, vomiting into a choked drain, green with morass, the slime and bile pouring from her mouth in a steady stream. 'Lisa and Eric,' her mind commanded. 'Lisa and Eric! Move, move.'

Her mind and body felt extremely weak, and it was only the thought of Lisa and Eric which gave her the strength and courage to move towards a small group of people surrounding Alex's body. Jim, Fonzo, and Sanch were nowhere to be seen. The ultimate betrayal. The street was emptying rapidly now, and Pavana pushed her way through the group of quietly murmuring people. Alex's head lolled in Stoner's arms, and the tears were streaming down his face. When he saw her, he said, 'I told him to stop this march, didn't I, Pavana? I told him. We told him. Everyone told him.'

Pavana knelt beside Alex's body, taking a limp, cool hand into her own. His mouth was open, his eyes staring as if he contemplated an infinity of unmitigated horror. She placed her cheek against his palm, examined his nails clogged with dirt and gazed into his poor eyes. She wanted to close them, but she couldn't. It was too final.

'Oh Alex,' she whispered over and over, dimly aware of the ambulance attendants removing Alex's hand from her lips, watching in numb despair as they placed him on a stretcher, drawing a sheet slowly up over his body and face. It was even more inconceivable then that Alex could be on that stretcher beneath that sheet. She looked around the faces in the crowd, expecting to see him come wending his way through the crowd to accost Stoner, to demand that he take both of them to Lisa and Eric immediately.

She was still kneeling on the ground beside Stoner, staring at Alex's blood in the dusty road. Stoner seemed unaware that his fingers clawed the dirt near Alex's blood. His maddened grief was terrifying. Once he asked of the crowd in general. 'Is Alex dead?'

But nobody replied and neither did Pavana, who felt uncertain herself of the answer. A few hours ago she had watched him washing his face and hands, running his fingers through his thinning curly hair, and now it seemed he was gone from her life, this time permanently.

She kept her eyes on the swirling red light of the ambulance moving recklessly through the streets, on its way to the hospital, its siren blaring, people scrambling out of its way, cars moving swiftly aside to let it drive freely through. Why did it have to go so fast if Alex was truly dead? Why didn't it go more slowly, in a more dignified manner?

She was weeping now for her children, for Alex, for Stoner, for her parents, for herself, for all that had been tried and for all that had failed, for all the misunderstandings, the lies, the betrayals, for her greater understanding of the underside of a humanity who loved winners, as Alex had understood only too well. She kept looking around, expecting Jim, Fonzo or Sanch to appear, but they never did.

Sorrow, anger, terror, coalesced into a gigantic burden within her, as she continued to kneel in the road, peering into Stoner's face. His eyes were tightly closed, and she forced herself to speak softly.

'Stoner, where are Lisa and Eric? Can you please tell me where they are? I must tell them that their father is dead.'

Chapter 57

Stoner didn't open his eyes but stretched blindly out with his two hands until they touched her body.

'Did you say Alex is dead, Pavana?'

She bit her lip to hold back the wild sounds raging in her throat. The pain in her chest was excruciating.

'I feel dead, too,' Stoner said, opening his eyes. 'Maybe he loved me.'

'Maybe,' Pavana whispered, willing herself to stand, to move closer to Stoner. She desperately wanted to shake his shoulders again, to force him to look at her, tell her where Lisa and Eric were, but Alex's blood on his shirt and trousers continued to sap her strength. She glanced up and down the street, uncertain which way she had come.

Groups of people stood a little distance away, staring at Stoner who was removing his bloody shirt, spreading it out on the ground. Slowly, delicately, he scooped up the dirt, darkened with Alex's blood, and placed it on his shirt. Knotting it carefully, he sat on his haunches, holding the bundle in his hands like an offering to a god whose understanding, love and forgiveness he craved.

She reached down and touched his bare shoulder.

'Stoner,' she said, trying to speak gently, 'where are Lisa and Eric?'

As she spoke, a police car braked at the kerb and several officers walked to the spot where Alex had been shot. Stoner stared uncomprehendingly at Pavana, and at the officers who grasped him by both elbows, pulling him to his feet.

'Please accompany us to the station, Mr Bennett. You are wanted for questioning.'

About to rush after Stoner, she saw P.C. Smith hurrying along the street towards her. Pavana reached out to him eagerly, her heart beating heavily. Her burden was so great, she felt unable to speak.

'We've found your children, Miss Leslie,' he called, while still a few feet away. 'They are quite unharmed. Exhausted, scared, worried about you, but safe.'

'Oh thank God!' Pavana said. 'Thank God! Where are they?'

'They're making a report at the station. We found them on the road leading to your parents' house. They'd been hidden in an unfinished hotel about a mile or so back from the road. The place is practically abandoned, surrounded by bushes and absolutely filthy. The man guarding them received a message this afternoon and just left them there, on what was to be a fifth floor of the hotel, no roof or anything as yet.'

'And they found their way to the road?' Pavana asked, running her tongue over her lips which were dry and cracked.

'Yes, they did. The building is about three miles from your parents' house, Miss Leslie. We did search that building several times. It's well known for harbouring vagrants, drug addicts and the like. But according to your children's report, their guard was always warned of our arrival and they were taken into the bushes where they sometimes had to stay for several hours.'

'They must have been so scared,' Pavana whispered.

'They don't admit to having been frightened, but I am sure they must have been. Still are. We usually raided the building at night or early morning.'

'Do they know about . . . ?' Pavana asked, staring down at the place in the road where Alex had lain.

'Yes, I had to tell them. They were so anxious about you, wanting to telephone Belize City. I had to explain.'

303

'Of course,' Pavana said, glad that the world didn't seem quite so empty any more.

'I'm so sorry Mr Abrams is not here to see our success. I could see you cared about him very much. I hope you don't mind my saying it.'

'A lot of people cared about him,' Pavana said. 'No, I don't mind.'

'The car is about to leave, Miss Leslie, shall we go?' He gestured towards the vehicle in which Stoner sat, between two officers, still holding his shirt filled with earth. Pavana shook her head.

'I'll walk, if that's all right with you.'

'Of course. It's not very far.'

She stumbled along, trying to keep up with P.C. Smith's swift strides, buffeted alternatively by waves of relief and joy that Lisa and Eric had been found, and by overwhelming grief over Alex's death. Like Stoner, she still could not really accept the fact that he was dead, and as the station loomed in the distance, her sense of unreality grew.

'At least a lot of people used to care about him, didn't they, P.C. Smith?'

'Until these heads of agreement, now dead, I understand, and if you'll pardon the word, I would say a fair number did.'

He gave a sudden shout.

'There they are, Miss Leslie, coming to meet you!' P.C. Smith was pointing his hand through the crowd, his voice high with excitement and triumph. 'Safe and sound.'

Pavana's heart thudded, and she repeated his words, 'Safe and sound!' praying fervently that this was true.

She squinted her eyes, holding her breath, as Lisa and Eric, weaving their way through lingering pedestrians, came tearing towards her, their feet bare, their arms stretched out eagerly towards her, their voices travelling above the noises in the road.

'Mom! Mom!' she heard them call. 'Are you all right, Mom?'

Pavana wanted to run to them, but couldn't. She felt so very tired, so weak. She stumbled along, her own arms open wide, calling, 'Lisa! Eric! Lisa! Eric!' waiting to see their eyes, their expressions, which would tell her whether or not they were truly safe.

They wrapped their strong, youthful bodies around her, peered into her face as she closely examined theirs, wiped the tears from her eyes, assuring her that the scratches on their faces, arms, and legs didn't bother them in the least. They were so beautiful, her children, the most beautiful children in the whole wide world, and she felt so relieved, so abjectly humble, so thankful to have them back with her again.

'I'm all right, I'm all right,' she responded to their frantic questions, gazing at their anxious faces, peaked and grimy, their dark eyes glassy, their clothing torn and stained. She looked at their feet, caked with mud and dirt.

'They took our shoes away,' Eric explained.

'There were no railings on the stairs, Mom, and we had to climb more than a hundred stairs to reach the top, sometimes several times a day. I thought we would fall off, especially when they were pushing us down the stairs at night to hide in the bushes.' Lisa paused for breath. 'I was horribly afraid walking about in the bushes barefooted.'

'Even at night,' Eric continued, 'they kept our blindfolds on. We mostly ate stuff out of tins, and drank soft drinks. We were thirsty all the time.'

As she listened eagerly to the twins relating their experiences, their voices rising far too high, she felt a desperate urge to get them away, to reach home as soon as possible. They were moving along the street too slowly, but she felt so weak and tired, as they must do.

'Guess who called the station while we were there, Mom?' Eric asked, holding on to her arm, as if he would never let go.

'Uncle Julian!' Lisa said, her face brightening. 'He said we should fly home and he'd meet us at the municipal airport!' She put her arms around Pavana's neck and squeezed her tightly.

'Shall we?' Pavana asked, her strength reviving a little. Good old Julian, always true to his word.

'Yes, oh yes,' Eric said. 'Let's get home.'

As they were about to set off again with P.C. Smith, Eric and Lisa looked back along the street where groups of people still stood, talking and pointing to the spot where Alex had fallen, as they would do, most likely, all evening and into the night.

'The officers told us about Mr Abrams,' Eric said, a slight catch in his voice.

'We feel so sorry, Mom,' Lisa said. 'We know you tried ... how much ...'

Pavana nodded, not meeting their gaze, grateful that P.C. Smith seemed eager to explain to them again what had happened. They listened, their faces sober, their eyes fixed on the distant ground.

'He died like a hero, anyway,' Eric said. 'Not many people would or could have done what he did.'

'Only I don't expect he thought he *would* die, eh, Mom?' Lisa asked.

'No, I'm sure Alex didn't expect to die,' Pavana said.

She placed her arms around their waists and held them tightly against her own body, willing herself to shut out that last sight of Alex's face caught in that weird surprise of death. She could almost taste his flesh on her tongue, and the acrid smell of his death filled her nostrils. As they huddled together in the street, staring as if mesmerized at the place where Alex had been shot, P.C. Smith looked at his watch and said, 'The last flight leaves at five, Miss Leslie. It's after four o'clock now.'

'Let's take a taxi to the airstrip,' Lisa said, pulling on her arm. 'Let's get home.'

'Come on, Mom,' Eric said. 'We need to get home. I expect we'll soon be able to forget all about this, eh?' He looked at her with a question in his eyes, and Pavana knew he was not talking about Alex's death but about her feelings towards him.

'After a while, I am sure we will,' Pavana said, smiling a little though she really wanted to weep, as she knew she would do, though silently, for years to come, perhaps for as long as she lived.

As they followed P.C. Smith to the station, the noise of the cars and trucks and buses hurtling down the street, the drone of an aeroplane overhead, the voices of pedestrians raised in excitement and disbelief, the laughter and games of children playing in the streets, the hawking cries of vendors on the sidewalks seemed to Pavana to be horrifyingly, unnaturally loud.

These sounds, signalling the resumption of life's routine, seemed out of place, ordinary, belonging to another period of time, one which had ended. Shouldn't there be mourning in the streets, the blowing of trumpets, the beating of drums, some signal that another less innocent era had begun? What happened in a country when one or more of its heroes died?

But perhaps Alex had been a hero only in her own heart, and in Stoner's. Hadn't they always expected too much from Alex? She was certain that they had, far more than he ever expected from himself. But if there is a God, or if there are gods, then Alex is with him, or near to them, Pavana thought to herself. For he had instinctively sacrificed his

306

life in order that Stoner might live. This thought would certainly give new meaning to those times when she did pray.

In the twin-engined aircraft, Pavana sat between Lisa and Eric, who slept, their heads on her shoulders. Through the window, she stared down at the villages, towns and the rivers, winding through the dense green jungle, thinking of Alex whose dream it had been to one day sit in the House as an elected representative of the people.

Returning to the ministry, to Belmopan, would be that much more difficult now. But she would do it and, as Gail had urged, continue trying to do her best, win, lose or draw. She understood very clearly, as Alex obviously had done, that sometimes in the heart of defeat is hidden eternal victory.

THE AFRICAN AND CARIBBEAN WRITERS SERIES

The book you have been reading is part of Heinemann's long-established Caribbean Writers Series. Details of some of the other new titles available are listed below, but for a catalogue giving information on the whole Series, and on the African Writers Series write to:
Heinemann International Literature and Textbooks,
Halley Court, Jordan Hill, Oxford OX2 8EJ

ZEE EDGELL
Beka Lamb

Joint winner of the Fawcett Society Book Prize, Beka Lamb is the story of ordinary life in Belize. It focuses on a girl's victory over her habit of lying and her relationship with a friend. The novel records a few months of this girl's life and portrays the politics of the small colony, the influence of the matriarchal society and the dominating presence of the Catholic Church.

BERYL GILROY
Boy Sandwich

A novel conveying the ways in which three generations of a West Indian family have been affected by life in Britain and how, after time, the third generation desires to take the family back to their homeland and regain a sense of belonging.

Frangipani House

Set in Guyana, this is a beautifully written protest at institutions which isolate, and a way of life which denies respect and responsibility for the weak.

MORDECAI AND WILSON
Her True-True Name

Short stories from 31 women writers, that display the range and variety of Caribbean cultures and tradition, and express the longing, pride and passion of the Caribbean identity.

EARL McKENZIE
A Boy Named Ossie

Ossie, a young Jamaican boy, is the tool through which Earl McKenzie expertly portrays the reality of life in rural Jamaica; its humour, warmth and ambitions, as well as its terrors and tribulations.

MARLENE NOURBESE PHILIP
Harriet's Daughter

Set in Toronto, two girls, Margaret – a second generation West Indian immigrant – and Zulma – fresh up from a joyous life with her grandmother in Tobago to a tense and unhappy relationship with her mother and step-father – become friends and comrades in various adventures.

EARL LOVELACE
The Wine of Astonishment

Earl Lovelace writes about the survival of a small community with a lyricism and understanding which has established an international reputation.

A Brief Conversion and Other Stories

A collection of short stories telling of ordinary people and everyday subjects, but through a rare combination of literary excellence and accessibility each is invested with a unique magic

MYRIAM WARNER-VIEYRA
Juletane

Helene comes upon an old diary. It belonged to a Caribbean girl who turned to writing as an escape from her traumatic marriage to a polygamous husband. Juletane met her husband in France, and moved to Senegal where she found herself sharing her life with two other wives. Helene finds herself making similar choices, and the diary begins to influence her life too.

This is the first translation of a powerful feminist novel that spans the African and Caribbean literary traditions.

VALERIE BELGRAVE
Ti Marie

An historical romance set in Trinidad in the years of transition from Spanish to British rule. This period (1777–1802) saw the advent of slavery and the emergence of a whole range of racial tensions that were to mould the shape of Trinidad. In this climate, a part Amerindian, part African, part Caucasian girl falls in love with an English nobleman. The tale of their romance encapsulates the mood of a new society coming to birth.

NAMBA ROY
No Black Sparrows

The "Sparrows" – four impoverished orphaned children – eke out a living as petty traders whilst under constant threat from the police.

STEWART BROWN (ED)
Caribbean New Wave

This anthology offers a taste of the energy, commitment and talent of a whole new wave of Caribbean writing.

HAROLD SONNY LADOO
No Pain Like This Body

Set in a Hindi Community in the Eastern Caribbean, the vivid, unsentimental prose of this novel describes the life of a poor rice-growing family during the August rainy season. Their struggle to cope with illness, a drunken and unpredictable father, and the violence of the elements is set against a sharply drawn village community.